THE DREAD PIRATE ARCANIST

FRITH CHRONICLES #2

SHAMI STOVALL

CAPITAL
• STATION BOOKS •

DREAD PIRATE ARCANIST

FRITH CHRONICLES #2

Published by
CS BOOKS, LLC

This is a work of fiction. Names, characters, places, and incidents either are the product of author imagination or are used factiously, and any resemblance to actual persons, living or dead, business establishments, events, or locales, is entirely fictional.

Dread Pirate Arcanist
Copyright © 2019 Shami Stovall
All rights reserved.
https://sastovallauthor.com/

Cover Design: Darko Paganus
Editor: Erin Grey, Sallianne Hines

IF YOU WANT TO BE NOTIFIED WHEN SHAMI STOVALL'S NEXT BOOK RELEASES, PLEASE VISIT HER WEBSITE OR CONTACT HER DIRECTLY AT s.adelle.s@gmail.com
ISBN: 978-0-9980452-6-9

ACKNOWLEDGMENTS

To John, for being the first to see.
To Beka, for making this possible.
To Gail and Big John, for all the support.
To Ann, for being an amazing best friend.
To Brian Wiggins, for giving a voice to the characters.
To Ryan, Tiffany, Mary & Dana, for putting up with me in the author group.
And finally, to everyone unnamed, thank you for everything.

A CELEBRATION OF GRIFFINS

Today the griffins of West Landin would choose who to bond with. The city officials gathered before the dawn, prepping for the evening celebrations.

I watched from afar on a rocky cliff that overlooked half the isle, the pre-morning winds disheveling my inky black hair. I had never visited the Isle of Landin before now, but I had heard amazing tales of their fearsome griffins since I was old enough to remember stories.

While the hopefuls of West Landin would have to prove themselves to the griffins in a Trial of Worth, I had already been tested and found worthy.

My pulse quickened with anticipation. For fifteen years, I had imagined bonding with a mystical creature and becoming an arcanist. Eight months ago it had become a reality, but it hadn't yet sunk into my heart and gut. Giddiness still twisted my insides with each new breath.

I turned to the shadows next to me, well aware that my mystical creature—my eldrin—lurked in the darkness.

"Luthair," I said. "Do you know much about griffins?"

"They are stubborn beasts," he replied from the void of

my shadow, his voice more sinister than his true demeanor. "And griffin arcanists are strong, courageous, and skilled at combat."

"Amazing."

As a knightmare, Luthair lived within the darkness, merging with it like salt in water. He didn't need to materialize to speak, and he could slink along next to me without anyone knowing. While some would consider that creepy or unsettling, I enjoyed his presence and trusted him in all things.

I returned my attention to the sprawling city. Unlike the small Isle of Ruma, where I grew up, West Landin housed thousands of people, had a massive port, and had constructed a seaside fortress to deter pirates. Their cobblestone roads, twice as wide as ours at home, snaked beyond the city limits to a valley filled with sheep, goats, and horses.

When the sun rose, the oranges and reds of dawn cascaded over the island, washing it in a familiar glow. The Isle of Ruma had wonderful dawns, just like this one. The nostalgia overwhelmed me for a moment, so powerful it almost hurt.

I missed my adoptive father, Gravekeeper William.

My days as his apprentice had seemed torturous at first, since I had never wanted to become a gravedigger, but now I understood how much he had influenced my life. He had been the best father I ever could've hoped for. I last saw him after I bonded with Luthair, a short time after my fifteenth birthday.

"Volke?"

"Yes?" I replied, recognizing Illia's voice straight away. I didn't even need to turn around. I knew she would walk over to speak with me.

Sure enough, she ambled to the edge of the rocky cliff,

one hand on the brim of her sailing cap. Then she offered me a smile.

"Are you out here daydreaming?"

"No." I slipped my hands into my pockets. "I wanted to spot some of the griffin cubs. I've never seen one in person before."

Illia sarcastically lifted an eyebrow. "You weren't thinking about the Isle of Ruma?"

"W-well, I *might* have thought about it for a moment."

"Yeah. I know." She stared down at West Landin, her only eye unfocused. "I've been doing the same thing."

The wind played with her hair, revealing the twisted knife scars on the right side of her face. Her sailing cap kept everything in place, so I didn't catch sight of the old wound for long, but I knew it was there.

I still remembered the first night that Gravekeeper William had brought her home. She had been five years old, and the injury hadn't yet healed. The pirate fiend who had taken her eye had cut in deep, damaging the socket. She had to rest in bed for weeks, her skin pale and dappled with sweat.

Illia glanced over. "Volke?" She frowned. "What's wrong? You're not thinking about home anymore, are you?"

"It's nothing," I said as I stared at my boots. Illia didn't like having attention brought to her scars, and I didn't want to upset her.

"You can't hide things from me." Then she smacked my shoulder and half smiled. "You'll tell me sooner or later."

Instead of arguing, I nodded and allowed the conversation to end. The morning sun warmed the isle, and the breeze brought ocean mists ashore. I could've stayed on the rock cliff with Illia for the entire day, enjoying the atmosphere.

A small ferret-like creature—a rizzel—bounded toward us, hopping along like only weasels could. His snow-white fur shone in the morning light, and his silver stripes had a metallic sparkle.

"Illia!" he cried out as he scampered over to her feet. "Why would you leave me?"

In a flash of sparkles and sorcery, the rizzel disappeared and then popped into existence on Illia's shoulder. She stroked his head as he curled around the back of her neck, hiding in her wavy brown hair.

"What is it, Nicholin?" she asked.

"Master Zelfree wants us all to gather near the edge of the woods."

"Right now?"

"He said *before dawn*, but it took me forever to find you." He arched his back and squeaked. "I can't believe you left me! I'm your eldrin! Arcanists don't leave their eldrin—it's unheard of!"

Illia chuckled, but gave no explanation.

All arcanists bore a mark on their forehead—a seven-pointed star etched into their skin. Illia's, while faint, had the image of a rizzel intertwined with the star, symbolizing her connection with Nicholin. When I touched my own forehead, I could feel the cracked arcanist star just below my hairline. Unlike Illia, my star had a sword and cape, representing my bond with a knightmare.

"Did you see any griffins?" Illia asked.

I had almost forgotten the reason I perched myself on the cliff. I shook my head. "No. I can't see their aerie from here, and the bonding ceremony doesn't start until dusk, so I'm sure they're still resting."

"Do you want to wait until you see one? I bet they'll wander around town before the Trials of Worth begin. We

4

can always tell Master Zelfree that Nicholin got lost or something. It won't be a big deal."

"I wouldn't want to lie. *Honesty. Without it, we cannot learn the truth about ourselves.*" I said the last bit with dramatic emphasis.

Illia groaned. "Please, Volke. For me. Stop quoting that damn staircase."

"You know I like the lessons from the Pillar. I think they're good rules to live by."

Nicholin crossed his little ferret arms. "You're wrong. They're lame."

"What?" I balked. Then I turned to the darkness. "Luthair, back me up. They're good, right?"

"Indeed," he said, his gruff voice echoing from my shadow.

"See? Luthair agrees with me. They're definitely awesome."

Nicholin and Illia exchanged knowing glances and huffed in sarcastic exasperation. If it were anyone else, the mocking would bother me, but I knew Illia didn't mean it. She gave me a hard time, just like when we were kids. With all the nostalgia in my veins, I welcomed the teasing.

"I guess we have to find Master Zelfree," Illia said. "C'mon. Let's go."

We walked away from the cliffside, seagulls serenading the dawn with a symphony of caws. The rocks created a natural path, making the trek down an easy one. Illia kept close to me—closer than usual—and I wondered if she was awash in sentimentality as well.

Today would be easy. As members of the Frith Guild, we had been called to the Isle of Landin to protect those attending the griffin bonding ceremony. Until the celebrations began, however, we didn't have much to do. Perhaps

Illia and I could convince Master Zelfree to allow me to continue my reminiscing in town.

"I'm glad we became arcanists together," Illia said. "That's how I always imagined it when we were younger."

"Yeah. Me too."

She smiled and took in a breath, as if she might continue the conversation, but the words never came. We got all the way to the edge of the trees before she turned her attention back to me. She met my gaze with her one eye. I think she wanted me to say something. Maybe about our past? I didn't know, and the longer she stared, the more disappointed she looked.

Illia lifted a hand and covered the scars over her damaged eye socket.

"Uh," I began.

Illia waited.

Nicholin perked up, his ears erect. "Hm? What's that?"

My breath caught in my throat. What did Illia want me to say?

Thankfully, Master Zelfree emerged from the woods, saving me from the awkward moment. He sauntered over, bags under his eyes, his dark coat and pants wrinkled from long hours of work. He ran a hand through his black, shoulder-length hair. His fingers caught in a few places, betraying the fact he hadn't brushed it in a while.

If I didn't know he was a master arcanist from the Frith Guild, I would've assumed he was a hungover drunkard who had stumbled away from the festivities.

"Master Zelfree," Illia said, her eyebrow high.

Zelfree had a strange arcanist mark—his star had nothing intertwined with it. His eldrin, Traces, was the shape-changing *mimic*, after all. The bangles on his left wrist were most likely her. That was how she had hidden herself in the past.

"You two finally decided to show up, huh?" Zelfree said. "You're late for the exercise."

"What exercise?" I asked.

"Don't worry. It's something simple."

Zelfree's shirt—black, like the rest of his clothing—was open enough to expose his bare chest and guild pendant, a silver symbol that marked him as a master arcanist. My bronze pendant told the world I was an apprentice, but I wasn't ashamed of my lower status. I loved my pendant with every ounce of my being.

"You all have been through a lot," Zelfree muttered. "And your training as arcanists has been erratic. For the next couple of months, everything will be simple. We'll take it slow while I assess your abilities, and then we'll work our way to more challenging assignments."

"I thought we didn't have to do anything until dusk?" Illia asked.

"We don't have to do anything *official* until dusk." Zelfree pulled a flask from inside his coat and unscrewed the top. "But I want you to practice your magic in the meantime. I split the other apprentices into pairs and sent them on their way."

Nicholin bounced on Illia's shoulder. "On their way? Where?"

"I hid apples around the daisy woods, and I want you to collect them using your magic and your magic alone."

"What? That's kids' stuff! My arcanist and I can handle anything. *We* took on Gregory Ruma's leviathan. *We* stared into the jaws of death and survived!"

"As an arcanist of the Frith Guild, you won't always be

fighting giant leviathans in the waves of the ocean." Zelfree cocked half a smile. "Sometimes we'll be asked to find missing mystical creatures or locate hidden caches. Since none of those things involve *traumatizing duels to the death*, I figured this would be a relaxing way to practice your basic magic."

"The apples are hidden throughout the entire wooded area?" I asked. The daisy woods covered a few acres of the island. The task felt daunting, even if it didn't involve combat.

Zelfree shrugged. "Apples aren't native to the islands. They're bright red, and I've placed them in precarious spots. It shouldn't take the six of you long to find them all." He took a swig from his flask. "Whichever team comes back with the most apples will get to spend time with the griffins before the ceremony."

My chest tightened. "Really?"

"And the pair who finds the least amount will have to wipe down the deck of our ship."

Illia and I both groaned. No one wanted ship-cleaning duty, especially since the sailors would have a good laugh at our predicament. Arcanists stood at the top of the social hierarchy, and seeing one swab a deck was a novelty—like watching a crown prince take out the garbage, or a knight commander clean all the training weapons. We'd be mocked for the entire journey home.

"Interacting with the griffin cubs sounds amazing," Illia said.

Zelfree nodded. "The mayor of West Landin asked the Frith Guild to protect the new arcanists until they reach the mainland. They'll sail with us all the way there."

"Protecting them from what, exactly?" she asked. "You never told us why they wanted the Frith Guild."

"Pirates are in the area."

The statement killed all mirth in the conversation. Illia grazed her fingers over the scars on her face. I had seen her react that way a million times before, every time someone mentioned nearby pirates.

The last thing I wanted was to deal with sea thieves and cutthroats.

"Any questions?" Zelfree asked. He swirled his flask as he spoke, and I couldn't help but take note of it.

I pointed. "I thought you said you were cutting back on the drink."

He downed the rest of his "breakfast" and walked past us. "Don't worry. I've limited myself to a single serving. Soon I won't need it to wake up."

Normally I was the tallest person in any group—six feet —but when Zelfree went by, he straightened his posture, standing an inch or so higher. I had never noticed before, probably because he slouched most times. It surprised me.

"Okay," I muttered. "I suppose we'll get started with the apple hunt then."

"Treat this like an urgent mission. The apples are baby mystical creatures. Recover them quickly and efficiently."

My thoughts didn't dwell long on his statements. The idea that I could see the griffins up close—before the ceremony!—excited me more than anything else. We had to find enough apples. It would make for a perfect day, and an amazing tale to write William about.

Illia took my elbow and pulled me toward the trees, a smile on her face.

The slender daisy trees grew sixty to ninety feet in the air, and in dense clusters. Their wide canopies caught the humid breeze and rustled with excitement. The white trunks, striped with brown, would make it easy to spot something crimson.

I kept my gaze up, hoping to catch a glisten of fruit among the branches.

"I'm going to make sure you see those griffins," Illia said as she let go of my arm.

"Me?" I asked. "But aren't you excited too?"

"Of course." She smiled, more to herself than to me. "When I was younger, griffins were my favorite mystical creature. I used to daydream that one would learn I had escaped from pirates, and that it would think I was so courageous it had to fly to our island just to bond with me."

Nicholin swished his tail. "I don't know if I should feel jealous or sad that I'm not a griffin."

"No, no, no," Illia said as she hugged Nicholin close. "That was me as a little girl. Now I know I wouldn't want to be bonded with anyone but you."

He made an odd purring noise, like he wasn't built for it, but still attempted regardless. "That's right! We're meant to be together."

Still—I had heard the excitement in her voice. If Illia wanted to meet a griffin, I would make sure that happened.

Somehow.

Thirty feet into the daisy tree woods, I spotted a rodent hole. While Illia went off to check some shrubbery, I knelt on the dirt and examined the burrow. I had dug enough graves to recognize when soil had been freshly tossed, so it was clear to me this entrance had been tampered with by human hands. Would Zelfree hide an apple here, of all places? I thought he had said they would be clearly visible. Best to check, regardless.

"What're you doing?"

The snide voice snapped me out of my concentration. I glanced up, and all excitement curdled in my system. Zaxis

Ren. He stood with his arms crossed and his green eyes narrowed in a condescending stare.

"I'm searching for apples," I said.

"In the dirt? Like an animal?"

I got to my feet and brushed the soil off the knees of my trousers. "Sounds like someone hasn't had breakfast."

"Heh. You think you're so funny."

Zaxis confused me more than anyone else. We had known each other our whole lives, and while it had been an antagonistic relationship when we were young, I thought we had worked past that during our time in the Frith Guild. Still, he fluctuated back and forth on whether we were being cordial.

Today wasn't one of those days, it seemed.

His phoenix, Forsythe, glided through the trees on scarlet wings edged with gold. Occasional dustings of soot rained down from his body as he moved, and he swirled around us once before elegantly landing on the ground next to Zaxis. Phoenixes had the bodies of herons, with long necks and delicate frames, but their majestic tails appeared similar to that of a peacock, with vibrant designs and curved feathers.

Zaxis's arcanist mark had a phoenix laced between the seven points of his star. I admired it for a moment, remembering the Trials of Worth on our home isle. I had wanted to bond with a phoenix more than anything back then.

Forsythe's gold eyes stared at me for a moment. "Good morning." His voice was imbued with a regal cadence.

"Morning," I replied.

Zaxis huffed and then motioned to a cloth sack of apples on the ground behind him. "Forsythe, don't bother talking to this biscuit. We have a game to win."

From what I could see, Zaxis had already gathered four

apples, all glistening red, almost the same dark shade as his hair.

"I'm not stopping you," I said, motioning to the woods. "You can leave and keep searching if you—"

Illia emerged from the nearby shrub, an apple in hand. "Volke, look. I already found one!"

"Oh, Illia," Zaxis said as he brushed off his coat. "I didn't see you." He straightened his posture. "Beautiful island, right?"

She acknowledged him with a quick nod and then smiled at me. "I think we should hurry. If there was an apple here, I think the others might not be searching as thoroughly as they should."

"Okay," I said.

Before I could return to searching the rodent hole, Forsythe investigated the burrow with his long neck and beak, rooting through the fresh soil. He grabbed the stem of a hidden apple and plucked it from the dirt. He set it at Zaxis's feet and fluffed his feathers, revealing the bright glow of his fiery body underneath.

"I found one, my arcanist. Aren't you proud?"

Zaxis flashed me a smirk as he stroked his phoenix's head. "Oh, yeah. Good job."

I gritted my teeth, half-irritated at myself and half-irritated at Zaxis. I should've ignored him and focused on my search.

Illia walked over and took me by the elbow. "C'mon. What're you waiting for?"

"This is nice weather we're having," Zaxis said to her, smiling wider than usual. "Pleasant and cool without too much wind."

"Uh-huh," she muttered. She tugged my arm. "Volke?"

I nodded. "Right."

I shot Zaxis a look before walking off, amused by his failed attempts at engaging Illia. Did he really think *the weather* would interest her? He wasn't as suave as he thought, though I did feel sorry for him. Not many people tried to strike up a conversation with Illia. For both their sakes, I wished he had done better.

Once we left Zaxis's presence, I turned my attention to the shadows. "Luthair, help us look for the apples."

"By your command, my arcanist."

2

ZELFREE'S APPRENTICES

The smell of the ocean mixed with the vegetation, creating a scent unique to islands. I shifted through the undergrowth, watching the bright blue lizards scurry away the instant I exposed them to the sunlight. It reminded me of younger times—the exciting discoveries of wild animals hidden around every corner.

The thoughts got me chuckling.

"I found an apple here," Luthair said.

I perked up and spotted his shifting shadow one shrub over. Sure enough, tucked between the roots of a daisy tree, and covered in twigs, was a red apple.

As I reached for it, a pigeon dove at me for the fruit. It scratched, pecked, and cooed, and—while annoying—it wasn't strong enough to pierce my clothing. White-crowned pigeons were common to the islands and considered docile, but this bird fought like its nation would lose the war if it came home empty-handed.

I swatted at the bird. "Stop!" Then I focused my knight-mare magic.

While phoenix arcanists evoked flames, I evoked an aura

of terror—haunting visions that preyed on the target's worst fears. The use of my magic burned me from my palm to my elbow, a harsh reminder that I was second-bonded, and that my sorcery didn't flow with ease, like everyone else's. I was the only one who had to deal with a crippling side effect, and the sting remained with me no matter what magic I used.

The white-crowned pigeon darted away at great speed, but it didn't go far. The bird stopped at a nearby daisy tree and huddled over a nest, its whole body shaking.

I bent down and scooped up the apple. Dirt marred the fruit's waxy skin, and I cleaned it on the side of my trousers.

The chirp of chicks, while faint, echoed between the tree trunks. The pigeon's nest was filled to the brim with her family.

With a heavy sigh, I glanced from the nest to my apple, debating how much I wanted to win. Then again, Master Zelfree never said we had to bring him a *whole* apple.

I withdrew a knife from my belt and cut a chunk from the side of the ripe fruit. "Luthair, can you take this to the pigeon?"

"Of course, my arcanist."

I dropped the apple chunk on the ground. Shadows formed and snatched the food from the dirt. In a matter of seconds, the darkness slunk across the ground, up the tree trunk, and slithered over to the nest. The shadows tucked the piece of apple into the twigs of the bird home, careful not to disturb the mother or her chicks. Once my terrors faded, she would be able to eat it and feed her young.

"I got another one, Illia," I called out. Hopefully she wouldn't care about the damage I had done to it.

Illia walked out from a cluster of trees and waved me over. "I found one, too."

I joined her in a small clearing, and she pointed to the branches thirty feet above us.

An apple had been wedged between two trees that had grown close together. The daisy trees were too thin to climb, and I didn't know if Illia could teleport such a distance. There wasn't really a place for her to land, either. The branches couldn't support more than a few pounds.

"Do you think we can shake it free?" I asked.

Luthair huffed. "Your master said to use magical methods."

Nicholin leapt off Illia's shoulder and bounded to the base of the tree. "This is all me. Stand back, everyone!"

He disappeared with a pop and sparkle and reappeared twenty feet above us, his little arms wrapped around the trunk of the tree. He didn't hang on well. He slipped downward, his tiny claws digging into the bark. After he slid a few feet, Nicholin teleported again, this time to the same height as the apple, his breathing heavy.

"I—" he inhaled and exhaled, "—got this."

The instant he touched the apple, Nicholin teleported. The fruit came with him, but he couldn't make it the entire distance to the ground. Instead, he appeared six feet above us. As he fell, the apple slipped from his grasp, and they tumbled through the air at different speeds.

Illia caught Nicholin in her arms. I ran for the apple, but missed. My heart sank, fearing the fruit would explode on the dirt, but shadows rose and buffered the fall, catching the apple in an inky tendril. I bent down and scooped it from the darkness.

"Thank you, Luthair," I muttered.

"I shouldn't be the one practicing my magic," he said. "Woods are filled with shadows—the more there are, the more you have to manipulate."

"Right..."

"Your master wanted you to treat this like an actual assignment. If you were looking for young mystical creatures, you would have to use all your knowledge and sorcery to safely gather them."

I held the apple close, Luthair's words sinking deep into my thoughts. What had I been doing? My first solution had been to shake the tree, rather than manipulating the shadows to snatch the apple for me. I needed to change how I thought about problems. I was an arcanist now.

"I'll try harder," I whispered.

Illia walked up behind me and placed a hand on my shoulder. "Are you okay?"

"Yeah. Let's go."

I handed the apple to Illia, and she placed it in her bulging belt pouch. Together, we had four, but we had been searching for an hour. I doubted we would win at this rate.

I examined our surroundings. With a wave of my hand, I tried to manipulate the darkness. A sharp agony of magic pulsed through my chest. I grimaced and closed my hand into a fist.

"Illia," I said, trying to distract myself. "Phoenix arcanists manipulate fire, and leviathan arcanists manipulate water, and I can manipulate shadows..." In theory.

She turned to me, her eyebrows knit. "Okay?"

"What do rizzel arcanists manipulate?"

Silence.

All arcanists could manipulate something, determined by the ability of their eldrin. Unlike evocation, where the arcanist *created* something using their magic, manipulation involved controlling an element, animal, or physical object already in existence. Nicholin could evoke a white flame of teleportation, but I had never seen him manipulate something in the environment.

"I don't know," Illia whispered. She stared at the ground while we walked. "I've been meaning to ask Master Zelfree, but I'm afraid to look foolish. Every other apprentice knows what they're doing."

"Have you seen me using my magic?" I asked with a playful smile.

"I'm serious, Volke. Even if it's harder for you, Luthair knows what you can do. He already went through the learning process with Mathis." She petted Nicholin and sighed. "My eldrin is so young. Even *he* doesn't know what he can manipulate."

"Just because I don't know what I'm capable of doesn't mean I don't know anything," Nicholin piped up. "I'm still amazing! I bet whatever I can manipulate will be awesome. Like, *time* or... something."

"That's impossible."

"Nothing is impossible! For me, anyway."

Illia stopped walking and glared. "Volke, focus. Stop thinking about what rizzels can manipulate and think about where Zelfree would hide those apples. I said I wanted to win, so that's what we're going to do."

The crunch of leaves interrupted our conversation. Atty Trixibelle stepped out from between two clumps of trees.

Her blonde hair shone in the patchwork of light that pierced through the leaves. While Illia wore a buccaneer's outfit—wide pants, long tunic, and an ankle-length coat— Atty wore a white robe with a hood, fastened with a leather belt.

She also held a small ball of flame in her hand, no doubt using it to shine light over the shadowy undergrowth. The fire didn't touch her skin—it remained half an inch above her palm, flickering with inner life and fueled by her phoenix magic.

"Volke," Atty said the moment she spotted me, her eyes wide. "You showed up."

"Hello. Uh, why is that a surprise?"

"We couldn't find you earlier. And you weren't here when we started hunting for apples."

Illia stepped between us. "Hello, Atty. Sorry, we can't talk. We're busy."

"Same as Adelgis and I." Atty's smile seemed reserved.

She had been amazing during our island's Trial of Worth. She never got flustered or bothered by anything. Such focus impressed me.

Atty tapped her chin with a finger. "I can't wait to play with the griffin cubs. I hear their fur is as soft as ten rabbits."

"That's a shame," Illia said. "Because Volke and I are going to be the winners of this little exercise." She patted me on the shoulder to punctuate her statement.

Nicholin puffed out his chest. "That's right. *We'll* be the ones petting griffins."

"Really?" Atty replied with a tone of faux confusion. "That's odd. It looks like you only have four apples." She motioned to a pouch hanging from her belt—a pouch that held five apples. "And Adelgis is just as determined to see the griffins as I am. He's never seen one up close either."

Silence settled between us. Illia glared, her hands tightly balled into fists. What had gotten into her? I'd never seen her taunt anyone into competition. Most of the time Illia didn't even care about structured games. Or rules. Or trophies. Or fame.

Were the griffins *that* important?

Atty stepped past us and headed toward the next patch of undergrowth. "I'd love to stay and chat, but I don't want to

19

disappoint Adelgis." She gave us both a wave. "It must be nice for siblings to partner together. I'm sure you'll make a great team. I'll have to stay on my toes if I'm going to keep the lead."

"Goodbye, Atty," I said as she glided off into the surrounding woods.

"Farewell, Volke. Perhaps we'll be partners next time."

The last statement caught me a little off-guard. Since when did she want to partner with me? I doubted we had interacted for more than thirty minutes in our entire lives. Then again, I wasn't offended by her offer. The opposite, in fact. It was flattering.

Illia straightened her hat. "I can't believe her."

"What's wrong?"

"Did you hear her?" Illia flapped her hand like it was speaking. "*It must be nice for siblings to partner together.*" She exhaled and headed into the woods with long strides. "Atty doesn't know us."

Nicholin huffed. "Yeah, she doesn't know us!" He snuggled close to Illia's neck. "What, exactly, are we upset about?"

"Never mind. Let's go. Now we *have* to beat Atty, just so we can wipe that smug look off her face. Can you imagine her cleaning the deck of the ship? That would be hilarious."

"I suppose," I said as I jogged to catch up to her. "But you don't need to be so vindictive about it."

Illia quickened her step. "I'm just... forget it. Let's get these apples and meet a couple of griffins."

Nicholin squeaked in delight. "Yes, I need to test Atty's claims! Nobody has softer fur than me, thank you very much." He stroked his side and smoothed his own fur to a silky sheen.

I returned my attention to the surrounding area, tense. I

would talk with Illia later. She had gotten upset in the past when people mentioned our "relation." It was obvious to anyone with functioning eyes we weren't real siblings. I had messy black hair. She had wavy brown hair. She had sun-kissed skin—like everyone on the islands—but mine was more honeyed and golden.

I thought it was a compliment when people recognized us as family. They respected the fact we were adopted and didn't draw attention to our differences. Yet Illia hated it. I suspected she wanted us to be friends rather than family—or maybe something *more* than friends—but I didn't like thinking about it.

I cherished our relationship the way it was. Why did anything need to change? And what if it did change, but then could never go back?

I just... didn't want to risk it.

We were siblings. Nothing more, nothing less.

Master Zelfree's voice echoed between the trees as he shouted, "The exercise is over! All the apples have been found."

My heart sank into my gut.

Damn. We definitely didn't win, not when Atty and Adelgis had five apples. But would we be the ones swabbing the deck of our ship? I hoped not.

"Dang," Illia muttered. "We should've gone with a better tactic from the start."

Illia and I picked up our pace and headed toward the sound of Zelfree's shout. Some daisy trees grew in such tight clusters that neither of us could fit between them. We ended up navigating a woodland maze until we came to a clearing bathed in midmorning sunlight.

Five people waited for us—Master Zelfree and his other four apprentices.

Atty greeted me with a sly wave.

Adelgis stood next to her, a tall man of sixteen with crisp pants, a button-up shirt, and a coat hanging on one arm. His black hair was pulled back in a loose ponytail, and to my surprise, he had apple bits splattered across most of his fine clothes.

"Are you okay, Adelgis?" I asked.

He glanced over, took a breath like he might offer a tirade, and then forced a slow exhale. After a few calming breaths he answered, "Some things are outside our control. Thank you for your concern, Volke. I will be fine once we make it back to the ship and I'm allowed to change."

Adelgis refused to touch the apple bits, like he was afraid of getting his hand sticky or of smearing the fruit into the cloth of his expensive shirt.

The last two in the clearing were Zaxis and Hexa.

Zaxis had a hand on his hip, his sack of apples at his feet. His total count came to six whole apples and one crushed apple... which was odd. He shot me a glare when he caught me staring.

"What're you looking at?" he snapped.

"N-nothing."

"Hey, Illia," Hexa said with a smile. "There you are! I didn't see you all morning."

Illia nodded, and so did Nicholin, both even going so far as to wave.

Out of everyone in the clearing, Hexa was the most *distinct*.

She wore a long coat with no sleeves, showcasing the scars on her arms. They were claw marks: some old, some new, and some so deep I shuddered in empathic pain. During her Trial of Worth, she'd had to fight with a hydra, and the more scars she got, the better, apparently. Her cinnamon hair, spun in tight curls, had been pulled back to reveal her ears—pierced in more places than I ever imagined ears could be pierced.

Occasional dustings of soot rained down from above thanks to Atty and Zaxis's phoenixes. I moved over a few feet to avoid it.

Hexa's hydra sat on the ground, curled around her feet, his yellow eyes scanning us in a slow and deliberate manner. Any time someone looked in his direction, he flashed his fangs and flared his spike-scales.

Pleasant.

The only eldrins not visible were Luthair—who hid in my shadow—and Adelgis's ethereal whelk, a strange creature capable of hiding in the light.

Master Zelfree glanced between us. "Now that you're all here, why don't you tell me your apple count?"

"We have four," I said, motioning to the apples in Illia's pouch.

Illia dumped them on the ground and avoided making eye contact with anyone, even going so far as to cover the scars on her face with her right hand. I recognized the telltale signs of embarrassment. She especially avoided looking in Atty's direction.

Adelgis stared down at the crushed apple on his clothing. "We have five." Then he shot Zaxis a sideways scowl.

"What?" Zaxis barked. He turned to Master Zelfree and kicked his bag. "We have seven. We win."

"What happened between you two?" Zelfree asked.

Adelgis started with, "I was reaching for an apple hidden in a bush when—"

"I got to it first," Zaxis concluded. "Then Adelgis tried to take it because he said he saw it before I did, but that's not how it works. He wouldn't let go of the apple, so I had to take it from him."

Adelgis motioned to his outfit sullied by the splash of apple parts. "Zaxis *crushed it* and then shoved the core in his bag."

"If you had *backed off* like I had told you, that wouldn't have happened!"

"Wait, wait," Zelfree said, holding up two hands. "Let me get this straight. In the exercise where I said the apples represented lost baby mystical creatures, you *splattered* one across your fellow apprentice?"

I had to stifle a laugh. Illia held her hand over her mouth, and so did Hexa, both of them shaking with restrained chuckles.

"I'm a phoenix arcanist," Zaxis said with a huff. "If these were real baby mystical creatures, I could've healed them. Everything would've been fine."

Zelfree dragged his hand down his face. "Gods, help me. I already need another drink."

"*Hey!* You said we needed to find the apples, not coddle them."

"That's right," Hexa said. "And we found the most, so we get to see the griffins before the ceremony."

I hated losing to the others, and hated the thought of cleaning the ship more, but it couldn't be helped. Illia and I had started late, and I hadn't even been using my magic to gather apples.

"I don't think this competition was fair," Adelgis said matter-of-factly. "As an ethereal whelk arcanist, my eldrin and I can hear thoughts. If there had been baby mystical creatures lost in the woods, we could've picked up on their distressed state. This task favors those with keen physical sight, nothing else."

Zaxis forced a sarcastic smile. "You're just jealous."

"We would've been tied for number of apples if you hadn't destroyed one in your overzealous attempt to win."

"I was willing to do whatever it took—you were just too polite. Guess who came out on top?"

"Quiet down," Zelfree snapped. After we had silenced ourselves, he crossed his arms. "If I had known you lot would be this competitive, I would've gone with something—"

The sound of galloping drifted into the clearing. Zelfree stopped talking and listened. The sound got louder and louder, and the speed with which the hooves hit dirt got my heart rate up.

No one rode that fast to deliver good news.

The dense trees near the clearing prevented the rider from bursting onto the scene. Instead, the horse whinnied as it came to a stop, and a rider dismounted with a grunt. Everyone remained still and silent until a denizen from West Landin shoved his way through the undergrowth.

"Master Arcanist Zelfree," the man said, squinting from the patchwork sunlight shining down on us. "I'm so glad you're here." He wore thin leather armor and carried both a sword and a flintlock pistol.

Zelfree stepped forward and slid his hands into his pockets. His haggard expression and slumped shoulders didn't really carry the air of *master arcanist*, but the rider seemed to recognize Zelfree instantly.

"What can I do for a member of the city guard?" Zelfree asked.

"I bring awful news, I'm afraid. Ryllin, the griffin ruler, and one of his children have disappeared. No one knows where they are, not even Kahtona, the griffin dame."

Two adult griffins lived on the Isle of Landin, both of

whom had lost their arcanists. They had decided to return to the island of their birth to preside over future bonding ceremonies. These two were the parents of all the griffin cubs—there was no way they would miss the Trial of Worth, not when it was their own flesh and blood who would be bonding.

Zelfree narrowed his eyes. "When were they seen last?"

"Last night," the guardsman said. "Ryllin had separated himself from the other griffins, but no one thought much of it."

"No one has seen him this morning?"

"Not a soul. People think his cub went to find him, but no one knows where the little griffin is either."

"Why wasn't anyone concerned when Ryllin separated himself?"

"He had been patrolling the isle, checking for pirates." The guardsman emphasized his speech with his hands, waving them around with each word. "Ryllin had been gone for hours. Everyone assumed he was just tired and had gone to sleep."

Illia glanced over to me, her gaze hard. I gave her a single nod, understanding from her body language that she was concerned. And I agreed—it was odd behavior, especially on the eve of a bonding ceremony. What had Ryllin been thinking? It didn't make sense.

"Will you help find Ryllin and his cub?" the guardsman asked.

Zelfree smiled. "Of course. The arcanists of the Frith Guild will handle the matter. Tell everyone in town to leave the search to us, understand?"

"Th-thank you, Master Arcanist! It's a relief to know it's in your capable hands."

"Don't get too excited. The guild charges for its services."

The man fidgeted with the edge of his leather gloves. He nodded after mulling over the information. "That may be true, but it is a relief. I'll deliver the message straight away, Master Arcanist. And I'll pray to the heavens that you find Ryllin and his cub without incident."

He entered the woods, mounted his steed, and galloped away, slower than before, but still with great haste. Once he was far enough away that he could no longer be heard, we all turned to face Zelfree. Our master took out his flask, opened it, and then stared with a frown at the empty container.

"Good thing I've been preparing everyone for this all morning," Zelfree quipped.

Atty perked up. "We're really going to search for lost mystical creatures?"

"Someone has to do it."

"But why do you think they left the safety of the city? Could something be wrong?"

"That's a possibility." Zelfree shook his left arm.

The pair of bangles on his wrist shimmered and morphed into a gray-furred cat. Her eyes—one rose in color, the other gold—shone with inner magic. She leapt onto Zelfree's shoulder and swished her three-foot-long tail.

I always found myself intrigued by the appearance of a mimic—it was both beautiful and exotic.

"We can handle a disgruntled griffin," the mimic said with a purr at the end of her words.

Zelfree stroked her head and scratched behind an ear. "Traces, we'll go into town, and you transform into one of the griffin cubs."

"Of course, my arcanist."

"The rest of you will pair up again and search the area behind the woods. I'm fairly certain if the griffins had been

27

in here, you would've found them between discoveries of apples."

Adelgis furrowed his brow. "Excuse me, Master. You won't make this a competition again, correct?"

"Oh, it's a competition." Zelfree smiled. "I've seen how it motivates you all. And I'm not going to count the apple victory, not after you two killed one of our hypothetical baby creatures. The new deal is: whichever pair finds the griffin cub will get to see all the griffins before the ceremony."

Zaxis half-barked, half-growled, "That's not fair!"

"Don't talk to me about *fair*. You're lucky I don't make you sit this one out." Zelfree pointed at him. "I don't care how many injuries you can heal. Not even a bruise, understand?"

"What if we find the adult griffin?"

"I'll handle the adult. Under no circumstance should you approach him."

Everyone nodded, though Adelgis and Zaxis exchanged quick glowers—so fast I doubted Zelfree even noticed.

Illia faced me, and I knew she wanted to partner up again. Before I could accept or deny, Zelfree snapped his fingers, drawing everyone's attention.

"You won't choose your pairs this time around," he said. "It's clear to me that you don't understand your own strengths and weaknesses. None of you picked a partner who would help you search—you all just picked people you got along with."

I glanced around the clearing.

Me and Illia.

Atty and Adelgis, prim and proper.

Zaxis and Hexa, gruff and forceful.

I could see it.

Zelfree pointed to a seething Hexa. "You're pairing with Adelgis."

Hexa rubbed her scarred arms and then turned her wild grin to Adelgis. I couldn't tell what Adelgis thought, because he hid his emotions behind a neutral expression and forced smile. Probably wasn't a good sign. Hexa looked ready to wrestle a rabid alligator, while Adelgis probably wanted nothing more than to change into a fresh outfit.

"Whatever you think is best, Master," Adelgis said.

Hexa walked over and punched his arm. "We'll make a great team. You can hear the thoughts of the cub, right? We've as good as won."

"Well, the cub needs to be close, and—"

"Don't make excuses now! You said you could do it, so I want to see it."

"Right..."

My chest tightened. I didn't want to be paired with Zaxis. Anyone but him. He was in a mood today, and I knew whatever happened, it would be a hassle from start to finish. I'd have a much better chance at participating in the griffin bonding ceremony if I partnered with Illia or Atty.

Zelfree pointed to Illia. "You're with Atty."

Illia and Atty stared forward with slight frowns, shock written into their wide eyes. They didn't even exchange glances.

"Thank you, Master," Atty replied. Then she bowed her head.

Illia said nothing and instead gave me a quick glance. She had this *I'm sorry* look, like she blamed herself for the failure of the first task and wanted to make it up to me. I shook my head, hoping she would understand I wasn't disappointed or angry.

But if she was with Atty... that meant...

"That leaves you two," Zelfree said.

Curse the abyssal hells.

I was stuck with Zaxis.

He walked over to me, his arms folded tight across his chest. He wore the sleeves of his long coat rolled up to his elbows, and the top few buttons of his shirt were undone, exposing his collarbones. Wiry and tall—but not *quite* as tall as me—he carried himself like he was willing to fight, which sometimes meant more than height.

"I get stuck with the loser," Zaxis said as he eyed me. "Makes sense we would *balance each other out*. I give it my all, and you barely give it anything."

"What's your problem today?" I asked under my breath. "You know I try to win every competition I'm in."

"Heh." He flashed me half a smile. "I just wanted to rile you into a good performance. I've noticed you sometimes do better if I prod you into action."

Zaxis thought he could get a better result out of me if he offered insults? I almost yelled at him for that comment, but I bit back my words. The longer I mulled it over, the more I realized…

He might be right.

Dammit.

"We aren't going to lose," Zaxis said, an edge of heat to his words. "Got that, Volke? I won with the apples, and I'll win here."

"Don't worry. We have the same goal."

"The griffin cub is your top priority," Zelfree said as he headed to the edge of the clearing. "It should be simple to convince it to return to town. And if words don't work, it's just a child without an arcanist. His magic won't overpower yours. But if you find the adult…"

He turned and faced us, his expression more intense than usual.

"Come and get me," Zelfree concluded. "Even without an arcanist, an adult griffin can have powerful magic. Understood?"

Everyone replied in unison, "Yes, Master Zelfree."

"Good. Now go out there and find that cub. I want this wrapped up before evening."

Dusk marked the beginning of the bonding ceremony. That didn't leave us much time.

3

LOST

*Z*axis and I hurried from the daisy woods, his phoenix weaving through the branches as he followed us in the air. Illia and Atty went in the opposite direction. I didn't know if they had secret knowledge on the location of the cub, but I doubted it. The griffin could be anywhere—they were capable of flight a few days after hatching, and the Isle of Landin wasn't *that* big.

Our master disappeared behind a set of trees while Hexa and Adelgis headed in the direction of the docks. Not a bad idea. With a boat, one could easily move around the island. I slowed down, half-tempted to tell Zaxis this idea, but he continued forward at full pace.

I jogged to catch up with him. The shadows moved alongside me, indicating Luthair's presence. None of us spoke until we reached the road, and even then, we traveled all the way out of the woods before Zaxis grabbed my upper arm.

"We need a strategy," he said.

Forsythe swooped down, a trail of embers behind him,

and landed on the ground, his black talons digging into the dirt.

Zaxis stroked his head. "Did you see anything?"

"Yes, my arcanist," Forsythe said. "Look to the southern sky."

Zaxis and I turned our attention upward. High above, near the tufts of ivory clouds, I spotted an adult griffin. She glided on her giant eagle wings, carried by the ocean winds. Her amber fur rippled with the breeze, and her beak shone with a sharp edge.

"Is that the missing griffin?" Zaxis asked.

I shook my head. "It can't be. That griffin is female. It's probably the dame, Kahtona."

He squinted. "You can see her private bits all the way from here?"

My face heated in an instant. "N-no, of course not! Female griffins have the heads of eagles. Male griffins have the heads of lions."

"Oh. I didn't know that."

"I read stories about griffins when I was younger. There are a lot of famous griffin arcanists. Haven't you ever heard of Freega the Dauntless? Or Captain Quint of the *Dawn Racer*? They both had griffin eldrin."

Zaxis scoffed and looked away from Kahtona, but his vacant gaze betrayed the fact that the cogs of his mind still struggled with our problem. He pondered for a moment and then pulled me close.

"What do griffins eat?"

"Fish."

"Every idiot knows that," Zaxis growled. "Tell me something more specific. You must've read about their eating habits when fawning over those legendary arcanists of yore."

It took me a moment, but I recalled half a dozen books I had read as a youngster.

"Griffins wait on cliffs and rock faces until they spot fish just below the surface of the water," I said. "Then they launch, grab them, and fly to a perch to eat. Their favorites are seatrout and spadefish, usually found in bays."

Zaxis smiled wide—more devious than I liked. He patted my arm, reached into his belt pouch, and withdrew a folded piece of parchment. I watched with rapt fascination as he unfolded a map of the island, including the two cities, West Landin and East Landin. The detail included the small daisy woods and main road where we stood.

"When did you get a map?" I asked.

"When we were in town."

"Smart thinking."

"Preparation," Zaxis said. "Without it, we leave our fate to chance."

Although I tried to stop, I couldn't help but smile. Zaxis repeated a lesson from the Pillar? I knew he studied the steps, just like I did, but I thought he was in the same boat as Illia—the lessons were all a silly waste of time.

Zaxis narrowed his eyes into an irritated glower. "Don't give me that doofy smile. I only said that because I know it *also* motivates you." Then he knelt and smoothed the map out on the road. "Now knock that off and help me look for a bay. The griffins have to eat at some point, and there aren't any islands close enough to fly to."

The Isle of Landin had three bays, each a glorious fishing location that the locals visited on a daily basis. If the griffin cub *was* there, why hadn't anyone spotted it yet? I shook the thought from my head. The missing griffins had just now become a concern. If someone had seen a griffin this morning, they wouldn't have thought much about it—a common sight not worth noting.

The bays were on the north, east, and west sides of the island. The western bay was the largest and made for a safe port into the city of West Landin. The griffins weren't there, obviously, or someone would've reported it. The eastern bay was where the city of East Landin made their port. The northern bay was rockier than the others, which was why no city had ever sprung up there. It would have plenty of caves and crags near the water, perfect for griffins to rest and eat the fish they caught.

I pointed to the northern bay—named Granite Shark Bay—and tapped my finger along the shore.

"This area here is ideal griffin fishing grounds," I said.

Zaxis nodded. "That's what I thought, too."

"You think we should head there?"

"It makes sense. And if we don't find them there, we can work our way to the east bay."

It wasn't a bad plan. The main road went up the island through the middle, stopping near Granite Shark Bay in the north. It would be an easy cart ride, and likely faster than taking a boat around the island.

Forsythe flapped his wings, creating a gust of warm air. "I knew you two would devise a solid strategy. You have such a calming demeanor, Volke."

"*Hey*," Zaxis barked. "Whose eldrin are you, anyway? I was the one with the map. This was all my idea, basically."

"I'm sorry, my arcanist. I thought—"

"And he doesn't have a *calming demeanor*. He just *daydreams* all the time." Zaxis snatched the map and folded it up in a few quick motions. "Even this morning, when we were supposed to gather to train with Master Zelfree, Volke had to go stare out over the ocean, like he was a character in a sappy romance, pining over lost love."

My face flushed, but anger burned away the embarrassment. He thought I was daydreaming? What did he know? And how did he even know where I was? If he knew about Zelfree's request to train, Zaxis could've told me, but instead he left me on the cliff. What was his problem?

"Let's get this over with," I said. "That way you won't have to suffer through me daydreaming any longer than necessary."

"I'm glad you're focused." Zaxis pointed to a group of carts down the road. "Let's catch a ride with them. C'mon, I don't want to fall behind the others."

The smooth cart ride made for pleasant travel. Zaxis and I sat in the back with Forsythe perched on the side. Three sacks of melons accompanied us in the cart, but I didn't mind. They had a pleasant smell, like sweet honey, and I had been tempted to buy one.

"I can't believe so many arcanists from the Frith Guild are here," the cart driver said. He held the reins of the horses with calloused hands, and his gray hair had a dull shine under the intensity of the afternoon sun. "I'm happy to give you arcanists a ride anywhere you want, no matter the time of day."

"Thank you," Forsythe replied. "Most generous."

"My wife would give me what for if I didn't help out you pirate-slayers. Those cutthroats have gotten worse and worse. Someone needs to deal with them, I tell ya."

I pondered the statements, wondering when Zelfree would have us deal with pirates. He seemed to want us to avoid any stress or trauma, but I didn't think that would be possible. Arcanists of the Frith Guild dealt with adversity. Everyone knew it. Zelfree couldn't shield us forever.

White steam from one of Landin's mountains wafted skyward. It disappeared before it touched the clouds, but I couldn't help but stare. What was over there?

I tapped Zaxis on the shoulder. "Do you see that?"

"That's steam from the Sapphire Springs," he said. "What of it?"

"Natural springs? The kind with hot water?"

"Yeah. Everyone on the Isle of Landin uses them during special occasions." He gave me an odd sideways glance. "There's a tradition of swimming in them after the griffin bonding ceremony."

"Oh," I muttered. "That must be nice."

"Bathing in the Sapphire Springs brings good luck," the cart driver said with a chuckle.

I patted the shadows next to me. "Think that's true, Luthair?"

"Mathis and I bathed in the Sapphire Springs once," he murmured. "Our fortune turned around for a time afterward."

The information got me pensive.

I had never considered myself lucky. Quite the opposite, in fact. Illia was my sister, but misfortune was my true sibling. Every detail about me—my thief of a mother, my murderer of a father, and the many years spent as a gravedigger—all spoke of a past marked by the black hand of misfortune. Even my childhood hero, Master Arcanist Gregory Ruma, was a man brought low by the death of his wife. He ultimately became a villain who killed thousands.

If that wasn't bad luck, I didn't know what was.

Although I had managed to turn my fortune around, I

swear more things went wrong than right—like the universe was out to test my patience.

I wouldn't give in, though.

Perseverance. Without it, we fail at the first problem.

Even if everything went wrong, I would keep moving forward. But...

A little luck wouldn't hurt. Hopefully we would get to bathe in the Sapphire Springs before we left the Isle of Landin.

Zaxis turned away and tucked himself in the corner of the cart. He held out his hand and created a small candle's worth of flame in his palm. Then he snuffed it out and did it all over again. He had done that on and off the entire trek, just creating and extinguishing flame. It looked mindless and tiresome, but he stared at the fire with an intense gaze.

"Are you okay?" I asked.

"Yes," he replied, curt.

"I think you've mastered evoking flame."

"Maybe. Not as good as Atty, though."

Ah.

That one statement explained Zaxis's attitude today.

He didn't want to lose—*to Atty*. It made sense. He and Atty both bonded to phoenixes at the same time. People would forever compare them. Who was the best? It was easy to measure between them, whereas comparing Illia and me would be difficult. I had a second-bonded knightmare and Illia had a rare and unusual rizzel. Those couldn't be quantified simply.

This also explained why Zaxis had crushed the apple when fighting over it with Adelgis. Atty and Adelgis had paired together, after all.

"Has Atty gotten better lately?" I asked.

Zaxis huffed. "She practiced with Master Zelfree before

dawn. He kept saying things like, *I'm really impressed with your ability* and, *I've trained phoenix arcanists in the past, but none like you.*" Zaxis squeezed his hand into a fist, killing the fire. "He's never even looked twice in my direction. Even when he's mad, it's like he'd rather I disappear than deal with me."

"You're reading too much into it."

"Heh. Whatever. I know what's going on."

Zaxis started up his fire practice again, his flame hotter, and brighter than before. He glared at it each time he snuffed it out of existence.

I wasn't sure what to say. I knew the feeling, but words never made me feel better, so what could I offer to Zaxis?

"We're going to be the ones to find those griffins," I said.

Although it took a moment, Zaxis glanced over with half a smile. "Exactly."

I relaxed against the side of the cart, satisfied I had done my part to pull Zaxis from his funk. Then again, his practicing reminded me I should be doing it too. I stared at my hand, remembering the pain from earlier, and sighed.

Did I really want to flinch and grimace in front of Zaxis? I would look pathetic, especially after his masterful display of evoking flames.

Before I could decide, however, the cart driver pulled the reins of the horses, jerking them to a stop. The sacks of melons shook, and two fruits escaped their confines.

"What's going on?" Forsythe asked, flapping his wings.

Both Zaxis and I stood.

A woman hustled down the road, her eyes red and her face shiny with tears. She held her skirt to prevent it from catching underfoot.

"Louis," the woman called out, her voice strained. "Thank goodness."

The cart driver dismounted with a grunt. "What is it, Camilla? You look awfully worn."

"It's my boys." Her eyes widened when she caught sight of Forsythe perched on the back of the cart. "By the heavens —you have arcanists with you!"

"From the Frith Guild, no less. But what's this about your boys?"

Camilla ran past him, her attention focused solely Zaxis and me. "Please, mighty arcanists. You must help me."

"What is it?" I asked.

"My boys went missin'. Both of them bolted out of town when the news spread of the lost griffins. They thought... they were sayin'... they'd be the ones to find the cub. But they're much too young. Only twelve and ten. What if somethin' happens? They're a clumsy pair. Likely to fall off rocks if they go climbin' too high without supervision."

"Of course we'll help," I said.

Zaxis grabbed my shoulder and turned my attention to him. "What're you doing?" he hissed under his breath. "We're looking for the griffins, first and foremost. Plus, we don't just help random mothers find their missing kids. We get paid for our services, remember?"

"But arcanists of the Frith Guild always help people in genuine need," I whispered.

I had read countless stories about the noble spirit of the Frith Guild. Sure, they took coin from cities and towns to rid the waters of pirates, but many arcanists went above and beyond any contract, and some even went from island to island with their healing magic or medicine—all free of charge. How could we turn our back on a poor, distressed mother?

"If the kids are looking for the griffins, we'll probably

run into them," I continued, my voice low. "It won't take much of our time to make sure they head home."

Zaxis opened his mouth like he had a retort, but he stopped himself short. Then he glanced back to the mother and held his arm up with dramatic flair. "Fear not, gentle woman. We, mighty arcanists of the Frith Guild, will help you find your boys." He stood straight and smiled. "What do they look like?"

I almost couldn't hold back my laugh. What was *that*? *I* had been the one who wanted to help, not *him*.

Camilla's expression lit up as bright as a lighthouse. "Oh, thank you! Thank you. My boys are named Leo and Grant. Leo is the elder, with short hair, brown as mud. Grant has a mole on his cheek, cute as a button. You'd know it as soon as you saw him."

"We'll keep an eye out," I said.

Zaxis nodded. "They're as good as found."

"You're doin' me a great kindness," Camilla said. "Thank you again! Thank you both so, so much!"

Our cart driver, Louis, retook his seat and urged the horses forward. "We best be on our way then."

I smiled to Camilla as we passed. Tears streamed down her face and caught in the lines of her smile. It shook me for a moment—she had full confidence in us, like there was no way harm could befall her children now that Zaxis and I were on the case.

"Forsythe," Zaxis said. "Take to the sky, would you? Maybe you can spot two runaway kids playing on the road."

"By your command, my arcanist."

The phoenix flew from the cart with a couple of powerful beats of his wings. It would probably be faster than sending Luthair to search.

"That mother is overreacting, ya know," Zaxis muttered as he crossed his arms. "I'm sure her kids are fine."

I hoped Zaxis was right. I understood why the boys would run off. If they "saved" the griffin cub, perhaps they could prove they were worthy enough to bond with—and bonding with a mystical creature would be worth any punishment. Still, it was reckless for kids as young as they were to get involved. Most mystical creatures didn't bond with children. What if the kids got upset after being rejected and then did something foolish?

"I'm worried about them," I said.

"Keep your eyes on the prize. Even if we don't find the kids, they'll have to come back home once the griffins are found."

He had a point. There wouldn't be a reason for them to keep searching after that.

Then again, what if Leo and Grant hurt themselves in the process of looking for a griffin, just like their mother feared? What if they were stuck somewhere and calling for help, but no one was around to hear their cries? What if we found the griffins and headed home, only to unwittingly leave them to a slow and painful death at the bottom of a rocky cliff?

The look on their mother's face remained in my thoughts.

She trusted us to bring her kids back.

I refused to let her down.

4

CLIFFSIDE ENCOUNTER

*Z*axis and I left the cart and headed toward Granite Shark Bay. The path was well worn, but not wide enough for a horse. Fishermen passed us with wooden cages and thin nets, all filled to bursting with fish. The fishermen bowed their heads and stepped aside for us to pass, each with a smile, as though gazing upon us was akin to witnessing a miracle.

Although I knew arcanists were revered—I had admired them my entire life—it felt odd to be on the receiving end. I hadn't yet done anything worthy of admiration. Our mentor, Everett Zelfree, had saved islands' worth of people, fought pirates, and brought mass murderers to justice. Our guildmaster, Liet Eventide, had protected cities from hurricanes, helped the land become fertile enough for farming, and even led assaults against raiders in the icy north. *They* were arcanists of legend.

I was...

Nobody.

"What's with that look?" Zaxis asked. He glowered at me

for a moment. "You should be paying attention to our surroundings."

"Sorry," I muttered.

I pushed the thoughts from my mind. The rocks of the northern bay were dark in color, darker where the water occasionally splashed. They jutted upward, like tiny mountains, some curved at the top, allowing for birds to perch comfortably. Forsythe did just that, his soot wafting down onto us when the wind blew. He flew from one rock to the next, glancing between them with his golden eyes.

"Master Zelfree said we picked the wrong partners for the apple hunt," Zaxis said as we walked. "But I had picked Hexa for a reason."

"Why was that?"

"I figured her hydra could search the ground, and my phoenix could search the air. We'd cover all angles." He elbowed me. "Tell me, if you could partner up with any other apprentice for this task, who would it be?"

The question caught me off guard. Was it a trick? Did he want me to say *him*? Was this him secretly asking for a compliment?

Zaxis must have seen my questioning gaze because he huffed and turned away, his ears red.

"Not me, *fool*," he said. "I meant among the others. Who would you prefer to be searching with?"

"Well..." I mulled over the options, even though I knew the answer. "Probably Atty. I know her the least, and we've never done anything as a team."

Zaxis chuckled. "Yeah. Sure. Those are the reasons." Then he shot me a scrutinizing glare. "You wouldn't pick Illia?"

"Illia and I are great at cooperating. If we partnered up, I'm sure we could find the griffins."

"What do you think about me and her partnering up? We'd work well together, right?"

"Uh... I guess."

I didn't care for the way Zaxis asked his questions. He wasn't talking about this assignment—that much I had surmised. Did he mean courting Illia? I almost laughed. She wouldn't go for Zaxis. He wasn't her type. And I was certain William wouldn't approve.

Right?

I crossed my arms, more bothered by the hypothetical than I should have been. Even imagining Illia and Zaxis alone somewhere got me tense.

"Tell you what," Zaxis said with a smile. "How about the next time we get to choose our partners, I'll recommend you to Atty, and you recommend me to Illia, okay?"

I turned away, feigning an interest in some distant rocks. "I never really convince Illia of anything. She usually gets *me* doing something."

"C'mon. You could put a good word in for me."

"Well, I suppose I could say something nice about—"

"Perfect," Zaxis interjected. "That's all I needed to hear."

All he needed to hear? Feh. He made interacting with him a chore. At times I felt like we weren't even having a conversation—he just waited for his turn to talk. Then again, he was talented, and while *he and I* never got along as kids, he had never made fun of Illia, even when the others used to laugh at the scars on her face.

We made it to the end of the road and stopped.

Granite Shark Bay was surrounded by tall, jagged cliffs on opposite sides. Narrow walkways led to the water, and some steps had been carved into the rocks to allow for upward travel, but it remained treacherous. Fortunately, the rock barrier in the bay prevented large waves, which kept most of the walkways dry.

I stared at the cliffs. Caves were everywhere, like the holes of a worm through an apple—some small, others large. I ran a hand through my hair, wondering where I would even start. The salty breeze helped me relax.

Zaxis glanced at the rock steps and then back to the road. He pointed to a group of fishermen not far from our location. "How about one of us questions the locals, and the other searches the rocks? We'll cover twice as much territory."

"Sounds good to me."

"I'll talk to the fishermen." Zaxis straightened his long coat. "Of the two of us, I have more charisma."

I rubbed at the bridge of my nose. "Fine. Whatever. Just remember to ask about the missing kids, too."

"Of course, of course," he said, dismissing the comment with a wave of his hand. "Here. You take the map. Mark down the areas you think we should explore together."

I took the paper and tucked it into my trouser pocket. Then Zaxis headed toward the fishermen, his red hair flowing in the ocean wind. I waited until he was speaking with the locals before heading up the narrow steps. If I slipped, I didn't want him to see.

"Luthair," I muttered, taking one step at a time. "Did your old arcanist, Mathis, have difficulties learning magic?"

"No," Luthair said, no hesitation.

Fantastic. I got to be the *special one*.

"What was the first thing he learned?" I asked.

"He learned to manipulate darkness. When he started, he could only move the shadows, but in time, he realized he could solidify and harden them—first to a cloth-like consistency, then to something as solid as metal."

"I can harden shadows into metal?" I stopped walking halfway up, my eyebrows knit. That was amazing! Almost unbelievable. "How does that work?"

"A knightmare is darkness given form. My body feels like metal, but it isn't. Mathis realized this and began training himself to coalesce shadows into a solid." Luthair shifted from one shady spot to the other, keeping to the dark. "Remember when I caught the apple with tendrils of darkness? That's how."

I knew I could move shadows around, and I was aware it could take physical shape, but I didn't know I was *condensing* the darkness. That description made it easier to visualize the magic. I walked up the steps until I came to a cliffside cave and stopped at the mouth. The inside was nothing but an inky void. A perfect testing ground.

My heart beat hard against my ribs as I reached a hand out and tried to manipulate the shadows.

Pain flared from my palm, but I had been prepared. Although it hurt, I kept channeling my magic, focusing on my target and willing it to condense into something physical. The agony moved to my elbow. I gritted my teeth, confident I could overcome it.

Then I motioned the darkness toward me. Snake-like rivulets of shadow exited the cave, solid enough to disturb the dirt on the rocks. They were five feet long, three in total. Somehow, I could *feel* them, like a new limb, only distant. Could I grab things with them? Probably. They acted like pieces of rope. But the suffering became too great. I released my magic and gasped for air.

The shadow-ropes disappeared.

Sweat ran from my forehead and dripped onto my coat.

Luthair shifted through the shadows underfoot. "That was an admirable start."

"Th-thanks," I murmured.

"Don't compare yourself to Mathis, though."

"Why not? He was a knightmare arcanist, too."

"He started with shadow manipulation. You started with terror evocation. Additionally, it was over a year before Mathis and I ever merged to use our magic together. You and he have taken very different courses in training."

"Oh..."

After a few deep breaths, I stretched my arms and relaxed. This wasn't the time to train inside a cave. Zaxis was counting on me, and I needed to explore the nearby area. I marked the walkway on the map, noting that one nearby cave was deep. Perhaps we would have to go inside.

I headed for another set of stone steps, and then another. Each stairway had at least fifteen steps, maybe twenty. The cliffside was larger than I first thought—and there was still another one on the opposite side of the bay. It would take all day to search the area, and already my legs burned.

Would we find the cub before dusk? Dread crept into my thoughts.

"Maybe we should've just sent Forsythe to handle this," I said between pants.

Needing a rest, I stood on the bottom of a fourth set of stairs. I had run up the Pillar—a tall, 112-step stairway—but this seemed harder for some reason. Probably because each step was so small, and I remained tense the entire way.

When I glanced down, I noticed several crimson spots.

My chest tightened, as though my gut knew what they were before my mind did.

Blood.

I knelt and touched the spots. Cold. I wiped my hand on my boot, leaving a red smear. Fish could bleed—not as much as other animals, but still. Perhaps a seagull had brought its lunch up to the caves?

The rationalization didn't help me relax. Something felt... off.

I glanced up the stairway. Crimson droplets on each step. Much more blood than a fish had, that was for sure.

"Luthair," I whispered.

He formed out of my shadow, rising up in one deliberate motion. His ebony armor shone in the light—he was a full plate suit, from the gauntlets down to the tassets to protect the legs. His helmet would cover a man's face, but there was nothing inside, just an empty suit of armor. Luthair carried a sword and draped a red-lined cape over his shoulders.

In all ways I found him impressive, despite the fact his armor plates had cracks and his cape was tattered at the end.

"You should be on guard," Luthair said, his voice more ominous and distinct when outside the shadows. "This terrain is perfect for an ambush."

"What if someone is in trouble?"

"That doesn't give you license to act negligently."

I replied with a nod.

With unsteady legs, I made my way up the bloodstained steps. Wind howled between the rocks. Was there a predator nearby? Or perhaps a rogue? I glanced around with each step, my pulse quick.

When I reached the top, I heard a whimper. I caught my breath, but all I saw were several outcroppings of rock. They created natural balconies that overlooked the bay, though none had any railing. I turned my attention to the nearby cave. A faint snivel echoed within.

"Hello?" I called out.

Luthair grabbed my shoulder, his metal-like fingers digging into my muscle. "Wait."

"You hear that, don't you? There's a person inside."

"It could be a trap."

"Is s-someone there?" a voice answered from inside the cave. "Help! Please... my brother..." The words were broken by gulps for air, followed by a powerful sob.

All caution left me. I jerked my shoulder free from Luthair's grip and ran for the cave.

It was one of Camilla's little boys—it had to be!

"*Volke*," Luthair shouted. "Wait!"

He melted into a shadow, slithered across the rock at lightning speed, and rose up in front of me, preventing me from diving into the cave. I almost crashed into him, but I flinched back.

"I need to get in there," I said.

When I took a step to get around Luthair, my boot skidded on something slick. I stared down, wondering if it was algae and water, but the reality sent ice through my veins. I stood in a pool of blood.

So much...

My hand trembled as I ran it through my hair.

I stared into the cave, my sight adjusting to the darkness faster than it ever had before. The floor, smooth and sloped at a slight angle, stretched back twenty feet before halting in a harsh dead end. The ceiling, while jagged, was ten feet tall, and I wouldn't have to duck to move around. Ripples carved by years of seawater distorted the walls.

Sure enough, near the back were two boys—one with muddy brown hair, and the other collapsed on the ground, covered in crimson. Blood wept from cuts across both of them, and the smaller boy had the worst of it. He had curled into a ball, unmoving, chunks of flesh missing from his shoulder, like he had been bitten. Their tunics and trousers appeared soaked from top to bottom.

The older boy, Leo, looked up, his face coated with tears. "Help," he said, his voice raw and on the verge of cracking. "He's not... *he's not moving...*"

"Look there," Luthair said, pointing with a black gauntlet.

Beyond the boys, near the cave wall, was another crimson puddle, this one mixed with feathers. Blood ran in rivulets down the slant of the floor. It was the griffin cub—its wings shredded and its fur torn open, like something had gone straight for its insides. Was it still alive? I couldn't tell.

I found it hard to breathe.

What had happened here?

Luthair pulled his sword. "This cave has only one exit. You could get trapped."

I pushed him aside. "I'm getting the boys."

Before he could offer another protest, I dashed around him. A trail of red led straight to Leo and Grant. My stomach knotted so tight it felt like it was intertwining with my other organs.

A show of confidence would make all the difference in the world. I needed to let these boys know everything would be fine. I had to give them hope that their problems could be solved, so long as they put their trust in me.

"I'm an arcanist from the Frith Guild," I said as I knelt beside them. "What happened here?"

Leo rubbed at his face, the tears flowing so steadily he could've filled a pond with his sadness. "It-it attacked us. And the cub. P-please."

"What attacked you?"

I wanted to examine Grant, but I froze before touching him.

He had lost so much blood his skin had become a ghostly white. My throat constricted as I pressed my knuckles against his neck. Ice cold. Then a weak shudder as the child took in air.

Grant was on the verge of death, no doubt in my mind.

"Everything will be fine," I whispered. Then I inhaled and forced a cough. "Everything will be fine," I said again, more confident than before. "I'm going to get you both out of here."

"Ryllin," Leo said between sobs. "*Ryllin.*"

What?

Was he saying...?

The heavy beating of wings sent wind rushing into the cave. I didn't need to look up. I already knew. Ryllin—the missing griffin ruler—had returned. And the injuries on the boys... they were from him.

Luthair stood at the cave entrance, his sword held with both gauntlets.

There, on the outcrop of rocks, as large as two grown horses and with eagle wings that stretched ten feet in either direction, was the adult griffin we had all been looking for.

5

FINAL REQUEST

I stood and then stepped in front of the boys.

Never had I seen a creature so majestic, yet so terrifying. Ryllin's golden fur was matted with splotches of blood. The beautiful feathers on his wings had been torn and ripped out in places. His mane—the mighty mane of a lion—was tangled by the wind and dripping with sea water.

When he walked, the talons of his front feet scraped against the rock, creating an eerie scratch that sent shivers down my spine. His gaze was fixed on Luthair, his bright blue eyes discerning and calculating. Then he flashed his fangs and growled, filling the cave with a low rumble that emanated from deep within his massive chest.

"Ryllin," I said, confused. "What's going on here?"

As though snapped from a trance, Ryllin turned his head in my direction, his pupils widening.

He exhaled. "Arcanist. Finally, you've come."

His coherent speech surprised and relieved me. Clearly I didn't understand the situation. Ryllin could explain everything!

I jogged for the cave entrance. "I came as soon as I heard

the crying. Please help me carry everyone back to town. We need to—"

"Stand back!" Luthair said. He thrust out his armored arm to stop me. "No closer."

I stopped next to Luthair, half-tempted to yell at him. There were two children and a little griffin bleeding in the cave! We couldn't delay any longer!

But something was wrong. Ryllin kept his wings wide and his hackles raised. He took in ragged breaths, tensing, and his muscles rippled with each subtle move. He was so large there was no way to get past him without touching some part of his body.

Leo leaned over Grant. "P-please... don't hurt him anymore..." He wrapped his arms around his younger brother's body, shielding him as best he could. "Leave us alone!"

"What's going on here?" I demanded. "Ryllin, I've come to help. Talk to me."

The griffin stalked forward until he was ten feet from Luthair and me.

"Arcanist," Ryllin muttered, his gaze on me. "I'm unwell. A sickness has consumed me, spreading from the iron ball lodged in my breast."

Although I hadn't noticed before, I spotted a bullet injury above Ryllin's front leg. Arcanists, mystical creatures, and eldrin—anything with magic—had the power to heal themselves. But the hole dripped with a steady stream of blood, not closing at all.

I stepped forward. Luthair kept me from advancing any farther.

Ryllin continued, "Since yesterday, my thoughts have become jumbled. Fever heats my head, burning the back of my eyes." He looked away, his wings drooping. "There are hooks in my mind, rotting away all judgment."

"If you're sick, we can get you help," I said.

"It's the arcane plague, arcanist," he roared. "I have no doubt!"

My heart stopped for a moment—the realization hit me hard.

That arcane plague drove mystical creatures insane. I had seen it first-hand on many occasions. Mystical creatures went laughing-mad with lunacy, some even forgetting their own names. The twisted look on their faces as they gleefully lashed out still haunted my dreams.

"You're sane," I said. "It's not the arcane plague. If it were, I would know."

Ryllin dug his talons into the rock. "I tried to keep myself from the city, just in case, but when my son came looking for me..." He growled and flapped his wings, his eyes scrunched shut. "I attacked him. My own body betrayed me. I couldn't stop the lust for magic. *I couldn't control myself.*"

"My master will know what to do. Please let me help you. There might still be a—"

"Did you not hear me, arcanist? I slaughtered my own son!" Ryllin snapped his eyes open, the intensity of his expression rocking me. "And I almost killed those two boys when they came to help my cub. I'm a danger to all around me—a monster. Strike me down, I beg you. Do it before I lose myself completely."

I forced myself to breathe, but nothing quieted the buzzing of my frantic thoughts. "There has to be some other way. We just... haven't thought of it. Give me a minute."

"Corruption pumps through my body, driving me mad one heartbeat at a time. Soon I'll be a gibbering mess, a husk of my former self. End me while I can still comprehend the magnitude of my crimes."

"But—"

Ryllin roared with all the power of a lion god, the sheer force quaking through my limbs. His rows of fangs shone in the afternoon sun, his saliva pink with residual blood. For a moment, fear threatened to immobilize me, but the terror faded as quickly as it had appeared.

Knightmare arcanists couldn't be shaken through magical means. The griffin could roar all he wanted, but I held firm, and so did Luthair.

"Don't do this." I held out my hand. "Come with me. The Frith Guild will find some way to help you!"

"If you don't run me through, I'll eat those children." Ryllin took another step forward, his pupils mere slits. "Starting with their legs and ending with their throats. I'll leave their heads for their mother."

His cold and serious tone frightened me more than any roar. He meant every word, and it hardened my heart to the situation.

"I'll never let you hurt those kids again," I whispered.

"I'm counting on it."

Ryllin lunged forward.

In an instant, Luthair melted into the darkness and reformed from my feet upward, coating my body in ink and hardening into shadow plate armor a second before Ryllin slashed with his talons. He knocked me down, but my arcane defense held firm, preventing him from cutting my skin. I jumped to my feet—my shadow armor looked heavy, but it didn't hinder my movement. I pulled out Luthair's black blade, my body coursing with a new sense of vigor.

We had merged. Together Luthair and I would live and die as a single being.

Careful, he spoke straight to my thoughts. *He's much stronger than we are!*

In a dark cave, I should have had the advantage, but my use of magic was so limited I didn't know what to do with it. When Luthair and I were merged, we were more powerful, but it was *my* skill we relied on. Even if Luthair knew how to bend the shadows to his will, *I* didn't.

Ryllin coiled and pounced, his mouth open. I sidestepped, barely escaping his fangs due to the slight slope of the floor, and I stumbled backward. Then Ryllin rushed me a third time. He never gave me a chance to correct my footing. I leapt away, dodging his bite, but hitting the wall.

Slip through the shadows, Luthair commanded.

I focused my magic, forcing it through my body. It burned, but I couldn't feel most of it, not with the adrenaline coursing through me.

Like Luthair, I sank into the darkness—entering a shadowy void.

It felt like water rose up all around me. I flailed, kicked, and tried to visualize resurfacing, but it was difficult. Luthair made shadow-stepping seem easy. He flitted from shade to shade, moving with the speed of a hornet, emerging wherever he pleased, so long as there was a surface for the shadows to travel across.

I exited the darkness, on the opposite side of the cave, but my head spun, and I took a second gathering my thoughts. Ryllin clearly didn't know where I had gone. He glanced around, emitting a guttural growl.

With my sword in hand, I stepped forward and swung. Although I had taken some lessons, I wasn't the most proficient with a blade. I struck Ryllin in the flank, cutting a slice of his hindquarters. It wasn't enough to kill or even seriously injure. My swing had been too weak.

Ryllin whipped around and swiped at me. His talon caught the armor again, but this time with magical force. His strike broke through the hardened shadows and ripped my shirt beneath.

His movements were wild and reckless—deadlier than before. Then Ryllin smiled and laughed. It chilled me. It wasn't a normal chuckle, but one of a madman, his lip curled up high and exposing his fangs.

He was... losing himself. This situation cut deeper than any talon wound ever could.

I had already failed.

"I'm so sorry," I muttered, my voice a combination of my own and Luthair's.

Ryllin roared again, his prolonged cry tainted by anguish. His eyes glazed over and bulged outward, like a bloated dead fish. He laughed, giddy and chaotic.

Without warning, red-hot flames rushed into the cave from the entrance, washing over Ryllin and drawing his attention. I leapt for the kids, imposing myself between them and the heat. Luthair's armor protected me, but it wouldn't last forever against the fire. Even with my magic, the intensity of the flame burnt my eyebrows and singed my cheek.

Zaxis stood at the edge of the cave, bathed in the afternoon light, his phoenix on the rocks behind him. He lifted his hand and a second stream of fire washed forward.

"Zaxis!"

"Volke," he barked. "How do you always manage to find trouble?"

"Careful! There are children in here!"

His flames stopped in an instant and he took a hesitant step back. He squinted, and then shook his head, no doubt unable to see through the darkness of the cave. Zaxis had no idea where the children were.

Ryllin, burned, but not beaten, continued to laugh, his voice growing louder with each second. Then he ran for Zaxis, his talons at the ready.

An adult griffin could rip right through any man, and Ryllin was tainted by the plague—I couldn't allow him to attack!

I lunged forward, the shadows slowing Ryllin and aiding my speed. I stabbed my sword straight into the griffin's side, just under the wing. The blade sunk in between the ribs, piercing deep. I swear I felt his heartbeat as I forced the weapon into his chest. I never let go of the sword grip, even as hot blood gushed from the wound.

The force of my stab knocked Ryllin to the side. He collapsed by the wall of the cave, his breath coming out in one forced choke. He shuddered, his last moments filled with silence rather than insane mirth. Once he stopped moving, I took a breath, my body shaking.

He seemed thankful in the end, but the sight shook me.

Ryllin didn't deserve such a fate.

You mustn't falter, Luthair said. *There are people who still need you.*

I gulped down air, my stomach queasy from the thick metallic scent of gore. The shadows melted away from my body as Luthair and I became two separate beings. Without his added strength, I swayed on my feet.

Zaxis jumped to my side and steadied me. "I can't believe you did that," he whispered. "You could've been killed."

"I'm fine," I muttered. I couldn't feel much—no pain, no emotions—the situation hadn't yet sunk in.

"You're a fool. If I hadn't heard those roars, who knows what would've happened?"

"Yeah. Thanks."

Zaxis looked at my torn shirt and then glanced up to meet my gaze. "Well... I should also thank you. For what you did. Stopping the griffin, I mean. Before it got to me."

"Don't mention it." As much as I appreciated Zaxis acknowledging my skills—a rare and special moment—now wasn't the time. I turned around and took stock of the situation.

Leo shivered, his fingers twisted into Grant's shirt like he would never let go.

"Wait here," I said to Zaxis.

I jogged over to the children and removed my coat.

"Give your brother to me," I commanded.

"He's not moving." Leo clenched his teeth. "He's not..."

When I tried to take him, Leo clung tighter. He shook his head, his tears fresh.

I placed a gentle hand on his shoulder. "It's okay. You did a good job, but I'm here now. I'll make sure he's safe."

Although I said the words with confidence, I had no idea if Grant would make it. Still, I couldn't allow the boy to prevent me from getting Grant to safety. If there was any hope, it was outside of this cave.

Leo glanced up, his eyes still wet. He released his brother and gave a single nod.

"Please help him," he whispered.

I wrapped my coat around Grant and held it tight around his shoulder, trying to staunch the blood flow. Then I ripped off my shirt and tossed it to the shadows. "Luthair, gather up the cub. We should take them both."

Ryllin said his son was dead, but I had yet to check. It was better to take him, just in case.

I glanced around at the scarlet puddles, my body as stiff as ice. The arcane plague transferred to others through blood. I wasn't injured, so I didn't think I was at risk, but the griffin cub could be in danger. Luthair wrapped up the little one before Ryllin's vital fluid mixed with his own.

Leo and Grant didn't have to worry. The plague only transferred to magical beings, not to ordinary individuals.

I stood, Grant in my arms. "Can you walk?" I asked Leo.

He gave me another single nod.

"Good. Follow me."

Without waiting for confirmation, I ran from the cave. Magic still burned my insides, probably a lingering effect of the fight. It didn't matter. I didn't care how much it hurt me. I wouldn't let these kids down. I couldn't save Ryllin, so I'd be damned if I would fail Grant too.

"Zaxis," I said as I exited the cave. "Here. Please help them." I thrust the boy into Zaxis's chest. My lungs hurt, and my heart beat loud enough to drown out all other sounds, even the crash of waves against the distant rocks.

Each breath burned my throat as I watched Zaxis open the coat wrapped around Grant. He placed his hand on the boy's body. His magic wasn't flashy, but the warmth that exuded from the healing was enough to ease my worry.

Zaxis wasn't evoking healing or manipulating flesh—he was augmenting the child with magic and filling him with life. Phoenix arcanists had the blessing of both offensive and wondrous magic. Knightmare arcanists, on the other hand, didn't have a way to heal others.

Grant would be okay. He had to be. Zaxis would make this work.

Luthair appeared a moment later. He carried my shirt and the griffin cub, both held tightly against his shadow plate armor. After Zaxis had finished with Grant, he handed me the boy and then took the griffin. He did the exact same thing, his palm pressed against the golden fur of the cub. Would the griffin make it? I hoped beyond hope he would.

Leo emerged from the cave, his legs unsteady. "Is Grant alive?" he asked, his eyes wide. "Is my brother okay?"

As if awoken by his brother's voice, Grant opened his eyes and exhaled. His groggy expression showed more confusion than pain, and I couldn't help but smile.

"I'm here," Grant said. "I... don't hurt anymore."

6

THE THIRD ABYSS

Z axis, Luthair, and I carried the children down four flights of steps. Once we reached the road, I noticed a group of fishermen waiting for us. They gathered around and gawked, drawn by the bloodstains and were amazed no one was hurt.

Then the fishermen whispered and pointed. At first, I thought they were discussing Grant, but then I realized the griffin cub was also awake and now on the ground. He had the head of a lion, so I knew he was male, and his cat-like body bounded around the group as he hopped from one person to the next. His bright blue eyes teemed with life, and he flapped his tiny wings as he ran between fishermen.

"You saved me," the cub said, his voice so child-like I found it adorable. "Thank you, arcanists! Thank you!"

"That's the Frith Guild for you," one fisherman muttered.

Another nodded. "What even happened? Why are they covered in blood?"

The cub stopped in his tracks, half his golden fur coat matted and soaked in crimson. He folded his wings onto his body, his expression one of dreaded realization. It must have hit him then—he remembered what had happened.

Zaxis waved the fisherman away. "Give the kids room. I healed them, but they still need to get their bearings."

Excited whispers grew in intensity. The fishermen took a few steps back, but they kept their attention on the kids. Leo and Grant shared an embrace, and the griffin walked over and sat next to them, his lion tail swishing back and forth.

Leo and Grant knelt so they could embrace the griffin together, as a little group of three. The cub sniffled and returned the gesture, his lion-paws wrapped around the kids. He calmed down afterward, a smile on his face once he broke free.

"The bonding ceremony is saved," a person said from the crowd.

More cheering. Lots of nodding and shoulder pats.

Although everyone was in the mood to celebrate, I couldn't bring myself to share in the delight. I kept my unsteady hands in my pockets, and my shoulders bunched close to my neck. They hadn't seen Ryllin in the end. They didn't know the plague had gotten him. It was a horrible way to die. I almost didn't want to say anything, for fear I would kill the happiness of a bonding day.

Should I tell anyone? Perhaps it would be best to tell Zelfree first and let him break the news.

I glanced down, noting the blood on my trousers, stomach, and bare chest. My vision blurred, and my stomach twisted. What was I going to do about the potential plague outbreak? I needed to wash off and scrub every last inch of my skin.

Zaxis stepped close and placed his hand on my upper shoulder. His healing magic coursed through me, but I didn't need it. I grabbed his wrist and shook my head. He stared down at the mess across my body and then gave me a questioning glare.

"I'll explain when we get back to town," I whispered. "First, I'm going for a swim in the bay."

The capitol building of West Landin had a massive aerie—a tower for nesting griffins. While intelligent and capable, mystical creatures still adhered to their animal instincts. Griffins only laid eggs at the top of tall trees or towers, near an abundance of fish. The people of West Landin built the aerie with elevated ponds, trickling waterfalls that created mini rainbows, and hanging plants with long vines, all to keep the griffins of their island happy.

It was a glorious sight. But I couldn't enjoy it.

I stared at the cobblestone as I made my way inside the capitol building, my thoughts dwelling on Ryllin. He had said a bullet was what caused his plague, but that was impossible. Blood spread the corruption, which meant the bullet had been laced before it was fired. Some fiend had targeted Ryllin.

What kind of dastard would do that? It made me sick just thinking about it. I kept my hands balled in fists and tucked in my pockets the entire walk. The dull emotionless ache I'd had before seemed to have bloomed into hatred.

Leo, Grant, and the griffin cub walked on one side of me, and Zaxis on the other.

"My name is Bedivere," the griffin said. "This is my home." He motioned with a wing, and the boys glanced around with wide eyes and open mouths.

The capitol building entrance hall was a small room right before a grand staircase. Polished marble floors covered with rugs made for perfect walkways. Four attendants, each dressed in formal robes of white and black, rushed forward. Their clothes had a griffin stitched in gold over the heart.

"Are you okay?" one female attendant asked. "We must call Lady Kahtona at once."

Bedivere held his lion-head high. "I am fine, all thanks to these arcanists."

Without missing a beat, Zaxis stepped forward and smiled wide. "We are arcanists of the Frith Guild. We were hired to return your griffin cub, and here he is, unharmed."

The four attendants nodded and then rushed to bring us a pitcher of water and a few cups. I waved away the refreshments, and so did Zaxis. I didn't need anything. I just wanted to inform everyone what had happened.

Then the attendants rushed up the staircase and left Zaxis, Bedivere, Grant, Leo, and me alone in the front hall. I didn't mind. I slunk into the shadows next to the grand staircase. My home island of Ruma had a capitol building, but it was small and doubled as the town's library. I admired the white marble of the railing. Everything had an eagle, lion, or griffin motif. Even the vases were painted with the three creatures locked in combat. Ruma had nothing so fancy.

Two attendants returned with warm towels.

A man stepped forward. "Boys, we need to take you home."

Bedivere flapped his wings. "They're my guests."

"I'm sorry, but their mother and father must be worried."

Leo and Grant were escorted from the building, each giving the little griffin a sad look before they headed out. When the massive front door opened, Zaxis's phoenix swooped in, littering the entrance hall with a light dusting of soot.

Zaxis held up his hand. "Here, Forsythe."

His phoenix circled around and landed on the floor, his talons catching on the aquamarine rug. Forsythe shook his feet, but it didn't much help. Zaxis knelt and helped his eldrin free himself from the decorations.

"Let me perch on your arm," Forsythe said as he scooted close.

Zaxis shook his head. "You're too big for that now. And I'm not wearing my leather bracer."

"I'll be gentle with my talons."

After a short sigh, Zaxis held out his arm. Forsythe hopped on and steadied himself with a few flaps of his wings; his talons were long enough to wrap around Zaxis's forearm. As Zaxis stood, the strain of holding the phoenix was obvious, but not extreme. I doubted he could hold Forsythe for longer than a handful of minutes, but the bird blatantly enjoyed the perch.

Forsythe nuzzled Zaxis's neck and made cooing noises, not unlike a happy pigeon.

Zaxis grew red in the face. "You're embarrassing me."

The sole attendant in the room, a young woman with short brown hair, gave Zaxis a smile. "Thank you, phoenix arcanist. We are so grateful to have little Bedivere returned to us."

He shrugged and waved the comment away. "It was nothing. All in a day's work."

She didn't thank me, but I didn't feel like thanks anyway. *I* had been the one to kill Ryllin, after all. I wished I could just forget the entire ordeal.

Then Zaxis stood straight and brushed off his coat. He coughed and motioned for me to join him. I walked out of the shadows, my gaze drawn to the top of the grand stairway. An adult griffin stood at the top of the steps, her regal eagle-head indicating it was the dame, Kahtona. Her attention fell on Bedivere.

"My son," she said, her voice feminine and distinct.

"Mother!"

Bedivere ran straight up the stairs, his wings outstretched as though to help him glide upward. He dashed for the front legs of his mother and buried himself within her protective grasp.

Kahtona wrapped her majestic wings around the cub as she leaned down for a tight embrace. After a few seconds, she stood and stroked her son with her eagle-like front foot.

"Where is he?" Kahtona asked the room. "Where is my mate?"

Zaxis and I said nothing. The last attendant held her breath.

The golden amber of Kahtona's eyes glittered with intelligence, and she stared at me with a knowing gaze, like she understood I would be the one to provide the answer. I stared up at her, dreading the words. I took a breath, and then stared at the rug underfoot.

Zaxis placed a hand on my shoulder. He gave Kahtona another one of his signature smiles. "My friend has terrible news. Give him a minute to gather his thoughts."

Kahtona released her son. "Bedivere, head up to the aerie."

The cub widened his eyes. "But—"

She cut him off with a quick glare. Bedivere hunched down, his wings drooped so low they dragged on the floor as he moved away.

"O-okay," he muttered.

Once the young griffin had gone, I steeled myself for the situation and returned my gaze to Kahtona's.

"I found Ryllin," I said.

Kahtona didn't move. She waited, her expression unchanging, but I could tell—even from the base of the stairs—that her fur and feathers raised a bit, half standing on end.

I continued, "He was near Granite Shark Bay, in one of the caves. He... attacked Bedivere. And then attacked the two boys who had been searching for your cub."

The statement shook the attendant. She paled, and her brow furrowed. Was the staff of the capitol building close to the griffins? No doubt in my mind. They were likely the ones caring for them on any given occasion. They might as well have been family.

Zaxis made some sound like he wanted to say something, but he stopped halfway through. Instead, he removed his hand from my shoulder and gave me a worried look.

Anger pushed my next few sentences out.

"Ryllin said he had been afflicted with the arcane plague."

The dead silence that followed told me everything. No one wanted the plague to come to the Isle of Landin, especially during a bonding ceremony. There was no cure. Once a mystical creature contracted the affliction, it was only a matter of time before they sank into laughing madness.

"He had been shot," I said, damn near defiant, like I was arguing the reality. "He said the bullet was tainted. He attacked his son, and the boys, because he couldn't control himself. He lashed out by accident, and in the end, he regretted what he had done."

"In the end?" Kahtona whispered.

"I..." It took me a few breaths. "I killed him."

Seconds ticked by, but I didn't look away. Kahtona had to know. Ryllin had been her mate, and I had his blood on my hands.

"Tell them you saved us," Zaxis whispered.

I shook my head.

"Ryllin let me kill him," I murmured. "He was the epitome of a griffin in the end—noble and with a sense of justice." After another moment to gather my composure, I continued, "I'm so sorry."

"You needn't apologize," Kahtona said. "You've done the island a favor." She hardened herself—her muscles tense. "And... my son?"

"I don't think he was infected," I said so fast I almost tripped over the words.

"Thank the heavens." Kahtona breathed easy.

"But I don't know who shot Ryllin. I swear, as an arcanist of the Frith Guild, I'll figure out who did. Ryllin didn't deserve the fate I dealt him. He was—"

"I know who shot Ryllin."

The revelation caught me off guard. The entire walk here, I had debated with myself over how I would go about finding the scum that had infected Ryllin. How did Kahtona know?

"Ryllin had been patrolling the island," Kahtona said, her voice and gaze distant as she recalled the events. "That's when he saw it. The pirate ship. And not just *any* ship or pirate. He came back to me with a bullet wound and said it had come from the *Third Abyss*."

The *Third Abyss*? What a dreadful name for a ship.

There were five levels to the abyssal hells, each more terrifying than the last. The Death Lords ruled over the lost souls in the third level, *the third abyss*. Their realm, a watery wasteland filled with the screams of the tortured, had haunted my childhood dreams, especially on nights after I had dug a fresh grave.

Whoever named their ship the *Third Abyss* was a fiend, no doubt in my mind.

"When Ryllin started acting odd, I should've been more attentive," Kahtona muttered. She stared at the far windows, her wings unfurled. "The bonding ceremony stole my focus, but that's no excuse."

"The Frith Guild will handle this," Zaxis declared.

His statement seemed to invigorate both Kahtona and the attendant. They stared at him with hopeful expressions. Even I felt a little relieved, though I didn't know if Zaxis had the authority to make such claims.

The Frith Guild *did* hunt down pirates, though. And any group who was willing to bring down a noble griffin was nothing but filth. They should be ripped from the ocean and thrown back in pieces, chum for the sharks.

Zaxis continued, "We won't let those responsible get away with their dastardly tactics. You can rest easy knowing the pirates who hurt your mate will be brought to justice."

He said what everyone hoped to hear. They wanted retribution, just as I did.

"Thank you," Kahtona said. Then she lowered her head in a formal bow. "I will never be able to repay the Frith Guild for what they've done. You have my deepest gratitude."

I left the capitol building before Zaxis and Forsythe did. They wanted to stay and enjoy the finer things of life, but I just wanted to be alone for a while. We still had a few hours before dusk—before the ceremony—and I intended to stay on our ship until then.

Kahtona seemed at peace, and I knew why. If the Frith

Guild said something would be taken care of, *then it would happen*. She relied on us to avenge her fallen mate, even though I wasn't entirely sure how we would do that.

Or if we could.

I knew nothing about the *Third Abyss*. Not the identity of the captain nor the crew. No information on the mystical creatures. Nothing. I knew they spread the plague and that they had to be close.

Lost in my thoughts, I almost collided with someone as I descended the front steps of the building.

"S-sorry," I muttered.

To my surprise, it was Master Zelfree. He panted and shook his head. "Volke? Are you okay?" He grabbed my shoulder. "Are you hurt?" He spun me around as he got ahold of his heavy breathing.

This was the most energetic I had ever seen him.

"Uh," I said. "Are *you* okay?"

His mimic, Traces, the gray cat with a long tail, jumped from his shoulders and onto mine. She, too, glanced over me, her soft paws tickling my skin as she walked with graceful steps from one shoulder to the next.

"Did Ryllin hurt you?" she asked.

I shook my head.

"Then what happened to your clothes?"

Her feminine voice slid down my ear. Although I hadn't thought about my appearance until she said something, it was all I could think of now. I had left my bloody coat and shirt by Granite Shark Bay.

"I'm fine," I said, curt. Then I jerked my shoulder from Zelfree's grip. "Zaxis can tell you everything." But their concern sank into my thoughts. "Wait, how did you know I fought Ryllin?" Zelfree hadn't been in the capitol building when I explained it to Kahtona.

Zelfree took a step back. "I saw the corpse in the cave. Of all my apprentices, you're the only one who uses a sword. I got here as soon as I could, just in case..." He took a deep breath "Is Zaxis hurt? I saw fire marks on the cave wall."

"He's fine."

"No one was infected?"

"No." He knew Ryllin had the plague? "I think everyone is fine."

I hadn't realized until then, but Zelfree was drenched in sweat. Had he... run here? No. That was way too far. Perhaps he rode on a cart and then ran through town. Either way, Traces leapt to his shoulders and wrapped her tail around his neck, ending my train of thought. She tilted her head to the side as she gave me another quick glance.

"You're kinda cute," she said with a *tee hee* at the end of her statement.

Was the mimic... teasing me? I had never felt more awkward. What could I even say to that?

"I'm going back to the boat," I muttered as I stepped past them. I really didn't feel like company.

"Wait," Zelfree said.

I stopped.

"You should stay here. You've earned the right to see all the griffins, after all."

"I'd rather be alone." I was about to continue when I recalled my own promise. "Let Illia see the griffins in my place."

Zelfree snapped his fingers. "You better not wander off, do you understand? Straight to the boat and then straight to the ceremony."

"I won't go wandering by myself."

"Good."

Zelfree visibly relaxed. I had never seen him so

panicked, not even when he was fighting Gregory Ruma. What had gotten him so riled? My wellbeing?

"You should take this time to practice your magic," he said in a gentler tone. "No one will be around, so you won't have to worry about people seeing you struggle."

His statement shook me. How did he know I felt anxiety about practicing in front of others? Did he sense it about me? Had I acted anxious?

"I've practiced," I muttered. "Once or twice while searching. I even managed to make shadow tendrils for a moment."

"Listen to me." Zelfree placed a hand on my shoulder and met my gaze straight on. His dark eyes held more focus and intensity than I had ever seen in him. "Don't practice until you get it right—practice until you can't get it wrong."

I slowly nodded, the advice sinking deep. It reminded me of something Gravekeeper William would say. And I took it to heart.

"I'll practice."

"Good. Then get going. I'll send someone to get you once the ceremonies are about to begin."

7

OATH OF THE GRIFFIN

I stayed locked in the personal quarters of our boat until an hour before dusk, pacing back and forth, using my magic until it burned my bones. The pain didn't distract me from my thoughts, however. I dwelled on Ryllin. He didn't deserve what had happened. He had lived a peaceful life—raising children—protecting an island.

And a bullet ripped it all away in an instant, the moment it struck his chest.

Dammit.

I wished I could've helped him. Why did it have to happen? Why were the villains allowed to roam free when they had condemned Ryllin to death or insanity? Did those pirates even care about what they had done? Had they shot randomly, not knowing? Or had they delighted in this wanton violence?

"Wallowing in despair won't change what happened," Luthair whispered from the shadows in the corner. "You should surround yourself with friends. Levity will do you good."

"Did your old arcanist sometimes feel like I do?" I asked.

"Yes."

"And what did he do?"

"He paced around until he finally came to his senses." Luthair rose from the darkness, his cape gently flowing in an unfelt wind. "Then he surrounded himself with friends and family, just as I suggested. You two are so similar you may as well be related."

I half-laughed. "Sounds like it."

Mathis Weaversong. Luthair's first arcanist. He was a legendary swashbuckler who fought corrupted arcanists. If *he* sometimes felt like the world was unjust, then I knew I wasn't unreasonable.

But perhaps Luthair had a point. Worrying about it wouldn't change the past. And keeping a positive attitude would help me cope.

"We should get to the griffin ceremony," I muttered.

"I think that would be best."

I walked out onto the deck of the ship. The evening greeted me with a cool breeze. Our ship—a galleon with three masts, weighing over 1,000 tons—was named *the Long Ride*. In every way it showed wear. I walked around one of the masts, taking note of the knife marks in the side of the wood. The ship probably had stories to tell. It would've been nice to hear them, since I love a good high-seas adventure, but I currently had no enthusiasm for such things.

At the bottom of the gangplank, bathed in the light of the setting sun, stood Adelgis and Hexa. Adelgis wore new clothes, pressed and tidy, which included a blue jacket and coal-black trousers. He flashed me a quick smile.

"Volke, there you are. Master Zelfree sent us to get you."

Hexa wore the same outfit from earlier—a sleeveless coat to showcase her scars. Her young hydra sat at her feet, his yellow eyes glaring at me.

She waved. "C'mon. We don't want to be late."

I jogged down the gangplank and headed into West Landin. Adelgis kept my pace, but Hexa fell behind. She kept stopping to allow her hydra to catch up. He was small —a young hydra with only one head—and his stumpy little legs didn't take him anywhere fast.

"I told you to leave your hydra," Adelgis said with a sigh.

I stopped and turned around. "Do you want me to carry him?"

Hexa sneered like I had cut to the heart of her pride. "I can do it." She glanced down at her eldrin. "Raisen gets lonely. I didn't want to leave him anywhere without me. Everyone else thinks he's scary."

She knelt and patted Raisen's head. He leaned into her hand and closed his eyes. While I didn't want to tell her to stop, we still hadn't reached the city square, and we were short of time.

"Illia always carries Nicholin on her shoulders," Hexa muttered. Then she picked Raisen up—he had to weigh at least 40 pounds—and awkwardly brought him close to her head.

Raisen flailed about, grunting and hissing the entire time. Adelgis and I stood transfixed as Hexa attempted to perch him on her shoulder. It was like watching a ship crash against the rocks. The whole thing was terrible, and painful to witness, but I couldn't look away.

"Hydras have bulky bodies to support the weight of their many heads," Adelgis said. "They aren't the type of creatures who *climb*. They're more like alligators. Or beached whales."

Hexa grabbed Raisen's back legs, slung them behind her neck, and then held onto his tail to keep him in place. The poor hydra trembled and clung tight, his claws digging into

Hexa's clothes and piercing her skin. She sucked in air through her teeth.

"It'll be fine," she said with a wave of her free hand and then grunted. "See? He's good."

Raisen curled around her neck. "My a-arcanist," he said, his voice raspy. "Are you s-sure?"

"I won't let you fall. You'll be safe."

Once Hexa started walking, Adelgis and I trailed behind. Although blood soaked into her coat from Raisen's claws, she made no comment about it. A piece of me was impressed, but another piece of me wondered if she was making a point—or if perhaps she was borderline crazy. Who would carry a hydra? Even their scales looked sharp.

"Hydras are sedentary creatures," Adelgis said matter-of-factly. "They wait in caves or in canyons and strike out at creatures that stumble into their territory. Walking all around an island isn't their preferred—"

Hexa shot him a glare. "Are *you* the hydra arcanist, or am I? Raisen can handle this."

"But—"

"What makes you think you're the expert, huh?"

"My father studied mystical creatures his whole life! I lived and breathed his research." Then Adelgis threw his hands into the air and exhaled. "I told you that *twice* while we were searching for the griffins."

"Oh, yeah," Hexa muttered. "That doesn't matter, though. I've lived next to hydras my whole life. I know they get big and they don't like to move around. That's the point." She held Raisen close. "I want to travel with Raisen for as long as possible, before he becomes a *beached whale*, as you so elegantly put it."

Adelgis sighed. "I apologize."

"Everyone else has an eldrin that can go wherever they

do," Hexa said. "I just want Raisen close for a little while longer. Especially since tonight we're going to the Sapphire Springs. And you want to stay with me, right, Raisen?"

Her hydra slowly nodded, even though he continued to tremble. "I'm ready for a-adventure."

"See? He's not afraid of anything!"

Raisen roar-hissed, his many needle-like fangs shining in the last of the light.

It didn't take us long to reach the main road, but by then the sun had set. The citizens of West Landin filled the street from one sidewalk to the other, each holding a lit candle that flickered in the wind. They chatted and whispered, but the moment we drew near, they parted to allow us to pass.

"Thank you so much," one woman said. "We owe the Frith Guild a great debt."

A man nodded along with her words. "Bedivere would never have returned to us if it hadn't been for you."

While Adelgis and Hexa smiled, I avoided eye contact. I didn't want the praise. Someone else could have it. I had still failed Ryllin, and their words of gratitude only reminded me of that fact.

The bonding ceremony would take place in the middle of town, next to the statue of the first griffin who had come to the island. We were still half a mile of crowded streets away, I knew we would miss most of the festivities. The hopeful arcanists would have to compete in a Trial of Worth, but I didn't know what that entailed for the Isle of Landin. It intrigued me, though my depression kept me from hustling.

Hexa picked up her pace. The people not only parted for her because she was an arcanist with the Frith Guild, but also because Raisen started hissing and snapping at everyone who got close. The denizens of West Landin leapt out of the way, their eyes wide. Hydras had deadly venom, after all. No one wanted to get bitten.

Baked fish, curled into balls, passed through the hands of the attendees. At one point I was offered a tray, but I refused with a smile. Even Adelgis shook his head when they thrust some in his direction.

"Volke," Adelgis said, leaning in close to me. The crowds created a steady white noise of laughter, conversation, and sizzling food. Even a couple of inches apart, it was difficult to understand him. "Master Zelfree only asked Hexa to go get you—I came along on my own."

"Why?"

"I wanted to, uh, speak with you. About tonight."

His face grew a bright red, and he mumbled something to himself, too quiet for me to hear. Then he fidgeted with his hands—lacing and unlacing his fingers.

I lifted an eyebrow. "Are you okay? What about tonight? I think they just want us to stand on the sidelines and look official." A round of clapping echoed through the streets. "And it sounds like they've already started. We need to hurry."

Adelgis shook his head. "Not that. I've seen several bonding ceremonies. I meant... uh... visiting the Sapphire Springs afterward. I'm not, well, an islander. I'm not accustomed to, er, your *customs*, if you'll pardon the pun. I need your advice."

I grabbed his upper arm and half-dragged him down the road as I jogged toward our destination. Children gathered in groups, some wearing griffin masks, but I stepped around them with light footwork, taking Adelgis with me.

"What about the Sapphire Springs?" I asked. "You sit in them. Not much of a custom. No need for advice."

Then it hit me. I had forgotten about the good luck the springs offered. Maybe that was what I needed—a little luck. Maybe then I wouldn't stumble on people already infected with the plague. I needed something. *Anything.* I just wanted to save people, and if some luck could help me do that, I needed it.

"Please, wait a moment," Adelgis said.

I stopped and let go of his arm. "We're late."

Another round of clapping was followed by cheers that spread like a wave through the crowd, louder and louder until it passed.

He leaned in close, his face so red it rivaled a tomato. He couldn't even look me in the eye when he said, "I... don't want to be naked in front of anyone."

I waited a moment, thinking he would say something else, but he never did.

"Uh, okay," I said.

"When the citizens of West Landin said there were no dividers between each of the springs, I got even more anxious. I didn't know you islanders were so comfortable with nudity."

His words sank into my thoughts. I mulled them over, my eyebrows knit. "What do you mean nudity? And there aren't any dividers?"

"For, you know, the men and women." Adelgis crossed his arms, then uncrossed them, his breathing strained. "I'm not sure if I want to go through with this. That's why I wanted your advice."

"No dividers *at all*?"

He glanced up at me, confused. "You didn't know?"

Of course I didn't know! There weren't springs on the Isle of Ruma. This wasn't *my* custom. How would I have known this ahead of time? No one had warned me!

I took a calming breath, my own face hot and my palms sweaty.

"I've n-never been to West Landin before," I muttered.

Adelgis motioned me to follow him. We walked into the shelter of a nearby alleyway, between a shoemaker and a barber, shielded from the ever-increasing cheers and applause.

"So, you didn't know you'd be sharing the Sapphire Springs with people?" Adelgis asked.

"It hadn't crossed my mind."

"I suppose that makes me feel a little better. I still don't know what I'm going to do, however. I'd rather not participate, but I don't want to say why in front of everyone."

I half-laughed. "But you were okay telling me?"

He shrugged. "You seem trustworthy. Your thoughts are always genuine."

"You listen to my thoughts?" I snapped, half-angry, half-shocked. Why would he do that?

"It's not like that, I swear. It happened by accident—I hear thoughts in a radius around me. You got caught in my bubble, so to speak, when I was practicing. I apologize, I should've told you sooner."

The information relaxed me a bit. He had been practicing magic. I knew better than most that sometimes weird things happened when you weren't a master of your own abilities.

"It's fine," I said, curt.

"But it's still true. Your thoughts were genuine, and I admire that. So... what do you think I should do about the Sapphire Springs? Maybe I could feign illness? You would vouch for me, of course. I'll stay on the ship while everyone else participates. Will anyone be offended?"

Wait.

Everyone else?

"Atty, Illia, and Hexa are participating?" I asked.

Adelgis nodded.

The news unnerved me more than I thought it would. Even though the city of West Landin was in the midst of mass celebration, their cheering faded to the back of my mind. I was nearly sixteen and now an adult, but I hadn't *been* with anyone, in or out of bed. Ever. Most of my younger life had taken place in a graveyard. There wasn't much time to practice courting people.

The closest I had gotten was when I was eight. Illia and I had pretended to be married for a week. The game had been chaste and pure—the fantasy of children—but I still recalled picking flowers to give her every day, as that was what a "good husband" did for his wife.

Remembering that moment made everything worse. I would be naked in front of Illia if we both went to the Sapphire Springs. And so would she.

I shook my head. This was exactly what I wanted to avoid. Our relationship didn't need complications like this. It didn't need intimacy. Our love *was* chaste, and I didn't want it entangled with youthful lust.

Maybe *I* should feign sickness.

"You understand then, don't you?" Adelgis asked. "I prefer not to get undressed in front of anyone from our guild. For many reasons. You'll tell them I was ill and decided to stay on the ship?"

"Sure," I murmured.

"Thank you so much, Volke." He exhaled and smiled wide. "Thank you."

"Don't mention it."

He patted my upper arm. "You've taken a huge weight off

my shoulders. If you ever need a favor in the future, just let me know."

"I will."

With that, Adelgis exited the alleyway, obviously in a brighter mood than before.

I couldn't bring myself to rejoin the festivities yet. My thoughts dwelled on the many possible situations in which I might find myself. Especially with Atty. Or any girl from West Landin around my age. What if I made them uncomfortable with my inevitable staring? What an embarrassing and awful situation that would be.

And then there was Zaxis—I hadn't thought about him till last, but for some reason it irritated me more than it should have. What would he do? Would he be there with Illia, Atty, and Hexa? Should I... talk to him? Tell him I didn't like that he was participating?

"Don't be stupid," I muttered to myself.

What would I do? Berate him? Tell him he had to wait on the boat too? I didn't know. It was hard to think.

"What's wrong?" Luthair asked from the shadows.

"I... have never been intimate with anyone." My shoulders slumped. "I'm not sure I can be a *noble* arcanist in this situation."

"A knight knows the difference between intimacy and camaraderie. If the others are participating, then it's to show trust and strengthen that bond. You'll damage that trust if you think this is an opportunity to sate your own desires."

"I would never *sate my own desires*." I rubbed the back of my neck. "And don't say it like that! You make it sound like I'm trying to take advantage of someone."

The sounds of celebration pierced my thoughts, drawing me back to my immediate surroundings. I didn't know what

I would do about the Sapphire Springs, but I knew what I had to do right now.

I dashed out of the alleyway and made my way down the side of the road, where there were the fewest people. I apologized as I squeezed by, my only goal the city square. After a few short minutes, I reached my destination.

A griffin statue, thirty feet tall and made of patchwork marble, dominated everyone's attention. Its gigantic, outspread wings made a perfect perch for the five griffin cubs staring down at the stage. Kahtona stood on one shoulder of the massive griffin, and the other shoulder, Ryllin's position, remained empty.

Four people, all around my age, waited on the stage below the cubs. Two girls, two boys. They wore cloaks with griffin feathers on their shoulders, symbolizing they had passed the Trials of Worth.

I had missed the ceremonies. Which was a shame—I had heard griffins test a person's courage before they bond. What would a test of courage entail?

My heart sank for a moment, but then I realized they hadn't finished yet. There were five griffins, but only four people on stage. Who else would compete?

When I glanced around, I spotted Zelfree by the edge of the stage. Atty, Zaxis, Hexa, and Illia stood next to him. I made my way toward them, excusing myself as I scooted between people.

"A moment of silence, please," Kahtona said, her voice booming over the crowd.

In an instant, people hushed their speech. Some even held their breath. Despite the thousands of people gathered near the stage, it was quiet.

"As many of you already know, my mate, Ryllin, has passed. A boy by the name of Leo Rutledge told me everything. Ryllin had been driven mad by the arcane plague and attacked our youngest son, Bedivere."

The statement drew a few hushed whispers from the crowd, but Kahtona glared, and the silence returned in full force.

"This was the work of pirates. Those wicked cutthroats steal from our islands day in and day out, and today they stole the gift of life. I will *never* forgive their villainy. But... I must put it behind me. The Frith Guild has vowed to see justice served, and I will leave retribution in their capable hands."

The citizens of West Landin nodded, and a few added a proud, *hear, hear* to punctuate the statement. Several people wiped tears from their faces. I hadn't known Ryllin, but it was apparent he had been loved by many.

Kahtona took a shaky breath, her voice thick with emotion. "Bedivere would have been killed had it not been for a young child by the name of Grant Rutledge. He ran to stop Ryllin. Although the child was gravely injured, he managed to save Bedivere's life. In another show of bravery, Grant's brother Leo stepped in and protected both Bedivere and Grant—pleading with Ryllin until two arcanists from the Frith Guild arrived to set the situation straight."

When she mentioned me and Zaxis, I stopped making my way through the crowd.

"Truly, both boys have courage in their veins," Kahtona said. "Now, my son has something to say."

Bedivere stood and walked to the edge of the statue's wing. "Although there were many brave people who participated in the trials this year, I couldn't pick any to bond with because I already knew who I wanted my arcanist to be. We are bound by destiny and by the blood of my f-father."

Bedivere wiped at his eyes with the back of his front leg.

"If Grant Rutledge hadn't run to save me... I wouldn't be here today. I know I shouldn't bond with a child, since children change so much as they age, but Grant will not outgrow his bravery. If he will have me, I want him as my arcanist. No other will do."

The declaration sent both gasps and cheers rippling around me. One by one, the people searched for the child in their midst. It wasn't long before he was brought to the stage while people chanted his name.

The mayor handed Grant a cloak. The long fabric pooled at his feet and tears streamed down his face as he held it in place. He was shorter than the other four on stage, but he held himself tall, a smile stretched across his face.

"I know we shouldn't reward recklessness by bonding with children who fling themselves into a dangerous situation," Kahtona said. "But... this will be the last year of griffins."

A collective shock returned the crowd to silence.

"Without my mate, there will be no more cubs. Because of this, I need to leave the Isle of Landin and find another griffin—only then can I return to lead the island's bonding ceremonies."

Kahtona planned to leave? But she had no arcanist. Although she was still powerful from her first bonding, without an arcanist her magic would be limited. And she would eventually die of old age. Why would she risk everything to search the world alone?

"Fear not," Kahtona said. "I will not undertake this mission alone. Leo Rutledge, if you don't mind a second-bonded griffin, I invite you to accompany me, Grant, and my son to the mainland. Although you are young, I will guide you into the role of a powerful, and noble, arcanist."

Again, the crowd sought out Leo and brought him

forward. Like Grant, he wept while keeping a smile on his face. He said something as he bowed to the statue, but his voice was drowned out by the cheering.

Second-bonding wasn't common.

I touched my arcanist mark on my forehead. Unlike all the others I had seen, mine was cracked. The magic didn't flow correctly through my body. It wouldn't for Leo either, if he accepted Kahtona's offer. But becoming a second-bonded arcanist was still better than *not* becoming an arcanist.

The mayor placed a cloak on Leo as well.

Then all the griffin cubs leapt down from the statue and flew to the stage. Kahtona followed and landed near Leo. Once all the griffins had joined with their desired arcanists, they reached out their front feet. The people on stage placed their hands gently on the talons.

"The oath of griffin arcanists," Kahtona said. "Repeat after me."

The future arcanists nodded.

> *"I will keep my word and my honor,*
> *For they are the currency of kings.*
> *I will protect the oceans and the sky,*
> *As griffins have given me their wings.*
> *I'll never turn to cruelty or surrender to the night,*
> *I'll be a shepherd of humanity and show the world my might."*

The chosen on stage repeated everything in unison, like they had practiced the words a million times before. My chest swelled with appreciation and understanding. The Isle of Ruma had the Tower with its 112 steps—that was our oath—but this also worked. It articulated what arcanists should strive to be. They were protectors and vanguards. They held the evils of the world at bay.

Once finished with the oath, the griffins glowed a brilliant white, illuminating the area with magic that warmed the spirit.

A second later, the glow vanished. All six people on stage now had an arcanist star on their foreheads—one with a griffin laced between the seven points.

8

SAPPHIRE SPRINGS

I never did make it to the stage with Master Zelfree and the others.

Once the oath had been taken, the citizens of West Landin headed toward the mountain springs in droves. I got caught up in the mass migration, barely able to focus as people continued to shout, applaud, and celebrate. I thought about slipping into the shadows and sliding away from the crowds, but I didn't want to suffer the pain of my magic, so I allowed myself to be taken by the human current.

When we reached the base of the mountain, however, I headed off onto a secluded trail. It wasn't hard to find the Sapphire Springs. Glowstones had been dropped into the many small pools of hot water, lighting up the mountainside with blue firefly-like dots as far as the eye could see.

There must have been hundreds of springs, each a different shape and depth. The glowstones gave the environment an aura of magic and wonder. Although I still felt nervous about seeing the others, my anxiety waned the longer I stared.

This was a magical place, much like the woods outside the capital city, Fortuna, or the Endless Mire back on my home island.

"Have you made a decision?" Luthair asked. "The others don't seem to know where you are. You could retreat to the ship."

"I want that good luck," I muttered.

"Then what will you do?"

"I'll just... avoid everyone."

"So brave of you," Luthair quipped. "So confident."

I glared at the shadows near my feet. "Hey. It's easy for you to mock—you're basically nothing *but* clothes."

He remained silent, and I sighed in frustration. What was wrong with avoiding everyone? I had the perfect plan. I could get my magical luck, and I wouldn't have to deal with the awkward situation of staring at the sky the entire evening. Win-win.

I climbed the side of the mountain, keeping to the narrow goat trails. Some pre-teens sat on rocks along the pathway, but they didn't even acknowledge me as I passed. They kept their candles close and made jokes under their breath. It reminded me of the pre-teens on the Isle of Ruma. I supposed some things were universal.

The mountain went on forever. I could've hiked up the side for hours before reaching the top. Fortunately, there were plenty of springs to choose from, even near the base. Most were taken by entire families—mother, father, kids, grandparents—and none of them seemed to mind sharing. On the contrary, it looked as though they were having fun. Kids splashed the water, grandparents relaxed near the edge, and the parents snuggled close, sticking near the natural vents that kept the water warm.

Thankfully, salt drifted up from the rocks under the

mountain and made the water a pale milky white. Even with the glowstones, it was difficult to see anything beneath the surface.

Most natural springs had an odd smell. The sulfur alone stunk like rotten eggs, but the glowstones had a scent of their own. Together, the springs and stones mixed to create a lavender aroma. Standing near a small grouping of springs reminded me of a field of flowers.

I crept along the edge of the celebration, away from all the large and popular gathering points. My bad luck stalked me, however. I slid around a boulder and almost ran face-first into a woman. I only saw her pixie-short blonde hair before jerking my gaze up to the sky.

"I'm so sorry," I murmured as I scooted back around the boulder. "I'm, uh, looking for a specific spring."

She giggled, and I felt like such a fool. My whole body turned hot with a blush. My thoughts came in random jumbles. Growing up, I didn't interact with many people. Our island didn't have springs. I hadn't been prepared for the situation and it left me feeling lightheaded.

"There are some springs right here," the woman said, her voice effervescent and happy.

"N-no, thank you."

"I can show you around, if you'd like."

I closed my eyes and navigated with my feet. "You're very kind. But I'll pass." I slid to the other side of the boulder and continued up the mountain, her giggling following me for a few minutes. When it stopped, I was certain I had left her behind.

Why did I have to be so awkward? I had a rough idea why—it was my limited experience and observation. Grave-keeper William's wife had died before I went into his care, and all the intimacy I read in storybooks involved heroic situations; love at first sight or destined couples finding themselves after years apart.

I knew all of that was childish. *I knew.*

But that didn't help me now, and I didn't want to come across as a bumbling adolescent, so I had to avoid everyone. At least for tonight.

I had to.

After a moment of calming my nerves, I opened my eyes and hurried on.

Then I found it—a perfect spring. It was tucked behind a giant rock, and a stream of water flowed from another spring a good twenty feet above, creating a splashing sound that soothed my nerves and blanketed the area in a white noise. The glowstones illuminated the milky water, inviting me in with the promise of soothing relaxation.

Excited to get my "good luck," and leave this place before I ran into somebody else, I ripped off my coat, shirt, boots, and pants. Then I tossed them to the side and slid into the water, despite the initial sting of heat. I gritted my teeth and forced myself to sink until my shoulders were under.

Then I exhaled and relaxed against the smooth rocks.

"I'll just be in and out," I whispered to myself.

"What're you doing here?"

The gruff voice sent ice through my veins and hot embarrassment straight to my face. I whipped my head to the side and spotted someone hiding behind the stream of flowing water. No, not *someone.*

Master Zelfree.

He sat with a slight hunch, half turned away from me, his body submerged from the waist down, his shoulder-length black hair wet and flat. I hadn't realized how wiry he was—thin without being emaciated, but somehow an odd combination of muscled and gaunt. He appeared to be in his mid-thirties, but arcanists lived hundreds of years, so it meant nothing.

He had a tattoo of a dragon on his left shoulder blade, though, which surprised me more than anything else.

Zelfree held a bottle of rum, and Traces, his cat-like mimic, sat on his shoulders. She gave me an odd tilt of her head, and then smiled a feline smile.

"I-I'm sorry," I stammered. "I didn't see you."

"Clearly," he said.

"I, uh, wasn't going to stay long."

Zelfree took a long swig of his drink. "Did you practice your magic earlier?"

"Yes."

"At least you take advice."

Still flustered that I hadn't noticed him, I stared at every shady nook and cranny. No one else. Just us two. I breathed a sigh of relief, but the tense feeling of being surprised didn't leave me. Neither of us spoke, and for some reason that made things worse.

Thirty seconds.

A minute.

Two minutes.

I couldn't stand the silence, so I said the first thing that came to mind. "You're here alone?"

Zelfree lifted an eyebrow, like it was without a doubt the stupidest question he had ever heard. He motioned to the unoccupied spring with a sarcastic sweep of his arm.

I slid farther into the water, until it came to my chin. "Sorry. I meant, why didn't you stay with the others?"

"I'd rather not spend personal time with my apprentices."

The hard edge to his words bothered me. He took

another drink, this time with a glare, like he wanted to punish the bottle for existing.

He didn't want to spend time with us? I had no idea he felt that way.

Did he hate the fact I was here? He didn't glance in my direction. He just remained stiff.

I didn't know Zelfree that well. His old apprentices—all phoenix arcanists from the Isle of Ruma—had died years ago. Apparently, Zelfree had blamed himself for their deaths, but I learned later it had actually been Gregory Ruma who murdered them. Ruma had gone insane because of the arcane plague and thought that feeding the young phoenixes to his dead wife's eldrin would bring her back to life.

It wasn't Zelfree's fault that Ruma betrayed his trust. And I thought figuring that out would've helped with his drinking, but Zelfree still needed the bottle.

I sat up, my chest so warm it hurt to breathe. I kept my waist under the water, and I placed my arms on the side of the spring. "Uh, do you mind if I ask you another question?"

"Will it be as riveting as the first?"

My face grew as hot as the water, but I wasn't about to let him get a million digs on me. "Hilarious," I said. "Do you always set aside time to sarcastically mouth off to people a fraction your age?"

My comment made him laugh.

Then he turned to me, half-smiling. "You're funny when you're not stiff. And here I thought you had a coat rack for a spine."

I swirled my hand around in the glowing water and chuckled. "Yeah, well, I get nervous. All of this is new, including being in a guild and learning magic. I don't want to mess it up."

"I can see that. So, what did you want to ask me?"

"Why are you like this?"

The question lingered between us for a moment. I hadn't meant to sound so judgmental, but I truly wanted to know.

I continued, "I thought you'd be happier now that you knew you weren't responsible for your old apprentices' deaths. You seem miserable most days. No offense."

He took one last drink before tossing the empty bottle to the side. It clacked against the rocks and rolled on its side before coming to a stop.

"I've made a lot of terrible decisions," he muttered, his voice somewhat slurred.

"Like what?"

I didn't think he would answer me, but he smiled and rubbed at his forehead.

"Where do I even begin? Why don't we start with my last apprentices? I didn't watch them like I should've. As a mentor, I had a duty to be there for them. Protect them." He closed his eyes. "And I never should've gotten involved with one."

"Involved?" I asked.

Zelfree chuckled again. It didn't last long, though. Then he sighed, his shoulders slumped. "A mentor should never fall for one of his trainees. I was so stupid and lonely, and after three years of training—*three years* of traveling around the high seas with my apprentices—I let the loneliness cloud my judgment. When my apprentices were killed... it almost broke me."

I held my breath, unable to think of anything to say.

Zelfree had been in love with one of his past apprentices? The information stuck in my thoughts, painting a sad picture of what *really* happened back on the island where we killed Ruma—Zelfree killing the man who took everything from him.

"I tried to leave the Frith Guild," Zelfree said, his voice quieter than a whisper and almost masked by the trickling water. "I had failed in all my duties as an arcanist. But the guildmaster wouldn't let me leave. She kept trying to help me through it, and after a few years, I think she pulled me back from the brink, but my mistakes still haunt me." Zelfree placed a hand over his face. "Gods, I've never told anyone else that. Our love... it was a secret. No one discovered us. We would meet for midnight trysts and..."

He swallowed hard and never resumed his speech.

Traces got to her feet, leapt from his shoulder, and landed on the edge of the spring. She glared in my direction. "I hope you'll keep this to yourself, Volke."

I nodded. "Of course. I would never—"

"*To yourself.*"

Again, I nodded, but this time I kept quiet.

"That's why I didn't offer to accept any of the phoenix arcanists when you first came to the guild," Zelfree said, his words slower than before. "But after I... killed Ruma... I figured I had to be there for Zaxis and Atty. Now it just hurts. I want to avoid anything that reminds me of..."

"We don't have to talk about it," I said. "I'm sorry I brought it up."

"Don't be. It's actually a relief to finally tell someone." Zelfree exhaled, his gaze fixed on the warm waters. "Thank you."

I tensed, unsure of what to say. "You're welcome?"

Then I heard Zaxis speak, his voice right behind me. "What're you idiots doing over here?"

Zelfree glanced up, and the two of them met each other's gaze.

"O-oh," Zaxis said, looking away, his cheeks flushed. "I'm sorry, Master Zelfree. I didn't know that was you."

"Who did you think it was?" I snapped.

"Adelgis."

Unlike me—who had forgotten all about the need for a towel—Zaxis walked to the spring, already undressed and with his towel wrapped around his waist. He tossed it to the side before getting in the water, and I glanced away just in time to be modest.

For a few moments, the trickling waterfall was the only conversation between us. Then Zaxis moved forward, his head high. "Master Zelfree, I've been meaning to speak with you. I've practiced my evocation, and my flames are—"

"That's good," Zelfree said, curt. "Why don't you tell me about it when we practice in groups?" He stood and turned behind the falling stream of water. Without a word, he snatched up his own towel hidden behind a couple of rocks and secured it around his waist.

"I'll see you two back at the boat," he said. "Don't dilly-dally around here, either. Head straight there once you're done."

"Okay," I said.

Zaxis nodded.

Then Zelfree left us, his movements tense. Traces ran after and effortlessly leapt up to his shoulder. She purred and wrapped her tail around his neck.

The moment he was out of earshot, Zaxis turned to me. "See? What did I tell you? He hates me."

"I don't think he hates you."

"Uh-huh. He'll chat it up with *you* all night long, but the instant *I* walk over, he has to leave."

"You did start off by calling him—what was it again?— oh, right. *An idiot.*"

Zaxis continued to glow a bright red, almost the same shade as his hair. Then he sank beneath the water, waited a few seconds, and reemerged. He wiped the water from his face. "I said I didn't know it was him."

"Well, stupidity isn't a crime, so you're free to go."

"Don't get smart with me," he growled. "I'm not in the mood."

"Why are you even here?" I asked. "I figured you'd be in the *popular* spring or something."

"Eh. I'd rather spend time with you over random arcanists." He stretched and leaned back against the rocks, his red hair slicked back and showcasing his phoenix arcanist mark perfectly. "So, tell me something interesting."

"I... don't have anything."

"C'mon. Anything will do. I hate the silence."

I laughed once. "Yeah, me too."

"Okay, how about this? If you could bond with any mystical creature in the whole wide world, what would it be?"

After a deep breath, where the steam filled my lungs and relaxed me, I said, "I had never considered bonding to a knightmare when I was younger, but now that I'm with Luthair, I can't imagine anything else."

"Not even one of those ancient mythological creatures? You know, the ones so powerful they can create islands or warp time or something?"

"They're all dead," I muttered. "And even if they weren't, I doubt some *super secret powerful creature no one has ever seen in a thousand years* would want to bond with me. All the stories I read said they bonded to gods. No one is so arrogant as to think they measure up to *that* standard."

Zaxis splashed water in my direction. "Listen to you. Still talking like you're a poor-boy gravedigger. You're an arcanist now. Even if you're second-bonded, you're pretty talented. It's okay if you act like it."

"Eh."

"Besides," he said as he leaned back and ran a hand down his chest. "Some people *can* measure up, thank you very much."

I couldn't help but laugh. Zaxis joined in too, smiling wide.

"I'm joking," he said as he slumped back into the water. "I'm not that self-absorbed."

"So you're admitting you're at least partially self-absorbed?"

He splashed me again. "Shut up. I'm just aware I'm talented. That's not—"

Zaxis caught his breath, and I followed his gaze to beyond the spring. Then I couldn't breathe either.

Atty had walked over to the side of the water, her delicate body wrapped in a thin towel. I swear my heart stopped for a second, and my mind ground to a halt. She stepped into the spring, one foot first, and then the next, stopping on a shallow rock so that the water only reached her knees. Then she went to undo the towel.

I stared down at my chest so intently that I discovered new hairs I hadn't realized were there. When I blinked, I took several seconds, keeping my eyes shut as long as possible, until it sounded as if Atty had fully immersed herself in the spring.

I glanced over at Zaxis. He stared at the night sky as though his life depended on counting each individual star.

"It's a pleasant evening," Atty said, a smile in her voice.

Even though I knew the opaque water would cover her body, I couldn't bring myself to meet her gaze. I fixed my attention on the boulder behind her shoulder, aware she was submerged from the collarbone down.

"I like evenings," was all I managed to say.

I like evenings.

The statement echoed in my thoughts, reminding me I had no social graces whatsoever.

"Whelp," Zaxis said as he patted my shoulder. "I should probably find Forsythe, and that'll take me awhile. You two hold down the spring until I'm back."

When Zaxis went to stand, I grabbed his elbow and kept him down. He gave me a sideways glance and cocked an eyebrow, like I was insane.

"*Don't leave me,*" I mouthed.

Zaxis rested back into the water and whispered, "I thought you wanted some alone time with Atty?"

"I forgot to bring a towel," I murmured. "And what if she doesn't want to be alone with me?"

Clearly Atty didn't mind sharing the spring with us, but what if I made it awkward for her? I had already demonstrated I couldn't form a coherent sentence—my company was no better than a corpse who occasionally moved due to trapped gas in the abdomen. *And* we were now muttering about her, even though she was only a few feet away, watching us.

Damn. I should've stayed on the ship. Good luck wasn't worth any of this.

Atty ran her fingers through her long blonde hair. "What're you two whispering about? Am I a bother?"

"Never," Zaxis said. "We love your company."

She blushed, and for the first time since I had met her, she half covered her face with the strands of her hair, hiding her pink cheeks. It intrigued me, and the longer I stared the more I took note of her smooth and slender shoulders, far smaller than mine.

That was the breaking point. Luthair had tried to warn me, and I knew I couldn't handle this. My experience with intimate relations was nonexistent. Even being with Zelfree and Zaxis had been somewhat difficult. I grabbed Zaxis's towel, dragged it into the water, wrapped it around my waist, and then stood.

"What the—?" Zaxis barked.

"I'm sorry," I said, not looking at either of them. "I'll tell Forsythe to bring you another."

I made it halfway down the mountain before I managed to relax. My blood remained hotter than the damn spring, and since I gave Forsythe back Zaxis's towel, my clothes clung to the water still on my body.

What did Zaxis and Atty think? They probably talked about how much of a lunatic I was for running out of the spring.

I sighed.

The path back to town didn't have lampposts. That didn't bother me. It allowed for a clear view of the stars, and I saw well enough to navigate. Shadows had become my new domain ever since I bonded with Luthair. My sight adjusted supernaturally to the darkness, to the point I saw as clearly as though I walked through the afternoon sun.

And under the cover of darkness, I felt as though my magic would come easier and stronger. I would have to test that in the future.

"Hey, Volke."

The greeting startled me. I almost tripped over a fallen branch, but I managed to get my footing and turn around.

Illia stood near a copperwood tree with Nicholin on her shoulder. Hexa leaned on the trunk, her puffy hair tied back tight. Raisen rested on a small blanket, guarding an unattended plate of food near the protruding roots. I suspected Hexa and Illia had been having a private picnic, their eldrin and a lantern their only company.

Illia stepped forward, her hair fluttering in the evening winds. The moment her bangs fluttered too far from her face, she lifted a hand and covered her scars. The reaction irritated me. I wanted to tell her to stop, but that was unreasonable.

"That *is* you, right?" she asked. "I think you're the tallest guy on the island."

I ambled over to her, close enough so she could see me. "Hey, Illia. What're you and Hexa doing out here?"

She pulled her coat close. "Oh, we decided not to do the Sapphire Springs. I hate crowds."

"Sounds like you."

"Hexa and I made our own luck. Right?" She gave Hexa a quick glance, and for a long moment the two of them seemed to exchange a silent conversation.

"Right," Hexa said. "Our own luck." She pushed off the copperwood tree and rotated her arms. "Well, I have to go. I'll be back at the ship if you need me."

Her ungraceful exit didn't fool me. Illia wanted her gone.

"Goodbye, Hexa!" Nicholin said with a wave. "Goodbye, Raisen!"

Hexa strolled off down the road, her hands on top of her head, her fingers laced together. Raisen struggled to keep up, but going downhill seemed easier for him. Hexa hummed an unfamiliar song and I wondered if it came from her hometown. I didn't know much about her. She hadn't been raised on the islands, so she remained somewhat of an enigma.

I stared down at Illia. "Maybe we should head back to the ship, too."

"Let's walk around first." She held onto my elbow. "I haven't seen you since you fought the griffin. I want to hear all the details." Her grip tightened on my arm, and she rested her head on my bicep.

Although I enjoyed the closeness of her gesture, I pulled my arm away and rubbed at my shoulder. "Kahtona recited the story of Ryllin's death during the bonding ceremony."

Illia kept close. "I want to hear it from *you*."

Nicholin swished his tail and puffed up his white fur. "Yeah, buster. You should've come straight to us after that fight and spilled the beans!"

"Shh," Illia hissed. She placed a hand over his mouth. "It's fine. Just tell us now."

"There isn't much to say," I muttered.

We walked down the rest of the mountain. Illia couldn't see much, and I helped her avoid a few large rocks and twigs. The moment I placed my hand on her upper arm, however, she twisted her fingers into my sleeve and refused to let go. I didn't say anything, and neither did she. To my surprise, Nicholin offered me odd glances the entire walk— sideways glares, like he was making a point.

"Is something wrong?" I asked.

Illia shook her head. "We tell each other everything. C'mon. I want to hear the story."

"It just hurts, okay?" I tried to keep the anger out of my voice, but that proved difficult. "I feel like... the pirates used me. Does that make any sense? Like I was their tool of destruction, executing the last step of their plan. *I* killed Ryllin. Not them. *Me.*"

"There was no other way."

"That doesn't help," I said, curt.

Illia leaned heavily on my arm. "You sound really upset."

"The entire fight still troubles me."

"I'm sorry, I just—"

"It's okay," I said with a long exhale. "Now you know."

The evening winds rushed by, carrying leaves from the trees and petals from the flowers planted around West Landin. I shielded my eyes with my free arm and enjoyed the natural rustling brought about by the breeze. Once the winds calmed down, Illia picked at the button on my coat sleeve.

"Maybe we should talk about something else." She met my gaze with her one eye. "How were the Sapphire Springs?"

"Good. I guess."

So awkward.

"Did you share a couple's spring?"

"Uh, no. I was technically alone with Master Zelfree for a bit. And then Zaxis."

"You weren't alone with anyone else?"

I shook my head. It wasn't a lie. Atty and I were never alone.

Nicholin ran from Illia's shoulder to my arm, all the way up to my shoulder. I leaned away as he sniffed my face. "Are you telling the truth?" he asked. "I'll know if you're not!"

I lifted an eyebrow. "They were the only two I was alone with."

"A likely story!"

"No," Illia said. She grabbed Nicholin and ripped him off my coat. "Volke wouldn't lie to me. He's telling the truth."

I straightened my sleeves. "Is there a reason for the interrogation?"

"I just... wanted to know." She placed Nicholin on her shoulder and looked away, a slight smile on her face.

"We shouldn't be wandering around like this," I said, trying to steer us toward a shorter route back to the boat. "Pirates infected Ryllin with the plague. Even Master Zelfree thinks they're still nearby."

"Yeah," Illia murmured.

"And with a boat named the *Third Abyss*, you know these scumbags are unstable. I think it would be best if we got back to the others as soon as possible."

Illia let go of my arm.

I waited for a moment and then turned around, confused by her stillness. Then I noticed how pale she had become, and how she stared at the dirt, unseeing. I waited a second, but it didn't get any better. She lifted a hand to the scars on her face, even though they were tucked behind her hair, which was held in place by her sailing hat.

"What's wrong?" I asked.

She didn't answer. She ran her fingers over the old injuries, her single eye vacant.

Nicholin patted the top of her head. "Uh, Illia? You're not moving."

"What was the name of the boat?" Illia whispered.

"The *Third Abyss*," I said. "An obvious reference to the abyssal hells. Like I said—these fiends want to associate themselves with Death Lords. It's disgusting."

"Volke..."

"Yeah?"

She met my gaze, her expression haunting. "The *Third Abyss*. Those were the pirates who killed my parents. The captain... he's the man who... who cut out my right eye."

9

THE WENDIGO ARCANIST

I didn't know what to say.

Illia didn't say anything either. She stared for a long moment, her breathing gradually becoming strained, like it was difficult for her to get enough air.

Nicholin, never at a loss for words, patted her shoulder. "Hey, I'm with you. Don't worry. Those pirates don't know who they're dealing with. You're an arcanist of the Frith Guild now."

After a long exhale, Illia stroked Nicholin's fur. She half smiled and allowed her gaze to fall on him. "Things *are* different," she whispered. "I was just a little girl then."

I stepped close. "I'm here for you, too."

"Thank you, Volke."

To my surprise, she embraced me with a tight grip. I returned the gesture, holding her close. Illia wore clothing that hid her body, and while we remained together, I realized how small she was compared to me. For some reason, it got me worried, and I held her tighter than before.

Nicholin also got in on the hug. He squirmed his way between us, held both of our coats, and pulled us together.

"We should get back to the ship," I said. "I'm sure Master Zelfree is already there."

Illia let go of me and then took a few steps toward the main road. "You go back to the ship. I have... a lot to think about." She returned her hand to the scars on her face.

She didn't ask me for favors often. I wanted to do as she asked, but uncertainty ate at me. What if the pirates were nearby? Some pirates—especially arcanist pirates—had been known to raid towns. Their powerful eldrin could lay waste to buildings or walls, and the pirates would rush in to steal objects or people.

And plague-carrying pirates were the worst. What if they started a panic by intentionally targeting more griffins? The new arcanists couldn't defend themselves well.

A whole host of terrible things could happen.

"I think we should stay together," I said.

Illia turned to me with a lifted eyebrow. "I'll be fine. Nicholin and I won't be in any danger."

Nicholin puffed out his chest and held his head high. "We can *teleport*."

"I know that," I muttered. "But still."

Illia left the small path, but stopped once she reached cobblestones only a few feet away. "I need time. I promise nothing will happen. You head back, and I'll see you in the morning."

Morning? That long?

She didn't wait for me to respond. She headed for the outskirts of West Landin, straight toward the daisy tree woods. Nicholin glanced back several times, a slight frown on his ferret-like face.

I watched her go, knots forming in my stomach with each step she took. Illia had always been a solitary person, but that didn't mean it was safe to be alone now. If Ryllin could be brought down by those cutthroat pirates, then Illia was in danger, no matter what she said.

And rizzels acted as lures...

"Why do you hesitate?" Luthair asked from my shadow. "A knight never abandons a post."

"You heard her," I said.

"I did."

"She wants be alone. She'd hate it if I ignored her wishes."

"Tell me, if Illia died tonight in a pirate attack, would you ever forgive yourself?"

The hypothetical question hit me like a sucker punch. I glared at the shadows around my feet, half-angry, half-panicked. "Why would you ever say that?"

"Would you?"

"Of course not! I'd be haunted by that for the rest of my life."

"Then you must tell Illia," Luthair stated. "Don't hide feelings of compassion or concern. Explain yourself—tell her that life wouldn't be right if something were to happen. She'll never know unless you speak to her."

Luthair's words invigorated me. He was right. I hadn't explained myself properly to Illia. I needed to tell her that walking around to gather her thoughts wasn't worth the risk of running into pirates. Especially not pirates who were willing and capable of infecting Nicholin with the plague.

"Let's go," I muttered.

I ran toward the road, determined to catch up to her. I slowed my pace when I hit the cobblestones, my eyebrows knit.

I didn't see her.

Anywhere.

I thought the Sapphire Springs had given me good luck? How was *this* good fortune?

Then it hit me. She had teleported. But why? Had she been that determined to be alone? I shook my head. It didn't matter. She couldn't teleport far. She still had to be nearby, and I knew she had been heading in the direction of the woods. So that was the direction I went, walking along the outside of the city wall.

Since most citizens remained at the springs, West Landin had all the warmth of a ghost town. The ocean breeze brought with it a scent of salt, and when I stared out at the waves, I was surprised by my ability to spot the flotsam washed up on shore. I could see in the dark, but now it seemed like I might be able to see *better* in the dark.

The realization lingered with me for a moment, but then I resumed my run. I slowed near the edge of the woods, my lungs hot.

"Can I see better in the darkness?" I asked between strained breaths.

Luthair slid through the shadows on the ground. "It is a magical ability inherent to knightmare arcanists. The darkness is our domain. It will help you in all situations."

"Right."

A twig snapped, and I jerked my attention to a small grouping of trees.

Illia?

No.

A man stood on the other side of a tree trunk. Perhaps if I *hadn't* been a knightmare arcanist, he would've remained hidden in moonlight shadows, but I could see him as though it was the middle of the day.

"Hello?" I called out.

He lifted his head and glanced over, glowering in my

direction. He held a book in one hand as he made his way around the daisy trees. For a moment, he stared at my forehead—no doubt trying to make out my arcanist mark.

"Who goes there?" he asked, his voice rough, like he didn't speak often or his throat was sore.

I straightened my posture. "My name is Volke Savan. I'm a knightmare arcanist with the Frith Guild." I touched the bronze pendant around my neck. "Who are you?"

"You said... you were a knightmare arcanist?"

Once he walked onto the road, I got a better view of his attire. He wore high-trim leather boots, both shaggy and scuffed from years of use. He also wore a tattered buccaneer coat, and his loose white shirt fluttered in the evening wind, revealing that he had no guild pendant. Most disturbing were the weapons he carried. A short sword—a cutlass, specifically, curved for slashing—and a flintlock pistol. Neither were common for the Isle of Landin.

"I only snuck into town for this accursed journal," the man muttered as he slid the book into his coat pocket. "I never imagined I'd actually find you. And all alone."

Journal? I had no idea what he was talking about. His attire screamed *sea thief*, and it was all I could think about.

"Identify yourself," I stated.

"Your knightmare's name is Luthair... right?"

I didn't answer. I held my breath, so tense I could hear my heart beat in my ears.

The man brushed back his dark chestnut hair. The sides were cut short, exposing his pierced ears. Well, the bottom was pierced, but the top of his earlobe... both were black, a harsh contrast to his tanned skin.

And his fingers—from the knuckles to the tips—appeared black too, like frostbite had set in, rotting away his flesh. But it couldn't have been actual frostbite. If it were, he wouldn't have been able to move his fingers. He just *looked* to have frostbitten sections of his body.

I almost didn't notice his arcanist mark. He had the standard star with a wolf wrapped around the points. No, not a wolf. The creature had the body of a wolf, the antlers of a stag, and a skull-like face.

"You're a wendigo arcanist," I said.

The man chuckled. "You know your stuff."

He appeared young, perhaps a few years older than me at best, but arcanists had extremely long lives. Maybe he was decades older. I had no way to tell.

The last thing I noticed, and the detail that stilled my heart, was a tattoo on the side of his neck—three horizontal lines: 三. The exact symbol used for the third abyss in all textbooks I had ever read.

"And you're a pirate of the *Third Abyss*," I whispered.

My worst nightmare had been confirmed. There *were* pirates on the island. Right here. Right now. Illia could be anywhere, and this blackheart could have all sorts of tricks up his sleeve. Where were the others? Safe on the ship. Far away...

"You seem smarter than most," the frostbitten pirate said. "I'd hate for you to get caught up in my revenge. Call your eldrin and step aside."

Luthair subtly shifted around my feet, no doubt waiting for a surprise attack or for my command. But I didn't know the strength of this pirate. He could've been a master arcanist for all I knew. Fighting him was a terrible idea.

I took a step back, my legs unsteady.

The man narrowed his eyes. "I didn't give you an option." He snapped his black fingers. "Wraith. Hold the man down."

A wolf-like creature appeared out of nowhere and bit my

right arm, his fangs crunching into my bones. I yelled, surprised by the man's eldrin, and stricken with an intense pain that shot up to my shoulder. The monster yanked me to the ground, and I hit the dirt side-first.

Luthair rose out of the shadows, his plate armor forming in half a second. Before he could jump to my aid, however, frost coated the ground in an instant. The frigid sorcery blanketed everything, even the individual blades of grass. Ice sparkled under the moonlight, giving the whole area a chilly appearance of arcane power.

"Volke," Luthair called out. "I can't shadow-step across magic."

The wendigo holding me—its face more bone than flesh —didn't let go. It growled as it thrashed its head from side to side, jerking my arm around with it, tearing muscle with its sharp fangs. My blood splattered across the frost-covered road, and I grunted back a second shout of pain.

Wendigo were beasts with antlers, emaciated bodies, and unbelievable hunger. Sure enough, Wraith looked like a wolf that hadn't been fed in months. His long antlers curved up into sharp points. Worse yet, wendigo were known for their vile diets. They feasted on raw flesh, and raw flesh alone, hunting people lost in the snow of the far north, sneaking up on them with their invisibility.

Luthair pulled out his inky longsword—it, too, shone in the moonlight.

The pirate ripped off his coat and threw it to the side of the road. "I don't need my eldrin's help, and you don't need your arcanist. Luthair, we have unsettled business. I want revenge. One of us will kill the other; that's my promise to you."

Luthair turned his helmet in my direction. Although

hollow inside, I recognized the hesitation in his movements, as though my safety were all he cared about.

The man snapped his fingers, and Wraith placed a heavy paw on my chest, growling, his saliva mixed with the blood weeping from my arm. I gritted my teeth, unwilling to make any more noise.

"If you go near him, I'll order Wraith to rip out his guts," the frostbitten man said. Then he pulled out his cutlass. "Fight me. If you win, the two of you can go free."

Luthair returned his attention to the pirate. "A man gives his name before a duel, villain."

"Fain," the man said.

The name held no meaning for me, and without a surname, I couldn't draw any conclusions. Other than the fact this man was a pirate, I had no idea what his business with Luthair would be. I couldn't allow him to kill Luthair, no matter what past revenge he was talking about.

Fain lunged with his cutlass. Luthair parried with all the expert skill of a master swordsman. Then Fain gestured with his hand, adding another coat of ice over the area, creating a thick hoarfrost that made it impossible for Luthair to get proper footing.

This time, when Fain rushed forward, Luthair failed to block the blow. The cutlass hit his shadow armor and chipped it. When Luthair went to strike back, Fain nimbly moved aside, unaffected by his own icy terrain. In fact, it seemed to help him—much like the darkness helped me.

Fain slashed again, tearing through some of Luthair's cape.

I couldn't take it. I tried to wrest my arm from the wendigo's mouth, but he growled and yanked me back, as though he would drag me into the woods. I had to get a weapon, and I tried to claw at the dirt with my free hand, but it didn't help.

Luthair glanced in my direction. Fain took the opportunity to create another layer of ice, this time trapping Luthair's feet in a crystal-like prison of frost.

No!

At this rate, he would be slowly cut to pieces!

I focused my magic, agony flooding my veins, and I evoked terrors. The wendigo released his hold on my arm, shaken and half-crying. Even Fain staggered backward, his skin dappled with sweat and his hands trembling.

While they were distracted, I reached for the darkness and tried to imagine it condensing into something sharp. Wraith recovered from my fear and snapped his jaws at me, but I willed the shadows to attack. Dagger-like tendrils sprung up from the ground and pierced into his body—one even lashing him enough to puncture his eye.

Wraith hissed and leapt away, black blood pouring from the injury and spilling across the ground. Although my shadow-daggers weren't long, they were pointed enough to pierce straight into soft flesh.

But after that display of magic, I couldn't move. I remained on the ground, breathing heavily, everything hurting. Even if Luthair and I merged, I didn't think I'd be able to get up.

The wendigo bared his fangs and dashed toward me. He lowered his head at the last minute and gored me with the tips of his antlers, the points piercing my shoulder near the collarbone. I gasped and half choked on a yell.

This wasn't the first time I had been stabbed by antlers, and it brought back frightful memories.

I manipulated the shadows a second time, my anger and fear acting as righteous fuel. The dagger tendrils sprang up, far more powerful than before. They lashed out with such force that one sliced through the trunk of a tree, another cut deep into Wraith's side, and one even caught Fain in the leg, ripping open his left calf.

The darkness thrashed with wild havoc, and one tendril pierced Wraith's other eye, blinding him with a fearsome strike. Although mystical creatures could heal, it would take time—longer than this fight would last, that was for sure.

The wendigo leapt away from me, whining like only a dog could.

"Wraith!"

When I tried to manipulate the shadows a third time, I collapsed. My magic had drained me. Then my vision faded in and out, tunneling into darkness. I didn't have the strength to lift my head.

Fain rushed to his eldrin's side, but after that, I couldn't see much. Ice chilled my core, and I shivered on the ground, my mangled arm tucked underneath me.

"Volke! Get up!"

The next thing I knew, Luthair stood over me. I stared up at him, relieved he hadn't died. He knelt and examined my arm. His armor remained cracked, chipped, and torn, worse than before.

"Are you okay?" I asked.

"I will be fine," he said. "We should worry about you."

"Where is...?"

"The pirate and his wendigo shrouded themselves in invisibility and then fled."

I glanced around, my vision blurry. "How do you know they're not around here?"

"I've listened and waited. They ran into the woods and haven't returned."

Knowing we weren't in immediate danger eased the

tension in my muscles. I relaxed and breathed easy. "We should find Illia and head back to the boat."

"Indeed."

Luthair helped me to my feet and then offered a shoulder. I couldn't walk without his support, and I held onto the shadowy plate armor as best I could.

Off on the side of the road, forgotten by its owner, lay the pirate's buccaneer coat. I stared at it for a long moment, and then pointed with a weak gesture. "Luthair, pick that up, please."

We walked over together and stooped down to gather it. The pockets were heavy, filled with contents, including the book the pirate had spoken about.

"Let's take it with us," I said.

Whatever the book was, it was ours now.

We headed for the surrounding woods. We didn't get far before my legs refused to move. Luthair held me close, his ebony gauntlets tracing the injuries on my shoulder and arm.

"Heal this," he commanded.

I... couldn't. I didn't even know how. My healing had just *happened* before, like a dream while sleeping. How could I force myself to heal? Even when I imagined it and concentrated, nothing happened.

I rubbed my face. "Maybe I should find Zaxis."

"Then we need to return you to the ship."

"We should find Illia first."

"As you wish, my arcanist."

Luthair detached his cape and wrapped it tight around my injured arm, creating an impromptu sling. I hadn't known he could remove his cape—it intrigued me for a moment. The "fabric" felt cold and silk-like, as though made from the most expensive material in the world. I stroked it with my free hand, surprised by the lightness of the shadow cloth.

"Stay awake," Luthair said. "You mustn't lose consciousness."

Easier said than done. My body felt heavy, my head spun, and my vision continued to tunnel until the road next to my feet was all I could see. I had never been so ill, and a piece of me wondered if I had been infected with the arcane plague. The wendigo didn't seem deranged, though.

I almost laughed. Perhaps it was a normal sickness? The thought calmed my panic—that was the first time I had thanked the heavens for a regular illness.

"Volke? What happened?"

I glanced up. Illia rushed to my side, her one eye wide.

Where had she come from? I hadn't even noticed.

Nicholin squeaked. "We leave you alone for *two seconds* and look what happened!"

"I went searching for you," I murmured. "Because I was worried pirates would attack. Ironically, a pirate found me instead. Funny, right?" I offered her a weak smile.

"It isn't funny at all," Illia said. She held my shoulder, her hands trembling. "Why do you always get into danger when I'm not around?"

I chuckled. Zaxis had said something similar when Ryllin attacked. I did get myself into danger, but wasn't that the job of an arcanist? Better me than someone else. And I wanted to make that point, but my senses finally failed me. The last thing I knew, I was falling to my knees.

THE CARTOGRAPHER'S JOURNAL

I awoke to the creaking of a ship's hull.

With each wave, the vessel rocked, straining the wood. The groans of the ship reminded me of sailing with Gravekeeper William. He said that was how boats "spoke" to us. If there was a problem, we'd be able to hear it. He had a great ear for his personal ship and even knew if water had gotten into the hold, just from the sounds it made.

I opened my eyes. The ceiling of my cabin had been constructed with oak planks, and I recognized the odd knot just above me. I was back on the *Long Ride*—the Frith Guild ship we had taken to the Isle of Landin.

When I tried to move, I realized something was lying on me.

Illia had draped herself across my bare chest, her wavy hair spilled over my skin, all the way to my neck. She had tucked her head into her arms, her even breathing betraying the fact she had fallen asleep some time ago.

Although I wore no shirt, I still had my trousers on under the blankets. I relaxed and stared at the morning sun streaming through the porthole. I had slept through the night.

"Illia?" I muttered, my voice raspy.

She jerked up, her eye unfocused. Then she ran a hand over her face. "Volke?"

"What's going on?"

"You were injured. Some sort of magical disease is in your wound. Zaxis tried to heal you, but it keeps opening up." Illia straightened herself. She had been sitting in a chair next to my cot, and when she stretched, she did so with stiff movements. How long had she been sleeping? Long enough that her back bothered her.

I lifted my arm and examined the gauze wrapped around the teeth marks. Blood stained the cloth. I was still bleeding.

"When will it stop?" I asked.

"Master Zelfree says he knows a great healer in the capital. Everything will be fine."

"Oh, okay."

Illia smacked my shoulder with enough force to sting. I forced myself to sit up, rubbing at the spot she had whacked.

"What was that for?"

She glared. "What were you doing walking around by yourself?"

"I told you! I was worried. I went looking for you."

Illia lifted an eyebrow. "My magic is good for escaping things. You shouldn't have run around like you did. I'd be upset if something happened to you, Volke."

My chest tightened, but I also had the urge to laugh. That was the exact reason I wanted to make sure *she* made it back to the ship.

Illia placed her hand on my chest, her fingers chilly, but not outright cold. Then she pushed me down and pulled the blankets up to my shoulders. The cot wasn't comfortable, but it was better than nothing. I shifted around until I found a position I could live with.

She stayed next to me, her hands on top of the blanket, her gaze distant, as though she was deep in thought. I didn't say anything. As I waited, my body grew heavy with sleep. When she took a breath, I shook my fatigue away and focused.

"Volke," she whispered.

"Yeah?"

"I haven't told anyone else about my real experience with the pirates."

"I don't think it's necessary, if it bothers you."

Illia covered her scars with a shaky hand. "I remember everything about my time aboard the *Third Abyss*. The smells. The cargo hold. The people. Whenever I try to sleep, it's all I see."

I held my breath and listened to the creaking of the hull. I couldn't imagine being held captive on a pirate ship. A waking nightmare.

"It all happened so fast," Illia continued, her voice quieter than before. "The pirates boarded my father's ship and started taking everything they could carry. When my father and mother fought back..."

"Illia," I said. I brought my hand out of the covers and placed it on top of her knuckles. "You don't have to tell me if—"

She shook her head. "I want you to know." She closed her eye. "The arcanists on the *Third Abyss* are all bonded to mystical creatures who consume human flesh. Man-eaters. My parents... I could hear them calling for me when the creatures attacked."

I didn't want to hear the last of the story. I knew exactly

how it ended—and it hurt me to hear her say it. Sometimes I wished I could somehow change the past and make everything right. I wished there was some way I could've been an arcanist then and stopped those pirates from killing her parents and torturing her.

I just wished I could take away this sadness that obviously still haunted her.

Illia placed her forehead on my chest, tears streaming from her eye. "The captain of the *Third Abyss* found me. Calisto. That's what they called him. He cut my eye... with a thin blade. He said if I didn't struggle, he... he wouldn't kill me."

She took a few shaky breaths. "He's a manticore arcanist. He fed my eye to his... to his manticore eldrin."

My gut twisted in a tight knot as I recalled the legends of manticores. They ate people. Only people. Ferocious and gigantic, they were monsters with the leathery wings of a dragon, the tail of a scorpion, and the body of a lion. Like a deformed griffin of evil. I had read that manticores had three rows of fangs, and their venom corrupted those with magic, and killed anyone or anything without.

"I doubt he'll attack a Frith Guild ship," I said. "We have a master arcanist aboard, after all. I'm sure we'll be safe."

Illia kept her face hidden in the blanket and said nothing.

I placed my hand on her back and grazed my fingers along her spine. "He isn't going to hurt you anymore."

"I wanted to become an arcanist to stop pirates like him," Illia whispered. "How can I do that if I'm this afraid?"

"I'm sure the Frith Guild will think of something."

"I... I want to stop him." She gritted her teeth. "I want to *end* him."

"There are probably master arcanists out there hunting

him already. You should focus on your training. Once you've completed it, you'll become a world-famous pirate hunter, I know it."

We sat in silence for a long moment as she thought over my statement. I didn't know how the hero arcanists of the world would apprehend the crew of the *Third Abyss*, but I hoped they would be dealt with soon. The moment the ship and her crew were set on fire, Illia could finally put this behind her.

Illia sat up, her eye dry, even if her face was still glazed with tears. She had a cold look about her, like she had come to some decision that helped quell her fear and uncertainty.

"Everything will be fine," she whispered. She turned to me and smoothed my blankets. "Get some sleep. I'll be close by if you need anything."

―――――

A thump and a bang woke me a second time.

I sat up, sweat soaking into my blanket, my heart wild and my eyes wide open. The sounds had come from the deck beyond the door to my cabin, but that knowledge didn't calm my nerves. It took me a long moment to find my breath.

"Jeez," I whispered.

"Jumpy?"

The voice spooked me, and a shudder ran down my back. I snapped my attention to the only other person in the room—Master Zelfree. He stood next to my cot, a book in one hand, his mimic eldrin on his shoulder.

"W-when did you get here?" I asked.

"I've been here for the past ten minutes or so."

"Just... watching me sleep?"

Zelfree held up the book. "Reading."

"Oh. R-right."

"I was watching you," Traces said with a smile and a purr.

"Okay..."

The adrenaline in my veins kept me wide awake, even as I rested back onto my cot. The sun from the porthole window wasn't shining directly in, which meant it was likely in the afternoon, or perhaps later, or maybe the boat had turned, I didn't know. Confusion ate away at my logic. How long would I need to rest? Most likely until I was healed, sure, but when would that be?

"I came to get you," Zelfree said. "You need to clean the deck, remember?"

I faced him, my whole body sore and cold at the same time. He wanted me to clean the ship *now*?

Then Traces shook her head and laughed. "You're right, my arcanist. He's so gullible!"

"Relax," Zelfree said to me with a smile. "You looked like I had just asked you to walk the plank."

I half-chuckled. "Sorry. I thought you were serious."

"Of course not." He sank down into the chair next to my cot. "Luthair told me what happened." He tapped the binding of the book. "He said this was from the pirate you fought."

I ran a hand through my hair. "Oh, yeah. The wendigo arcanist said he had gone into town to get it."

"The reason we went to West Landin was because the pirates had been harassing the ships and merchants. The mayor had even received a letter from the *Third Abyss*, threatening to raid the city if they didn't open their port."

"Why?"

"The mayor thought it had to do with the griffin ceremony, but I suspect it was actually for this journal. It belonged to Martin Mercator. Do you know who that is?"

"Of course," I said. "He's a famous cartographer. Everyone from the islands knows of his exploits."

I always imagined becoming a cartographer if I hadn't become an arcanist. They drew maps of both explored and unexplored territory. Some cartographers, like Martin Mercator, hunted down famous shipwrecks or sites of magical interest. Although he wasn't an arcanist, he had produced so many helpful maps that everyone knew his name. He had a talent for drawing, geometry, and navigation.

"There is no duplicate," Zelfree said as he tapped the cover, "and the mayor of West Landin had been entrusted to keep it safe. He and Mercator are friends, you see."

"So, you think the pirates snuck onto the island to get that journal?"

The details made sense, when I thought about them.

The pirates infected Ryllin to cause panic and fear. The people of West Landin then put all their efforts into protecting the remaining griffins, especially the cubs. There was no doubt in my mind that all the city guards had been busy protecting the Sapphire Springs during the celebrations—with no one left in town to stop a would-be thief.

"What's in the journal?" I asked. "Why is it special?"

"A lot of maps to shipwrecks. Some with magical items. There are even a few smaller islands not on normal maps. I'm reading through it now, hoping to find something that stands out, but most of it is insignificant. Perhaps Calisto just wants to gather himself a small pile of easy-to-acquire treasure."

"Maybe..."

Zelfree half-laughed. "It was lucky you found that pirate

before he escaped. We might not have ever known this was something they wanted if it hadn't been for you."

"Lucky?" I muttered.

Was this the work of the Sapphire Springs?

I laughed aloud. Zelfree cocked an eyebrow, but I didn't even acknowledge him. *This* was my luck? Getting jumped by a pirate in the dead of night? Misfortune really *did* have it out for me. Even my "lucky" encounters were an excuse for me to come home broken and bleeding.

But the more I thought about it, the more my laughter melted away into melancholy appreciation. Although it would have been nice to stumble upon a couple of coins on the road, I preferred stopping the pirates from stealing the cartographer's journal, even if it meant having a messed-up arm.

Zelfree stood. "I think you might need some more rest. You're clearly delirious."

"I think you're right."

"It won't be long until we reach port. Tomorrow morning at the latest."

"Thank you," I said as I got comfortable. "I'll try not to die until then."

I opened my eyes.

The twilight of the setting sun drifted into my cabin through the porthole. Breathing took considerable effort, and I was warmer than I had been the entire trek. Baking. And sweating. I wanted to bathe more than anything.

When I tried to sit up, I realized things were on me. Not a person—multiple smaller *things*.

I glanced down at my chest and caught my breath in

shock. Nicholin had curled up on me and fallen asleep. Forsythe, Zaxis's phoenix, and Titania, Atty's phoenix, had bundled themselves in my blanket on either side of me, cooking me with the heat of their bodies. When I tried to move, Raisen's hydra head poked up from between my legs, his gold eyes glaring in my direction.

"Get some sleep," Raisen hissed.

"What's going on?" I propped myself up on my elbows.

Nicholin yawned and stretched, his rear near my face like some weird cat. I pushed him off my chest and sat all the way up.

"Hey," Nicholin barked. "What's the big idea?"

The phoenixes awoke and glanced over. Raisen breathed with a heavy rasp, still glowering in my direction.

"What are you all doing here?" I asked.

"Illia was worried," Nicholin replied.

Both Forsythe and Titania nodded.

"Zaxis thought you might be cold," Forsythe said.

Titania unfurled her wings. "Atty wanted me to warm you."

"Hexa said I should be nearby," Raisen added with a grunt.

Everyone had sent their eldrin to watch over me? Well, not Adelgis. His ethereal whelk was nowhere to be seen. When I glanced around, however, I spotted Luthair in the corner of the cabin, his arms crossed and his cape secured back on his shoulders. Although he had no face under his helmet, I could tell he had been staring in my direction.

I rested back down on the cot, taken aback by everyone's kindness.

Nicholin hopped onto my chest. He squeaked and waved his little paws. "These *turkeys* came here for your comfort, but I'm the one to protect you."

"You're all going to stay with me?" I asked.

The group of eldrin replied with enthusiastic nods.

I had soot all over my blanket, and I was afraid to move my feet with a hydra between my legs, but for some reason their presence put me at ease.

I felt my shoulder—where the wendigo had gored me with its antlers—and realized the injury was no more. Only my forearm refused to heal, apparently.

"Luthair," I whispered.

"Yes, my arcanist?"

"I've been meaning to ask you... Do you know the guy who attacked us? The man named Fain?"

"No," Luthair replied. "The name means nothing to me."

"You have no idea how he knew you? Or why he attacked?"

"It's a mystery, though Mathis and I did garner many enemies among the wicked. The more pirate arcanists Mathis brought down, the more the rest wanted us both dead."

"Huh... I see."

After a long exhale, I closed my eyes. I'd have to investigate this *Fain* fellow once I felt better. Nicholin curled back into a ball—making it difficult to breathe again—and went right to sleep.

As I slept, my dreams became a coherent narrative.

I was back on the Isle of Ruma, attending a dance at the town hall. Atty asked me to the floor, which angered Illia, and amused Hexa. When we got out into the crowd, Atty ran her hands over my body, a frown deepening on her face. I asked what was wrong, and she explained I was *lumpy*.

Then Zaxis danced with us—we were a group of three, smushed together in a tight circle, swaying to the romantic melody of a love song. Zaxis said he was *helping me* by *showing me how it was done*. Then he competed with Atty to determine the best dancer, going so far as to bite and kick at Atty while the people of Ruma watched from the sidelines.

Master Zelfree stood a few feet away, stroking his chin as he stared at me with a critical eye.

"You need to practice more," he said. "And stop being so lumpy."

I jerked awake, coated in a thin layer of sweat. The eldrin had gone, leaving me alone on the cot. I tried to sit up, but my head felt heavy. I ran my hand up my face and half gasped the instant I felt a tentacle suctioned to my temple.

"What the?"

Fueled by hysteric strength and panic, I jumped off my cot and grabbed at the thing. It was big—the size of my head —and wrapped around my skull like an octopus on a coral reef. My first instinct was to claw it off, which was more of a delirious overreaction, but I couldn't think straight.

"Calm down, Volke!"

With my heart beating hard against my ribcage, I turned to face the speaker. Adelgis stood next to me, both his hands up. I took a few deep breaths, the *creature* still on my head and stuck so tight I could feel its pulse through its many tentacles.

"Everything is okay," Adelgis said. He took a cautious step closer, like I might be a lunatic he needed to corral. "My eldrin is on your head. She isn't going to hurt you."

Tense and agitated, I reached one hand up to touch Adelgis's eldrin. She was cold, while being hard in some places and soft in others.

One by one, she detached her little tentacles and floated

away from my head.

Felicity—that was her name. Out of all the eldrin in the Frith Guild, she was, by far, the most peculiar.

For all intents and purposes, Felicity appeared to be a sea snail. A *giant* sea snail with a crystal shell. It glowed with a faint inner light, and her snail-body shone with an iridescent glimmer, like the outside of a soap bubble. She had six tentacles that hung from her underside, dangling in the air as she floated around like a ghost, untethered by gravity.

"Forgive me," Felicity said. "I tried to give you pleasant dreams."

"Is that what you were doing?" I asked as I ran a hand through my hair. "It felt like a nightmare."

Adelgis grabbed Felicity out of the air and held her close to his chest. "Ethereal whelks have power over people's dreamscapes. I thought it would be a good opportunity to... er... well, I thought you could use some pleasant sleep."

I narrowed my eyes. "Wait. Were you *practicing* on me?"

"I didn't say that."

I glared.

"Okay, *yes*," Adelgis said. He turned away, his eldrin still in his arms. "But we were doing a good job until you woke up."

I stared at him in disbelief. "Seriously? I think a fever brought on by my illness would've done a better job."

"W-what? Really? But I included everything you like. The Isle of Ruma, all of us, Master Zelfree..."

"Just because I liked all the pieces doesn't mean I liked how you arranged them!" I rubbed my temples, hoping the visions of my dream would fade away. Unfortunately, they remained crystal clear, like actual memories.

"I'll try to make your dreams better in the future," Felicity said with a snicker, her voice bubbly.

Hot in the face, I glared. "Maybe you should practice your dream manipulation on someone else."

Adelgis petted Felicity's bioluminescent shell. "Once I master this, I can give you any dream you desire. A fantastical adventure, an old memory, some tale you weave for your own amusement. It'll be helpful when I encounter mystical creatures. I can look into their dreams and see what they truly want. It'll help the bonding process. We can match up people with similar personalities and goals as their potential eldrin."

"And?"

"And... I'd appreciate it if you let me practice on you?" His voice took a hard upturn on the last word, making the statement into a sheepish question.

Really? It had to be me?

I groaned. "Very well."

"R-really?"

His shock baffled me. I offered a shrug, and he smiled wide.

"Oh, thank you so much, Volke!"

Felicity wiggled her tentacles. "Yes, thank you!"

"Don't get worked up," I said. "It's no big deal."

Adelgis forced a single laugh. "It is, though! You obviously don't understand what it's like to be lost in a large group. I'm the middle child of seven. I got overlooked quite easily." His expression settled into something neutral. "My father would go home and forget me in the lab on a few occasions—that's how easily forgotten I was."

"Really?"

"Well, it was kinda my fault. I, uh, didn't talk much. He taught me all sorts of things, but it was me, my siblings, his apprentices, some researchers... and I was short. Easy to miss."

I had never felt neglected—just shunned. The Isle of Ruma didn't care for me, but Gravekeeper William made sure to give me a good life at home. I pitied Adelgis at a certain level.

"And now I'm the *sixth apprentice*," Adelgis said as he threw up an arm in exasperation. "Who has *six* apprentices, anyway? An outrageous number. Of course Master Zelfree would have to favor some, and phoenixes have such flashy abilities. Controlling light and dreams pales in comparison. So, I understand why people overlook me, even in the Frith Guild."

"I, uh, never thought of it like that."

"Well, that's why I need to thank you," Adelgis said. "For giving me the time. It means a lot."

Perhaps I should speak with Adelgis more often.

A horn sounded from the crow's nest, interrupting our conversation. The sounds from the deck betrayed the sailors' commotion.

Land.

We had likely reached the capital city, Fortuna. Pirates didn't dare approach those docks. There were hundreds of arcanists in and around the city. Several guilds made their homes there, after all.

I walked over to the porthole. Water splashed across the glass, but between waves I could make out an island in the distance. Well, not an island. An *atlas turtle*—Gentel—a massive mystical creature bonded to our guildmaster. Our guild had built its headquarters on her soil-covered shell. I couldn't see it from the ship, but I knew it was there.

"I'm glad we're back to the guild," Adelgis said. "I feared we would run into the Dread Pirate Calisto."

I turned my attention to him, my brow furrowed. "Did Illia tell you?"

"Tell me what? About the pirate? No. Master Zelfree did. He said that's the man who captains the *Third Abyss*."

"He's a dread pirate? Is that different than just a normal pirate?"

"It's the title the navy gives pirates who have sunk more than five vessels. Dread Pirate Calisto earned that designation years ago. I've heard he's sunk more than twenty."

Felicity floated out of Adelgis's arms and headed toward the ceiling. "I loathe the idea of listening to that man's thoughts and dreams."

"Do you know anything else about him?" I asked.

Even hearing his name upset me. Why hadn't other arcanists stopped this pirate already? He sounded like a dastard, yet he still sailed the seas without fear? Arcanists of the Frith Guild shouldn't have been shaking in their boots. We should've been hunting him down.

"Calisto is actually known for sparing ships that comply with his demands," Adelgis said. He added, rather matter-of-factly, "And Master Zelfree says he's one of the most successful pirates around because of the loyalty of his crew."

"Pirates don't understand loyalty."

"Perhaps. Maybe they just fear him and his manticore eldrin. I know I wouldn't want to get eaten."

I retook my seat on the cot, my head dizzy. I rubbed at my arm, half-surprised to see someone had changed my gauze at some point. We were close to a healer, but I still felt tired.

"I'm going to sleep until we're docked," I said. I shot him a sideways glance. "How about you wait to practice on me until after I'm healed?"

Adelgis replied with a nervous laugh. "Yes, well, that would probably be for the best."

A FAVOR

Someone shook me. Again. And again. I opened my eyes, disgruntled and groggy.

"What?" I croaked.

"Volke. Please. I need you."

Illia's voice poured over me like a bucket of ice water. I sprang to attention, ready to fight. Had pirates attacked us? Was it the plague? Had Ruma come back to exact revenge? My mind played the wildest tricks on me. I must've thought of a million problems, all in half a second.

"What's wrong?" I asked.

She knelt next to me, her hands unsteady. "Shh." She stared at me with her one eye—not with fright, but determination.

I stared back, confused. "Illia?"

"I need you to do me a favor."

Once I knew it wasn't an emergency, I glanced around. "Where are Adelgis and Felicity?"

"I told them to leave." She scooted closer to me. "I didn't want anyone but you to hear this."

Why did she sound so desperate? And why wouldn't she just elaborate? She must have known her secrecy killed me inside.

"Master Zelfree said we're taking you to the grand apothecary," Illia said. She gripped my blankets. "To the master arcanist, Lady Dravon. Don't you remember reading about her?"

"Yes."

She was a prominent arcanist who conducted research all around the world on antivenins and cures. Centuries ago, she had been the first to counteract hydra venom, and her name went into all the history books. Then she settled down and allowed her research to spread throughout the healing guilds. If we were heading to her—if Master Arcanist Dravon really lived in Fortuna—I would be in the best of hands.

"Master Zelfree is about to come get you," Illia said. "When we get to the grand apothecary, I need you to cause a scene. I want to sneak into her laboratory and search for something."

Silence settled between us as I mulled over her request. Illia had never asked for something like this before. And the way she looked at me—with her lips tight and her eyebrows knitted—I knew she didn't want me to ask why. She wanted me to agree to this outlandish request without a second thought.

Illia's grip tightened on the blankets.

"I—"

Nicholin appeared in the room with a 'pop' sound and a burst of sparkles. His claws skittered across the wooden planks as he ran for Illia. "He's coming! He's coming!"

She stood. Nicholin leapt to her shoulder, his blue eyes

wide. Then she gave me one final glance, pleading with me. I wanted to reply, but she teleported from the room with another 'pop' and a puff of white and silver sparkles.

A second later, a knock sounded at the door.

"Come in," I called out, my heart beating hard, even though I hadn't risen from my cot.

Zelfree stepped into the cabin, a neutral expression on his face. "Good. You're up. Let's go. We've arrived at Fortuna and I'm taking you to get your arm looked at." He motioned to the door.

Fortuna, the capital city stationed on the end of a peninsula, acted as the largest port hub in the area. Even Gentel, a giant atlas turtle island, could fit among the docks, if she so chose. I had only visited once, but it had been long enough to become enamored with the city.

I slid off the side of the cot, still disturbed by the interaction with Illia. I took my time getting my shirt and coat, my hazy thoughts recalling every detail of our quick exchange. She wanted me to cause a scene. What did she want, exactly? It wasn't like I could break into song or dance. Why would she ever ask that of me?

I pulled on my boots.

"How are you feeling?" Zelfree asked.

"Uh, better. I don't feel that sick anymore, actually."

"That's because you slept a long time. Wendigo injuries don't go away without medicine, however. You might feel well now, but in a day or two you'll be collapsing again."

"Oh. So, where are we going?"

"To the grand apothecary, Lady Dravon. Her lab is near the docks, and I sent word ahead before we left the Isle of Landin. She should be prepared for us, and she'll have medication for your injury."

So Illia had been right.

I got up and followed Zelfree. As I walked off the *Long Ride* and onto the gangplank, I noticed Leo and Grant with their griffin eldrin. Zaxis, Atty, and Hexa stood around petting the griffins and feeling their fur. The two kids stopped talking and specifically offered me frantic waves.

I waved back, happy to see they were okay.

Both griffins bent a knee and regarded me with deep bows. I didn't know why, but that gesture embarrassed me more than the over-the-top waves. I replied with a nod and then continued onto the docks with Zelfree.

My shadow fluttered at the edge of my peripherals. Luthair had heard everything, but he hadn't yet offered me any of his insight. Illia said she wanted to sneak in, but what did she want to search for?

I paid little attention to the beautiful city of Fortuna as I stepped onto the main road. Windows shone in the midmorning light, carts hustled past, pulled by elegant horses—and a massive clock tower stood in the center of the city, complete with bells and a representation of the stars in the night sky etched on a steel dais. These marvelous testaments to civilization always impressed me.

Zelfree stuck close, and it was then that I noticed we were alone.

"The others aren't coming?"

"I told them to head to the guild," he said. "You and I won't take long."

Merchants and citizens alike parted ways when they noticed me and Zelfree. My arm, stomach, and head competed for *sorest body part,* but I kept my attention focused enough to return waves and nods. People admired arcanists. I wanted to be a good role model.

On our trek, I faced Zelfree, half-wanting to tell him about Illia's strange behavior. "Uh…"

He shot me a quick look, his eyes narrowed.

I floundered, turned away, and opted for a different conversation. "Do you think you could help bring the *Third Abyss* to justice?"

"I'm not going to take that assignment, even if it comes to the Frith Guild."

"Why not? I've read hundreds of stories where you brought down pirate crews with your stealth and guile. I thought you were an expert at this?"

"First off," Zelfree said, holding up a finger, "I've tried and failed to kill the Dread Pirate Calisto in the past. Second," he held up another finger, "running down pirates is how I lost my apprentices all those years back. I'd rather not have a repeat."

"Couldn't you leave us behind?" In my mind, stopping Calisto was a higher priority than training fledgling arcanists.

"Drop this issue. There are others plotting Calisto's demise. They'll handle it."

The finality of his tone ended all conversation.

After that, it didn't take long to reach Lady Dravon's apothecary lab. It was set apart from other buildings and much closer to the ocean than I had anticipated. Three large chimneys stuck out of the tiled roof, each billowing smoke into the sky. One pillar of steam looked green in coloration, and I could've sworn I smelled gravy.

Stone steps led up to the massive front door. Carved on the wood was none other than the legendary *caladrius*—a snow-white bird of healing. A caladrius could cure any sickness so long as it took the illness into itself. From what I knew, the caladrius had no rival when it came to restorative magic. They were the ultimate healers.

According to the books I had read, Lady Dravon had

bonded with *two* caladrius' in her lifetime. Her first eldrin had died when it took an incurable sickness into itself to save Lady Dravon's life. That was when she had vowed to find cures through other means besides magic. During her long journey around the world, she had found a second caladrius and managed to bond again.

Zelfree pounded on the front door. Then he glanced at me and glowered. "Why are you so sweaty?"

"Surprise, I'm sick," I quipped.

"Hm." He stared for a moment, like he wanted to press me for more details. Then he panned his gaze over the surroundings before returning his attention to the door. "You'll be fine. The wendigo bite won't kill you."

"I didn't think I would die... I was more worried I'd lose an arm."

Zelfree huffed out a chuckle. "Lady Dravon won't let that happen. Just relax. You're fine now that we're here."

While we waited, I glanced around, curious about what Zelfree had been looking for. Then I spotted something white near a tree planted next to the city wall. Although I hadn't gotten a perfect glimpse, I knew what it was.

Nicholin.

Which meant Illia was close by.

Why did she insist on sneaking into the lab? Why not just enter with Zelfree and me?

Zelfree grabbed my shoulder and turned me around to face the door. "Listen. Under no circumstance are you to engage Lady Dravon in extended conversation, got it? One word replies. Keep your mouth shut at all other times." Then he pounded on the door a second time, his face hard-set in an aggressively neutral expression.

Was something wrong? His tense demeanor worried me.

I wasn't versed in high-class etiquette, and I wondered if he thought I would embarrass him.

It was a real possibility. Especially if I had to cause a distraction for Illia.

Right before Zelfree knocked a third time, the hinges groaned and the massive door slid inward.

THE GRAND APOTHECARY

A short woman dressed in a crisp yellow, blue, and white robe stood inside. Her short golden hair had been pulled back in a tight ponytail, and her eyes had laugh lines at the edges. With one bright smile, she erased my worries.

Her arcanist star caught my attention right away—it was large and prominent, the wings and tail of a caladrius etched into the skin over her forehead, all the way to her ears and then down the side of her neck.

"Everett," the woman said. "My, you haven't changed at all. And look who you've brought! So strapping and handsome." She giggled as she gave me the once-over.

Zelfree pinched the bridge of his nose. "Please, don't."

"What? No hello?"

"We don't have time for pleasantries."

"Still no fun at all, I see." She laughed, her positively radiant demeanor enough to rival the sun. "I knew you two were on your way, so I decided to get the door myself. Oh, where are my manners? Hello, Zelfree's apprentice. People in Fortuna call me the grand apothecary, my colleagues call me Lady Dravon, but my friends refer to me as Gillie."

"Hello," I muttered. "I'm Volke. Nice to meet you, uh, Lady Dravon."

More than one word. Hopefully Zelfree would forgive me.

Lady Dravon lifted an eyebrow. "What did I just say? Call me Gillie."

"Er, but—"

"Any apprentice of Everett is a friend of mine—is that clear?" Gillie placed a gentle hand on my elbow and guided me into her lab. "Now come, come. I have medicine to give you. Plus, I have so many questions."

"We won't be here long," Zelfree stated.

"Well, you're not leaving until I've caught up with you, so the faster we get this over with, the faster you can leave!" Gillie laughed the entire way down the entrance hall, even as the front door groaned as it closed.

The inside of the lab surprised me. Tall bookshelves lined every wall, some filled with books and others stuffed with clutter. Golden glowstones hung from the ceiling on silver chains, creating a warm smolder of light that flickered off the glass jars and vials. The scent of gravy I smelled outside became a savory cinnamon, as though both a bakery and a jerky shop were hidden within the lab.

Four apprentices sat around a large table: two reading through books, one studying a bird in a cage, and another serving tea. I knew they were apprentices by the bronze badge they wore on the front of their robes. Each badge had a caladrius stamped into the metal, indicating their affiliation with Gillie's research lab.

None of them had arcanist marks, however.

Gillie led us past the table and through another door.

The next room amazed me. Ornate cages, some as big as I was, held hundreds of birds. Most were messengers—birds who carried letters from city to city, or island to island—but there were tiny hummingbirds flitting around in the mix. I stared at the bright blue and red ones as we walked by.

"Where are you, Alana?" Gillie asked.

A bird so white it put snow to shame glided down from the top of a nearby cage. She had the face of a parrot, and her beak shone with the luster of polished gold. With a couple of graceful flaps of her wings, she landed on Gillie's shoulder.

"Yes, my arcanist?" the bird said.

"I need you for a moment. Our guest is finally here, and his infection won't treat itself."

Alana turned her head around as only a bird could. Her vibrant blue eyes scanned me for a moment.

Gillie stroked Alana's ivory feathers. "This is my eldrin. Alana, meet Volke. Isn't he dashing?"

I stared, taken aback by how small Alana was. While young phoenixes could be the size of a puppy, she appeared more like a kitten, no heavier than a pound.

"I thought you had been bonded to your eldrin for several decades?" I asked.

"That's right," Gillie replied with a laugh. "I'm that popular, am I? Everyone knows me and Alana?"

"Don't eldrin grow bigger while bonded? Shouldn't Alana be... I don't know... large?"

"Oh, she is big! For a caladrius, anyway. Look here."

Gillie hurried over to a large cage with thin golden bars, an open door, and a massive bird bed made of silk and down feathers. A tiny hummingbird-sized chick rested inside, its feathers just as white and glorious as Alana's. To my fascination, it, too, had the beak of a parrot and blue eyes rivaling the azure hue of the ocean.

"Is that a baby caladrius?" I asked, breathless.

Gillie reached into the cage and scooped up the bird. "That's right." The tiny mystical creature fit into one palm, so tiny I was afraid I would kill it if I sneezed in the wrong direction. "Caladrius chicks weigh less than a gram. The largest grown caladrius on record is no bigger than a sheep dog."

"Please, Gillie," Zelfree said. "Treat the boy so we can go."

She gave him a sideways glance. "You never have any fun anymore, Everett. Don't you remember the long nights when we sailed from one island to the other, talking about everything from mystical creatures to buried treasure? You and Ruma were hilarious with—"

"*That was a long time ago*," Zelfree snapped. "Gillie. Focus. I have apprentices to train."

Gillie placed the caladrius chick back in the beautiful cage. She didn't shut the door when she walked away, but the chick didn't seem like it was going anywhere. It yawned and rested back down on its fluffy bed.

Without so much as a word, Gillie led us deeper into her lab.

The third room we entered seemed more like a storage area. Several journeymen were stacking and organizing supplies. They nodded as we passed, but otherwise kept their attention on their work. We walked past several doors, including one with a giant lock and chains. I stared at it for a long moment, disturbed by the heavy metal hinges and thick wood.

"What's in there?" I asked.

"Deadly poisons, lethal venoms, and plants that cause

people to hallucinate," Gillie replied matter-of-factly. "Oh, and plague-ridden mystical creatures."

"What?"

The shock of the answer sent a wave of ice through my body. The plague was *here*? In the other room? Why would anyone do that? What if they escaped? There were so many arcanists in the city of Fortuna who could be infected!

"I've been researching a cure," Gillie said as she opened a door that led to a long hallway. "And while I have medicine that seems to delay the full onset of the affliction, I haven't been able to remove it from a mystical creature yet."

It took me a few breaths before I managed to relax. Could she create a cure? That got me smiling. Thank the heavens. I had no idea where or how the arcane plague started, but I knew it needed to end no matter what. For everyone's sake.

Gillie led us through a hallway, which was just as cluttered as the storage area. Bookshelves lined the walls—not to hold tomes, but to add more space for vials, metal wires, and stacks of parchment.

Once we made it through the untidy hall, Gillie led us into a large study.

Her desk had a million quill pens and books, and the back part of the room was nothing but boxes, crates, and bizarre items. Claws, scales, feathers, fur, talons—even jars with eyeballs and rainbow-colored sand. The room was larger than my entire home back on the Isle of Ruma, but somehow it had less space than a coffin.

A single window, half-blocked by a dresser filled with loose papers, allowed a tiny strip of light to filter into the room.

"Take a seat," Gillie said as she motioned to a couch tucked into the corner.

I pushed a few books to the side in order to take a seat. Zelfree leaned against the wall by the door. He fidgeted with the bangles on his wrist, but his mimic never revealed herself.

"How are you feeling?" Gillie asked.

I shrugged. "Better now."

"Wendigo sickness is devious. It'll come and go, making you think you're healed when you're really not." Gillie rustled through the items in her room, examining materials. "Wendigo are fearsome creatures. They live in the snowy forests far to the north, and their Trial of Worth involves nearly freezing to death."

"Really?" Too bad Adelgis wasn't with us. He had said his father was a researcher. I bet he would've been fascinated by everything Gillie had to say.

"You betcha. They like to eat lost travelers, and their teeth are lined with a debilitating disease—that's what's causing your arm to hurt and bleed. It prevents magical healing and saps your strength."

I rubbed at the gauze over my forearm, the pain pulsing underneath. "Yeah."

"Did the wendigo stand on two feet or four?"

"It was the size of a full-grown wolf and stood like one too. It also had antlers."

Gillie pushed aside a stack of boxes and climbed into a corner of the room, even going so far as to get on a bookshelf. "That means it wasn't a true form wendigo. You're lucky! True form wendigoes have a bite that corrupts the use of magic. Very dangerous."

"Wait," I said as I scooted to the edge of the couch. "How do you know what the true form of a mystical creature looks like? I mean, I thought they were things of myth."

"They're real," Gillie mumbled as she opened small

boxes and checked the contents. "Just extremely rare. An eldrin gains its true form when its arcanist embodies the principles and telos of the mystical creature they're bonded to. Not many arcanists ever achieve such a feat—but it does happen."

I turned my attention to Zelfree. He gave me an odd glance in return, like he was irritated we were talking about anything other than healing my arm.

"Is she right?" I asked.

Zelfree sighed. "Yes." Then he pointed to the window. "You've seen Gentel. She's a true form atlas turtle."

"She is?"

I stood from the couch, despite my headache and dizziness, and stepped around the mess until I could stare out the glass. Gentel floated in the harbor, so massive she appeared to be an island.

"What do atlas turtles normally look like?" I whispered.

"Oh, let me show you!" Gillie said as she whipped around, her bright smile back in place. Even her caladrius perked up and spread her wings a bit.

I replied with an enthusiastic nod. Until I saw Gentel, I thought atlas turtles had gone extinct. Did Gillie know another atlas turtle arcanist? Or maybe she had an atlas turtle hatchling?

"No," Zelfree drawled. "We aren't here for that."

The door to the study opened and an apprentice from the front room entered with a platter of sandwiches and tea. "Lady Dravon? Did you want some refreshments?"

"No," Zelfree said, louder than before.

"But it's teatime, and—"

"*No.* Absolutely not."

Gillie shuffled around the clutter in her room and clapped her hands together once. "It seems our guests don't want snacks. However, I can't seem to find my tools in here, so we'll have to search the storage room. In the meantime, we can show Volke the baby atlas turtle in my care."

After a long exhale, Zelfree glowered. "What part of *no* don't you understand, woman? We're not here for that."

"Everett, why don't you help me search? You were always so adept at finding things when we were younger. And then we can discuss your sourpuss attitude, hm? I can help you regain a little humor."

"That sounds like a literal nightmare."

"Oh, you don't mean that!" Gillie giggled as she led Zelfree and her tea-serving apprentice from the room. "Volke, wait here. We'll be right back."

The door shut with a harsh *snap*.

Which left Luthair and me alone in the messy space. I pushed away from the window and made my way to the couch. With a huff, I threw myself on the cushions. Gillie seemed pleasant. I wished more people like her existed in the world. Life would be infinitely more interesting, that was for sure.

"Well?" Luthair asked from the shadows around my feet.

"Well, what?"

"Are you going to help Illia or not?"

I sat up straight. My head still hurt. "She wanted a distraction. What am I supposed to do? This place is bustling with people."

Luthair rose from the darkness, his armor coalescing until he stood in front of me, his tattered cape secure over his shoulders. "Perhaps you should break something."

Had I misheard him? Break something? That didn't sound like a suggestion Luthair would make.

"Why?" I asked.

"It's obvious Illia wants to walk around the lab without

anyone noticing. If something is broken, the apprentices and journeymen will rush to clean it."

"And you're okay with me vandalizing this place? I thought you adhered to honor and righteousness?"

"Many months ago, Illia helped when you asked her to break into Gregory Ruma's private quarters. Not an honorable act in the slightest. You didn't even explain yourself before asking, despite having a justifiable reason to investigate Ruma. Shouldn't you give Illia the benefit of the doubt?"

"Well—" Luthair's reasoning didn't leave room for disagreement. Illia had helped me in the past. Perhaps this was a moment where she needed me to believe in her. "—I'm not sure I could damage a place like this. Gillie is doing so much good."

"I noted several bookshelves of empty glassware. I suspect knocking one over would provide Illia a moment to walk around."

"Do you know why she wants to get in here?"

"No, my arcanist."

I couldn't think of a reason either.

I rubbed my hands together, the pain becoming a dull sensation that faded to the back of my mind while I dwelled on the problem. I could use my shadow powers to knock things over. No one would know. And the place was so unorganized—perhaps everyone would blame it on the mess.

Confident I wouldn't do *too* much harm, I stood, walked over to the door, and carefully opened it. The cluttered hallway was deserted. I stepped out. Luthair melted into the shadows and followed close behind me.

Sure enough, I found several bookshelves in the hall that functioned like extra storage space. They had beakers, bottles, and vials—all glass and all stacked on top of each other in small piles. The journeymen and apprentices were a single door away, in the storage room, diligently working.

With a deep breath, I concentrated on my magic. The lab was dark—perfect for practicing my shadow manipulation.

I waved my hand. The darkness hardened and moved around the base of the shelf. The glass objects clattered together, but nothing fell.

"Do not hesitate," Luthair whispered. "You needn't fear your own strength."

After a deep breath, I imagined grabbing the bookshelf with the shadows and knocking it over. Although a sting ran from my temple to my wrist, I kept my focus. A second later, the bookshelf toppled forward, as if shoved from behind.

The resulting *BANG* and *CRASH* sent shivers down my spine. I had never expected it to be so loud! The whole city probably heard what had happened.

The dimensions of the bookshelf didn't quite fit in the hallway. It was too tall, and when it fell forward, it hit the opposite wall, throwing its contents all over the floor. The glass shattered on the wood and flew in every direction. The entire hall had become a deathtrap for bare feet. I took a single step back, my boots crunching the debris, my heart beating so hard I could barely hear anything else.

"What was that?" someone shouted from the storage room.

"Is everything okay?" another cried. "Secure the birds!"

"Make sure the caladrius chick is safe!"

The many apprentices and journeymen ran into the hallway to appraise the damage. Sure enough, just as Luthair predicted, they grabbed brooms and dustpans to clean the space.

Then, because the universe hates me, a *second* bookshelf

fell forward. Gillie's mentees stared with wide eyes, the disaster worsening with each passing moment.

And then a third fell.

And a fourth.

The cacophony of destruction echoed in the hallway, drowning out my thoughts and practically battering me with physical force. I took another step back and hit something—at first I thought it was another bookshelf.

I whirled around and flinched. Zelfree stood next to me, his eyes glued to the utter annihilation of glassware. The dust settled after the last bookshelf collapsed onto the wall, creating a weird tunnel of cracked bookshelves and piles of glass shards. Seconds passed in awkward silence. When Zelfree turned his attention to me, I panicked.

"I was practicing my magic," I blurted out. "You said I should. So I did."

He ran a hand through his long black hair, never saying a word as he panned his gaze over the hallway for a second time.

"I, uh, thought I could manipulate the shadows to pick up a vial. I never meant for—well, I didn't think this would happen. Like it did."

Although I considered myself a terrible liar, this wasn't a bad explanation. Accidents happened, right? Hopefully he wouldn't be too angry?

Much to my shock, I spotted Illia and Nicholin in the storage room. Zelfree had his back to them, but Illia froze the instant she saw us. I met her eye, and we stared at each other. With a silent wave of her hand, she motioned to the door with the locks and heavy hinges. I shook my head.

The apprentices and journeymen rushed around the hallway, cleaning everything as fast as they could. No one had any energy to notice Illia's sneaking.

Zelfree glared at me.

My shoulders bunched at the base of my neck. "I'm sorry."

Illia and Nicholin walked a few steps, her boot crunching a small patch of glass.

Before Zelfree could turn around, I held up my injured arm. "I couldn't concentrate," I said, louder than normal. "The pain in my arm is what caused my magic to, uh, go everywhere. I really am sorry."

"It's fine," he growled. "I just don't want to sit here and help Gillie clean it up."

Illia and Nicholin teleported as Zelfree spoke, their 'pop' obfuscated by Zelfree's gruff speech. I exhaled once they had gone, but I couldn't help wondering if Illia would be okay. Why was she going into the restricted room with all the plague-ridden mystical creatures? Surely they were in cages, or at least tied down. She would be fine.

I hoped.

"By the stars."

Gillie stood on the far end of the hallway, an odd turtle in her arms. Her eyes went wide as she took in the mayhem, but the longer she stared, the more a smile crept across her face.

The turtle, however, gave the mess one look and then retracted his head into his shell as far as he could. Sea turtles couldn't put their heads fully inside their shells, however, so his face stuck out awkwardly, his neck scrunched up, giving him the appearance of having three chins. It *almost* distracted from the fact he had a bonsai tree growing out of his shell.

"You did always have a knack for causing trouble, Everett," she said.

"This wasn't me," Zelfree barked.

"But it *was* your apprentice?"

He didn't answer. Instead, he shot me a glare.

I replied with a shrug.

Gillie smiled. "I thought so. Come, come. Let's forget this mess. Everything will be fine." She waved us back to her study. "Once a season, I hire a few men from the local blacksmith to help me rearrange and tidy up. They are *adorable*. I try to find any excuse to have them move things for me." She fanned herself.

"The Frith Guild will pay for these damages." Zelfree took me by the shoulder. "I should've watched my apprentice a little closer." He squeezed my bicep hard.

I bowed my head. "I'm very sorry."

"Don't worry," Gillie said with a laugh. "I don't keep my valuable research out in the hallway! This will get sorted. You just get back on that couch. I have everything I need to straighten you out."

IMBUING

"This is a hatchling atlas turtle," Gillie said.

She held up the mystical creature. The little turtle had fin-like legs and a flat shell. Growing straight off his back, as though the roots were veins, was a bonsai tree. The plant and the turtle were each the size of a full grown cat, and Gillie had to hold him with the entirety of her arms.

Even as I admired the dark green coloration of the atlas turtle's body and the lush foliage of his tree, a small piece of me couldn't stop thinking about Illia. Was she okay? What if she got caught? What would I even say?

It was best not to think about it. If I dwelled, I was certain Zelfree would catch on, and then he would know everything.

"Hello," the turtle said, a hint of anxious fear in his youthful voice.

I had been staring at him for a long time.

I forced a chuckle. "You're so tiny. I guess it'll be amazing once you're grown, right?" I rubbed at the back of my neck, trying to come off as non-threatening as possible.

"I hope I get big one day."

"This little guy was sick," Gillie said as she handed the hatchling turtle to one of her apprentices. "I've treated him, and he'll be going back to his island within a fortnight."

The apprentice gave us a bow and left the room. Just Gillie, myself, and Zelfree remained.

I glanced out the window, transfixed by the giant island. The hatchling didn't even compare. Did gaining a true form substantially change a creature?

Gillie nudged my elbow and had me sit back down on the couch. Her caladrius watched as she unwrapped the bandages around my forearm. Pus and blood wept from the bite wound. Although Gillie didn't flinch or grimace, her eldrin ruffled her feathers.

"He bit you good," Alana said.

I nodded. "But if magic can't heal it, what're you going to do?"

"Medicine," Gillie said, smiling. She reached into the pocket of her robes and withdrew a pouch of powder. She opened it, sprinkled the substance across my forearm, and rubbed it into the injury. "Does that hurt?"

"A little."

"You shouldn't feel anything in just a moment."

Sure enough, the longer she rubbed, the duller the pain got. To my alarm, however, all feeling left my forearm, like it had fallen asleep. I figured it was part of Gillie's plan, but I still worried something had gone terribly wrong.

"What if the wendigo was carrying the arcane plague?" I asked.

"It wasn't."

"How can you be so sure?"

"Man-eaters—mystical creatures who require human flesh from time to time in order to live—are immune to blood-based illnesses, both magical and mundane."

The knowledge rocked me. "That doesn't seem fair."

Gillie laughed. "Phoenixes aren't affected by heat. Yetis feel no cold. Mystical creatures who consume humans won't pick up diseases. That's why I know so much about the wendigo, actually. I thought maybe wendigo magic could help fight the plague."

"O-oh. I see... But even if they're immune, couldn't they still pass it to others?"

"The arcane plague only latches to magic. That's why non-magical creatures can't be affected, and why none of the man-eater mystical creatures carry it."

"Sorry for the questions," I said.

"I've haven't been able to study a live wendigo yet, but once I do, I think I might have a breakthrough."

While plenty of mystical creatures ate meat, not many fell into the "man-eater" category. Those mystical creatures were often the preferred eldrin of pirates, which made the whole situation worse. People like wendigo arcanists didn't have to worry about becoming infected by the plague. They could just spread it without fear of any repercussions.

Gillie patted my knee. "Treating your arm will take a few moments. Why don't we enjoy some tea while we wait?"

Zelfree stepped closer, like he was about to protest.

"You two did wreck my lab," Gillie interjected. "I mean, would it kill you to humor me for an hour or two with a bit of company? I'm not even asking you clean the mess." She placed her hands on her hips. "I think this is an even trade."

Zelfree held back his protests. After a prolonged moment, he just exhaled and his shoulders slumped. "Fine."

"Oh, wonderful! I'll ask my apprentices to prepare us something special. Take a seat!"

Although I could feel irritation washing off him in waves, Zelfree sat next to me on the couch. He stared straight ahead, his expression set in a scowl. "Do you have any hard liquor?"

"I keep some in stock just in case you come over."

Gillie shuffled from the study, giggling to herself the entire way.

I didn't know how long we had been there, but hours had passed. At one point, I glanced toward the window and saw the sun setting behind the massive atlas turtle island.

That was okay, though. Gillie fetched us cakes, tea, water, tiny vegetable slices, mead, pastries, and various types of wine. She had her apprentices bring in a small coffee table—there wasn't really room, but she made them do it anyway. So, cramped together, we consumed the refreshments while my medicine set.

"And one time," Gillie said, teacup in hand, "Everett tried to collect honey from tyrant bees. Do you know how aggressive they can be? Honey badgers don't even mess with tyrant bees!"

I couldn't help but smile. "Did you actually collect their honey?"

Zelfree swirled his glass of wine. "Of course."

"It was a sight to behold," Gillie added. "That was the summer he learned mimics and mimic arcanists, could obfuscate their magical aura."

I hadn't ever seen Zelfree smile and relax like he did on Gillie's couch. He leaned back, the bags under his eyes noticeable, his whole body loose. If we were all quiet for a few minutes, I suspected he would've gone straight to sleep.

Gillie stared at him, an eyebrow lifted. "You look tired, Everett."

"Yeah, well, I've been busy."

"I wish you would've taken my advice and gotten married." She wagged a finger. "You need someone to fret about your wellbeing. Someone to tell you to get some rest and maybe make you a hot lunch. When was the last time you even considered finding somebody to be with?"

Zelfree tensed—his calm demeanor gone in an instant. "You know my motto. Keep your love-life, finances, and next move private."

"You can tell me."

He stared at his glass, as if contemplating how to even answer her question.

"Uh, Gillie?" I interjected. "Is my arm mended yet?"

She clapped her hands together once. "Oh, yes. Give it here."

I leaned forward and held out my arm. Gillie wiped away the medicine with a clean rag, and while I still had bite marks, the wound had stopped bleeding. Then she wrapped my injury in gauze.

While she worked, I glanced back at Zelfree. He met my gaze with something I interpreted as appreciation—a tilt of his head and a slight nod. He really *hadn't* told anyone about his relationship with a past apprentice.

I understood. It wasn't appropriate for a mentor and an apprentice to be together. And, at some level, I was certain he still blamed himself for everything that had happened. I could see it in the way he turned away, like he was afraid to form even this slight connection with me.

"I'm going to make you something," Gillie said, pulling me from my thoughts.

I turned to her. "Like what?"

"A magic item—a trinket. To help you in the future."

She withdrew a long phoenix feather and a shiny crystal

from her robe pocket. I sat forward, excited to the see the scarlet and gold. Although I hadn't bonded with a phoenix, they still had a special place in my heart. I loved their noble aesthetic.

"How do you make a trinket?" I asked.

Gillie widened her eyes. "You haven't been taught?" Then she playfully glowered at Zelfree.

He sat up and scooted to the edge of the couch. "Don't give me that look. He's still an apprentice, he's second-bonded, *and* he hasn't even been with the Frith Guild for more than a year. We've studied evocation, manipulation, and augmentation. Those are the basics. He doesn't need to learn anything advanced right now."

"Tsk, tsk."

Zelfree gritted his teeth, his glass of wine clenched in one hand.

Gillie laughed and waved away his attitude. "Oh, you. Relax. I'll just give him the rundown." Then she returned her attention to me. "You make trinkets through *imbuing*. Evoking creates magic temporarily, like fire or your terror. But *imbuing* is like fusing your magic to an object so that it's permanently magical."

I nodded. "Amazing."

"First, you need an object you're going to turn into a trinket." She held up the phoenix feather. "Then you need a magical adhesive." She held up the shiny crystal she withdrew from her pocket. "This is a star fragment." The crystal itself was no bigger than my thumb nail, and it glowed with a gentle inner light.

"A star fragment," I muttered.

"They're rare, but very powerful. It'll be our glue. Once you have those two things, you use the star fragment to stitch your magic into the object of your choosing."

I had heard of star fragments only in stories. Swash-bucklers would search the world over for such magical resources, much like explorers searched for gold.

Gillie twirled the feather in her grasp. Then it and the star fragment, glowed a gentle white, along with the arcanist mark on her forehead. With rapt attention, I stared, amazed by the powerful energy that flowed through the room like a subtle breeze. Papers rustled, and glass jars clinked together, but she didn't create a mess.

After a controlled breath, Gillie took the glowing feather and twisted it around the star fragment, forming a circle. She tied the ends with a bit of string from her pocket, all while the magic continued to shift through the room. Her caladrius remained on her shoulder, examining her work.

Finally, after a few minutes, the power waned. Gillie took a deep breath, and the feather stopped glowing. She smiled wide as she showed off her phoenix feather bracelet —a trinket.

The star fragment had disappeared during the process, and I wondered if it had been "burned up" to create the magic item.

"There," she said. "I could have used a piece of wood as the base item, instead of the phoenix feather, but wood doesn't conduct magic as well. You want to use objects with an affinity for your type of sorcery. Phoenixes can heal, so imbuing this feather with caladrius magic—peak healing magic—enhances the restorative effects."

Then Gillie handed me the trinket. I held it in both hands.

"Why didn't you use a caladrius feather?" I asked.

"A caladrius feather already has caladrius magic. You need something else—something that resonates with your sorcery."

Gillie petted her eldrin. "I hear knightmare arcanists make the world's best weapons and armor. The shadow they imbue is both hard and lightweight. Truly, a material unlike any other."

"Really?"

Gillie motioned for me to put the bracelet on. "That will safeguard you from infection in the future. As long as you wear it, this shouldn't happen again, even if a wendigo were to attack. You'll be immune to diseases."

I slipped the phoenix feather over my wrist and examined the shine under the light of the glowstones. "Thank you so much."

"You seem like a well-mannered apprentice." She leaned forward and whispered, "When you're not busting up other people's labs, that is."

My face filled with heat. I fidgeted with the bracelet. "I really am sorry about that."

She laughed. "Don't worry about it. I just like seeing that sheepish look on your face. It reminds me of Ruma, when he used to get caught in his antics." Gillie motioned for Zelfree to chime in. "You remember, right? You used to follow him around like a lost puppy. Remember when he tried to hide things in an underwater cave?"

Zelfree didn't answer.

"Not even our master could find that cave," Gillie continued with a longing sigh. "It made for some amusing conversations." She met Zelfree's eyes and stared. For a long moment, neither said anything, but I could feel the mirth draining from the room. Gillie frowned, her appearance much older than it had appeared a minute ago. "I've wanted to apologize to you, Everett... If I had a found a cure for the plague before Ruma had done all those unspeakable things, then—"

"Enough," Zelfree snapped. He set his glass down and stood. "We need to get going."

Gillie got to her feet. "Wait, please. The guildmaster... she's worried about you. And I am too. She said you weren't grieving, and—"

Zelfree snapped his fingers, and I jumped off the couch. Then he grabbed my shoulder and shoved me toward the door, his gaze so focused I didn't dare speak.

I stumbled into the hallway. Zelfree followed close behind, but he stopped and whirled around when Gillie gently touched his arm.

"I told you," he said in a low tone. "Stop meddling."

"I just want to help."

The hallway had been cleaned. Mostly. The bookshelves had been propped back up and shoved against the walls, but piles of broken glass sat along the edges of the hall. A path had been cleared.

To my horror, Illia opened the far door and crept into the hallway. She and Nicholin closed the door, silent but not invisible. She noticed me and flinched—an odd box held tight in both her hands. To Illia's credit, she made no noise, not even a gasp. Nicholin perked his ears, his blue eyes wide with shock.

What had they been doing this entire time? I couldn't believe they were still in the research lab! It must've been hours since I sat down and talked with Zelfree and Gillie. They had plenty of time to escape, yet they were trying to escape *now*?

"Luthair," I whispered.

His shadow dashed across the floor as he spoke in a quiet tone. "I'll handle it."

For some bizarre reason, Illia and Nicholin didn't teleport. They watched Luthair and followed him back out the door they had just come through—like they had no idea where they were going in the first place.

I turned back to Zelfree and Gillie, determined to distract them, but I stopped before I uttered a word.

They were talking to each other in harsh, but hushed, voices. Gillie shook her head and muttered something, her hand gently resting on Zelfree's forearm. He murmured something back, his whole body so stiff he could've been a statue.

When they noticed me staring, they ended the conversation.

"I'm done with this," Zelfree said.

He turned and walked down the hall, his boots crunching on bits of wood from the cracked bookshelves. I chased after.

We hustled through the storage area and I didn't see any journeymen. Zelfree continued through the room with the birds, and out to the entrance room. I never spotted anyone, and I hoped that meant Illia managed to escape without being seen.

Zelfree slammed his shoulder into the front door, opening it wide as he continued his long stride out onto the streets of Fortuna. The lamps were lit, and the docks were still busy with fisherman, giving the city a nightlife I had grown to love during my past visits. The Isle of Ruma went to bed with the sun and woke with the roosters. Anyone out late at night was considered a hooligan or miscreant. I enjoyed the change of pace.

I jogged to Zelfree's side. When I glanced back, I saw Gillie standing in the doorway of her research lab, her haunting gaze locked on us.

Traces leapt onto my shoulder, startling me enough that I almost tripped over the curb of the road. When had she transformed back into her cat self? Zelfree wasn't wearing his bangles anymore.

"Say something to him," she said into my ear. "He likes you."

"Doesn't he like you more?" I murmured under my breath.

"He never listens to me."

We rounded the corner, passed a dirty fish stall, and headed straight for the docks where our skiffs were tied. Zelfree didn't even look at me. He kept his hands in his trouser pockets and focused his glower directed straight ahead.

Although my throat felt tight and I had no idea what would make this better, I took a deep breath. "Uh, so, the Isle of Ruma has this staircase we all call the Pillar."

He said nothing.

"All the steps hold the values of an arcanist. One step deals with grief and acceptance and—"

Zelfree came to an abrupt halt. I jerked to a stop next to him, and Traces leapt off my shoulder, abandoning me. Zelfree didn't face me when he spoke.

"Have you ever buried a friend?"

"Well, I apprenticed as a gravedigger for a while—I buried people then." I forced a chuckle, hoping my pseudo-joke would amuse him.

It didn't.

After an awkward period of silence, I continued, "I've never buried anyone close to me."

"Have you ever buried someone you were supposed to protect?"

My mouth went dry as the reality of the situation set in. "No."

"Then—" he shot me a glare, "—keep your advice to

yourself. I've done this song and dance more than once. At some level, I'm becoming an expert."

The Frith Guild headquarters rested on the back of the atlas turtle island. It was a manor house built of brick and pale white ivory, standing three stories tall, with hundreds of rooms, a library, and a map room.

All the apprentices and journeymen lived on the third floor. The guildmaster and the master arcanists lived on the ground level, with the studies and recreation rooms in the middle. Each cozy room—still larger than what I'd had back on my island—came supplied with a bed and dresser.

The lamp in the corner of my room kept everything half-lit, but I didn't care. My dark vision made the light source unnecessary. I paced back and forth, my anxiety never waning.

Illia, Nicholin, and Luthair had yet to return.

I knew we had left them. If Illia couldn't teleport, she would need to take a skiff to reach the guild. And Luthair would surely return to me once she was safe at the manor house, which meant they were still out there somewhere.

"What was she thinking?" I said to myself as I quickened my step.

Part of me wanted to go searching, but I knew that was a terrible idea. Midnight approached. Where would I even start looking?

The sound of nails tapping on glass broke my chain of thought. I turned my attention to the window and sighed in relief. Illia and Nicholin waited on the other side, both grinning like master thieves who had succeeded in an epic heist. I ran over, opened the window, and motioned them in.

A shadow slid into my room with them, moving like a snake, but fluttering at the edges, like the wings of crows.

"What happened?" I asked as I closed the window.

Illia threw her arms around me, unable to control her giggling. I embraced her, just happy she was back, but still confused. Nicholin leapt from her shoulder and landed on my bed. In an instant, he curled up and snuggled himself into my blankets.

"It's been a long day..." He fluffed a bit of my bed and rested his head down. "You don't mind sleeping on the floor, right? I hate sharing."

Illia released me, her one eye shining in the dim lamplight. "Thank you so much, Volke. I never could've done this without you."

"Done what?"

She reached into her jacket pocket and pulled out a small box—the same box I saw her holding in Gillie's lab. It had the caladrius imprinted on the side, its wings wide and its tail feathers flared. The entire box appeared to be made from black wood and metal, both foreign to me.

"What is this?" I asked.

Illia stepped closer, until we were mere inches apart. "I couldn't teleport because the sorcery on the box prevents it from being taken magically. Even Luthair couldn't move it with his shadows."

I glanced to the darkness.

Luthair shifted about. "It's true."

"That doesn't answer my question," I said as I turned back to Illia. "What is it?"

"It took forever to get out of that room because the door was locked from both sides." Illia smiled wide. "I managed to pick the lock from within. Luthair helped, of course. It took longer than I liked, but it was all worth it."

"Illia. Tell me."

She held the box close to her chest, her fingers curled around the edges. "It's poison."

I waited.

Gripping it tighter, she lowered her gaze. "King basilisk venom. The deadliest poison in the world. One drop will kill an arcanist, no matter where it touches them."

A PLAN AT NIGHT

I took an immediate step away from the box.

King basilisks embodied the word *deadly*. Their gaze could turn people to stone, their claws had a toxin that paralyzed, their blood burned like powerful acid, and their venom specifically killed magic. Regular basilisks were also dangerous, but they paled in comparison.

Those who bonded with king basilisks became the most sought after arcanist assassins. The threat of their lethal magic and eldrin became so great that decades ago, the queen had ordered all king basilisks killed, and any new hatchlings born were considered an affront to the crown.

The Royal Navy carried out systematic purges of the islands the king basilisks were said to originate from. Since then, I'd say there were fewer than twenty still alive.

I motioned to the box. "You stole that?"

Illia never looked up at me. "Why are you even bothering to ask? You know the answer."

"Why?"

"Because with this... I can kill a master arcanist."

The most famous story involving king basilisks was

the tale of *Gali the Red*. He splashed a single drop of king basilisk venom on the tip of a spear and stabbed the master arcanist who ran his guild. But the venom soaked into the wood of the spear's shaft during the fight. Gali the Red then died from just *holding his own spear*—skin contact with the affected wood was all it took.

I stared at Illia, my chest so tight it hurt to breathe. "You want to kill the Dread Pirate Calisto."

She smiled. "I've already thought of everything. And now that I have this, I can be the one who kills him."

"Illia, I—"

She held a finger to her mouth, and I caught myself on the last word. Then she closed the distance between us, standing so close I could hear her breathe.

"I have to do this." She slipped the box back into her coat pocket. "And I want you to come with me."

"Where?" I whispered.

"Port Crown."

"But that's a pirate port. The worst in this region. Only cutthroats and sea thieves venture there."

Illia gave me a *that's the point* look before smoothing the collar of my jacket. "Calisto stops there when he sails through the islands. I'm sure he'll be there now, or sometime soon. All I need is to get close to him. One drop of king basilisk venom—by surprise—will be enough."

"How would you even find him? He won't walk around alone. He'll have his crew. He'll have his eldrin."

"I already thought of that." Illia's smile widened. "I'll lure him into a private location with *this*." She reached into her other pocket and withdrew the cartographer's journal. "He wants it, right? I'll send Calisto a note telling him I've come to make a trade. Clever, isn't it?"

I ran both hands through my disheveled hair. "Illia. This is a terrible idea."

Her smile disappeared instantly, her one eye wide, like she was genuinely caught off guard. "What? It's perfect."

"You want to meet the Dread Pirate Calisto, in Port Crown, so that you can kill him with king basilisk venom?" I half-laughed, somewhat sarcastically. "There are so many things that can go wrong. What if he sends someone else to collect the journal?"

She shrugged. "I'll teleport away."

"What if he does show up, but then he attacks you?"

"Again, I'll just teleport."

"What if you miss with your poison and—"

"I already told you," Illia snapped. She took a step back, her face a slight shade of red, her shoulders trembling. "Manticore arcanists can't teleport, Volke. I can get away. He'll never catch me."

"What if he does manage to catch you, though?"

"I evaded a full-grown leviathan *while in the ocean*." Illia turned on her heel and shoved the journal back into her coat pocket. "I told you I thought of everything. Plus, if anything unusual happens, I know you'll think of something to get us out of it. That's what you're good at. Rolling with the punches."

"Don't you remember what it's like to face a master arcanist?" I shook my head and paced the room again, my pulse high. "We couldn't even harm Gregory Ruma! He was fast and talented and had way more magic than we do. If Zelfree hadn't protected us, we would've been torn apart."

"We were on a deserted island with nowhere to go," Illia said as she turned around, an edge of pleading in her voice. "Port Crown is *massive*. There are tons of people and buildings. We'll be able to escape Calisto—that's not the part of the plan I'm even worried about. I'm more concerned with him showing up. If he *does* meet me, he's as good as dead."

"I don't know..."

She walked over, threw her arms around me, and twisted her fingers into my coat. She squeezed, holding me tighter than she even had before. "He killed my parents."

The statement stilled my thoughts and breathing.

Illia continued, her voice soft, "Please, Volke. I can do this. It should be me." She pressed her face into my shirt, her trembling never ceasing. "That's how all the great legends go, right? If I'm going to be the hero of my own story... shouldn't I be the one to kill him?"

"We're just apprentices," I said, unable to return her embrace. "There's so much about magic we don't even know."

My short time with Gillie taught me that. Imbuing, true forms, wendigo, diseases—the world was huge and wondrous. Just because Illia could flee from danger didn't mean she would always be safe. What if Calisto had some way to track her? Or what if he had his own equivalent of king basilisk venom?

And Port Crown was his home turf. We would be outsiders, unfamiliar with the buildings and terrain. What if someone *else* came for us? Like when Fain targeted me out of nowhere? What if someone wanted Illia's rizzel?

I gritted my teeth. "Illia, I think... you should return the cartographer's journal to Zelfree. We can ask the Frith Guild to handle this. They have master arcanists who have dealt with pirates in the past."

Illia shoved herself away from me, hard enough that I stumbled backward. With her jaw clenched, she crossed her arms and bunched her shoulders at the base of her neck.

"Volke," she said, her voice shaky. "You're supposed to be

the one person who helps me no matter what. I've always been there for you—why can't you be here for me?"

"This *is* me being here for you." I shook my head, my mind buzzing. "We need to think of a different plan. Something less reckless."

When I stepped closer, she flinched away, keeping herself guarded. That stung more than any words. After a few moments, I walked to the wall opposite of her and pressed my back against it, distancing myself as far as I could.

Minutes passed in strained silence. Her exhales came out with a rasp, like she would speak at any second, but never did. I waited, uncertainty gnawing at my thoughts. I didn't want to upset her, but how could she ask this of me? I wanted to be the voice of reason and help her come up with a strategy that didn't involve us venturing into a pirate port. Anything but that!

Illia stalked over to my bed and scooped up Nicholin. He yawned in her arms and curled himself up on her shoulders. Then she headed for the window.

"Wait," I said.

"Are you going to help me?"

The question lingered between us.

"No," I finally said. "This is too rash. We should think about this more."

Without another word, Illia climbed over the sill and clung to the ivy lattices on the wall of the manor house. I watched her go, unable to find the words to protest.

After she had disappeared, I hung my head and cursed the abyssal hells.

I couldn't sleep. I didn't even try. I paced until my legs hurt and my feet became sore, my thoughts a tangled mess of hypothetical conversations.

Hours passed.

What if I promised to help Illia in some other way? What if I begged a master arcanist of our guild to take this mission on personally? I touched the phoenix feather bracelet around my wrist. What if I paid a master arcanist to use the king basilisk poison instead of Illia? Would this trinket even be enough?

"I have to come up with a plan."

Luthair shifted beneath my feet, his shadowy body a thicker black than the darkness that clung to the corners of the room. "Perhaps you should speak to someone about this. You've lost yourself to doubt."

"Like who? Master Zelfree? That way Illia can think I was ratting her out?" I forced a sarcastic smile. "I'm all ears, Luthair. Who can help me with this?"

"Hexa."

His suggestion stopped me in my tracks. Hexa and Illia did get along well. As a matter of fact, Hexa was the only other person besides me that Illia spent any time with. They were even together while everyone else went to the Sapphire Springs.

"You're right," I said. "Maybe Hexa can help me talk some sense into her."

I exited my room, more pep in my step than minutes earlier. Only a handful of lanterns were lit for the evening hours, but I navigated my way with no need for any more light. The men and women of the guild were separated—men on the west side, women on the east. I wandered the hall, went past the grand staircase, and continued to the east, careful not to make much noise.

No one patrolled the halls at night. We were on a moving island, after all. Very few people could even get to the manor house, and what protections we did have were stationed outside. And we were all adults, not schoolchildren that needed scolding for being up in the middle of the night.

When I reached Hexa's room, I hesitated. If I pounded on the door, I would surely wake others.

"Luthair," I said. "Go in and wake her."

His shadow form easily slid under the door. I waited a few moments, hoping no one would stumble upon me while I stood like a creeper in a darkened corridor.

After a soft click of the lock, the door creaked inward. Hexa hadn't opened it, though. Luthair stood on the other side, his black full plate armor glistening in the low light. He motioned me in.

Hexa's room was identical to my own—except she had a bed for Raisen. Well, it was more a nest than a bed. It was positioned in the corner of the room, made of feathers, twigs, and ripped up blankets.

But Raisen wasn't in it.

And Hexa wasn't in her bed, either.

My throat tightened, and my gut twisted into knots. I turned my attention to the open window. Cold air crept in on the gentle ocean breeze. I walked over and leaned over the sill. The ivy lattice had been bent in a few parts, no doubt from the weight of a person climbing it.

Illia had taken Hexa with her.

Panic flooded my being. I ran from the room, my heart slamming against my ribcage. I don't know why, but I headed straight for Zaxis's room first, determined to get his help. Perhaps his phoenix could fly around the island and spot Illia before she got too far.

I reached his door in record time. Luthair slipped under

the moment we arrived, and I waited with bated breath until it opened.

But Zaxis wasn't the one at the door. It was Luthair.

I dashed around him.

To my horror, Zaxis wasn't in his room either. His blankets were disturbed, as though he had been sleeping, and there was a perch in the corner of his room for Forsythe, but everything sat cold and empty.

No.

No, no, no.

Illia had taken Zaxis with her as well.

I left the room and went to Adelgis's. When I reached the door, I stopped and motioned for Luthair.

"Open it," I commanded.

Had she taken everyone? Dread consumed me. A handful of apprentice arcanists couldn't face down the Dread Pirate Calisto.

Luthair opened the door. I walked in, half-expecting to see the window open and an empty bed. What I found was Adelgis. He stood next to his bed, wearing nothing but trousers, a thin white shirt in his hands. His lantern had been snuffed, and when he glanced over, his eyes never focused.

I saw him clearly, though. And I saw an odd mark across his ribs—like a giant yellow and purple bruise. A lump of *something* protruded from under his skin, no longer than a finger, or thicker than a slug.

"Adelgis?" I asked.

He grimaced and jumped away, sweat dappling his body.

"V-Volke?" He hastily wrapped the shirt around his chest, covering the bruises and lump. "Felicity, I need light!"

His ethereal whelk appeared out of nowhere, forming much like Luthair did. Her shell coalesced like tiny fragments of light coming together to form a tiny glowing ball. Her crystal and soft tentacles formed afterward. She floated a few feet above the floor, and in seconds, she grew brighter and brighter, until she illuminated the entire room better than any lantern.

I shielded my eyes and took a few steps back. "I'm sorry."

"*What're you doing in here*? How did you even get in?"

"I, uh..."

The surprise of the situation stole my words.

"Get out," he said. "I'll talk to you in the hall."

I left, unable to offer any protest. Once the door shut behind me, I didn't move. Where else would I go? I needed to speak with him. Maybe Illia was still here. Perhaps she hadn't gotten around to speaking with him.

Adelgis opened the door faster than I expected. He was fully dressed—boots, belt, his coat, and a shoulder cape. The cape covered the side with the bruises, and he smoothed it as he walked into the hallway. He had even pulled his hair back into a loose ponytail.

He stared at the floor as he spoke. "Volke."

"Uh, well, again, I'm really sorry."

"Is there a reason you barged into my room unannounced?"

"Yes." I shoved my hands in my pockets, both anxious and embarrassed. The emotions refused to mix evenly in my body. "Have you seen Illia?"

He lifted his gaze, his eyebrows knit. "She came by to ask me a couple of things."

"About Port Crown?"

"Yes."

Damn. She probably had gone to the others already. I just thought... she wouldn't leave unless I went with her. I guess nothing held her back, not even logic or caution. Or my absence.

"Are you okay?" Adelgis asked.

"Illia wants to go to Port Crown," I muttered.

"I did see a group of people untying a skiff from the docks."

I stared at Adelgis for a moment, disbelief still clawing at edges of my mind. Then I placed a hand on his shoulder. "How long ago?"

"A couple of hours."

"And you said *nothing*?"

"Why would I?" He lifted an eyebrow. "People are allowed to leave the atlas turtle, even at night."

I scratched at my scalp. "I... I'm such an idiot. I should've known this was what she was going to do. I should've just gone with her. At least then... I could be there to help her." Nothing felt right about the situation. Every moment apart from her filled my thoughts with hypothetical visions of her death.

Adelgis crossed his arms. After a long moment he asked, "You, uh, didn't see anything when you walked into my room, right?"

I waved away the comment. "N-no. It was dark."

He let out a short exhale and relaxed. "Oh, of course."

"Again, sorry for bothering you, but I need to go."

"You want to go after Illia?"

"She took Zaxis and Hexa with her."

I turned away, mapping out the plan in my mind's eye. First I needed money. I had gold leafs in my room. I would get them, take a skiff to Fortuna, and hopefully catch Illia at the docks. If she wasn't there, I'd hire a ship to take me to Port Crown—or as close as they were willing to get.

Creaks of the floorboards broke my concentration. I

glanced up and spotted Atty at the end of the hall. She held a cloak tight around her shoulders, her long golden hair hanging loose and disheveled.

"Volke?" she asked.

"Yes?"

"The apprentice in the room next to mine said she saw you in the women's hallway. Is that true?"

"I'm sorry," I said. "I went to see Hexa."

"But she's gone."

"How did you know that?"

Atty fidgeted with the clasp of her cloak. "I went to her room to investigate. She sometimes sneaks out at night to be with Illia." Before I said anything else, Atty walked down the hallway and stood closer to Adelgis and me. "This is about Port Crown, isn't it?"

I caught a breath, confused she knew anything. Had Illia gone to her too?

Adelgis motioned to the stairs. "It seems Zaxis, Hexa, and Illia have headed out for the pirate city under the cover of darkness. Volke was just saying how he needed to get there so he could see Illia."

"Truly?" Atty stared at me, her eyebrows knit.

I stared at her phoenix arcanist mark and nodded.

"Then what are we waiting for? Port Crown is dangerous. Neither the queen nor her navy have power there."

"We?" I choked out.

Adelgis patted my shoulder. "Of course. If I had known Illia was going to use my information to sneak off, I wouldn't have been so forthcoming. We should definitely stop her. Or at least protect her from knaves."

"I assume you don't want to get her in trouble?" Atty asked with a slight smile. "If we all go, and all come back in one piece, it'll be less likely that the guild will be harsh in their reprimand."

The shadows around us moved, and I knew Luthair didn't like that plan. He wanted to tell Zelfree what we were doing, but I *didn't* want Illia to get in trouble, and if Zelfree caught her with stolen king basilisk venom, she wouldn't simply get reprimanded.

"You two are willing to go with me?" I asked.

"We already said as much," Adelgis said.

Atty nodded. "Of course. We should leave soon, though. It isn't long before the journeymen get up to start their studies."

"I need to get coins from my room," I said.

The other two nodded.

"We'll pack," Atty said, "and meet at the skiffs in a few short minutes."

15

UNEXPECTED COMPANY

The quiet of the manor house helped refocus my thoughts. I descended the stairs, coins in my pocket, a small bag of supplies slung over my shoulder. Three people stood in the front room, and to my confusion, none of them were Atty or Adelgis.

Guildmaster Liet Eventide and two journeymen—Reo and Salest, both wearing copper pendants to signify their rank in the guild—were having a conversation. When I reached the last step, they stopped talking and turned their attention to me.

"Hello, V-Volke," Reo said as he straightened his thin-framed glasses. His arcanist mark had an ogata toad behind the star, its lithe body unlike normal bulbous toads. "What brings you here this twilight hour?"

I held my bag close. "I need to go into town before our training starts."

"Ah."

Guildmaster Eventide regarded me with a long stare. Unlike most arcanists, who appeared youthful despite their centuries of age, she looked as though she were in her sixties. Her silver hair, slung over her shoulder in a tight braid, glittered as though metallic.

She glanced behind me. "Have you seen your master this morning? He didn't report in when you arrived last night."

"I think Master Zelfree needed some alone time." I forced a chuckle and rubbed at the back of my neck. I wasn't lying.

"Did Gillie have a chat with him? I thought he would be better after seeing her. That woman would invite the reaper for tea if she thought he looked even a bit dour."

"They spoke for a few hours."

For some reason, the guildmaster pondered my statement. Then she turned her attention to the top of the staircase. The furrow of her brow distorted her arcanist mark—one that glowed with an inner light, unlike anything I had seen on anybody else. It was a giant star with an atlas turtle woven between the points. The mark went beyond her hairline and wrapped around to the side of her neck, disappearing beneath the collar of her long coat.

Journeyman Salest held up a book. His arcanist mark had a lightning bird intertwined around the star. "Um, guildmaster? I was wondering if we could head somewhere here in the future." He pointed to a page, his voice weak but distinct.

The guildmaster returned her gaze to the book. "Perhaps. First we must answer the many requests of the guild. I swear each island of the region has asked for our assistance." She had a tired edge to her voice that I had never heard before.

While they scoured the map in the book, pointing to each city that had sent messengers, I walked past them. I hoped none of them had heightened hearing or smell. My heart beat hard, and I knew I probably smelled of sweat and worry.

Reo kept his eyes on me as I went, his head slowly turning to follow my steps to the front door. When I reached for the handle, he said, "Stay s-safe out there, Volke."

I replied with a curt nod and exited the manor house.

The dying evening greeted me with an embrace of frigid wind that tousled my messy hair. I pushed through, undaunted by the chill. Atty and Adelgis were by the skiffs, just as they said they would be. I jogged down the long, winding path.

Illia wasn't on the Fortuna docks, and no vessel would take us to Port Crown.

I didn't blame them. Merchant ships rarely ventured there, and it wasn't like pirates stopped at Fortuna. Instead, Adelgis found a captain willing to take us to the Isle of Gott —the closest port to our destination. I thought we'd have to pay, but the crew insisted that we ride free. We were arcanists of the Frith Guild, and they wouldn't take our coin.

Part of me felt guilty about accepting their charity. I understood, however. If I were a captain, I would've given arcanists free rides all the time, especially if they hailed from the Frith Guild.

Outfitted and ready, our ship—*the Able Seaman*—cut through the waves at a remarkable speed. We chased after the rising sun, and it was only then that I realized I hadn't slept the entire night. I didn't feel tired, though. My mind was on Illia. If I had just gone with her, perhaps I could've talked her into a more sensible plan. Or maybe we could've executed her plan perfectly, and I wouldn't need to worry.

By my estimate, she had an eight hour lead on us. Depending on the type of ship she chartered and the weather on the water, we could make that up and meet her there. But the opposite could happen, too. We could arrive late—long after her confrontation—unable to do anything.

I rested on the railing of the ship and stared out at the cerulean waves. Gulls littered the skies, heralding the new day with a symphony of caws.

Atty wandered to my side, her white robes and ivory trousers a harsh contrast from the sailors wearing shirts, frilly neckwear, doublets, and black pants. Her phoenix, Titania, circled overhead before swooping down to the wooden railing and landing with grace.

"How are you feeling?" Atty asked. She pulled her blonde hair back with a tie, to keep her long strands from fluttering across her eyes.

"I'm worried about Illia."

"Oh, yes. Of course. I meant your arm. Does it still hurt?"

I rubbed my elbow and shook my head. "The grand apothecary took care of everything. I'm fine now."

"I came to visit you several times when you weren't feeling well." She turned her blue eyes to the ocean, the tips of her ears a slight shade of pink. "You, uh, never woke up, so I never got to say anything to you."

Instead, I got Adelgis waking me up with his dream snail.

I smiled, amused by my own joke. "I appreciate you coming to visit me."

"I also wanted to... talk to you about the Sapphire Springs."

She said every word without looking at me, the strain in her voice betraying her embarrassment. I couldn't blame her. I hated that I had to have this conversation.

"I'm so sorry," I said with a sigh. "I just, well, er—I'm not experienced with *people*." From my fight with Illia to my disgrace at the springs, I felt like I handled relationships as well as I handled my second-bonded magic—everything hurt.

Atty turned to me, but still didn't make eye contact, her attention on my shoulder. "You didn't flee the springs because... you disliked my presence?"

"N-no. Of course not. I tend to just avoid things I'm unsure about."

"You never ran away from me while we lived on the Isle of Ruma."

We had never been undressed in front of each other on the Isle of Ruma.

"Things are different now," I said. "We're adults, and I don't feel confident with that title yet, if that makes any sense."

"It does," she quickly said, more hopeful than before.

I breathed a sigh of relief. "Oh, good."

"My mother never wanted me to spend time with others my age, because she thought they would distract me from my studies and make me *impure*." She had said the last word with a cringe. "I've always wanted to know my fellow arcanists, though." Atty moved closer, her flushed expression gone and replaced with a genuine smile. "And my mother *never* would've allowed me to attend the luck ceremony on the Isle of Landin."

"Really?"

"No." Atty looked away, laughing to herself. "That's why I figured, *heck with it*, my mother's not here, I'm an adult—I can make my own decisions. I told myself I would participate, and then I'd finally get to bond with people in the group."

"And?" I asked, wishing I didn't already know my part in the story.

"It turned out half our fellow apprentices didn't even go, and Master Zelfree left before I could even see him." Atty sighed and stroked Titania's head. "I think I idealized it in my mind—like the magic in the springs would make us a tight-knit coterie."

"Did it give you good luck?"

"I did find a star fragment," Atty said with a shrug. "But a local merchant had reported it missing, so I returned it. He gave me a gold leaf for my honesty, so I had something to show. What about you?"

"That was the night I found the wendigo and got bitten."

She lifted both eyebrows. "How... lucky."

"Well, I stole the cartographer's journal from him. That was a kind of luck. I guess."

After a short chuckle, she went back to playing with her hair. "So you didn't return to the springs after you left?"

"No. Did you?"

"No. It was painfully awkward once you fled. I know Zaxis the most out of the group, but he avoided me like I had plague. We sat in silence for a full five minutes before Forsythe brought him a towel. Then he just... left me."

Oh, Zaxis... But at least I wasn't the only one.

Why did I have to be so weird about things? Clearly Atty just wanted to get closer to everyone. It made the ending to her story all the sadder. I wondered how long she sat in the spring by herself.

Before I could continue the conversation—and apologize a second time for acting like an incompetent boob—Adelgis walked over, cheer in his step. His eyes lit up when he noticed the feather-bracelet on my arm.

"Volke, is that a magical item on your wrist?"

I pulled back the sleeve of my coat to expose the phoenix feather.

Titania perked up, her heron-like neck longer than I remembered. "Is that one of mine?"

"I don't think so," I said. "Gillie—er, the grand apothecary—gave this to me."

Adelgis held out a hand. "May I see it?"

I nodded, and he grabbed my arm.

With a keen eye, he studied every inch before releasing me. "A lesser trinket. Probably made with one star fragment. Still, it's constructed with phoenix and caladrius magic, so I bet it's great at protecting you from diseases."

"You're familiar with magical items?"

"Of course. My father makes them all the time. He and the grand apothecary of Fortuna are good friends."

"Oh, so you know Gillie?"

Adelgis smiled wide. "I like to call her Lady Dravon." He sidled up to me and Atty. "I've even been to her innermost workshop. She keeps it locked at all times because of all the amazing ingredients and resources she has there."

His bragging got me thinking. Then it all hit me at once.

"Did you know Gillie had king basilisk venom?" I asked.

Adelgis nodded. "I've seen it."

"And... did you tell that to Illia?"

"I told her all about the grand apothecary when she asked, including all the bizarre things Lady Dravon keeps in her workroom. I didn't think much of it at the time. I just like telling people about how useful magical research can be."

Curse the abyssal hells!

I turned away from Adelgis, almost unable to control my anger. *He* was the reason Illia wanted to break into Gillie's place to begin with. She had talked to him before we got to

Fortuna and formulated her crazy plan on the assumption she could steal herself the deadliest poison in the world.

Oblivious to my seething, Adelgis continued, "You see, trinkets have a low level of magic. Artifacts are magical items constructed with *vast* amounts of magic, and often constructed from powerful mystical creatures. Or perhaps a special piece of a creature." He pointed to Titania. "I once saw an artifact that created flame. It was made from the heart of a phoenix—the source of their fire. Very interesting."

Atty brought a hand up to her collarbone and glowered. "Maybe you should stay away from Titania."

"Er, I wasn't saying I would do that! I'm just trying to make a point. Trinkets are limited, but artifacts can do almost anything so long as you have enough fuel and the right resources. Don't you like imagining stuff like that?"

"I don't like imagining someone using Titania's heart to make a bracelet."

Titania puffed her feathers out, and soot fell all over the deck of the ship. "I don't like it either, thank you very much."

I pushed away from the railing, not in the mood for any more conversation. "I need to get some sleep." I headed for the hold, not bothering to hear their responses.

The ship rocked against the high waves and powerful winds. A mild storm had found us, and I hoped it wouldn't delay our trip. As it stood, the trek from Fortuna to the Isle of Gott required eight days under normal conditions. A whole week would pass before we reached Illia, and I didn't want even one extra day to be added to that.

I counted down each hour with a heavy heart.

Atty and Adelgis both shared my cabin. The *Able Seaman* was a merchant ship first and a passenger ship second. There wasn't an ample amount of room, so Adelgis and I took one bunk cot, and Atty shared the other with her eldrin. Fortunately, Adelgis and I both had eldrin that could "hide in plain sight," and neither required sleeping spaces.

"How upset do you suspect Master Zelfree will be when he finds all his apprentices have left?" Atty asked. She stared at her palm while she spoke, her eyes focused on something I couldn't see.

I leaned back on my narrow cot. "Oh, I suspect he'll be pretty damn upset."

"Do you think he'll remove us from his tutelage?"

"I don't know. Maybe? I'm sure he'll give us a stern reprimand. I can already see it."

I hoped beyond reason he wouldn't drop us as apprentices.

Adelgis poked his head over the edge of the top bunk, his long black hair unsecured. "His thoughts are quite dark at times. He has an active imagination."

"You shouldn't listen to other people's thoughts like that."

"It's not my fault all my magic involves strange techniques."

If I had to use one word to describe Adelgis, it would've been *bizarre*. In all ways I considered us different. Still, his ability to hear thoughts had come in handy before, and I was certain it would come in handy once we reached Port Crown.

I glanced at the porthole. Another hour down.

At night, I practiced my swordplay with Luthair.

His ebony blade didn't weigh as much as a normal sword of that length, and the edge effortlessly sliced through the air. If I weren't careful, I could take someone's arm clean off.

"Always face your opponent," Luthair said as he corrected my stance. "That means you have to move when they do, but keep your weight evenly distributed on both feet. If you lean too heavily on a single foot, it'll be easy to topple you with a single blow."

I focused on steady breathing.

"Since you're inexperienced, you're best served to end the fight quickly. A swordsman with skill will notice your amateur fighting style and capitalize on it."

"I thought I'd been doing well?" I turned to Luthair and frowned. "That's what you said."

"Skilled swordsmen have trained since as young as seven years old. You're far behind, even if you're learning at an accelerated rate."

Since seven? I supposed that made sense. I trained with Gravekeeper William at seven. He showed me how to cut and measure wood for the funerary boxes. He also taught me the difference between a casket and a coffin—a casket has four sides, shaped like a long rectangle, while coffins have six sides with a wide shoulder area.

I didn't know why such details floated into my head, but Luthair must have noticed my vacant expression.

He kicked out his greaves and almost tripped me.

I caught myself and stumbled backward.

"You must focus," he said. "We don't get much time to train together. You should use it to the fullest."

I nodded. "R-right. I got this. I'll pay attention."

"Good. Now keep your sword at shoulder level, and

strike with one fluid movement by bringing your sword forward and above."

I stepped right, trying to imitate his instruction.

Luthair nodded his empty helmet. "Always step to the side before a strike—whichever side is the opponent's weakest."

"How will I know?"

"If the opponent is right-handed, step to your right. If the opponent is left-handed, step to your left."

Simple enough.

I kept my sword at shoulder level.

"With your sword up, you have an easier time of blocking an opponent's blow."

I swung my sword forward and down in a slow-motion overhead arc.

Luthair corrected my grip. "Almost. Good progress. With a strike like this, gravity helps take your blade into the body of your opponent."

"Why a sword?" I asked.

As though confused by the question, Luthair hesitated for a moment. Then he tilted his helmet head. "What do you mean?"

"Well, if you can make anything out of shadows and use it as a weapon, why not a spear? Or an axe? Or a rifle?" I glanced down at the hilt of the shadow blade. I admired the arcane detail.

"Mathis forged this sword," Luthair said. "It's a magical object, like a trinket, but much stronger. The core of that blade is the fang of a behemoth. Mathis had just learned to imbue his sorcery and chose to fashion a sword. He could've picked anything, I assume, but this weapon called to him. It's part of being a knightmare arcanist."

I lifted my gaze. "Will I forge a weapon?"

"I... don't know. I'm already a fully formed shell of armor. The time of weapon crafting happens when a knight-mare reaches maturity. This is the cost of second bonding. I've never heard of a knightmare with two weapons."

So I was stuck with Mathis's weapon for all time. Although I didn't mind the sword, I would've preferred something like a rifle. The thought of a knightmare gunslinger amused me. The long-range shots would've made fighting people at a distance much easier. Plus, until Luthair had started teaching me, I had never wielded swords before.

"Let's try the strike again," Luthair said, pulling me out of my thoughts.

"Okay. I'll swing faster this time."

I had been on lots of ships in the past, and some parts of the experience were always the same.

We ate dried meat and fish, and drank ale—water didn't keep well on long trips, but mild alcohol was safe. Some-times the ship would provide biscuits, but that was usually on the passenger vessels. Since the gunners didn't have much to do on a peaceful trek, they would sweep the deck and keep it clear of water that splashed aboard. The boatswain—the person in charge of the sails—would often climb up and down the rigging until everything was secure.

I enjoyed watching the sailors work. It kept me distracted.

Only one day left until we reached the Isle of Gott. From there, it would be a few hours' sail into Port Crown. We were close.

Atty and Adelgis stayed with me at all times. Although

Atty sometimes needed more privacy than Adelgis and I, it wasn't long. She would change or wash with great haste and never interacted with the crew unless I was nearby. I doubted she was afraid—her phoenix magic could easily burn everyone on the *Able Seaman* to a crisp—so I wondered why she stuck so close the entire trek.

I never asked her, though.

A powerful wind washed over the deck of the ship, ripping the caps off most of the sailors. Mine flew off, but bits of shadow, like black string, reached up and snatched it from the air. I grasped it and placed it back on my head. "Thank you, Luthair."

He shifted around my feet, but made no reply.

"That was strange," Adelgis said as he smoothed his clothing. "The wind felt magical."

He could sense that? I didn't know how to tell one way or the other.

A heavy hand landed on my shoulder. I whipped around, my blood hot and my mind set on a fight. Instead, I caught my breath and flinched, taken aback by the sight of Master Zelfree.

"How did you get here?" were the first words out of my mouth.

Adelgis and Atty both turned at the same time, their eyes wide and their expressions set to *guilty*.

Then I noticed his arcanist mark. Normally it was an empty star, but he had a sylph wrapped around the points. Sylphs were air creatures—small and humanoid with tiny wings. They could ride the breeze like a man rides a horse. Sure enough, his mimic fluttered into view in the form of an adorable sylph no bigger than my forearm. She had long sparkly hair that flowed as though caught in a permanent wind. Her dress fluttered, but never revealed anything compromising.

Zelfree grabbed the collar of my jacket, breaking my fascination. "What are you doing here?" he barked. "You up and disappear without so much as a note? *Are you touched in the head?*"

I ripped my coat from his grasp and hardened my gaze. That obviously wasn't the reaction he had been expecting—he dropped his hand and waited, one eyebrow raised.

"Illia is heading to Port Crown." I took a step back. "I'm not returning to the Frith Guild until I know she's safe."

Atty and Adelgis nodded along with my statement, muttering *that's right* and *we're in this together.*

Zelfree was dumbfounded for a split second before anger took over. "Are you all insane? You should have come to me the instant Illia left. I could've cut her off long before she made it to Port Crown if I had known what was going on!"

I shook my head. "This doesn't involve you."

"What was that?" He half laughed, half-huffed. "That's the most insubordinate thing an apprentice has ever said to me."

"You don't understand. This is a personal matter. Illia wants to kill the Dread Pirate Calisto because he's the one who killed her parents. He's also the one who took her eye."

The news sent a shiver through the group. They all turned to me, even Traces in her sylph form. I had forgotten that no one really knew what had happened to Illia. The information settled over them like a wet blanket, dulling emotions and turning them all pensive.

"I'm her brother," I continued, my chest tight. "I should've gone with her, but now I have to catch up. She isn't a child. I couldn't have sent you to *fetch her*. She never would've listened. This... it's more complicated than that."

Traces landed on Zelfree's shoulder, her cute little girl expression stuck on *oh my*.

Zelfree ran a hand through his disheveled hair. He exhaled, and then took a deep breath, mulling over my words and staring at the deck like he was plotting its death. When he glanced up, he met my gaze with a cold intensity. "She's going to attack Calisto in Port Crown?"

I replied with a single nod.

He waved his hand and the breeze picked up, filling the sails of the *Able Seaman* with a powerful force. The ship sliced through the ocean as it gained speed.

"You're helping us get there?" I asked.

Traces giggled. "We wouldn't leave one of our apprentices in a pirate port!"

"I'll help you," Zelfree said. "Port Crown isn't a place for apprentice arcanists. It's a cesspool of criminals and blackhearts. And Calisto is the worst of them all."

16

PORT CROWN

Tower Isle, home to Port Crown, came into view just as the sun touched the ocean. The crimson skies created an ominous backdrop for the island's jagged mountains. Fog haunted the beaches, a creeping wall of gray and white.

With Zelfree's magic, we made it there sooner than I expected, but if Illia had no trouble on the water, she'd still likely have a few hours lead on us. Would she be okay? I hoped so.

We had left the *Able Seaman* behind on the Isle of Gott, and the *Coral Driver* we were now aboard was nothing more than an island-hopping vessel, barely large enough to hold twenty people. Adelgis, Atty, and Zelfree stood close, and while Adelgis and Zelfree pulled their coats tight as the chill set in, Atty didn't seem to realize the temperature had crept downward. Her phoenix had perched itself on the railing next to her, the soot from Titania's feathers sprinkling onto the deck.

"I've heard you can get anything in Port Crown," Adelgis muttered. "They trade mystical creature parts to make valuable items, capture people to sell to the nations beyond the ocean, and some mix concoctions deemed illegal on most islands."

"How would you know that?" Atty asked, her eyes narrowed.

"My father does research in the city of Ellios, and he once received materials procured from Port Crown. His colleagues debated the ethics of using such things, since there was no way to determine if they were obtained in a legal manner."

"Like... phoenix hearts?" Atty petted her eldrin, her hand unsteady.

Adelgis replied with a slow nod.

The conversation didn't surprise me. I had read all about Port Crown from the books and journals in Gravekeeper William's library. The queen and her navy had no power over Tower Isle, even though it had once been the port for privateers—arcanist captains who were given letters of marque to hunt pirates and raid vessels that came from across the ocean. But when the queen stopped issuing those letters of marque, the privateers became resentful. They turned into pirates themselves, plundering ships from our island nation, and also ships that were exhausted after a long trek over ocean waters.

The thought of pirates got my blood running quick with fire. I gripped the railing of the *Coral Diver* and exhaled. "Why doesn't the Frith Guild come here and stop these scoundrels? Surely, with the backing of the navy, these fiends wouldn't stand a chance?"

Zelfree pulled a flask from his pocket and then pointed to the jagged mountains. I followed his finger and squinted. Perched on the top of the rocks, bunched in a group of three, were rocs. Not R-O-C-K, like the minerals found on the ground, but R-O-C, the mystical creature of sea storms.

Rocs were gargantuan birds with wings the size of sailing ships, and their eyes could see details all the way to the horizon. One breath and they froze the clouds—one flap of their wings and they created a gale force wind that kicked up a tsunami.

"The rulers of Port Crown are all roc arcanists," Zelfree said with a half-smile. "Their eldrin grab boulders from the mountains and throw them on enemy ships. If that doesn't work, they alter the weather, create a storm, and fly into the ships with their massive talons. Fighting them on their home turf is foolish. And I haven't even addressed what the other pirates can bring to the fight."

The news drilled into my thoughts, spiraling them into dark places.

Tower Isle was set apart from our island nation. While most islands formed a wide half-crescent, angling toward the west, Tower Isle was the last bit of land before taking to the ocean in the east. There wasn't an easy way to attack Tower Isle, not without significant loss—and there was a good chance roc arcanists could escape an attack.

I hated it. The situation reminded me I didn't have the power to right all the injustices in the universe.

One roc stretched his wings wide and screeched as it yawned. The sound shook me to my bones.

Zelfree took a long swig on his flask. "Okay, listen up. Once we get to the docks, you should flaunt your arcanist mark, but don't use magic unless you absolutely need to." He offered each of us a glare. "This is the kind of city where the first sign of violence is an invitation. We don't want to get into a senseless brawl. We're here for Illia, Zaxis, and Hexa. Then we leave. Understand?"

We muttered our acknowledgements, but no one could take their eyes off the encroaching fog. The captain turned the *Coral Driver* and fearlessly plunged into the mist. The thick earth-bound cloud lowered the temperature another couple of degrees, and I shivered.

"Everyone stay calm," a deckhand shouted. "We'll be passing through the gates soon."

The gates?

The crew scrambled to lower the flags and secure everything to the sides of the deck. Nautical flags were how ships communicated information while out at sea. Every ship used three—one for their nation, one to signify if they had arcanists among their crew or passengers, and one to communicate the state of emergency, if any. Even pirates waved flags, but in Port Crown, all were to be removed before entering the city. It was to signify that this was a place devoid of allegiances.

It seemed as though each person on the ship held their breath as the *Coral Driver* neared land. Only the creaking of the hull heralded our arrival, and the near silence allowed me to concentrate enough to see shapes hidden in the fog. We sailed between two large rocks, probably the opening to the Port Crown bay. But why would we need to stay calm? Most cities had a port bay. This wasn't new.

The answer came in the form of a roc leaning down from the stone gates. Its massive head—large enough to hold a man whole in its mouth—emerged from the fog like a dream. The roc's cream colored feathers ruffled as it scanned the deck of the ship with piercing coal-black eyes.

The colossal creature opened and shut its beak when it got within a few feet of the passengers. A couple of people threw themselves onto the deck and covered their heads. Others trembled and held loved ones close.

Up close, I noticed the edges of the roc's beak were sharp enough to be a gargantuan pair of scissors—or a guillotine.

One snap and it could slice through steel, no doubt in my mind.

A roc was the dragon of birds, and when it exhaled, the scent of blood washed over the *Coral Driver*. Then, as silently as it had descended, the roc pulled its head back. The creature returned to resting on the rock gate.

Once the roc had retreated into the fog, the passengers collected themselves.

"I thought it was going to eat Titania," Atty muttered, holding her eldrin close.

Adelgis shook his head. "The roc only had thoughts of catching specific people. Like it's acting as a sentry."

I exhaled, unaware of how tense I had become during the encounter. There was no way I could fight a roc. It was too huge—like Ruma's leviathan, those creatures couldn't be fought through conventional means.

The *Coral Driver* lowered her sails and crept into the dock at a leisurely pace. Adelgis tapped my shoulder once we were close enough to see the other ships through the fog.

"There it is. The *Third Abyss*. Calisto is here!"

We all turned our attention to the direction he pointed.

By the abyssal hells—it was a man-of-war style ship! 200 feet long, with 124 cannons, the man-of-war ships were some of the most deadly on the waters. The ship could accommodate 1,000 men with its four decks, and the four masts allowed the ship to sail at eight or nine knots.

We were too far away to see the crew, but the shifting shapes indicated some were still aboard.

I almost didn't notice the bizarre color of the ship. Everything was a dirty-white or gray, different than any wood I had seen on a large ship.

"What is that?" I whispered.

Zelfree glared at the vessel as we sailed by. "That's ghostwood. You see the fog around here? Ghostwood grows naturally on this island—it always creates a thick mist, even when cut down."

"The ship... creates fog?"

"That's right. Fog thick enough that it makes fighting it one hell of a task."

"How do *they* see through it? Wouldn't that hinder them as well?"

"I'm not sure, but I know Calisto has his methods."

No wonder Calisto had yet to be caught. He hid in a bank of fog no matter where he sailed.

Dockhands awaited us at the port. In a matter of minutes, the *Coral Driver* was secured to the pier, and a gangplank lowered.

Zelfree removed his jacket and threw it around Atty's shoulders. She gave him a surprised look and then shook her head.

"I'm not cold."

"Keep it. You look too delicate for this place. White is a color that stands out amongst this filth."

Without further comment, Atty wrapped the coat around her and secured the buttons shut. It hid her white robes for the most part, and gave her a bulkier—and more formidable—frame. Perhaps people would assume she had weapons tucked away in her inner pockets.

Zelfree took another drink from his flask and then splashed some on his hands. He patted each of us on the shoulder as we left the ship.

Adelgis cringed the moment Zelfree's whiskey-palms hit his clothes. "Is this necessary?"

"You all look too fresh. Trust me. We want to blend in as much as possible."

With a few expert movements, Zelfree popped the collar

of his shirt, lowered his hat, and tucked the long strands of his hair up into it, hiding most of his distinguishing features. I tried to imitate his technique, but I hadn't brought a hat. Instead, I messed up my hair—more than usual—and kept my coat collar up to my chin.

The docks reeked of alcohol and fish. Inns lined the walls of Port Crown, each with posters more risqué than the last. I didn't stare at any of the women, even the ones that were just drawings, for fear of offending Atty. To my amusement, she stared for a long while, a frown on her bright red face.

Zelfree removed the bangles on his arm. Then they glowed a soft white and transformed into an ethereal whelk —just like Adelgis's eldrin. The arcanist star on Zelfree's forehead shifted to show the spiral shell.

"We're going into the city," Zelfree said, a harsh seriousness to his tone. "Don't leave my sight. We'll speak with a few of my contacts and then head to a tavern I know to be safe. Keep your eyes peeled for the others."

We all nodded in unison.

Although the sun had set, lamps and glowstones kept Port Crown pulsing with life. They also kept the fog within the city to a minimum. A light haze hovered over the area, like a thin layer of smoke.

We entered through the dock gates, and the crowds that lined the roads and walkways were unlike any I had ever seen. Homeless beggars sat on the corners with pans held out in front of them. Sailors from all types of ships congregated in front of bars and taverns. Merchants clogged the road with booths that stretched from here to deep within the city.

A constant barrage of noise made it difficult to think. Titania flew away from Atty and took to the sky. Could she see individuals in this cramped environment? Perhaps eyes above could speed up our search.

Zelfree led us through the throngs of people. Whenever some ruffian bumped into him, he would growl and shove the person away, often with a curt remark. Although I thought it rude, it seemed to work. Fewer and fewer thugs seemed interested in bothering us.

I jogged to his side. "Why have your mimic transform into an ethereal whelk?" I asked, my voice almost drowned by the commotion all around us.

"It's rare enough that few will know what it can do, and I need to hear thoughts if we're going to get out of here quick."

My eyebrows shot to my hairline. "Won't that anger people?"

"You saw the *Third Abyss* on the pier. Calisto is here. Either we get Illia tonight, or we may never do it. I don't have time to be polite."

His statement cut like a knife deep in my chest. If Port Crown was outside of our nation's laws, perhaps this was for the best. Read thoughts, find Illia, and leave.

There were more arcanists in Port Crown than I had ever imagined. On any other island, the ratio of arcanist to non-arcanist was about 1 to 1,000. Here, I spotted arcanist marks so frequently it felt like the ratio was 1 to 500, or maybe even 1 to 250. Harpy, imp, troll, pixie—so many types of arcanists, it was hard to keep track.

And everyone displayed their weapons, even if they had no magic. Cutlasses were popular. So were flintlock pistols and rifles. A few people carried long knives and hatchets. It was all a warning not to start trouble.

"Can we visit the market?" Adelgis asked from the back of our ranks, his gaze set to the many streets filled with vendors, despite the late hour. "There's bound to be interesting things here."

Zelfree shook his head. "Don't wander off."

"Can't we just walk down the road? If we're going to listen to people's thoughts, I could investigate without disturbing the locals."

"No. The markets here will disturb you, trust me. We don't need to be embroiled in anything other than the task at hand."

Despite the warning, Adelgis kept his attention on the merchants. While the idea of finding rare magical components and trinkets interested me, nothing mattered more than finding Illia. Unfortunately, the city was larger than I thought. We turned down road after road, Zelfree in the lead, his pace quick.

I didn't care where we went. I searched the crowd with a single-minded focus, even after my feet began to hurt.

Some roads twisted and became narrow alleyways. In those moments, Zelfree made sure to keep us close. He seemed to know every crag within the city, and shielded us from the worst of the scum.

How long would we search? The evening pressed on, and I thought we might never find the others.

Then, like a flash of light in the darkness, I caught sight of a tattoo on a man's neck. It was three horizontal lines: ☰. Just like the tattoo Fain had on his neck—a marker for the crew of the *Third Abyss*.

I grabbed Zelfree's shoulder and pointed.

He headed in that direction, and I hung back with Atty and Adelgis. I couldn't hear anything, but lip reading Zelfree wasn't hard. He asked if Calisto was in town, and the pirate promptly gave him the finger.

To my surprise, Zelfree didn't argue. He ambled back to

us, his gaze set to the ground. "Calisto's in a nearby gambling hall. *The Gold Grotto*."

"Let's go there," I said the second he ended his sentence.

"We aren't actually here to find Calisto. I asked about him because Illia will likely be nearby."

Adelgis rubbed his hands together. "And shouldn't we avoid contact with Calisto at all costs? Going into the gambling hall would be, uh, *a gamble*, pardon the pun."

Atty nodded. "I'm not sure we should just enter through the front door."

"But Illia is looking for him," I said. "Well, assuming she hasn't already tried her plan... If she's going to head anywhere, it'll be this gambling hall. We can catch her before she confronts him."

"But what if we run into Calisto?"

"I can slip into the shadows." My shadow-stepping was good enough to get away, even if it wasn't good enough to end up at a specific location.

Zelfree nodded along with my words. "All right. I have a plan. Volke, you and I will enter the casino and check around inside. I saw a white hart arcanist a few streets back. If I use that magic, we can stealth around with little chance of getting caught. Atty, Adelgis—you two stay right over there at the *Final Retreat*. Tell them you're looking for a room that smells nice."

"That smells nice?" Atty repeated, her nose already scrunched. "As in, all the other rooms smell terrible?"

"It's a code phrase," he snapped. "It means you're with the Frith Guild. The *Final Retreat* is run by a friend of mine."

I had almost forgotten that Zelfree used to act as a spy and double agent. All the tales of his great adventures had him infiltrating pirate crews and sending crucial information back to his guild. It was no wonder he knew so much about Port Crown and where to go to stay safe.

"How long will you be gone?" Adelgis asked.

"No more than thirty minutes. Volke and I will inspect the *Gold Grotto*. If Illia is there, we'll speak to her. If she's not, we'll post ourselves around the building until we spot her or the other two." Zelfree pulled out his flask and downed the last of his alcohol in one long swig. Afterward he coughed and tucked the empty container back in his pocket. "If Illia already tried her plan, I'm sure someone will be willing to spill the beans on that story. Volke, let's go."

"Right," I muttered.

17

THE DREAD PIRATE CALISTO

I didn't care for the white hart arcanist mark Zelfree came back with. Although majestic and beautiful, I couldn't erase the memory of the plague-ridden white hart I had encountered in the Endless Mire. Its bulging eyes had haunted me to this day.

My thoughts drifted as Zelfree dragged me to an alley between buildings. Although Port Crown had a lot of light, there were still dark corners to hide in.

"Let me see your boots," he said as he knelt.

Zelfree touched both, and for a brief moment they felt warm.

Once done, I took a step back, confused. They didn't seem different. "What happened?"

"White hart magic can distort sound. I've made it so your boots won't make a noise."

Half-disbelieving him, I stomped my foot down. Nothing. No slam or click—dead silence, as though I had fallen deaf. I knew white harts were masters of stealth, but I didn't know their arcanists could manipulate how others heard things.

"Did you memorize all the techniques of every mystical creature?" I asked. "How did you know you could do this as a white hart arcanist?"

Zelfree stood, brushed himself off, and touched various pieces of our clothing. "I'm a mimic arcanist. I can sense magic, and I know someone's capabilities as long as I'm close to them. Once my mimic has changed, I gain access to those abilities."

"Wow. That's so... useful. Mimic magic sounds awesome."

"*Shh*," he hissed. "Hold a part of my shirt. Don't let go. Once I've shrouded us in invisibility, you can't break contact with me. The moment you do, the magic will fade, understand?"

I nodded and grabbed a bit of the shirt on his shoulder.

"Under no circumstance are you to attack anyone here. Even if Illia is in trouble, leave the fighting to *me*. You're here to convince Illia to abandon this mission, if we manage to find her. Nothing else."

He held my upper arm and shook it once.

"*Nothing else.*"

"R-right," I said.

Without warning, a wave of pressure washed over me. I closed my eyes, and when I opened them a second later, it was as if the whole world had been color-muted. I could still see colors, but they appeared duller and gray at the edges. The only things not affected by this discoloration were Zelfree and me. It took a second to absorb what had happened—invisibility had swaddled us.

"Follow me at arm's length," he commanded. "Don't speak unless I say something first. Tap my shoulder if you need anything. We can see each other, obviously, so keep most communications restricted to nonverbal motions."

I nodded.

That made Zelfree smile. "Good."

"What would you have me do?" Luthair asked from the shadows around my feet.

Both Zelfree and I jumped. I kept my grip on his shirt, however, even when he tried to go in the other direction. After a few calming breaths, Zelfree said, "Just remain hidden. Keep to the corners. If I need you to leave, I'll say something."

"Understood."

I didn't know where Traces had gone to. In the form of a white hart, I doubted she could go with us into the *Gold Grotto*, even if she had master stealth. White harts were large, after all.

Zelfree exited the alleyway, and I kept closer to him than most shadows. The denizens of Port Crown never glanced in our direction. If eyes turned our way, they kept going, failing to focus. The front doors to the *Gold Grotto* were heavy and wide—it took a few seconds for them to swing shut once open. Zelfree dragged me inside the second a couple of drunk sailors stumbled in.

Smoke filled the building, and I choked back a cough. Everyone had a pipe, cigarette, or cigar. Glasses of rum, ale, whiskey, and grog were passed to the card tables, sometimes by the dozens. The chatter and laughter reached thunderous levels, to the point that Zelfree really hadn't needed to silence our clothing. If we had walked in here with a war drum; I doubted anyone would've noticed.

Hundreds packed themselves around the ongoing games. Dice clattered on the wood, and coins clicked in their glass jars stationed in the middle of the tables. I glanced around, desperate to spot Illia, but it was difficult to see through the ocean of people.

Bar maids carried everything on large silver trays they held above their heads, blocking more of my view. Zelfree darted to the wall and hurried along the edge of the room. He didn't give me much time to investigate, so I kept my eyes wide as we dashed around the gambling patrons. I was unwilling to blink, just in case I missed Illia in the split second I had to spot her.

Zelfree stopped near the back of the room. I almost collided with him as he turned to face me. "There's a wendigo arcanist here."

"Where?"

"Close by. He's probably invisible, like us. But I can still feel his magic."

"What if we bump into him?"

"Then we'll get caught." He shot me a sarcastic glare. "And stop looking around. That's not helpful. Stay focused on my movements."

"What if Illia is—"

"She's upstairs."

"Really?" My heart sped up and I was tempted to drag Zelfree to the nearest set of stairs. "How do you know?"

"I just told you mimic arcanists can sense magic. Stop acting like a jackanapes and pay attention! There's a rizzel arcanist above us. It's faint, which means it's a weaker arcanist—that fits Illia."

I took a deep breath and regretted it. The smoke clogged my throat, and I had to cough into my hand. "Do you sense a manticore arcanist?" I asked between stifled rasps.

"Yes. He's here. I haven't spotted him yet, but he's hard to miss. Just stay close."

Zelfree dragged me toward a large door opposite the front. We waited until one of the bar maids opened it, revealing a long hallway and steep stairs. We rushed in before the door swung shut, though the heel of my boot caught the wood. No one seemed to notice with the commotion raging in the main gambling room.

We walked up the stairs, Zelfree keeping his back to the wall, even as he went upward. I mimicked his movements. Without the rowdy crowds, I could finally hear myself think. Plus, it became apparent then that my clothing didn't rustle. Not my coat, my pants—nothing.

We reached the second floor and Zelfree stopped midmotion, like a rabbit caught in the garden.

A swanky man stood in the middle of the long hallway, his hand on the knob of an opened door. "Calisto will be with you shortly." He had a voice tinted with haughty importance. "Stick to the deal and all should go well." As he shut the door, he smiled.

Everything about him reeked of gaudy self-importance. He wore a fine suit similar to the gentlemen of the mainland, and kept his large beard and mustache tamed with scented oil so potent I could smell it from twenty feet away. His hair was trimmed in such a way as to display his arcanist mark: parted in the middle and greased into place so thoroughly it wouldn't move in a hurricane.

As the man walked by us, I noticed the creature wrapped around his arcanist star was a grifter crow. Those crows were trickster creatures with a love of money and luxury. Weak creatures, though. Their magic was often nothing more than parlor tricks and sleight-of-hand. Even a grifter crow arcanist of hundreds of years couldn't stand up to a mildly trained phoenix arcanist.

Once the grifter crow arcanist was halfway down the stairs, Zelfree moved toward the door that had been open. He stopped just before he reached the handle. Then he whipped around, his gaze hard-set, a hint of panic on his shallow breath.

I wanted to ask what was wrong, but he had said not to speak unless he did first. Instead, Zelfree reached for the door, silenced it with his magic, and gently pushed it open.

He ran inside with me a whisper-distance away. The door made no noise as it moved. We made no noise. Everything was as silent as the dead. Zelfree closed the door behind us, but my attention was stolen by the sole other person in the room.

Illia.

She stood by the far window, staring out to the streets below. Although she had worn a hat, long coat, tall boots, and a bandana wrapped around her forehead, I still recognized her. She had a specific lax posture where she rested her weight back on one foot, and the wavy brown hair poking out from the back of the hat screamed *her*.

The room was nothing more than a private bar. Three tables, a liquor counter, and nine chairs were the only furnishings. I thought we would head straight for Illia and leave, but Zelfree yanked me by the collar and ducked behind the bar counter as fast as he could take us.

A second later, the door opened—this time with a squeak.

Illia turned on her heel, her spine stiff and her arcanist mark covered by the bandana. It was only then that I noticed she wore an eyepatch over her missing eye.

Three people entered the room. Even with the colors muted from our invisibility, I could make out every distinct feature on their persons.

The first was a woman with a low-cut shirt and a scarlet feather in a wide-brimmed hat. Her long black hair hung free, all the way to her waist. She had the curves and allure of a woman who knew how to move her body, but the moment I spotted her arcanist mark, I stopped thinking about that.

She was a kappa arcanist.

While kappas weren't the strongest of eldrin, they were deadly fish-people that ate the flesh of children. And... they all had the same Trial of Worth. Kappas would only bond to mothers who offered up their first born as a meal.

Only. Never an exception.

The second to enter was a burly man with a thick beard and a peg leg. He carried a long rifle and held a cigarette between his lips, dragging a line of smoke into the room that had once been clear. His arcanist mark was just as horrid as the kappa.

He was a snallygaster arcanist.

Again, they weren't the strongest of eldrin, but they exclusively ate the flesh of people, especially those sick, elderly, or young. Half-lizard, half-bird, snallygasters were mutated dragon creatures who flew on crooked wings. Their Trial of Worth involved offering a piece of yourself for them to eat.

I shuddered when I glanced at the man's peg leg for a second time.

The last man to enter didn't need an introduction. I knew him immediately—the Dread Pirate Calisto.

He wore a tailored coat that fell to his ankles, the collar of which had the fur of a crimson lion's mane stitched into it. His shirt, a dull black, blended well with his copper-auburn hair. He carried pistols on his belt, knives on his boots, and various bracelets on his wrists.

To my fascination and curiosity, his manticore arcanist mark glowed, just like our guildmaster's. And it stretched into his hairline, down around his neck, and appeared to continue past the collar of his clothes.

Why did his mark glow? I wished I had asked our guild-master before I left.

All three of them had the horizontal lines tattooed on their neck, but only Calisto's was woven into his arcanist mark.

They walked into the room and shut the door. When the group attempted to walk around the middle table, Illia held up a hand.

"That's close enough."

Calisto stopped and rubbed at his copper-stubble-covered chin. He smirked, and although he had to be over a century old, he appeared no older than twenty-five.

Why wasn't Illia just attacking them? She could've waited behind the door and surprised them before they even knew who they were dealing with. Manticore arcanists had sorcery that improved their strength and speed far beyond human limits. Why would she ever risk seeing them used in person? Especially by a master arcanist like Calisto?

"You want to run the show, huh?" Calisto asked, his voice smooth, but weighty. "That's fine. So long as we get to make our little trade. You *do* have the cartographer's journal, right? I'm a man who doesn't like to waste his shore leave."

Illia reached into her coat pocket and withdrew the journal.

All at once, the three pirates perked up, Calisto going so far as to genuinely smile.

"I'm impressed," he said. "But first show me the page with the compass. I don't care about the rest."

Illia narrowed her eye. "Compass?"

"Page eighty-four, lass. Open the journal so I can see it's still there."

She flipped it open to the desired page and flashed it for the room to see. Sure enough, a picture of a strange compass was drawn across the left-hand side, along with a ton of writing on the right.

The kappa woman exchanged a glance with the peg-legged man. "See, Spider?" he said. "You owe me two leafs. The girl has what we wanted."

The woman, *Spider*, frowned as she reached into the depths of her coat. A second later, she withdrew a small sack of metal that clinked as she threw it onto the table in the middle of the room. Gold leafs spilled across the wood, and a few fell to the floor, each gold coin the size of a sand dollar.

I held my breath. There had to be hundreds of leafs in that sack—more money than ten years' worth of hard labor.

Calisto hooked his thumbs in his belt loops and nodded to the coins. "There's your payment. Just like we agreed."

A tense second passed as Illia brought the journal close to her chest.

I clenched my fists. Why wasn't she using her poison? She could do it now!

"You're awfully young to be stealing from the infamous Frith Guild," Calisto continued, the teeth of his smile straight and perfect. "I'm always looking for talented people. If you want to make a steady amount of coin, you should consider joining my crew on the *Third Abyss*. You'll want for nothing."

With a shaky hand, Illia pulled the eyepatch off her face, revealing the twisted scars and missing eye.

Spider sneered. The peg-legged man chuckled.

"Calisto," Illia said, her voice raw with emotion. "You... you're the man who killed my parents. The man who cut out my eye."

The statement rocked me—why would she tell him that? —but after a moment of contemplation, I finally understood.

Illia wanted to confront him. She wanted him to know what he had done.

"I know," Calisto replied. "I recognize my handiwork."

Illia's voice had been low at first, but it grew bolder with each word she forced out. "You're a monster who terrorizes innocent people. I don't want your *offer of employment*. I don't want your *coins*. I came for your life."

Calisto hardened his gaze, but his smile never waned.

Spider's frown shifted into a tight grin. "I told you, Breen —I'm never wrong. This girl doesn't wanna make a trade. *You* owe *me* two leafs."

The man, *Breen*, grumbled as he unsheathed his cutlass. "For once I'd like one of these exchanges to go down exactly as planned."

Spider pulled a sleek pistol from her holster. "I guess we'll be taking that journal by force, then."

The two thugs went to step forward, but Calisto lifted a hand. They froze, their attention on him. He motioned them back with a gentle flick of his wrist, and they slowly complied with his command.

"You heard the girl," Calisto said. "*I'm* the one that did all those terrible things. You two can stay out of this. It's between me and her."

Confusion flashed between them. Spider offered a forced giggle. "You must be joking."

"I'm not. I remember this one. She's the girl who set fire to my ship and managed to escape." Calisto tilted his head. "How old were you then? You had to have been young."

Illia gritted her teeth. "You're a c-corrupted soul with no

remorse. I... I was nothing but a little girl when you maimed me."

Her voice came out in strangled shaky bursts, like she was holding back a sob or a shout; it was hard to tell. Her tone agitated me, but Zelfree placed a heavy hand on my shoulder and squeezed hard. I didn't move from our hiding spot.

Calisto laughed. "Corrupted soul? That's a new one. Most people just go for *murderer* or *bastard*. Kids are gettin' creative these days." He moved aside two of the chairs and then kicked the table loaded with gold coins. It easily slid across the wood floor and collided with the far wall. It crashed to its side. The gold leafs went everywhere.

Illia flinched, but she didn't move from her spot.

The room was clear between them. No obstacles. Nothing to hide behind.

"You've got a lot of moxie, lass," Calisto said. "You stole a journal just to get me all to yourself? You even prepared a little speech. That takes guts." He lifted his arms. "Well, here I am. Come at me, and let's see what you've got."

With an unsteady hand, Illia slipped the journal back into her coat. She watched Calisto with an intent gaze, as though she couldn't believe he would just wait. Sure enough, he didn't move. Illia took her time as she withdrew the black box holding the king basilisk venom. The other three regarded it with lifted eyebrows and curious expressions, which meant they likely had no idea how lethal the contents could be.

Illia undid the latch. The box had a smooth velvet lining that protected a single vial. She picked it up and allowed the container to fall to the floor with a loud clatter. The vial wasn't large—it couldn't hold more than a few drops of venom.

It wouldn't take much to kill someone, though.

After a deep breath, Illia removed the glass top. Her hands still trembled, but she held the venom firmly enough to prevent any spilling.

"This is for my parents," she whispered.

I almost called out—to tell her to stop—but I couldn't find my breath. I was so tense everything seemed to move in slow motion.

Illia arched the vial out in front of her, throwing the poison at Calisto. With speed far beyond the average man, he pulled out a long dagger and held it up to block the droplets of king basilisk venom. But *right before they hit his blade* they glittered and vanished, only to reappear on the other side of the weapon and splash across Calisto's face.

She had used her magic to teleport the poison!

Part of me wanted to jump out from behind the counter to congratulate her. Masterful!

The quiet of the room persisted. Everyone waited, but nothing happened. Calisto relaxed, sheathed his knife, and brought his hand up to his face. Three dots of blackish-blue venom had splashed across his cheek. With one clean motion, he wiped the deadly substance onto his finger.

"What's this?" He licked it from his hand and then smiled. "King basilisk venom? Tsk, tsk. That's highly illegal to carry without the proper papers."

Spider and Breen took a few steps backward right after the words *king basilisk venom* were muttered.

Illia's eye remained open and wide, sheer disbelief written into her frozen stance and knitted eyebrows.

I couldn't breathe. Calisto just *licked it*? How? He should be long dead!

Calisto laughed with an earnest sincerity. "Don't look so shocked. You're not the first person to try to poison me, lass.

You aren't even the first person to use king basilisk venom. Again, it's impressive for someone your age, but you'll have to be original."

He undid the top buttons of his shirt and pulled it open. Around his neck, dangling below his collarbone, was a pendant made from the shattered fragment of a unicorn horn. He smoothed it against his muscled chest.

"I killed a unicorn arcanist just so I could get the horn to make this artifact," Calisto said. "Unicorns are immune to all types of poison and venom. And now so am I."

Illia ran a hand up her face, her fingers catching on the bandana. My heart sank as she scrunched her eye shut and clenched her jaw. I told her this wouldn't work—I knew in my gut—but I had secretly hoped everything would go off without a hitch. I didn't want to see her fail.

"Poor lass looks distraught," Breen said as he hefted his trousers.

Calisto kept his shirt half-open and shrugged. "These types always come with a surprise after their first attempt fails." He motioned for Illia to come at him. "Let's see it. We don't have all night."

Illia didn't look up. She dug her fingernails into the bandana, her whole body trembling.

Why didn't she just leave? Teleport away? I knew she didn't have any other plans. She had been so confident with the first.

"She doesn't have anything else," Spider drawled. She placed a hand on her prominent hip and swished back her hair. "That was it. All her eggs in one basket."

Calisto waited, and when Illia didn't move to do something else, he chuckled. "*That's it*? One dose of poison?"

His thugs started laughing and he joined in. Spider and Breen even muttered a few asides, their amusement over

Illia's failure enough to keep them chortling long after the fact.

Illia stared at her boots, her one eye red, her shoulders bunched at her neck.

"Okay, okay," Calisto said, holding up his hands. "Fun times are over." He took a step forward and cocked his head to one side. "I usually get upset when urchins try to kill me with amateur tactics, but they're never as brazen as you are."

Still, she said nothing.

"I'll tell you a secret, lass. I actually feel sorry for the people I raid and kill."

Illia snapped her glare upward. She lowered her hand and balled it into a tight fist. "You're a disgusting liar."

"Hear me out. It's like pointing a gun at a dog. The dumb mutt doesn't know it's in danger until it's already dead. That really pulls at the heart strings."

His goons took steps to the side, widening their reach, their hands still on their weapons. I wanted to move to intercept, but Zelfree kept his grip on my shoulder. The air in the room thickened—no more jovial demeanors.

Bloodlust had a distinct scent.

Calisto smiled. "That's why I always give people an opportunity to surrender. I told your parents I'd let their ship go if they handed over everything I wanted, but they refused... Look what it got them."

The mere mention of her parents shook Illia a bit.

"Here's your chance. You're facing down the barrel of a gun. Give me the cartographer's journal, or I promise you a fate worse than what your dear ol' mammy and pappy got. My men haven't had a proper shore leave in many months, and my manticore has been begging for young flesh. You'll be lucky if the latter gets to you first."

Illia took a deep breath and stood up straight. For some

reason, in the low light of the lamp, in the dim back room of the gambling hall, she looked more like a woman who had seen the worst of what the world had to offer and lived through it.

"I'll never give you this journal," she whispered. "I don't even know why you want it, but I'll make sure it burns."

Calisto huffed. "Tsk. You should've just taken my offer when I asked if you wanted to join my crew." He snapped his fingers. "Fain."

Everything happened so fast that I almost didn't register it correctly. Fain, the wendigo arcanist who had been invisible, appeared behind Illia, his frostbitten hand already in her jacket pocket. He stepped back, the journal in his grasp, a smirk on his face.

Illia whipped around to snatch it away from Fain, but the instant her back was to Calisto, he shot forward, his celerity in a league of its own.

18

THE OCCULT COMPASS

Before I could act, Calisto crossed the room. His manticore magic enhanced his strength and speed beyond anything I could hope to rival, and when he reached Illia, he already had a dagger in hand.

Fain, with black fingers, gripped the cartographer's journal close. Illia reached for it, but then Calisto stabbed her, his blade sinking in through her jacket and straight into her soft organs.

Illia cried out and stumbled forward.

I couldn't help it. I let go of Zelfree's shirt and focused on my magic, allowing the burning of my second-bonding to fuel my rage. The shadows in the corner of the room lashed out with sharp tendrils, breaking furniture, cutting up the bar counter, and smashing the lanterns on the wall.

Zelfree gritted his teeth. "Idiot, I told you not to do anything!"

As if he knew I needed him, Luthair merged with me in an instant. The cold sensation of his dark armor calmed me a bit, but not enough to erase the fury.

With a flash of white and glitter, Illia teleported before the fight could continue.

I caught my breath. It took me half a second to realize what had happened. Although my worst fear had come true —Illia getting hurt—she had managed to escape the danger, just barely.

I, however, still stood in the thick of it.

The darkness in the room confused the four pirates. They glanced around, their pistols, cutlasses, and daggers at the ready. Calisto's glowing arcanist mark didn't provide much visibility, but it did highlight his presence.

"What's goin' on?" Breen shouted.

Calisto turned on his heel, glaring. "A knightmare arcanist. I *hate* knightmare arcanists."

I could still get away. I could slip into the shadows— perhaps out the window, or at least into the hallway by travelling under the door. But the journal remained in the hands of the sea thieves, and I couldn't allow them to have it.

I reached a hand up and willed the shadows to grab the cartographer's journal from Fain's hands. In one swift motion, the dark tendrils wrapped around the book and yanked, taking it from Fain.

"What the?" he spat.

Excellent, Luthair said, his voice in my own head.

Zelfree's arcanist mark shifted from the white hart to that of a knightmare, just like mine. He grabbed one of my shadow gauntlets and then waved his hand at the window. A claw of darkness shattered the glass, startling Fain, who jumped away and pulled a blade.

Calisto ground his teeth. "Don't let them escape!"

Too little, too late.

Zelfree dragged me into the inky depths of the darkness

as we shadow-stepped across the floor, up the wall, over the window sill, and outside—the sensation of moving through the darkness akin to icy waters. I couldn't tell our location once we left the building, as the vertigo scrambled my thoughts. Slipping through the void always confused me, but Zelfree seemed to manage without a problem, like he had long since mastered knightmare magic.

When we emerged, we were in the same alley where we had left Atty and Adelgis, but now it sat empty.

I swayed on my feet, my head spinning from the speed at which we had fled. After a few seconds, I staggered and hit my knee, my body still sore from my magical outburst. Damn my second-bonding.

"Get up," Zelfree growled. "We can't stay here."

The sound of more glass breaking drew my attention. Gasps, shouts, and grumbles from the people of Port Crown echoed down the street. I stood, and Zelfree dragged me over to the edge of the building. With his back against the wall, he glanced around the corner. I leaned out, my armor melting into the evening darkness and keeping me inconspicuous.

Calisto stood on the sidewalk, a ring of broken glass all around him. Had he jumped down from the second story? He appeared uninjured—almost energetic and restless. He held his dagger, Illia's blood still on the blade, and glanced around the crowd.

"S'that Calisto?" a few men muttered, their raucous voices cutting through the other conversations.

"His ship's at port."

"Somethin's up."

"A girl with one eye has stolen something from me," Calisto shouted, commanding enough to silence the others. "I'll give fifty gold leafs to the man who finds her." He twirled his weapon in his hand, drawing everyone's attention to the steel and crimson glistening in the lamplight. "And an extra twenty-five leafs if you find a knightmare arcanist."

An outrageous amount of gold for a simple task. Sure enough, the generous announcement riled the crowd, their eyes wide and their fingers on the hilts of their weapons.

"I want them alive," Calisto continued, smiling. Then he brought the dagger to his nose and inhaled. After a short moment—while people chaotically hustled around him—Calisto turned his intense gaze north, in the opposite direction of the ports.

Zelfree ducked back into the alley. "Dammit. C'mon."

He grabbed my arm and dove at the ground, like someone diving into water. He plunged into the shadows, taking me with him. The second trip wasn't as bad as the first. I had no idea the route he took, but I didn't get dizzy or confused. In the darkness I couldn't breathe; it was as though my body had become as thin as a shadow, prohibiting my lungs from functioning. That panicked me a bit, and I knew that my reaction prevented me from mastering this skill.

We emerged from the shadows in the middle of a second-story hallway, the worn wood and faded brass door handles betraying the building's age. Zelfree and I both gasped for air the moment we came up, but I was the only one to stumble into the wall. A stale scent of potpourri wafted around us. It reminded me of the cheap inns found at every port.

Relax, Luthair said. *The shadows won't harm you.*

"I'm pretty sure suffocating me is a form of harm," I quipped, my voice somehow a mix of mine and his.

Zelfree didn't give us time to chat. He grabbed the front

of my inky armor, opened a nearby door, and shoved me through. Once inside, he slammed the door shut and glanced around the room.

Atty sat on the end of a nearby bed, her phoenix on her lap—the curved feathers of Titania's glorious tail wrapped around Atty's waist. She stared at us, stiff and anxious.

"Where is Adelgis?" Zelfree barked.

She held Titania close. "He stepped outside to—"

"*What*? I gave you both just one instruction!" Zelfree ran his hands through his long hair, his jaw clenched. "By the abyssal hells, it's like herding cats." He threw his arms down, whipped around to the door, and threw it open. "Where'd he go?"

"The market around the corner. He said he'd be right back."

"I'll get him. Nobody is to leave this room!"

Zelfree didn't wait for a reply. He slammed through the door and stormed down the hall. Then I heard nothing. No doubt he had stepped into the shadows.

After a few calming breaths, Luthair melted away, becoming a separate being once again. The break in our connection always rocked me—I hadn't realized how much raw power we had when merged. I felt drained afterward, almost ragged.

Atty got off the bed and walked over, her brow furrowed. "Are you okay? What happened?"

"We need to leave," I said, breathless.

"Did something go wrong?"

"Calisto... He knows we're here."

I staggered to one side and then caught myself. While rubbing at my temple, I hobbled to the window. The denizens of Port Crown rushed down the streets, some grabbing people and ripping off hats or head coverings. Anyone with a missing eye was grabbed and examined. It was a common feature among sailors, though. During ship battles, the cannonballs would smash through a hull and send splinters in every direction. Those splinters had the luck of the abyssal hells. I swear they found eyes more often than any other body part.

Where was Illia? She had teleported away, but now she was in constant danger—a fear I'd had from the beginning. How would we find her before anyone else did?

Titania stretched her radiant wings. "Should I take to the skies?"

"Zelfree said to wait here," I muttered. "Let's actually do what he wants this once."

A moment later, stomping filled the hallway beyond the door. Zelfree slammed his way in with Adelgis close behind. Judging by the disorientated look on Adelgis's face, I suspected he didn't enjoy shadow-stepping either.

"Listen," Zelfree said, his voice hard-edged. "We haven't much time. Manticore arcanists are deft hunters. Calisto is after Illia. I've no doubt in my mind he'll find her before she escapes the island. We need to get to her first."

Adelgis pulled himself from Zelfree's grasp. "W-wait. You didn't let me explain myself. I went listening for thoughts regarding Calisto. I heard something extraordinary from the marketplace. It—"

"Will it help us find Illia?" Zelfree growled.

"Er, no."

"*Then I don't care.* Our one and only goal is to get the others. *Focus.*"

"Why not use the white hart magic?" I asked. "We could slip through the crowds unnoticed."

"I can't." Zelfree glanced at the door and then back to me, his anxious energy infectious. "I can only mimic the sorcery of nearby creatures. The white hart is too far away now." He cracked his knuckles and stared a hole into the floor. "Damn. We'll need to hunt her as well."

In the next instant, Zelfree's arcanist mark shifted from a knightmare to a manticore—a lion with dragon wings and a scorpion tail. I turned my attention to the rest of the room, half-expecting to see Traces nearby in the shape of the grotesque manticore, but I saw nothing.

"Where is your eldrin?" I asked.

"I left her on the edge of the city. I couldn't risk her shapeshifting in the crowds. It'd give us away."

His manticore arcanist mark didn't glow like Calisto's.

Curious.

I didn't have time to inquire about it, but I took note.

"Illia wasn't at the docks, right?" Atty asked. "You would've sensed her there? Is there a place like this inn where she could go to hide?"

I shook my head. Illia had never visited Port Crown before, and as far as I knew, neither had Hexa or Zaxis. How would they know about a safe haven like this?

"Illia hates crowds," I said, thinking aloud. "She'd hide someplace far from here. Probably not even in the city." We had lived our childhood in a graveyard, and even then the corpses were sometimes too many people for Illia's comfort.

"Perfect," Zelfree stated. "That gives us an advantage. Calisto's manticore magic will allow him to sniff out her blood. He'll search every alley Illia teleported to on her way out of town, but we can race straight to the walls." He snapped his fingers. "Atty, when we leave, let your phoenix watch from the sky. Adelgis, if you can, listen for any thoughts that may be *relevant* to what's going on. Volke, I want you to keep your head covered. No one can know you're a knightmare arcanist."

I replied with a curt nod. "Luthair, can you find something for me to wear?"

A piece of the shadows slithered out of the room and into the hallway. He returned a few moments later with a black and white bandana, the cloth folded into the shadows and moving across the floor as though alive. I snatched it up and wrapped it tight over my forehead.

Zelfree motioned to the door. We left as a group, not a word between us.

The patrons of the inn didn't pay us much mind. They gossiped with each other and stayed indoors, no doubt opting to avoid the commotion outside. I didn't blame them. The lowborn pirates would surely do whatever it took to get their 50 leafs. No one wanted to come between a cutthroat and his gold.

When we entered the street, Zelfree kept close to me. Men with torches searched the darkest alleyways, and twice a group approached us. The moment they caught sight of Zelfree's arcanist mark, however, they backed away, their eyes wide. Manticore arcanists had an infamous reputation, after all.

Anxious energy kept me restless. Until we found Illia, all I could think of was what would happen if Calisto managed to surprise her. Anxious, I shoved my hands into my coat pocket and flinched when I realized I had the journal.

Of course. I had ripped it from the clutches of the wendigo arcanist. While merged, I hadn't even thought about where the shadows stashed it—a piece of me must have tucked it away without thought.

Zelfree walked the street at a leisurely pace, and I turned to him with a glare. We wouldn't make it to the walls before Calisto by meandering through the city!

He returned my gaze with a hard glower. "We don't want

to draw attention to ourselves," he growled under his breath. "We can't *run* like the guilty fleeing the scene of a crime." He grabbed my shoulder and pointed me toward a massive carriage. It rolled down the street, drawn by draft horses, heading straight for the walls of the city. "See that? When it passes, jump on the back."

Zelfree motioned for the others and gave them the same instruction.

The carriage carried more than just people—the back acted as a cart for supplies. Barrels and crates were tied down at all angels, preventing anything from falling. It was a carriage for traders. The goods they carried were no doubt samples they were intending to show to the locals.

Zelfree, Atty, Adelgis, and I jumped onto the carriage once it passed. I was surprised by how much room there was. Atty and I could sit on the cart portion, while Zelfree and Adelgis clung to the ropes. The carriage went faster than our walking speed, and people cleared out of the way, allowing us to traveler faster than before without drawing attention.

I remained tense, though. In order to distract myself, I opened the journal to page eighty-four, curious to see what Calisto was willing to kill for.

THE OCCULT COMPASSES OF LIVIA BRITE

For decades I have searched for the three Occult Compasses of Master Arcanist Livia Brite. These artifacts were crafted from the eyes of an all-seeing sphinx, a mystical creature now extinct. To my knowledge, only three compasses ever existed, and two of them have been destroyed. This I can now confirm.

Many thought the third had suffered a similar fate, but in reality it sits in the hold of a sunken ship by the name of the Endless Havoc. The captain reported it stolen so he could take it for himself, only to smash against the rocks near a deserted island.

While I found the Endless Havoc's location, I was unable to reclaim the many lost treasures within. Instead, I have recorded my steps to its location, so that someone may return in the future to secure the last known Occult Compass.

The other page was covered in details, including an approximate latitude and longitude, along with instructions for finding the exact rocks *the Endless Havoc* had crashed against. Although I found it interesting, I had never heard of an Occult Compass, nor had I read anything about Livia Brite.

Adelgis leaned near, reading over my shoulder, his honeyed skin growing paler and paler.

"Is this what Calisto wanted?" he asked, his voice softer than a whisper.

I nodded.

"This is dreadful."

Zelfree turned to us. He opened his mouth, but stopped once he noticed the journal.

"I took it," I said.

He slammed it shut and glared. "Why can't you follow simple instructions? You weren't to do anything!"

"But... Calisto wanted it, so I figured he shouldn't have it."

Zelfree gritted his teeth. "If he had this journal, we could've waited him out—hidden until he got bored and went searching for his treasure. Now he'll *have* to chase us. Do you understand what you've done?"

I wanted to answer, but he shoved the journal back into my hands and then leapt off the back of the cart.

"We're here," Zelfree growled. "But in the future, when I give you an order, make sure you follow it."

He disapproved of what I had done? I had thought he'd be pleased—the villains would walk away with nothing if we managed to escape this accursed port town.

Atty jumped off, and I followed suit. Adelgis stumbled as he dismounted, but then he jogged to my side and grabbed the sleeve of my coat.

"The Occult Compass locates mystical creatures," he said as we squeezed down a narrow walkway, just within sight of the city's walls. "You can attune it to any creature you want, so long as you have something from it. The hair of a rizzel will lead you to more rizzels, or the shadowy blade of a knightmare will lead you to more knightmares."

Calisto wanted to gather mystical creatures?

I knew pirates sometimes sold creatures they had kidnapped. They could make a small profit from such endeavors, but oftentimes mystical creatures weren't sitting defenseless on a beach somewhere. They were found around breeding grounds near special feeding areas—like the charberry tree on the Isle of Ruma—and those places almost always had a city or a powerful arcanist, guarding it.

What use would it be to find mystical creatures if they were protected?

Zelfree took my upper arm and pushed me forward. "Here's the wall. Both of you keep quiet. Unless this conversation will help us leave Port Crown, I don't want to hear it."

Adelgis said nothing, his gaze vacant as he turned it to the tall stone structure in front of us.

Fog from the ghostwood forest wafted over the wall, and I knew right away that Illia would want to hide herself in the dense mist beyond the city. It would provide a natural cover, and perhaps she knew of a place to tie a boat.

Zelfree approached the guards and greeted them with a quick jut of his chin. They nodded in return and allowed us to leave. They probably hadn't yet heard of the bounty on Illia's head. Or the extra reward for finding a knightmare arcanist. Or else they might have checked us, if only to cash in on the reward themselves.

For once, luck seemed to be on my side.

"There you are," a creature croaked, its voice a rasp that grated at my ears. "I found you."

I craned my head back and stared at the top of the wall. There, between the battlements and merlons, sat a half-lizard, half-bird—a snallygaster. It was larger than I expected, perhaps the size of a goat or ram, and it was stocky with fat. Its body had the overall appearance and low stance of an iguana, and its wings had been stolen from a raven.

The snallygaster lashed it tongue about. "You won't escape the *Third Abyss*."

And then it screeched.

Loud. Painful.

An alert to our location.

19

THE GHOSTWOODS

Atty held up her hand. "Begone, fiend."

A stream of brilliant fire emanated from her palm and washed over the wall of the city. The snallygaster hissed and rolled off the wall, straight into the city. A moment later, it flew upward, its wings working hard to keep its gluttonous body in the air. A trail of smoke wafted from its singed tail.

Zelfree ran a hand through his hair. "Dammit." He turned his attention to the off-white and gray trees all around us. Then he inhaled deep. "Go. Into the woods."

"Which way?" I asked.

He pointed. "There. She's bleeding. I can smell it."

Manticore magic allowed him to detect blood from so far away? They were man-eaters. I shouldn't have been surprised.

I glanced back at the city. "What about Calisto?"

"The fog won't slow him. We need to hurry."

Atty dashed past the tree line and into the grim mist that blanketed the area. She held up a hand and evoked a torch-like flame, creating a beacon for us to follow. The fog didn't want to cooperate, though. Normal fog would've burned and evaporated, but the fell haze resisted. The longer we pushed forward into the woods, the thicker the gloom became.

While chasing after the others, I tripped on a root and slammed into the trunk of a twisted tree. The bark had knots that looked like screaming faces, each with open mouths that spewed fog at a steady rate. The sight rocked me. I jumped back, my hands shaking, and I quickened my step until I reached the others.

Insects swooped down from the tree branches in swarms. I batted them away, but they kept aiming for my face, distracting me as I struggled to keep up. Even Atty seemed to have trouble. She slowed and swished the torch-fire around her head.

"What are these?" she asked.

It was hard to get a good look at them, what with the fog and their fingernail size. They appeared to be red mosquitos, but their proboscis stretched longer than any I had ever seen.

Adelgis undid his coat and threw it over his head. "They're wisp bugs. If given enough time, they drink the fluid from your eyes and then try to burrow into your brain."

The unsettling information helped no one, and even stilled Atty in her tracks. Her hands trembled, and before I could say anything, she waved her free hand around in a half-arc, filling the ghostwoods with a rush of fire.

"*Stop*," Zelfree hissed.

She ceased her magic a moment later, having accomplished her goal—the wisp bugs had burned to a crisp. The few that survived the inferno buzzed back to the trees, no doubt to some sort of horrid nest made of nightmare fuel. Adelgis probably knew all about their lifecycle, but I didn't want the disturbing information rattling around in my thoughts.

After a deep breath, we resumed our trek. Zelfree maintained the lead, but the dense forest soon prevented us from outright running. More than once, a tree would appear from the fog, blocking our path. Zelfree glanced over his shoulder every few seconds, his expression growing dire.

Then he stopped. "Keep going in this direction," he commanded. "I'll catch up with you."

I shook my head. "But—"

"It's okay. I'll delay Calisto."

Zelfree took Atty by the shoulder and pointed into the fog. She nodded, as though they had a silent conversation between them. Then Zelfree broke away from the group and jogged back the way we had come.

He had manticore magic. He wasn't defenseless.

But still. My growing anxiety squeezed at my chest, making it difficult to breathe.

"We should keep going," Atty whispered.

Adelgis, whose coat remained over his head, nodded.

We stuck close together. Our heavy breathing mixed with the evening sounds, creating the ambiance of a dreadful dream. I swear I heard hisses from the roots and growls from the branches. Unable to see anything, my imagination filled all the blanks in the worst way possible.

"Ah!"

I jerked my attention to Atty, but it was too late. My foot didn't connect with the ground. I fell forward and hit a steep slope in a tumble. Twigs and underbrush clawed at my skin, but halfway down I managed to remember something Zelfree had taught me. *Shadows don't fall.*

I slipped into the darkness and then reemerged at the base of the hill a moment later. My body tingled from a slight pain, like my limbs had fallen asleep. Perhaps I had gotten better at mastering my second-bonded magic, or perhaps the anxiety of the situation numbed me to everything else. I couldn't tell.

Atty and Adelgis didn't fare as well as I did, however. I heard their grunts as they slid into the trunk of a ghostwood tree. I jogged over, my heart rate higher than it had been seconds earlier. Where were we? Was this the right way?

We couldn't afford to get lost.

I helped Atty to her feet, my hands unsteady. "Are you okay?"

"Y-yes," she said as she brushed the black and gray leaves off Zelfree's coat. "Are you?"

"I'm fine."

I reached down to help Adelgis, but he sucked in air through his teeth and jerked away. When I knelt to get closer, he placed an arm around his side.

"I'm hurt," he said. With a gentle touch, he probed along his ribcage. "There's pain, but I think I'll be fine. I need... a few minutes."

"We don't have a few minutes." Then I motioned to Atty. "Can't you heal him faster? With your phoenix magic?"

She bit her lip, her eyes wide. "I can't."

"What do you mean?"

"I mean... I've never been able to heal people." She brushed her disheveled blonde hair behind her ears. "I've tried. It just... doesn't come to me."

"You can't use healing magic *at all*?"

Atty shook her head.

I stood, my body chill and stiff. Wind rustled the leaves and soared across the knotholes, creating an unnatural howl. I couldn't detect the sounds of animals. I couldn't detect much of anything, really. It worried me, because I knew we weren't alone in these ghostwoods.

Fighting to think of a plan, I walked around the nearest tree, my gaze on my boots. I almost couldn't see the ground I stood on, but with enough concentration, I managed to detect the rocks and detritus. Then I stepped on something, and my foot sunk into the ground, a soft squish instead of the usual crunch of dead leaves. With my breath held, I knelt, panicked by the blood soaking the dirt.

Zelfree had said Illia was bleeding.

I got up and ran a short distance forward. Sure enough, about twenty feet away, I found another splattering of crimson on the forest floor.

She was teleporting toward her point of safety. If we kept going in this direction, perhaps we could catch up to her before anyone else.

"Luthair," I said. "Can you carry Adelgis?"

"Yes, my arcanist."

"Then let's get him and continue."

Forming from the darkness, Luthair stepped out of the shadows as a suit of armor. He clinked as he rushed to Adelgis, but the noise wasn't loud and didn't echo through the woods. With careful movements, Luthair scooped Adelgis into his arms and held him close to his breastplate.

Two dots of light came into view seconds before they soared overhead. It wasn't until they were inches from me that I recognized Titania and Forsythe—their phoenix wings ablaze as they shot between the trees. They disappeared into the fog, their speed concerning.

A screech heralded the arrival of their pursuer. The snallygaster emerged from the fog at a slower, bumbling pace, his black wings blending with the surroundings. The beast swooped close to me, his curved claws outstretched. I ducked and avoided the attack, but the snallygaster circled around one of the ghostwood trees. He landed with a heavy slam of his stumpy legs, only a few feet away. Then he walked forward, his spiky jowls and dewlap swaying with each step.

Atty moved forward. "How dare you chase my eldrin!"

Her fire flooded the woods in a wide burst. The snallygaster brought his wings up to shield his body, but otherwise didn't avoid the attack. Once the flame had dissipated, it was apparent the mystical creature had been singed, but not charred.

"Wretch," the snallygaster hissed.

His neck bulged, like a frog about to croak. A second later, it seemed as though he had puked up his intestines—a thick ball of undulating flesh laid out in front of him, the mucus of his insides sticking to the twigs and dirt. A thick tongue-like limb was still attached to the snallygaster, connecting the disgusting fleshball and its creator. Then the intestines untangled themselves at a frightening speed, revealing whip-like tentacles that lashed outward.

One tentacle grabbed Atty by the ankle, another wrapped around my left forearm, and one slithered into a nearby burrow and ripped out a rodent, as though the creature's insides were simply attracted to life, rather than acting with a directed purpose. The squealing rat was yanked into the snallygaster's mouth before I even had a chance to act.

Luthair leapt away, Adelgis still in his black-armor arms. He nimbly avoided the snallygaster's tentacles with expert footwork.

The tentacles pulled me and Atty. She fell backward and hit the ground on her hip as the fiend dragged her toward his mouth. I stumbled forward, but managed to remain standing, though I couldn't rip my arm from his slimy grasp.

Atty created another torrent of blazing fire, this time hot enough that sweat poured from my armpits and forehead. The snallygaster protected himself again, his wings seemingly unharmed by heat. Although flames washed over his tentacles, the slime kept them from burning.

"Atty, wait!"

While I had found it difficult to focus earlier, the stress of the situation tightened my concentration. I gritted my teeth and evoked my terrors—a sense of dread that filled the area with nightmarish visions for everyone but me.

The snallygaster screamed and retreated, his eyes wide.

Atty covered her ears and closed her eyes, and the moment the monster let go of her leg, she pulled it close to her body.

Without letting go of Adelgis, Luthair unsheathed his sword and threw it to the ground. It "fell" into the shadows, and with only a gut feeling this would work, I reached for my own shadow and withdrew the blade from the darkness.

I slashed through the thin tentacle holding my arm and took a step backward. The bit of flesh writhed on its own, twisting on the woodland floor. I stumbled, shaken from my own magic use.

"Do it now," I shouted.

Still affected by my terrors, Atty hesitated. For a split second, I worried she wouldn't be able to react, but she recovered faster than the snallygaster and unleashed a pyre of destructive magic. The creature couldn't bring his wings up in time. The flame seared the snallygaster's iguana-like face, melting his scales and charring his eyes.

With a horrid scream that chilled the adrenaline in my blood, the monster leapt into the canopy, busting through branches and heading upward, despite the many obstacles.

His intestines trailed behind him like the tail of a disgusting kite.

"Good teamwork," Atty said as she offered me a weak smile.

I nodded and half-laughed. "We should stick close together. I'll let you know beforehand when I'm going to use my terrors."

"O-okay."

Titania and Forsythe flew back a moment later, their warm glow a welcome sight.

"This way," Forsythe said as he swooped around us. "My arcanist and the others are waiting."

We followed as a tight group: Luthair in the middle, Atty on point, while I followed from afar, my sword in hand. I feared the snallygaster would burst through the branches above at any moment, and I tripped more than once as I kept my gaze upward. Luthair's sword was light, and didn't slow me, and I felt much safer knowing I had it close.

The clinking of shadow armor and my heavy breathing, rattled in my eardrums. We must've run for a few solid minutes, and although I still had fight-or-flight energy from the battle with the snallygaster, I could feel it waning.

Forsythe and Titania curved around a large tree—one so gigantic it could be hollowed out to make a two-bedroom house. Hundreds of knot-faces twisted together up the side, their mouths open and spewing mist like someone with the flu spews their lunch.

We made our way around and came to a thinning section of the ghostwoods littered with giant rocks. I caught my breath the moment I spotted Zaxis, Hexa, and Illia. They sat on top of a larger boulder, one with a flat surface and elevated above the ground.

"Illia," I said, breathless.

I dropped the sword into the shadows and ran to the rock. The three of them glanced over, their expressions a mix of shock and confusion. I pulled myself up, finding the stone surprisingly smooth, and got to my feet once I reached the top.

Blood dappled the boulder. Illia had removed her coat, revealing her slashed shirt and her injury underneath. Although I had feared the worst, the wound wasn't deep. It didn't even look open.

Zaxis stepped around Illia, his arms crossed. "What're you doing? How did you even get here? And find us?"

I pushed him aside—he barked a quick *hey*, but I ignored him. With stiff movements, I approached Illia, ready to apologize and tell her everything I had considered over the last week without her.

Hexa moved in front of me and shoved my shoulder, nearly knocking me off the rock. Her hydra slithered between her legs and flashed his fangs.

"This doesn't involve you," Hexa said, sterner and more serious than I had ever seen her. "Why'd you even come, huh? To drag Illia back?"

"I—"

"We don't have time for childish arguments," Atty said from the ground. "Please, focus. We must leave the woods immediately."

Hexa shot her a glare.

"Zelfree hasn't returned, the snallygaster managed to escape, and I fear Calisto may be here at any moment."

20

WATER CAVE

"You led Calisto to us?" Zaxis said, incredulous. "Did you even stop to think that we have our own plan for escape? We don't need you rushing in with the damn pirates! That's a whole new level of incompetence."

Adelgis shook his head. "What plan? We can't outrun him. Even this conversation is costing us."

"We'll be fine, no thanks to you."

I ignored the conversation, uninterested in their bickering.

Illia wouldn't look at me, even when I kept my attention on her. She never glanced over, her gaze was set in the opposite direction—intentionally avoiding eye contact with me. When I tried to approach her a second time, Hexa shoved me again. This time it sent fire through my blood, and my first thought was to throw her from the rock.

She must've sensed my shift in attitude because she tensed and met my anger with a glower.

Zaxis's voice pierced through my agitation. "We're not leaving through the woods. We have a boat."

"We're nowhere near the docks," Adelgis said with a scoff. "Which one of us is the incompetent one now, huh?"

"Don't get smart with me! You idiots were the ones who brought Calisto to us. We have everything under control here."

"A manticore can track blood! *We* weren't the reason Illia messed up—you all still would've been in this situation had we been here or not."

Zaxis glared. "Tsk. Whatever. Shut up and follow us to the skiff."

The two phoenixes circled and then flew off into the fog.

While I wanted to help Illia, both Zaxis and Hexa were by her side to offer her an arm. She held onto Zaxis, her injury mostly healed, and together they leapt down from the boulder. Hexa followed close by, her hydra hustling to keep up.

I jumped down and exhaled, my frustrations building with each second.

Adelgis, still in Luthair's armored arms, furrowed his brow. "Volke?"

"What?" I snapped.

"I think I can walk on my own now."

I nodded to Luthair, and he set Adelgis down with a gentle motion.

With everyone together, we headed away from the woods. Despite the sparsity of ghostwood trees, the mist remained thick. Illia, Zaxis, and Hexa seemed to know where they were heading, though, and they pressed forward at a confident speed, weaving around large rocks and rotting stumps.

A sudden chill washed over the area, and frost formed over the blades of grass. Everyone stopped and glanced around, but visibility was limited to a few feet in every direction.

I gritted my teeth. "Wendigo magic." I motioned for them to continue. "I'll handle this."

Luthair melted into a shadow and then formed back up around me, the sleek sensation of his armor a welcome change from the chill of the fog. Once solidified, I hefted the sword and glanced over my shoulder. Everyone took off and left me—except Adelgis. He kept himself hidden behind a boulder, his attention set on the gray mist.

"Leave," I said, my voice a frightening mix of mine and Luthair's.

"You said it was a wendigo, right? I can help."

We didn't have time to argue. Ice crept over the rocks and clung to the air, thickening the already dense fog. I widened my stance, ready for the creator or his arcanist to come this way. They had to be chasing us, and I was the only one who could afford to get bitten in a fight. I had to be the one to stop them.

The grass crunched with movement, even though I saw nothing. Was it both the arcanist and his eldrin? Just one? I couldn't tell.

It drew closer, the invisible creature rushing forward at an ever-increasing speed. When I swung my sword, the blade whiffed through the air and connected with the ground. I had expected to hit something, and the shock of missing threw me off-balance.

While still invisible, the wendigo crunched his jaws down on my right forearm. My shadow plate protected me from the fangs, but thick frost spread over my gauntlet, sticking in the knuckles and grooves of the fingers.

I focused my magic, willing the shadows to condense and become solid. The pain in my chest was sharp, and I inhaled deeply. I wanted to cut the beast with the darkness, but it released my arm and danced away.

My breath now visible, I turned and swung again—this time slower. I didn't connect, and the wendigo bit at my ankle. His icy rime seeped past the greaves protecting my shin and burned every inch of skin it made contact with.

I lifted a hand and evoked my terrors, desperate to halt the invisible beast's movements. The wendigo released my ankle and whined, but it never became visible. I slashed with my blade and hit nothing. Even if it was stunned and shaking from the nightmare visions I had given it, that didn't matter if I couldn't connect.

Without warning, a flash of light illuminated the area. The shine stung my eyes and burned portions of my armor. I felt the sear of the shadow-plate like it was my own flesh and instinctually brought the cape around to shield me from the radiance.

Adelgis had his hand up; the light emanated from his palm. His magic cut through the fog, clearing a small area around us. It also broke the wendigo's invisibility—shattering the magic that kept it hidden from my sight.

The emaciated wolf stood a foot away from me, his antlers laced with ice and his skull-face devoid of emotion. I loathed the wendigo's deathly visage. It reminded me of decay and starvation.

Although frost coated two of my limbs, I lunged forward with a heavy overhand swing. The wendigo, shaken by my terrors, attempted to step aside, but I caught the fiend in the withers, slicing flesh up to his shoulder blade.

The wendigo fell backwards, his teeth bared and his hackles raised. He emitted a low rumble of a growl that could shake the dead. I struggled to hold my sword, my right hand so numb I no longer had any feeling in my fingers—it was as if the cold continued to spread, its temperature plummeting with each passing second.

With a shimmer of magic, the wendigo disappeared from sight, melting into thin air as invisibility wrapped around his body.

Adelgis flashed his light a second time, dispelling the obfuscation. The shine burned my armor again, and I grimaced away.

He doesn't mean to harm us, Luthair spoke to my thoughts. *His sorcery is just meant to combat anything that obscures sight —including shadows.*

But the accumulation of damage, pain, and exhaustion was catching up with me. The wendigo came in for another attack, fully visible. I tried to dodge, but nothing moved right. My body didn't respond fast enough, and the beast bit down on my iced gauntlet, adding more magic to my already frozen forearm.

I couldn't shake it off, and when I brought my sword up and around, I didn't have the strength to follow through. My strikes were weak and growing worse by the moment. If I could just focus... I could use the shadows to grab the wendigo... but even that seemed impossible.

Someone emerged from the fog and rushed toward me. I braced for impact, fearing one of the pirates.

To my shock, Master Zelfree grabbed the wendigo by the back of the neck and ripped him from my arm. His strength shocked me—but then I remembered his manticore magic. Zelfree effortlessly threw the wendigo against one of the rocks. The beast yowled and collapsed to the ground, its antlers cracked.

Zelfree turned to face it, but the wendigo scrambled to its feet and ran from the fogless clearing, its tail between its legs.

"Master Zelfree," I said, the gruff tint of my mixed voice echoing between the rocks.

"What're you two doing?" He grabbed my upper arm and shoved me forward. "I saw that light from a mile away! We don't have time for this."

"It was magic."

"It doesn't matter! Everyone will know where you are. C'mon. We have to hurry."

I half-ran, half-jogged, my ankle still coated in the wendigo's ice. Zelfree pushed Adelgis along, herding him close to us as we headed in the direction of the others. To my relief, Zelfree didn't appear injured. Had he delayed Calisto? I found myself checking behind us more often than was healthy, my thoughts plagued with dread.

It didn't take us long to reach Zaxis, Hexa, Atty, and Illia, along with their eldrin. They stood by a collection of rocks and perked up the moment we got close.

I stumbled as I neared the group, my leg stiff and heavy.

Atty rushed to my side. "Volke, are you okay?" She knelt and held her palm an inch above the frost. With a controlled wave of her phoenix fire, she melted a significant portion, restoring feeling to my leg.

"Thank you," I said.

"Let me see your arm."

While she helped me, I noticed Illia staring. When we met each other's gaze, she turned away. Then she placed a hand on Hexa and used her magic. A flash of white and sparkles later, Hexa was gone.

Illia had teleported Hexa without travelling along with her.

It took me a moment to grasp the concept—I thought Illia had to travel with the person teleporting. Perhaps she had improved her skills.

Then Illia did the same with Zaxis.

Then the hydra and the two phoenixes.

Zelfree turned his attention to our surroundings. "Where did you send them?"

"There's a cave under these rocks," Illia said. "That's where we hid our skiff. You can take the narrow waterway in the cave all the way out to the ocean."

"Is that right?" Zelfree's arcanist mark twisted and shifted until he had a rizzel wrapped around his seven-pointed star. "You all are more clever than I thought you were."

Traces teleported to Zelfree's shoulder as a false rizzel, her white and silver fur shimmery, even in the fog. She nuzzled the base of his neck. "Those pirates won't be busy forever."

"Let's go then."

Once Atty finished melting the ice from my arm, Luthair detached himself from me. I swayed on my feet, but Atty held my shoulder and steadied me.

"You need to be careful," she whispered. "You look wretched."

I didn't know whether to laugh or sigh. "Sorry. I'm—"

"We don't have time for this," Zelfree growled. He placed his hand on Atty's back and teleported her away. Then he yanked my arm and brought me close. "Calisto is after you and Illia *specifically*. If he catches sight of you, don't engage him. Just run. You have shadow-stepping powers. You can slip away. Understand?"

"Y-yes."

"Good."

Magic enveloped me, and for a brief moment, it felt as though I could reject its pull—which meant I could shrug it off and remain here. I didn't, of course; instead I trusted Zelfree to send me to the right location.

Teleportation wasn't like my shadow-stepping. When I travelled through the darkness, I couldn't really see or breathe—I moved with some sort of kinetic sight that didn't fully make sense to me, no doubt because of my amateurish understanding of magic. Teleporting, on the other hand, felt like someone had pushed me off the side of a cliff. I jerked and caught myself—similar to waking from a dream where I thought I had fallen—and found myself in an entirely new location.

We were underground—that much I knew instantly.

Glowstones had been placed on a few nearby rocks, but I didn't need them. I stood in a narrow cave, the sound of water trickling on rocks echoing all around me. A small stream led toward the coast, a rickety skiff floating on its waters. The boat had been tied to a stalagmite to keep it from drifting out of the cave.

The red and black hue of the rocks glittered under the blue illumination of the glowstones, giving the area a purple aura of magic.

Nicholin sat on the bow of the skiff, his ears perked. "Volke? Is that you?" He blinked out of existence and appeared on my shoulder a second later, a purr rumbling in his tiny body.

"Nicholin? What're you doing here? Why haven't you been with Illia?"

"She said rizzels act like lures for other creatures! I had to stay hidden." He hugged my neck, and I could feel him smile as he pressed his face against my cheek. "You came to help us! I knew you would. Why do you have to be so dumb and stubborn sometimes?"

"He didn't come to help," Hexa said, glaring. "He brought Zelfree here to take her back."

Nicholin's tail puffed to twice its normal size. He flattened his ears and then teleported off me. When he reappeared, his back was turned and his little front legs crossed. "Hmph! Of all the things. How disappointing."

It hurt to see him reject me so thoroughly, but I didn't know what to say.

Illia and Zelfree had yet to teleport into the cave.

"Shouldn't we be hurrying?" Adelgis asked. He rubbed his arms and shivered. "Won't Calisto and the others be here any moment?"

Zaxis waved away the comment. "They can't get in the cave. The entrance is far from here, and there's a good twenty feet of rock between us and them. As far as they're concerned, we up and disappeared into the fog."

"I see." Adelgis let out a long exhale. "Thank the stars."

I gave our surroundings a second glance. Stalagmites and stalactites marked the ground and ceiling with teeth-like formations, the narrow river widening between them. Other than the glowstones, we had zero light, which meant we were deep in the cave and far from any entrance. Even the air seemed thin, like we could pass out if we weren't careful. The pirates would not find us here.

"Help me gather these rocks," Zaxis said. "We should still make our way to the ship."

As he and Adelgis gathered the glowstones, Zelfree and Illia appeared together with a flash and light sparkle. I wanted to approach them, but their stony expressions stopped me cold. Neither spoke as they helped untie the skiff.

Apparently Hexa, Zaxis, and Illia had bedrolls and a satchel of food, but the skiff could not accommodate seven people *and* their supplies. They left everything on the stone shore of the cave.

Illia got into the dinky boat. There were two wooden plank seats, one at each end, and she opted to sit near the bow. The skiff rocked with her weight. Nicholin leapt into her arms. Zelfree got in afterward and sat at the back, balancing the skiff enough for everyone to cram on.

"Are we sure this is safe?" Adelgis asked.

Zaxis pushed him aside and huffed. "The water is less than five feet deep. Even if the damn boat caught fire, we'd be fine. Stop acting like an infant."

Zaxis got onto the skiff and sat on the same bench as Illia. The seats weren't built for multiple people, so they squished together, but she didn't seem to mind. Zaxis wrapped his arm around her and brought her even closer.

Then Hexa walked past Adelgis and stepped into the boat. She, too, went for the bench at the bow and sat on the other side of Illia, squeezing in. Although jam-packed, none of them complained.

Raisen hissed as he dragged his fat hydra body up into the boat. The phoenixes perched themselves on the side— one on the port, one on the starboard. Luckily for all of us, Luthair could remain in the shadows and Felicity could remain incorporeal. Traces returned to her bangle form and wrapped herself around Zelfree's wrist.

The skiff rocked more and more, but after a few minutes it settled again.

"Would you mind assisting me, Volke?" Atty asked, her fingers laced together as she held her hands in front of her.

I held out my hand and helped her into the boat. She took a seat on the back bench next to Zelfree, but he stood up afterward and stepped behind the seat, balancing himself at the end of the boat.

I got in, and Atty scooted over to allow me room. I sat on the bench, her legs pressed against mine. She smiled and leaned onto my arm to allow for more room. Adelgis got onto the skiff a moment later and sat on my other side, pushing me into Atty. While I thought our proximity was a concern, she made no indication of discomfort or worry. It distracted me longer than it should have—my mind was torn in several directions when I imagined what the others thought of our tight-knit seating arrangement.

Atty glanced up and met my gaze, her blue eyes quite vibrant, even in the gloom of the cave. She offered a tepid smile, and I forced one of my own, if only to be polite. My whole body ached, and her weight exacerbated the problem. But I would never complain.

The glowstones had settled at the bottom of the skiff, clumping on either side of Raisen. The illumination cast a dim bubble of light around the boat, giving us visibility only for a few feet ahead.

The shallow stream wasn't much of a waterway. Several times the wood of the skiff scraped along the bottom, the rocks threatening to tear a hole in our vessel.

"A ship is waiting for us at the mouth of the cave," Zaxis said. "It's our getaway vessel."

Adelgis shivered. "So, uh, what... happened? One minute we were searching for Illia, and the next we're fleeing from town."

For a long moment, no one answered.

"Illia was attacked by the pirates," Zelfree finally said, terse.

"And she didn't manage to kill Calisto?"

Silence settled over the group.

What were we supposed to say to that? I was certain it bothered Illia. Her whole plan had been ruined, and now the enemy would know exactly what she was after. She no longer had her poison or the element of surprise.

"Calisto deserves everything coming his way," Zaxis said in a low tone. "Even if we didn't get him now... he needs to die."

Hexa nodded along with those words. "That's right. He's terrorized countless people, and Illia deserves to—"

"Enough," Zelfree barked. His voice echoed down the cave for an extended period of time. Once the noise died down, he shook his head. "We aren't going to talk about this until we reach your *getaway ship*, do I make myself clear?"

The others became quiet.

Our skiff drifted at a slow pace. More than once we needed to guide it by pushing off the rocks. The lack of conversation didn't help me relax. My muscles remained stiff and any slight noise—even Nicholin sneezing—got me flinching.

"Why can't we speak?" Adelgis asked, his teeth chattering. "I still haven't told you about what they were selling at the markets."

Zelfree snapped his fingers. "We aren't safe yet. Not until we leave this forsaken island long behind. I don't want any arguments, or scheming, or plotting, or discussions—we're going to focus on staying together and making it out of here, *in that order*."

"But..."

When Zelfree shot Adelgis a glare, we all returned to a state of awkward silence.

Atty turned to me and shrugged. I didn't know what she meant by it, but a moment later she rested her head on my shoulder. I tried not to think about it, but my mind wouldn't cooperate. Neither would my body. I grew hot and rigid, trying to act as though I didn't notice her casual comfort with me.

The ride out of the cave seemed to last three lifetimes. I took shallow breaths the entire ride and focused my attention on the blue light cast on the ceiling from our glowstones.

After what felt like an excruciating length of time, the first rays of a new day drifted into the cave, guiding us straight to the entrance. Far beyond the rocks, and away from shore, was a ship stationed on the waves of the ocean. Zaxis, Hexa, and Illia had planned the perfect getaway after their scheme to kill Calisto.

It was a shame the whole endeavor had ended as it did.

21

HEADING NORTH

Our getaway ship, a two-mast galleon, was called the *Seawolf*.

While the sun rose from the horizon, we boarded the *Seawolf* and thanked the captain and her crew. Zaxis had paid them to wait, and the sailors had even cleared a cabin for us. They outfitted the room with sleeping hammocks, a common practice for smaller ships that were tossed around by the waves. The free-hanging hammocks rocked with the current, unlike cots, which were so stiff that they would throw a sailor out of bed if the waters got rough enough.

Zelfree ordered us to the ship's galley to get food. I hadn't eaten for the last day, but I didn't feel hungry. My attention remained on Illia, and when Zelfree took her from the group, my anxiety came back in full force. Somehow, despite being close to her for the last few hours, I hadn't managed to say a thing to her.

I needed to fix that.

Under the pretense of needing to use the head—the toilet area on most sailing vessels—I skulked through the shadows, using my magic to bypass any obstacles on my trek to see Illia. She and Zelfree had gone to our collective quarters and shut the door tightly behind them. When I approached, I lifted my hand to knock, but stopped before I connected with the wood, stilled by Zelfree's hard-edged words.

"What you did was foolhardy. I've known drunkards with better decision making abilities."

"You don't understand," Illia said.

"I know better than you realize! Volke told us what the man did to you, and I've had my fair share of personal encounters with dastards like Calisto. Your actions are still inexcusable."

When Illia replied, her voice was louder and more defiant than I had heard in years. "I read all about the hero arcanists of the Frith Guild. They would've done something!"

The moment of silence between them made me realize I wasn't breathing. I took in a shallow breath and stared at my boots. Luthair shifted in the shadows and I could feel his disapproval like the breeze from the ocean.

I didn't care. I couldn't bring myself to leave.

"Give me your guild pendant," Zelfree said.

I almost couldn't believe it. He... wanted to remove Illia from the Frith Guild?

"I—" Illia took in a ragged breath. "You can't do that."

"I'm your master. At any time I feel like you're unsuited for the guild, I can remove you from it."

"Because I tried to kill one of the worst pirates of all time? *That's* why you want me to leave?"

Zelfree—at least, I think it was him—slammed his hand on the bulkhead of the ship. "Don't you dare delude yourself into thinking your actions were noble." The ice of his words hit me hard, and I wasn't even the one he was chastising. "You stole from an apothecary's workshop, endangered your fellow apprentices, and angered a crew of deranged lunatics *all for your own personal vendetta*. This wasn't about anyone other than yourself."

Illia took a deep breath. "I'm... an arcanist. I can do this if I want. If I had succeeded, you wouldn't have been upset."

"Again, you're proving to me more and more that you don't understand." He growled out a curse—something I couldn't catch. "If you want to gallivant across the world fighting pirates who wronged you, then you don't need a guild. Nothing was stopping you from living out all your revenge fantasies the moment you became an arcanist."

Illia said nothing.

"But when you joined the Frith Guild, you accepted the mantle of a protector—someone who puts the needs of others before their own. Someone who puts aside their own pain and suffering so they can provide their strength to people who need it more, even if it means the ultimate sacrifice."

His words reminded me of Gravekeeper William. Although William had never become an arcanist, he had served as an officer in the Queen's Navy. He said he did it to help the world in the best way he knew.

"Why did you join the Frith Guild?" Zelfree asked.

Illia took in another strained breath. "I... admire the guild."

"No, you don't. I watched you when you applied. I've seen you every day since you joined. You came to the Frith Guild because *Volke* did. If he had gone someplace else, you would've gone there too."

She didn't deny his claims.

"If you can't even be honest with yourself, you'll never

understand why you're not suited to be here. The hero arcanists in all those tales didn't endanger everyone around them for vengeance. They rose to face the darkness because they had accepted that burden. They didn't use their strength for personal goals—they gave it to the guild. That's what it means to be part of a group with aspirations higher than personal gain. What it means to be a soldier. Or an officer. Or a knight."

Again, Illia offered no response.

Zelfree's tone softened. "Gregory Ruma and I had been friends. Do you think I wanted to kill him? But I... had to put that aside to do what was necessary. Now, give me your pendant. If you still want to be in the Frith Guild when we get back, you can take it up with the guildmaster."

They exchanged no other words. I waited, straining my ears, hoping Zelfree would change his mind. A second later, he threw open the door and stepped out, almost colliding with me.

I flinched back, and we exchanged glances. He didn't comment on my spying. Instead, he continued out to the deck of the *Seawolf* with a cold expression that couldn't hide the exhaustion he exuded.

Tense and awkward, I hovered around the doorframe for a moment, well aware Illia knew of my presence. Should I speak with her? The right words weren't coming. How could I ever make any of this right?

If she couldn't be part of the Frith Guild, I wouldn't be either, of that much I was certain. I'd never abandon her again.

Determined to tell her just that, I lifted my gaze. She stood near the porthole, her whole body leaning heavy on the bulkhead, her back to me. Nicholin scurried across the floor until he reached my feet. I hadn't realized he had been in the room.

Then he motioned me away and grabbed the underside of the door in order to close it. I didn't interfere. If Illia had told him she wanted privacy, I would respect her wishes. I shouldn't have been eavesdropping in the first place.

Curse the abyssal hells! What was I even doing? Somehow I had failed her at every turn. I should've been there for her. I should've said something to Zelfree. I should've—

Nicholin stared up at me, his blue eyes big. "Illia wants to be left alone, but I want to be held." He stood on his back legs and held up his paws.

Although he could easily teleport to my shoulder, I knelt and scooped him up. Nicholin buried himself in my arms and curled into a tight ball. I stroked his plush fur, unsure of what he wanted. After a short time, he relaxed and sighed into my coat.

I turned and walked back out onto the deck. The morning sun created an azure sky worthy of epic paintings, but I couldn't enjoy it.

"Volke! There you are."

Adelgis made his way over to me, his long hair untied and caught by the ocean winds. He didn't even bother taming it; he just positioned himself so that I blocked the breeze.

"Do you have the cartographer's journal?" he asked.

It took me a moment to register his words. I reached into my coat pocket, unsure if I still had the book. Luckily, it was there. I pulled it out and handed to Adelgis, balancing Nicholin on my other arm.

"Oh, thank the stars you didn't lose it." He took the

journal and then motioned toward the stern of the ship. "You should come with me. I think you'll want to hear this."

Together we made our way back to the galley. The tiny room had two tables nailed to the floorboards, four long benches, and a cooking station with a large iron pot. Crates of salted pork and ship biscuits were tethered to the walls.

Zaxis, Hexa, and Atty sat at one of the tables, their expressions neutral.

"We'll arrive at the Isle of Gott before sundown," Zelfree said.

"What?" Hexa asked.

Zelfree gave Zaxis and Hexa a glare and they perked up.

"I'll need to have a talk with both of you before we get back. I understand you were helping Illia, but your actions were still reckless beyond reason."

They exchanged a quick glance, but didn't reply.

"I don't think we should go to the Isle of Gott," Adelgis said as he stepped forward, the journal held tight in his hands.

Zelfree shook his head. "It's the closest port. We can get a faster ship there."

"But that's the place Calisto will look for us first."

"I suspect he thinks we're still on the island, near Port Crown. Additionally, I doubt he wants to find Illia so bad he'll charge off after a group of arcanists. It's risky, even for him. And trust me, I know him pretty well."

"He'll come for this." Adelgis held up the journal. "So I think we should try to outsmart him and head somewhere else."

Zaxis leaned forward on the table. "Oh, yeah. You were jabbering on about the journal earlier. Illia said Calisto wanted it, but I never knew why."

"It's because of this Occult Compass." Adelgis flipped

the pages until he got to the entry. "See here? It locates mystical creatures. If you place a small part of a creature onto it, the arrow points you to the closet one."

"Uh, okay? I mean, that's great, but everyone knows where we can find mystical creatures without the damn compass. Go to any island. Ruma has phoenixes, Landin has griffins—I'm pretty sure the Isle of Muafikin has unicorns."

Adelgis snapped the journal shut and shook his head. He fidgeted with the binding and stared at the floor for a moment, as if gathering his words and courage.

"While we were in Port Crown, I went to the market to find exotic mystical creature parts."

Atty narrowed her eyes. "That's why? I told you that was a terrible idea. We don't need things like phoenix hearts. It's gross."

"W-well, regardless of whether it was a good idea, I over-heard something." He glanced up and met Zelfree's gaze. "Calisto recently spent a good portion of his gold leafs. The pirates in the market had all heard the same rumor. He purchased a *scale of a world serpent*."

Although Adelgis had been speaking at a normal volume, the last statement felt like it had been shouted. I didn't need expert levels of deduction and reasoning to guess what Adelgis was afraid of.

Fairy tales spoke of mystical creatures from ages past—creatures so powerful they were considered eldrin only to gods. The world serpent was one such creature. It was, according to legend, as massive as an entire fleet of ships, and capable of swallowing a full-grown leviathan whole.

Not only that, but these ancient mystical creatures had magic beyond compare. The world serpent didn't evoke fire or lightning—it created new islands, volcanos, and mountains. Its scales were said to repel all forms of attack, including sorcery.

These legendary creatures were once real, since pieces of them had been found all around the world, but as far as I knew, no one had ever seen one. They were extinct. Gone. They had all vanished after the age of gods. Any tales about them were now considered nothing more than children's nursery rhymes.

Did the Dread Pirate Calisto want to find a world serpent? Was his plan to use the scale on the Occult Compass and follow it to where the mythical beast rested?

"He won't ever find one," I said when the room remained quiet. "Right? There aren't hatchling world serpents roaming around anywhere. Even if he had the compass, it wouldn't get him anything."

Zelfree stroked the stubble on his chin. He stared at the table, the bags under his eyes prominent in the low light of the galley.

"Maybe." Hexa shrugged. "I remember some explorers came through my home town once. They wanted to find eggs of ancient creatures, because they thought they could still hatch."

"That's nonsense."

She leaned back and shook her head. "I dunno. It'd be worth a shot to me."

"Any piece of a world serpent would make for powerful magical items," Adelgis said. "Even if Calisto didn't find a hatchling world serpent, what if the compass led him to other parts? I mean, haven't you guys heard of Xelvia's Fang? It's a sword with no equal—a magical artifact crafted from the tooth of a world serpent. Calisto could be trying to gather things like that."

"Okay, so let's keep the journal away from him," Zaxis said with a shrug. "Seems simple enough."

Atty laced her fingers through her blonde hair. "Won't he chase us if we keep it?"

Adelgis nodded along with her words. "That's why I'm saying we shouldn't head to the Isle of Gott! Calisto will go there straight away. It's the closest port, and everyone stops there before heading to the other islands."

"Not stopping there will add four days to the trip. Does this ship even have four days' worth of supplies?"

Zelfree crossed his arms and said, "I'll speak with the captain."

Everyone turned to him, but no one offered any response.

"We'll head north," Zelfree continued. "Instead of going west. It'll only be three days until a port that way."

"So, you're concerned?" Adelgis asked.

Zelfree didn't respond, which confirmed Adelgis's fear.

If Calisto managed to harvest the corpse of a world serpent, he would have the makings for powerful magical items—perhaps devastating weapons. A man as sadistic as Calisto shouldn't have any more advantages.

Heading north would lead us into another nation's territory, but that wouldn't be a big problem. No one on this ship was a wanted criminal. It just meant it would take us longer to get back to the Frith Guild.

Zelfree walked over to Adelgis and took the cartographer's journal from him. "I'll keep this safe. The rest of you just sit tight. The Frith Guild will handle everything with Calisto. No half-baked plans and no one leaves this ship. It's my one goal on this trip to make sure you all get back to the guild manor without any further incidents."

My whole body ached. Every time I tried to relax, something or someone would bother me. And I didn't want to use one of the hammocks. Illia remained in our collective sleeping quarters, and I couldn't bring myself to face her, which left me with hardwood benches or coils of rough rope.

Neither helped.

Instead, I leaned on the railing and watched its wake. It didn't make me sleepy, but it gave my mind something to focus on.

As the sun set in the distance, my nervous anxiety waned. It seemed Adelgis guessed right—Calisto was probably heading for the Isle of Gott, but we were heading north. The *Seawolf* would be in a safe port long before he managed to discover us.

Nicholin stayed on my shoulders the entire day, though he didn't speak much. Instead, he would cuddle against my neck at random moments. Even now, as the winds picked up, he refused to leave my shoulder.

"You're taller than Illia," he said, staring out over the ocean. "That's weird."

Before I could reply, Luthair rose from the harsh shadows cast by the masts. I turned to him, surprised he would make his presence known without me calling for him.

"Are you okay?" I asked.

His empty helmet nodded.

"Then... what're you doing?"

"Forgive me. While my default position is to allow you to make your own decisions and mistakes, I feel it's necessary for me to intervene. You should speak to Illia. This prolonged silence between you is nothing but damaging."

Nicholin's ears stood straight. "I agree. Good plan. I support this."

"You came out of the shadows to scold me?" I huffed as I pushed away from the railing. "I guess I shouldn't be surprised. That does sound like you."

"I only comment because I don't wish to see either of you suffer."

"What if she doesn't want me to see her? You saw how she acted toward me."

"You won't know until you exchange words."

"She wants to see you," Nicholin added. "And also, if you don't go, I'll bite you in all the soft parts of your body."

"W-what?" I barked. "Why would you—"

"Because Illia is my arcanist and I want her to be happy! No more depression. She needs some cheering up."

I didn't like his pushy insistence, but I *did* want to speak with her. And what had I been planning anyway? Sleeping on the deck of the ship? Avoiding her until we reached land? That was childish and silly.

"Fine," I said with a shrug. "I'll speak with her. But if she wants me to leave, I'm not staying."

"I'll make sure the others give you some privacy," Luthair said.

Oh, so *that* was why he formed. I smiled, grateful Luthair was willing to help me like he did. Then again, that was what eldrin did. They helped their arcanists with *all* their goals, no matter how trivial or minor.

I was lucky to have an eldrin like Luthair.

Nicholin leapt from my shoulder and landed on Luthair's. Then—for some reason—Nicholin climbed onto Luthair's helmet and pushed himself through the face guard, squeezing his body through the tight space. Once inside, he twisted back around until he was staring out the eye slit, his blue gaze barely visible.

"How do I look?" Nicholin asked, his voice echoing inside of Luthair.

I patted Luthair on the shoulder, his shadow-metal cold and unmoving. "You, uh, are okay, right?"

"Yes, my arcanist."

"You don't feel anything?"

"I am just the suit of armor. You needn't concern yourself."

"O-oh, right. Good."

Nicholin stuck out his paw and waved to me.

It was... weird...

I buried it deep in my mind, hoping the sight would soon be forgotten.

Then I headed toward the sleeping cabin. I hadn't seen much of the other apprentices or Zelfree, despite the small size of our vessel. I hadn't been in the mood to speak with anyone, and they all seemed preoccupied by the news of the world serpent.

Ancient times had never fascinated me as a child. I always wanted to read about swashbucklers and legendary arcanists—they felt more real and immediate. Everything else was just a myth, basically. People said a world serpent could create new islands, but no one *knew*. Gregory Ruma, on the other hand, had done countless things that were all observed and documented. He founded my home island, and that was a feat I couldn't be more grateful for.

When I reached the cabin door, I hesitated. What would I say?

I shook my head.

No. Now wasn't the time to reflect. I had to push forward,

like jumping straight into the waves in order to acclimate to the chilly ocean.

I opened the door, slowly and with a cough to announce my presence. Illia sat in a hammock at the far end of the cabin, her attention on the wall in front of her. She glanced over her shoulder, but there were no lit lanterns, so her gaze fell to the floor, unfocused.

"Illia," I said, my voice far quieter than I intended. I cleared my throat. "Illia. It's me."

She lifted her head and turned around in her hammock. "Volke?"

"Yeah. Uh, do you mind if we talk?"

"I don't mind."

Perfectly capable of seeing in the dark room, I weaved between hammocks and made my way to Illia. She kept her attention on my footsteps until I was inches from her side. Then she glanced away and fidgeted with the hem of her shirt. It was the same one she had worn when confronting Calisto, and her blood stained the back and side of it.

"Why didn't you change?" I asked.

Illia flinched at my voice. "I... didn't feel like it."

Even her pants had the blackish crimson of dried blood.

Unwilling to argue with her about her attire, I took a seat on the nearest hammock and rubbed at my knees.

"Illia. Listen—"

"I know," she blurted, cutting me off. Then she whirled on her heel and pressed her forehead on the bulkhead. "I've been ridiculous. I never should've gone. I never should've done any of this." She spoke so fast it was almost hard to understand her. "I should've just kept everything to myself."

"That's not what I came to say."

"Did you come to say *I told you so*?" Illia pushed away from the wall, but she didn't face me. Instead, she ran her fingers through her wavy hair and pulled it forward enough to cover her whole face, not just the scars. "I didn't even think Calisto would be that prepared, but it was so obvious. *Of course he would be.* What was I thinking?"

"It wasn't *that* obvious." I rubbed the back of my neck. "For a brief second, I thought you had actually gotten him."

Illia faced me, her one eye wide. "Why did you bring Master Zelfree here? You could've come to get me without him."

I stood from the hammock, my heart beating fast. "Illia, I didn't mean to bring him. I actually came to help you." I wanted to comfort her—hold her, *anything*—but I restrained myself. "I'm so sorry. I should've been there for you. When I learned you had left, I immediately went to the docks."

"Then how did Zelfree get here?"

I combed my disheveled hair with my fingers. "I don't know. He just *showed up.* I told him it wasn't his business, but I think he's really concerned about losing you."

Illia scoffed and looked away, her eye glassy with tears. "I doubt that. You heard him. I'm not fit for the guild."

"We can convince the guildmaster to give you a second chance, I'm sure of it."

She forced a laugh. "What's the point, Volke? Obviously I'm a screw-up. I don't deserve to be here."

"Everyone makes mistakes."

She took a step back, her gaze shifting to one of anger. "You don't! You wouldn't have done this. But I'm..." Illia shook her head. "I don't know what I'm doing."

"Illia, what're you talking about? I mess up all the time. Remember how I said I was going to be a phoenix arcanist?" I half-chuckled, half-sighed. "There are lots of things I've wanted to do but never did because I ruined it. But you were always there to help me afterward."

The boat creaked as it swayed on the waves. Illia turned to me, tears spilling from her eye and rolling down her cheek. "Me?"

"Always you. That's why... I should've been there. We're in this together, no matter what mistakes are made. I'm sorry I forgot that."

Illia rubbed at her face, clearing away some of her tears before she threw her arms around me in a tight embrace. I returned the gesture, thankful she didn't hate me. I never wanted to disappoint her, and any trouble she got into should be mine to share.

She twisted her fingers into my coat and buried her face into my shirt. "Volke..."

I gently rested my chin on her head.

We remained that way for several minutes, the sounds of the ship and ocean our only companions. Then she pushed away from me, her hands trembling.

"Stay with me," Illia said. "I don't want you to go."

"Okay. We should probably get some rest."

"This hammock. Stay with me here."

I sat on the hammock, and Illia sat next to me. Although the hammocks had been built and secured with large men in mind, I still worried it would snap. Instead, our weight pressed us into the middle, forcing us close, her hip digging into mine. I didn't care, and it seemed neither did she.

Illia rested her head on my shoulder. "Is this okay?" she whispered.

"Of course it's okay."

She was much softer than I thought she would be.

"You don't mind if the others see us like this?"

I shook my head.

Then again, I imagined Zaxis wouldn't like this.

That didn't matter, though. I knew what I wanted—and that was for me and Illia to be close. Perhaps Illia wanted more than this, but our relationship as adopted siblings was enough for me. I never wanted to lose it, and this entire trek to Port Crown made me realize how far I was willing to go to keep it.

I didn't want to risk changing the dynamic between us. So, even if the others thought this was intimate, it wasn't.

I closed my eyes and rested my head on top of hers.

22

OPEN OCEAN

At some point I had fallen asleep.

I awoke as Illia got out of the hammock. I almost fell forward to the floor. Somehow, I had been asleep while sitting up. I jerked to one side and watched as she slid into the hammock next to mine, the dark skies indicating it was still evening. Sleepy and drained, I lay down and quickly drifted back to sleep.

After what felt like two seconds, I awoke again, but the warm glow beyond the porthole told me dawn would soon be upon us. I had slept for hours, yet it didn't feel that way.

Dreams lingered at the edge of my consciousness. Something about buried treasure and living out a legendary tale I had enjoyed in my youth. And also hard lumps under my skin—always being afraid someone would find out.

I stared at the oak wood ceiling, awake enough that my legs twitched with restless energy. Illia remained in her nearby hammock, fast asleep. Others had come into the cabin as well, likely during the night.

The boat rocked at an even rhythm. William said a steady sway meant easy sailing. If we were lucky, the winds would hurry us along. While I enjoyed sailing, open ocean journeys—anything away from the islands—could result in terrible disaster. If we crashed or were found by pirates, there would be little to be done about it.

With a long yawn, I swung my legs out of the hammock and stood. Then I headed for the door, my gaze drawn to the warm glow in the cabin. Zaxis rested on a hammock wearing just his guild pendant and trousers. Forsythe slept on his bare stomach. The phoenix had his head curled around to his wing, his heron-like neck long and elegant. When I stepped past, the creaking of a floorboard woke the bird.

"Volke?" Forsythe asked. His feathers puffed outward, revealing more of the fiery glow emanating beneath his feathers.

"I'm sorry, Forsythe. Go back to sleep."

"Where are you going?"

"I want to walk around for a bit."

His feathers smoothed, and he tilted his head to the side.

Zaxis grumbled and then sat up. He cradled Forsythe in one arm and rubbed his eyes. "Hey," he whispered, his voice rusty. "I need to speak with you."

"Can we do it outside the cabin? People are trying to sleep."

I motioned to Illia and then glanced around for the others, but the only other one on a hammock was Adelgis. To my surprise, Felicity floated in the air over his head, her shell dull when not exposed to light. She waved with a tentacle, aware I could see her despite the dark. I replied with a shy wave back.

Where was everyone else?

Zaxis stretched for a moment, even going so far as to groan, and followed me to the deck.

The ocean winds slapped me out of grogginess and straight into irritated. I pulled my coat close. Zaxis, on the other hand, didn't even bat an eye. He stood in the breeze, still just in his trousers, his skin unmarked with goosebumps.

He ran a hand through his messy red hair, and I noticed the sweat dappling most of his wiry body.

"Are you okay?" I asked.

Zaxis placed his phoenix down on the deck. "Just hot. Forsythe does this to me."

"You asked me to cuddle with you," Forsythe said.

"I said, *you should stay close*," Zaxis snapped.

"But then you brought me over to your hammock."

Zaxis shoved his hands into the pockets of his trousers and forced a shrug. "It wasn't like that. I was just concerned."

"Yes, my arcanist." Forsythe leaned from side to side, his golden gaze filled with confusion.

Although frigid air swept over the deck at a fierce rate, the night crew of the *Seawolf* carried on with their work. Across from Zaxis and me, standing on the elevated quarterdeck near the stern, were Zelfree, Hexa, and Atty. Gravekeeper William had said quarterdecks were reserved for officers, so I had never set foot on one before. Then again, the status of guild arcanist—even an apprentice guild arcanist—eclipsed that of most naval officers according to the Queen's law.

Zaxis crossed his arms over his bare chest. "What's with you?"

I turned back to him, half-lost in my thoughts. "Huh?"

"You and Illia. What's going on between you?"

"Nothing."

"Uh-huh." Zaxis stepped close to me, his breath a hot

rush of mist every time he exhaled. "What was that back on the hammock, then? You two just being *siblings*?"

The statement dug itself under my skin. *This* was why I never wanted anything to change between me and Illia. People wouldn't understand—and I didn't want to risk our relationship cracking under outside pressures.

"We were both exhausted," I repeated, curt. "It would've happened with anyone."

Zaxis rolled his eyes. "Tsk. You're either lying to me, or you're lying to yourself." He met my gaze and then jabbed a finger into my shoulder. "Look, it's getting awkward for everyone else, too."

"Maybe you should mind your own damn business."

I regretted the harshness in my words, but I also didn't need judgments from the others.

Zaxis tensed, but he didn't move away, almost like he anticipated a fight.

"I'm just telling you what they think," he said. "You can do whatever you want with that information."

Despite his typical aggressive attitude, Zaxis's tone didn't hold any animosity. He sounded... genuine. Like he was warning me—protecting me from some sort of problem in the future. And while I hated the topic of our conversation, I appreciated his candor.

"Thanks," I forced myself to say.

He huffed. "Whatever. I just want to make sure you're not trying anything with Illia."

As I mulled over his comment, Atty and Hexa appeared at the edge of my peripheral. Atty held Titania on her arm, and Raisen waddled behind Hexa, his hydra head bobbing up and down as he moved.

"What were you two doing?" Zaxis asked.

Atty stroked her phoenix's majestic feathers. "Master Zelfree wanted us to get some training done."

"Magical training," Hexa added. "He wants us to master the basics of manipulation. He says it's fundamental to growing our sorcery."

Zaxis shot me a *told you so* kind of look. "Guess who didn't get invited to the training session?" he muttered under his breath.

"I didn't get invited either," I whispered. "You *were* sleeping."

"Walk over there and see what he says. I bet you he'll demand you start training."

Atty allowed her phoenix to fly off toward the crow's nest. When she walked past me to get into the cabin, we exchanged a quick glance. She smiled wide, but didn't say anything. I suspected she didn't want anything to be strained between us, and she kept all her thoughts to herself. Was Atty bothered by Illia and me? Perhaps.

Hexa didn't keep her thoughts hidden, however. She walked over and stared me down.

"Illia trusts you," she said. "And where I come from, you don't break your loyalties. Especially not as an arcanist. You stand with your blood-brothers and blood-sisters until the bitter end."

"I apologized and told Illia I would be there to help her no matter what."

Hexa loosened a bit and then patted my shoulder. "Good. Because *I* won't forgive you a second time."

A part of me wanted to remind her that Illia and I had grown up together. Hexa wouldn't come between us, no matter how much she disapproved of my behavior. I did appreciate her looking out for Illia, though. Not many people made friends with Illia—her curt demeanor and social hesitation didn't make for easy conversation. Hexa didn't seem to have much tact, however.

Hexa walked into the sleeping cabin, leaving Zaxis, Forsythe, and me on the cold deck. Well, and Luthair too. I could see his shadow shifting about. I wondered why he kept silent most of the time, and my attention focused on him for longer than I wanted.

"I bet all her practicing with Zelfree is why she's better at magic than I am," Zaxis said, breaking the quiet between us. "I practice all the time, but I don't think I'm doing it right."

"You should stop thinking you're not as a good as Atty."

"Why's that?"

"For starters, you'd be less insufferable."

He shot me a glare.

"And more importantly, apparently Atty hasn't learned how to use her augmentation at all. She can't heal—not even the slightest injury." I gave Zaxis a hard look. "Why don't the two of you work together, huh? You could teach her healing. She could tell you what Zelfree's been teaching her."

For a long moment, he said nothing. Then he turned away, a thoughtful expression on his face. "Not a bad idea, for a former gravedigger. I'll probably do that." He sighed. "But I still think Zelfree doesn't want me as an apprentice. I'm willing to bet you anything he'll avoid training with me, even if you go over there and suggest it."

I shoved my freezing hands into my trouser pockets and shrugged. "Fine. Get ready to owe me."

I ambled across the deck, careful not to slip when the boat rocked. The early morning crew didn't move with much energy. They untied a few barrels at a leisurely rate, one even going so far as to use them as a seat for a moment while he wrote something in a journal.

No one stopped me when I walked up the seven steps to the quarterdeck, though the wind gave it an honest try. I had to squint my way past the strong breeze in order to get to Zelfree. He stood at the stern, his elbows up on the railing, gazing out across the ocean. His black coat fluttered in the air currents, but Traces sat on his shoulders, keeping the collar from moving.

When he didn't acknowledge my presence, I figured I had to announce myself.

"Hello, Master Zelfree."

He didn't turn around. "What is it?"

Some greeting.

"Atty and Hexa said you trained with them." I rubbed at my neck. "I wanted to do the same."

"You should get some rest."

"I'm not tired."

Zelfree pushed off the railing and turned to me with a slight frown.

He really didn't look good. Bags under his eyes, a slouch to his shoulders, his stubble becoming longer each day—he looked more like a stowaway that hadn't eaten in days rather than a master arcanist. I suspected even the sea rats would feel guilty for stealing his food.

"*You* should get some rest," I said.

"I can't." Zelfree pinched the bridge of his nose. "Let's just practice your manipulation before the sun gets over the horizon." Then he pointed to a coil of rope. "See if you can control the shadows enough to cut small bits of fiber off the excess rigging."

"Uh, well, what do you think about Zaxis joining us? He's also awake."

"I'd prefer to keep this one-on-one."

At first I had thought Zaxis might've been overthinking

things, but Zelfree's rejection made Zaxis's paranoia seem real. Was our master avoiding him?

"You trained with Atty and Hexa at the same time," I said.

Zelfree narrowed his eyes into a glare. "That was different."

"Really? Because it seems weird that you'll spend time alone with some arcanists, but not others. Especially after what happened with your last batch of apprentices."

Traces raised her hackles and arched her back. "I said never to tell anyone about that!"

"I haven't." I held up my hands and shrugged. "I'm just making observations."

Zelfree gritted his teeth and mulled over the comment. It took longer than I expected, and I almost said something, but he returned his gaze to me with a cold seriousness about him that hadn't been there before.

"Zaxis reminds me of Travin," he said, his voice strained, like he hated every word he spoke. "In more ways than one. They look similar; they have the same attitude." Zelfree turned his gaze to the deck. "It's... difficult not to think they're the same person."

Travin?

I had heard that name before...

Then it came to me. Travin Ren had hailed from the Isle of Ruma. He had bonded with a phoenix on my fifth birthday—on the last Day of the Phoenixes. Had Travin been apprenticed to Zelfree? And was he the one that Zelfree had fallen for?

It all made sense when I thought of it like that. Zelfree didn't want to be reminded of his past love—so he avoided anything that stirred up old memories.

"Zaxis thinks you dislike him as an apprentice," I said. "He doesn't understand what you've gone through."

Traces rested back on Zelfree's shoulders, but she maintained a tense posture with her ears flat against her head.

"I never told Zaxis what happened," I said again. "But I think you should. Then Zaxis would understand, at least."

The sun finally crested over the horizon, washing the *Seawolf* in a wave of orange and yellow. I shielded my eyes with my arm, but I kept my attention on the waves. Nothing beat a morning on the ocean. The shimmer of the waters created a sparkle not unlike the stars—it was as if the ocean and the night sky had traded places.

"It's foolish to hang on to this as long as I have," Zelfree said. He kept his gaze low. "I should've moved on by now."

I returned my hands to my pockets. "I don't think it's foolish."

Zelfree shot me a glower.

"W-what? I don't! I mean, you shouldn't let it eat you from the inside, but losing someone close can feel like the whole world depopulated. You obviously cared for him. You shouldn't regret those feelings. Not now, not ever."

I remembered the many times Gravekeeper William spoke about his late wife. He had never let it hinder his work, but he did celebrate their anniversary, even decades after her death. He knew how to keep her memory sacred without letting it destroy him.

"Besides," I muttered. "Don't you remember what happened to Gregory Ruma? I doubt his wife wanted him to dwell like he did. Maybe he could've remained a hero if he just—"

"I understand," Zelfree snapped. Then he exhaled, removing the anger from his tone. "I really do understand."

Traces lifted her ears and then gave me a cat-like smile. "Hm. I knew there was a reason I liked you."

"Enough," Zelfree growled. "We don't need to keep discussing my personal affairs. It's getting ridiculous. You're right. I'm Zaxis's master, and I never should've forgotten that."

I smiled. "So you don't mind if I go get him for training?"

"Fine. Go get him and we'll—"

A bell rang, cutting Zelfree off.

We both turned our attention to the crow's nest. The barrelman—the unlucky sailor stationed at the top of the tallest mast—continued clanging the bell. Sailors across the *Seawolf* stopped their work and glanced upward.

"It's the *Third Abyss*," the barrelman shouted. "Off the bow, to the south! The *Third Abyss!*"

My vision tunneled, and an icy grip tightened on my chest, preventing me from breathing. I rushed over to the railing and glanced back at the bow, expecting to see a ship in the distance.

I didn't.

Just a bank of fog on the water.

The ghostwood of the *Third Abyss* cloaked it in a sinister veil that stretched in both directions for hundreds of feet. I couldn't see the ship at all—the mist was too thick.

In the next second, a million thoughts cascaded through my mind. The *Seawolf* had 24 cannons, less than the standard for galleon-type ships. And the only master arcanist on board was Zelfree. The *Third Abyss*—a man-of-war battleship—had over 100 cannons, and it could have more than Calisto as the master arcanist, I really didn't know. Plus, the fog would obscure our vision and allow them to get close enough to board before we could even retaliate.

The *Third Abyss* could easily overtake us, no doubt in my mind.

The open ocean was like a cage. Nowhere to go. Nowhere to hide.

Luthair formed out of my shadow, his black armor gleaming in the morning sunlight. Although he had no facial expressions, his posture told me everything. He placed a gauntlet on the hilt of his sword and kept his stance wide, a tension to him that he rarely exuded.

"What're we going to do?" I whispered.

"I'm not sure, my arcanist. But one should always be prepared for the worst."

I turned to Zelfree, who remained on the quarterdeck, his gaze unfocused. When he made no move, I walked back over to him, panic chilling my blood.

"Master Zelfree?" I asked. "What should we do?"

Traces swished her tail and curled tight around the back of his neck. "We'll think of something."

It took a few moments—my heart beat hard against my ribs and echoed in my ear canals—but Zelfree eventually lifted his head and walked with purpose. I followed him off the quarterdeck, unsure of his destination. The other apprentices made their way out of the sleeping cabin with groggy expressions, no doubt awakened by the ringing of the warning bell.

"Luthair," I said. "Go inform them about what's happening. I'm going to stay with Zelfree."

"Yes, my arcanist."

Luthair turned and headed in their direction.

Zelfree entered the captain's cabin, and I kept on his heels. To my surprise, it was empty. Perhaps the captain had gone to the head or the galley, or was off talking to his first mate about their tactics.

We didn't have much time.

The absence of any sailors didn't bother Zelfree, though. He strode straight for the captain's desk, opened a drawer, and withdrew a quill pen and inkhorn. Typically, the captain wrote letters or updated his maps with the pen and ink—why did Zelfree need it? Was he going to write Calisto a letter?

Before I voiced my questions, Zelfree withdrew the cartographer's journal from his coat pocket. He placed it on the desk and turned to page eighty-four. The instructions for finding the Occult Compass were written on one page, and an illustration of the compass was masterfully drawn on the other.

"Read it," Zelfree said. "Memorize it quickly."

Without question, I did what he said. The steps to reach the shipwreck weren't complicated. I could remember them long enough to write down later. Once finished, I noticed Zelfree dipping the quill in ink. He motioned me aside and then scratched two extra lines of directions into the journal, both of which would take someone drastically off course.

I gawked at the handwriting—it appeared identical to the cartographer's!

"Are you secretly Martin Mercator?" I asked.

Zelfree finished his writing and gave me a smirk. "Of course not. I studied forgery for years. You don't become a master spy with amateurish penmanship."

"Are you... planning to give this to the pirates?"

"I need to leave soon. Don't waste my time with idiotic questions."

"You can't leave! We need you here."

Zelfree glared. "Calisto wants this journal. And he wants you and Illia, because you took this from him. But trust me when I say, he wants me more. If I bring him the directions to the Occult Compass, I can persuade him to leave the *Seawolf* alone. None of you need to get caught up in this madness any longer."

"Persuade?" I asked, almost laughing. "You're not going to talk to him, right? That would be crazy. Or suicidal. Or both."

Zelfree snatched up the journal, the rings under his eyes darker than before. "We don't have much of a choice. We're not going to outfight him. We're not going to outrun him. This is the only way."

"But what if—"

"Listen. You're my apprentice. It's my duty to keep you safe until your training is over. I'll handle this. You stay with the others and head back to the guild. If you make it back before I do, tell the guildmaster where I am."

If we make it back before him?

How would he even escape?

As if answering my unspoken question, Traces transformed herself into a rizzel and then leapt onto my shoulder. She squeaked as she made herself comfortable.

Zelfree placed a heavy hand on my opposite shoulder, his grip tight. "Once I'm done with Calisto, I'll be back. Promise me you'll get everyone to the guild."

"Me?" I whispered.

"You're mature enough to handle this. Now promise me."

"Of course. I promise."

Zelfree forced a smile, but there was no mirth behind it. Something about the way he slid his hand off my coat gave me a terrible sense of foreboding. His grim expression didn't help, either.

Then he left the captain's cabin with the altered cartographer's journal in hand.

23

DIRE STRAITS

While the correct directions to the Occult Compass remained fresh in my mind, I wrote them down on a blank sheet of parchment I found in the captain's desk. My hand shook the entire time, making the words difficult to read, but I understood what I had written.

Traces, still in her faux-rizzel form, swished her tail. "You should bring this to the guildmaster."

"Why aren't you going with Master Zelfree?"

"When I'm in my natural mimic form, I'm quite vulnerable." She tilted her head. "And I can only maintain a shapeshift through concentration. If I were attacked and wounded, I might change back, thus taking my arcanist's new magic and making me a liability. Calisto will kill me the moment he knows I'm around. Then Zelfree wouldn't be an arcanist anymore."

"I see..."

Zelfree had an amazing set of powers—the ability to sense nearby arcanists, and know their techniques was useful all by its lonesome—but having a fragile eldrin was a major drawback. It made sense that he left her in protected areas while he risked himself in all the fighting.

I folded the parchment and tucked it into my coat pocket. Uncertain of what to do next, I returned to the deck, my movements rigid.

The crew hurried to lower one of the dinghies. Zelfree waited as they prepped it, all the while speaking to the captain. I watched from afar, unable to make out their conversation over the yelling of the sailors.

Atty jogged over to me, and Titania flew down to the deck and landed next to us.

"Volke, have you heard the news?"

I nodded.

Titania fluttered her wings. "We're continuing north! Master Zelfree is heading out without us."

Sure enough, Zelfree boarded the dinghy and allowed the crew of the *Seawolf* to lower him to the waves. I held my breath, grateful for the easy weather. Dinghies didn't fare well out on the ocean waves. Most were so small they would get toppled.

Once detached from the ship, Zelfree rowed the boat toward the fog. He didn't need to put in much effort—the mist crept toward him at a steady pace.

"All sailors to their stations," the captain called out. He motioned with his arms, giving hand signals to the sailors too far away to hear properly.

Atty placed a hand on my shoulder. "What're we going to do? Master Zelfree didn't leave us instructions."

"We're going to head back to the guild," I said. "We need to tell Guildmaster Eventide what happened. Plus, we need to give her directions to the Occult Compass."

It needed to be in the hands of the Frith Guild.

Although she had seemed nervous a moment ago, Atty

calmed once she heard the plan. She straightened herself and turned her attention to the waters. "What if the *Third Abyss* chases us?"

"Then we'll be forced to fight."

"Do you think we can win?"

I shook my head. "We won't have much of a choice, though."

Silence settled between us. The morning sun, while glorious, cast a harsh red hue into the sky, like even the weather knew of the impending bloodshed. I walked to the railing and kept my gaze on Zelfree until he disappeared into the fog. The *Seawolf* didn't slow, but neither did the *Third Abyss*. Zelfree had been confident they would leave us alone once he spoke to Calisto...

But what would happen to him?

"He picked rizzel magic so he could have options to escape," Traces whispered to me. "Everything will be fine. Just you see."

I hoped so.

Zaxis, Hexa, and Illia ran up to the quarterdeck and watched the fell mists from the highest point. Atty stuck close to me, and no matter where I looked, I didn't spot Adelgis or Luthair. Were they still in the sleeping cabin? It was the only explanation.

I could have gone and checked, but my anxiety wouldn't allow me to leave. I kept my attention on the fog from the *Third Abyss*, counting every second in obsessive detail.

Those villains terrorized everyone. I just wished I had the power to stop them—to protect the *Seawolf* and her crew —to help Zelfree and make the oceans a safer place.

But I couldn't.

I knew it, and the reality twisted in my gut, hurting me more than the sting of a blade piercing my skin.

"The fog's two and a half miles out," the barrelman shouted.

I gripped the railing tight and tried to remember what Gravekeeper William taught me about judging nautical miles. The distance to the horizon was approximately 1.17 times the square root of my eye height above the water. I suspected I was twenty feet up, which meant the horizon was 5.2 nautical miles away.

The barrelman slapped the side of the crow's next. "Two miles out!"

Doing math helped distract me a bit, but it wasn't enough to quell the ice in my veins or the dryness in my throat.

How was the *Third Abyss* gaining on us? My first thought went to the kappa arcanist. Kappa typically resided in rivers, so they had powers over water. It no doubt aided the ship in chasing us.

The longer I stared, however, the more I noticed the fog drifting away. I half-smiled. Hope welled in my chest.

"Two and a half miles out!"

Audible sighs of relief washed over the ship. The deckhands manning the rigging regarded each other with chuckles and slight nods. Even the captain managed to relax.

"Three miles out."

Had Zelfree convinced Calisto not to chase us?

I glanced at Traces. She stared back with bright blue eyes. If Zelfree died, she would know instantly. Since nothing had happened to her, I suspected he was still okay… but I still worried.

"Let's speak with the others," I said.

Traces nodded.

The other apprentices gathered in the sleeping cabin. Luthair and I stood in the back corner, my thoughts dwelling on Zelfree even though we needed to formulate a solid plan of our own.

Having everyone in the same room—along with all their eldrin—made the quarters feel small. Atty sat on a hammock with Titania in her lap. Hexa stood near the door, her scarred arms crossed, her hydra at her feet. Adelgis paced along the far wall and glanced out the porthole whenever he passed it.

"We're still heading north," Zaxis said. He swung in his hammock, one leg off, one leg on. He hadn't bothered to dress himself yet. "And once we reach Port Rask, we'll be safe from Calisto."

Illia sat in the hammock across from him, her one-eyed gaze drilling a hole into the floor. "When will Zelfree return?"

Traces, who hadn't left my shoulder, perked her ears straight up. "My arcanist will return once he can."

"We need to get back to the guild," I said. "If Adelgis is right, and Calisto is after an Occult Compass, then Guildmaster Eventide should know."

Adelgis stopped walking and turned to me, his eyebrows knitted. "Didn't Master Zelfree give them the cartographer's journal?"

"He altered the directions to the compass before he went over. I have the real directions." I pulled the parchment out for dramatic effect. Everyone turned their attention to me, each examining the folded paper.

"Then *we* should get the Occult Compass first," Hexa said, her voice loud, even when speaking in a casual tone.

Zaxis pointed to her and smiled. "Yes. That way, even if those dastard pirates figure out what Zelfree did, it won't matter. *We'll* have the compass."

"Wait." I held up my hands. "Zelfree didn't change all the directions. He just added a few at the end. If we head there, we'll likely run into the *Third Abyss*, or at least pirates from the ship that are searching the area. We can't risk that."

"I agree," Adelgis said, nodding.

Illia stared at me, searching my gaze for a long moment. "I also agree."

The group brought their attention down on Atty. She didn't acknowledge them. Instead, she stared at the blue sky beyond the porthole, her posture straight and her arms wrapped around her phoenix. Although it appeared as though she were daydreaming, everyone knew the truth. She wanted time to mull over the situation. If she voted to get the compass, we would have a lot more to discuss. But if she wanted to return to the guild, there would be no need for arguments.

"How disastrous would it be if the pirates came across this compass?" Atty asked.

I crossed my arms and shrugged. "Well, let's assume they'll find a world serpent corpse or something. If their plan is to make magical items, they would still need one other component. From what I understand, an arcanist's magic can only be bonded to an object through the use of a magical adhesive, for lack of a better term."

Adelgis's eyes went wide. He snapped his fingers and walked across the cabin to me, smiling wide. "Yes! That's exactly correct! Trinkets and artifacts require star fragments to bond arcanist magic and make them permanent. You can have all the phoenix feathers in the world, but if you don't have any star fragments, you won't be able to make them into useful items."

"So," I continued, "even if they had world serpent parts, they would need star fragments to do anything with them."

Atty turned to me. "Does that mean we don't have to worry?"

"We should worry," Zaxis interjected. He got off his hammock, Forsythe in his arms. "You know those pirates have star fragments. It's the number one thing stolen from ships. They're rare, super expensive, and every arcanist wants them. I bet you they have a whole bunch of star fragments on their ship right now."

The added hypothetical got everyone reevaluating their position. During our moment of silence, the creaking of the boat echoed throughout the room. I turned to Luthair, hoping he would say something, but his empty helmet "stared" back at me with nothing.

I sighed. I had promised Zelfree we would return to the guild, which meant I needed to convince them.

"This would be better left to a master arcanist," I said. "All of it. And once the arcanists of the Frith Guild know about this, I'm sure it'll be handled in an instant."

The others exchanged glances and slowly nodded.

"The Frith Guild is legendary," Hexa muttered. "That's why I travelled all the way to Fortuna after bonding. They're amazing."

"Right? We should leave it to them."

Hexa regarded me with a serious expression, her eyes calculating. "I'm switching my vote. I say we go back to the guild."

Zaxis set Forsythe on the floor and huffed. "Really? No one else thinks these pirates are insane and need to be stopped no matter what?" He held a hand out to me. "Volke?

Nothing? I thought you admired heroes who risked life and limb to stop disaster. What kind of hypocrite are you?"

"Stop that," Atty said, glaring. "Think about it this way—we know exactly where the pirates are heading. If we intercept them with master arcanists on our side, there's a good chance we can get rid of the *Third Abyss* once and for all."

That logic held up and got me excited. Maybe we *could* destroy the *Third Abyss*.

"It's settled, then?" Adelgis asked. "We'll head to Port Rask and find a fast ship to take us back to Fortuna?"

Everyone nodded, even Zaxis, though it didn't look like he enjoyed participating.

It took two days to sail the rest of the way to our destination.

Traces grew quieter and quieter with each passing hour, but whenever I asked about Zelfree, she reassured me he was still alive. Her voice never convinced me, though. Perhaps he wasn't dead, but she was worried about him. What could I do?

Again, I found myself powerless to alter the situation.

Why did the pirates have to be so much stronger? Why did we have to sit back and watch while their claws raked across the lives of good and simple folk?

A deep-seated hatred built in me with the passing of each new day.

When the *Seawolf* docked at Port Rask, our group disembarked. Unlike Port Crown, which had a bustling city filled with markets, taverns, and entertainment, Port Rask would've been lucky to see more than a hundred people pass through in a single day. A rickety fish shack stood out as the most prominent and active social scene—five people sat around chatting. You could buy fish and booze—a common combination—and nothing else.

"Why is this place so... barren?" I asked.

Traces tilted her rizzel head. "Oh, it used to be popular, maybe fifty years ago. Then gold was found in a mountain to the west. A new port city popped up and stole all the talented people from this area."

"I see."

"That's not entirely true," Adelgis said as he walked by me. "A master golem arcanist guards this port. My father says he's talented."

Traces turned her head. "I was getting to that part. He protects the—" She stopped herself short with a sharp gasp.

I reached up to pet her soft fur, but Traces went limp and fell from my shoulder. I reached out to grab her. Thankfully, Luthair manipulated the shadows in time to catch her before she hit the dirt of the main road. Then he set her down.

Everyone stopped and paid attention.

Traces shimmered and reformed into a cat, her body unmoving and her eyes held shut.

I knelt next to her, my hearing fading in and out as thoughts buzzed in my head.

"Are you okay?" I asked. I touched her side, careful and gentle.

She took in a shallow breath.

"Traces?"

Zaxis ran over. "I can heal her."

But she didn't look hurt. Zaxis touched her and nothing happened. She remained on the ground, her breathing ragged.

The others formed a circle and muttered things I couldn't hear.

When Traces finally stirred, it was to tilt her head to the side. "Everett..."

"He's dead?" I asked. It was all I wanted to know—all I feared.

"He's injured..." She mewed and shuddered. "It hurts so much..."

Thank the good spirits! Whatever had happened, we could still fix it.

I gathered her up and held her close to my chest. "We'll take you to Gillie. Hang on."

"Everett... my arcanist..." Then Traces mewed a second time. "I must see him. He needs my help. He's dying."

24

INTO THE FOG

"What're we going to do?" Hexa asked.

What *could* we do? We were already on our way back to the guild. We didn't have a ship of our own, and who would be willing to intercept the *Third Abyss*? Plus, Zelfree wouldn't want this. I could already hear him yelling at me—telling me that he'll handle everything and we should all stay away.

Traces shuddered in my arms. "I need to get to him."

Her insistence added to my panic. How injured was Zelfree? Why did she need to get to him?

As if he was reading my thoughts—and he probably was—Adelgis straightened his posture. "An arcanist's magic grows weaker the farther away they are from their eldrin. Perhaps Traces and Master Zelfree are so far away that he can't properly heal."

I hadn't known that. I supposed it made sense. Arcanists only had magic because of their bond, after all.

Zaxis stood and smacked his fist into his other palm. "Master Zelfree is in trouble. We can't go back to the guild now. It's even *farther* away from where the Occult Compass is. If we take Traces there, we'll be the ones killing Master Zelfree."

"I should've stuck with my gut," Hexa said. Then she muttered a curse and shook her head. "If we had the Occult Compass, we could've traded it for Zelfree or something."

"Ashes to that! We should rescue Master Zelfree."

"That sounds reckless," Adelgis muttered.

Zaxis waved the comment away. "Listen to you. What a coward."

"I don't want to go in without a plan. That doesn't make me a coward."

I tuned them out, more concerned with the situation than their incessant bickering. I really wanted to keep my promise to Zelfree. He wanted us safe more than anything, but I didn't become an arcanist so I could hide away while everyone else handled the problems of the world.

Traces nuzzled into the folds of my shirt and curled her long tail around my arms.

What would Zelfree do? I already knew the answer. He had somehow followed me out on the open ocean and helped us find Illia without a moment's hesitation.

I turned away from the group. Luthair must've sensed my anxiety because he rose from the shadows and took his place by my side. The citizens of Port Rask pointed, but I ignored them too.

"Doubt is your biggest weakness," Luthair said, no apology in his tone. "You doubt your own competency, you doubt your magic—and now you even doubt your ability to make decisions."

"I just want to make the right ones."

"Inaction is often the worst choice of all."

Illia walked over to my other side, Nicholin on her shoulders. She stared at me with her one eye, and then turned her attention to the waters. "Whatever you think is best, we should do."

"You don't have an opinion?" I asked.

She didn't answer.

"Because I'm not always right. You don't have to give up on yourself after one mistake. I could really use your input. I have no idea what we should do."

Nicholin fluffed out his chest. "Oh, if we need a leader, I'm all in." He waved a paw through the air. "We need to save Master Zelfree! Zaxis is right—if we head back to the guild, we'll be taking Traces farther away. We'll be killing him."

"You think we should all go?"

"No. Six of you would be too much. You'd risk getting caught. I think if three of you went—maybe two—you could get to Calisto's ship and rescue Zelfree."

Adelgis rubbed at his forearms. "What would the rest of us do? Just wait here?"

"Go back to the guild," Nicholin said. "Or... do what Hexa suggests. Get the Occult Compass—that way we have it as an option. Plus, we're members of the Frith Guild, dammit! We shouldn't let these pirate dastards have an inch!"

His squeaky little speech—while hasty and lacking crucial details—got me smiling, despite my ever-mounting fears.

"I like that plan," Zaxis said. "We should stop these pirates right here and now."

Illia glanced over, her gaze harder than before. "You want my opinion? I agree with Nicholin and Zaxis. That pirate filth deserves nothing. I want their whole ship to burn —I want everything they care about to slowly fade." Then she exhaled. "But this is what Zelfree was talking about. He said I get wrapped up in this feeling... and that's not becoming of a Frith Guild Arcanist."

"Zelfree didn't say you couldn't have those feelings," I said. "He just meant they can't be the sole reason you lash out against someone."

Illia opened her mouth like she might protest, but after mulling over my comment, she stopped herself.

"That's not the sole reason now," Nicholin said. He stood on his hind legs, lifting himself higher. "We should commandeer a vessel and head straight for them!"

"No," Luthair stated, his dark and gruff voice silencing the group.

Even I didn't know what to say. He had never been so adamant before.

"Mathis and I dealt with many pirates," he continued. "And nothing here will compare to the *Third Abyss*. Instead, I want to share a technique Mathis would use to infiltrate enemy ships."

"Oh, really?" Hexa asked. She moved in closer. "Go on."

"If Mathis knew where they were headed—as we do— he would wait ahead of them. We would hide ourselves near the shore, or in the waters, and the pirates would come to us, unaware of our presence."

"The Occult Compass is near an outcropping of rocks," Adelgis added.

Atty combed her blonde hair with her fingers. "Do those sea thieves even know we're after them? We might have the element of complete surprise."

"The fog of the *Third Abyss* creates an ideal situation for slipping on and off the ship without much fear of detection," Luthair said. "Saving Master Zelfree is a real possibility."

The finality of the statement settled over the group.

We had a plan. A reckless plan, but we didn't have many options, or that much time. If half of us went to the *Third Abyss* and half of us went to the Occult Compass, surely one group would succeed.

The determined expressions of the others told me they knew it too.

I hated going against Zelfree's wishes, but I refused to let him die. He deserved much more than the cruel torments of a dread pirate.

We split into two groups. Illia, Zaxis, and I would head to the *Third Abyss*. Zaxis had healing—something Atty lacked—and Illia could teleport. Traces insisted I come along, since I could step through the shadows, but I suspected she just wanted me to keep her safe.

Adelgis, Hexa, and Atty would head to the Occult Compass. They took the real directions to the Occult Compass and hired a small ship to take them to the coordinates. It wasn't difficult to convince a captain, especially when no one mentioned that Calisto had his eyes on the area.

One of the locations mentioned in the cartographer's journal was a grouping of skerries—rocky islands devoid of life. Zaxis managed to find a ship that would take us there, and Luthair was convinced the *Third Abyss* would sail by, unaware we were waiting for them.

The timing would be tight. Smaller vessels could sail between groupings of skerries, but man-o-war ships were too large. The *Third Abyss* would have to take a longer route to ensure its safety. We could take a short route and hopefully be there long enough beforehand to prepare.

"Nicholin, I need you to stay with Adelgis," Illia said.

Her rizzel puffed out his fur and squeaked. "It was my plan! I want to go fight pirates."

"You know why you can't stay."

He wouldn't be far—the shipwreck with the Occult Compass would be in the same skerry area—but it still worried me now that I knew distance played a factor in the potency of sorcery.

Zaxis whistled for Forsythe. "You go with them too. Your glowing body will get us caught, otherwise."

Forsythe didn't complain. He circled overhead and then headed out with the second group.

We set our course for the skerries.

The rocks of skerries remained slick whether they were wet or dry. I hated venturing onto them when I was younger. I had fallen on my face more than once and even cracked a baby tooth.

When our dinghy reached the skerry, I opted to stay in the boat. Nothing grew on this rocky island. A landscape of dark brown, gray, and black stretched out before us, both lumpy and jagged. The evening brought with it dark clouds, like it wanted to wear black for an impending funeral. I glanced down at Traces, and she glanced up at me with her two oddly colored eyes.

"He's still alive?" I whispered.

She nodded. "Just suffering."

The information sent anxiety through my system. Why did we have to wait for everything? Travel times, eating, planning, preparing—the old legends of master arcanists never included all those frustrating details! And now I knew why.

Illia shivered as she paced along the rocks. The clouds overhead added to the darkness, and while it forced her to widen her eye to see *anything*, the low light actually honed my vision.

Unaffected by the weather, Zaxis stood on a rock jutting out of the skerry. He crossed his arms and stared off into the distance. "So, we'll know they're here because of the fog, right?"

"Yeah," I said.

"And you two are prepared to infiltrate a pirate ship, right? You aren't going to get cold feet?"

I shook my head, as did Illia.

We had come too far to back down now. Hexa, Atty, and Adelgis were counting on us. If we got Zelfree *and* the Occult Compass, we could head straight back to the guild as heroes. But if we were caught, it would all be over. I couldn't even imagine how we would make it out.

Well, Illia would escape. Just not me or Zaxis.

"You should shake your doubt," Luthair said from the shadows.

Traces kneaded my shirt with her claws, like only cats could. "I'm already feeling a little better. Zelfree must be closer than before. Don't mess this up at the final hour."

Yeah, some pep talk. *Don't mess it up, Volke!*

Inspirational.

Illia placed her hand on my shoulder. I flinched, surprised by her close proximity. I calmed when I noticed the corner of her mouth twitch up into a half-smile. "We can do this together."

She always knew what to say.

Zaxis glanced over and snapped his fingers. "Hey! I'm

here too, dammit. I've got enough confidence for ten people. You two should learn a thing or three from me."

"I've been on the *Third Abyss* before," Illia said as she ran her fingers along the scars on her face. "If you had seen half the things I did, you wouldn't be so foolhardy."

He slid down the side of the rock and landed on both feet with a level of skill I found impressive. Then he sauntered over and huffed. "My old man didn't have many inspirational things to say, but he did teach me one valuable lesson."

"Your father is a blowhard," Illia said with a roll of her eye.

"He said, *don't be afraid of the challenge—be afraid of failure.*"

"I'm not impressed."

"I get it now." Zaxis took a seat on the side of the dinghy. "We shouldn't be afraid of the halfwit pirates or their bloodthirsty manticore—we should be worried about Master Zelfree. If we fail, they'll kill him. Righteous rage makes for good fuel."

"That's preposterous," I said.

Luthair stirred in the shadows. "I see some merit in his words."

"Honestly?"

Before Luthair could offer an explanation, a shift in temperature stilled everyone's breathing. Although the other two couldn't see through the void of a cloudy night, I could tell they knew something had changed. I stepped out of the dinghy, my sight set on the bank of fog rolling our way.

"They're here."

Seeing the approach of the *Third Abyss* grounded everything in a way my imagination never could. I had been tense before, but now it felt like I'd never be able to relax. Illia grabbed my forearm and motioned to the far edge of the skerry—the side the *Third Abyss* would sail by. As a group of three, we made our way over, careful not to slip on the slick rocks that made up the tiny island.

The ghostwood mist rolled over us before we made it to our desired location. We quickened our steps, and Illia slipped. Zaxis leapt for her side in an instant, still as sure-footed as ever.

"I've got ya."

She pulled out of his grasp, her face red. "Thank you, Zaxis." We took a few more steps, and she added, "And I've been meaning to thank you for everything else. For accompanying me to Port Crown. And all of this. So, thank you."

He smiled. "Call on me anytime. I'll be there for you."

It hurt to hear the conversation, but I didn't say anything. Instead, with all the grace of a comedy routine, I also slipped. Zaxis caught me by the armpit and helped to steady me before I broke another tooth.

I glanced over to give him thanks, but he cut me off with a smirk.

"How're you so good at this?" I demanded as I ripped my arm away.

"I'm a show pony at heart."

Despite the situation, his comment got me chuckling. Then he slapped me on the arm, drawing me back into our dark and dreary setting.

"Stop daydreaming," he said. "Focus."

Zaxis had a way of simultaneously being irritating and entertaining. I sometimes wished he would just stick with one, though.

In order to reach the far point of the skerry, we had to wade through knee-deep ocean water. Boots only protected feet for so long, and after slogging through the icy shallows, I swear I couldn't feel my toes. The rocks slanted down, making it difficult to go any farther without swimming.

Traces hissed at the ocean and then transformed into metal bangles that wrapped around my neck. Could she breathe in this form? Did she have thoughts? They were odd questions I didn't have time to ask her.

Then I heard the creaking of the hull. The eerie sound bounced off the rocks, creating a disturbing echo.

"It's close," Illia said. "You two should grab on to me. I'll bring us the rest of the way."

I placed my hand on Illia's left shoulder, and Zaxis placed a hand on her right.

"Hold your breath," she muttered.

Her magic gripped me, and I felt like I could resist, but I allowed the sensation to sink into my flesh and bones. Half a second later, I gasped. Cold water rushed over me as we plunged into the ocean. I kept my hand on Illia and swam for the surface, but before I got there, we teleported again.

Another dunk into the waves made it difficult to concentrate. I never let go of her, though. After two more instances of jumping through the water on waves of teleportation, we appeared next to the *Third Abyss*.

I didn't have long to take in the gray wooden planks of the hull, but I recognized it immediately. We splashed back into the water, and Illia swam with us to get closer. The ship sailed at a leisurely pace, but as a person in the water, it seemed lightning fast.

Once we broke the surface, Illia gasped and shook her head. "One more time," she choked out.

Then we vanished and reappeared on something solid. My legs buckled—I hadn't been prepared to stand—and the three of us toppled to the floor. In an instant, we all leapt to our feet, water dripping from our coats, shirts, and trousers. I took in ragged breaths, still a bit disoriented from the trek.

I glanced around.

The lanterns had been extinguished, leaving the tiny storeroom we had entered in a state of darkness. Crates lined the walls, and barrels had been tied to the floor.

We had made it to the *Third Abyss*.

25

TRAVERSING THE THIRD ABYSS

"**W**here are we?" Zaxis whispered. "I can't see a thing."

I coughed up a bit of seawater—my mouth salty from the effort—and then examined our surroundings. We had entered a storage room, but man-o-war ships had four decks —which had level Illia taken us to?

Illia leaned against the bulkhead. "I'm sorry. I've, uh, never done something like that before. I don't know where we are..."

"What if you had teleported us into the wall or something?" Zaxis asked. He grabbed a box and steadied himself. "Could we have died?"

"I don't think it works that way. It's hard to describe, but... teleporting is like being blind, groping around in the dark. I can *feel* pockets of air where I can *jump* to. I knew we could enter here, but I didn't know what here was."

At the far end of the room, I spotted massive sandbags.

"We're on the bottom level of the ship," I said.

Zaxis turned in my direction, his eyes unfocused. "How do you know?"

"Large ships need extra weight to keep from capsizing. It's called ballast weight. They use rocks or iron—in this case, sandbags. You only store the ballast on the bottom-most deck, so that's where we have to be."

"Why would you ever know that? Weren't you a gravedigger?"

Illia sighed. "Gravekeeper William knew *everything* about ships. He must've taught us a hundred useless facts."

"Not useless if they come in handy now," Luthair muttered.

His gruff voice startled the other two, but I was starting to become accustomed to it. I enjoyed his interjections.

I glanced around, intent on finding a ladder or door. The gray wood of the ship gave everything a deathly appearance. A haze lingered in the air, like the fog wanted to form, but there wasn't enough space.

Shaking a growing feeling of dread, I wove between barrels and took note of the differences. According to William, barrels with metal rings held liquid, and barrels without the metal rings contained anything else. Most barrels here had metal rings. Rum? Or perhaps oil? Likely flammable, since they were stored on the bottom-most deck, as it would be the first to take on water.

Then Zaxis snapped his fingers and created a small ball of fire in his palm.

"Don't," I snapped.

He closed his hand and snuffed out the flame. "I can't see."

"I can. Just wait there."

I heard him mutter, *since when can he see in the dark?* but Illia never answered.

It didn't take me long to find a door and narrow stairway. I glanced up, careful not to make noise. Lights emanated from the decks above, and the echo of conversation lingered at the edge of my perception. I closed the door and stared at the wood, imagining the layout of a man-o-war in my mind's eye.

Four decks.

Above us would be another layer of supplies and store rooms. Above that would be the gun deck—the area for the heaviest cannons. Above that would be the main deck, meant for lighter guns and crew quarters. Then came the actual deck with the swing guns, shrouds, and rigging. The officer's quarters, captain's quarters, and navigation would be under the quarterdeck.

But where would they keep Zelfree? Likely somewhere below deck. Less chance of escape.

I crept back to Zaxis and Illia. They hadn't moved since last we spoke.

"Hey," I said under my breath. "I found the stairs up."

Zaxis shook his head. "Why not teleport?"

"We might pop into existence right in front of someone," Illia replied. "We were lucky we didn't run into anyone while getting in here."

"It's night. Most of the crew has to be sleeping."

"We shouldn't risk it," I said. "Just let me guide you to the stairs."

With slow movements and careful steps, we made our way to the door. Before I had a chance to open it, the bangles around my neck shuddered. I flinched. Traces transformed back into her cat-self and stepped onto my shoulder.

"You're wet," she murmured. "Disgusting."

"I'm sorry."

"Be careful. I can sense Calisto."

My mouth went dry, but I shook the panic from my thoughts. "Close by?"

"No... somewhere far above us. But we have to avoid him —no matter what."

I wished I had a mimic's ability to detect nearby arcanists. It would be helpful in more ways than one.

I opened the storage room door and peered into the stairwell. No one in sight, just the lights and noises of men talking on the upper decks. Luthair slithered ahead of me as a shadow, gliding up each step until he reached the deck above us. He waited, and I took the gesture to mean all was clear.

While climbing the steps, I tried to remember the subtle things Zelfree had done when moving around Port Crown. He had disguised us, altered our scent, kept to the edges of rooms, and strode through the streets with the gait of a thug. I didn't know how to imitate his actions exactly, but I attempted to keep close to the walls as I traveled up the stairwell.

When I reached the next deck, a shout of pain caught my attention—followed by the lash of a whip. I grew icy and still, my thoughts focusing on the noise. It came from beyond a door. A lit lantern hung above the doorframe, and I stepped up close, my pulse fast.

Were they torturing Zelfree?

Another crack and scream sent a shiver down my spine. We wanted nothing more than to rip down the door and tear those pirates apart.

Illia grabbed my shoulder, freeing me from my tunnel vision. "Do you hear that? Send Luthair in to check."

I forced myself to nod.

Luthair slid under the door and disappeared into the room. He returned in a couple seconds. Then I heard another lash, but no cry of agony.

"It's the wendigo arcanist," Luthair said from between my feet.

I rubbed my forehead, my hands shaky. "He's hurting someone?"

"No. He's being punished."

The information startled me. I hadn't been expecting to find a pirate in distress from fellow pirates. Then again, they were sea thieves and cutthroats, not the cuddle squad. But why would they turn on a fellow arcanist?

Zaxis moved closer to the wall, his clothes drying faster than the rest of ours. His red hair puffed, defying gravity. "Listen in," he whispered. "See what they're doing."

I gave the stairwell another glance. No one. Then I placed my ear against the wood of the door. It helped me hear a little better, but not much. Traces also placed her ear on the door.

I detected voices.

"—and Calisto's tired of giving you second chances," a man said.

He sounded familiar. It didn't take me long to place it. *Breen.* The snallygaster arcanist I saw with Calisto in the *Gold Grotto.* He had a deep rumble to his voice that was hard to mistake.

"You failed to get the journal, then you failed to get the journal a second time, *and then* you failed to follow the pukes who stole it from us? And now, the final drop of water in the bucket, you fell for a simple trick from our hostage?"

Another crack of the whip, this time accompanied by a sharp yell.

"Calisto liked your brother," Breen said. "Kalroux pulled his weight with the best of 'em. But not you. You're a disappointment, mate. I think Calisto keeps you around cuz of nostalgia. Kalroux was his go-to man."

"Kalroux?" I whispered.

I couldn't place the name, but it triggered something in my thoughts. Perhaps I had read it before?

Then I heard the shuffle of boots on wooden planks. The sounds grew louder, and I knew they were heading for our door. I jumped back and glanced around, uncertain of where we would hide. Fortunately, Illia didn't hesitate. She grabbed my arm and Zaxis's shirt—the next second she teleported us back to the ballast deck.

I listened hard.

Breen and a few others entered the stairwell. They didn't head down—toward us—but instead traveled upward, their heavy steps echoing the entire way. After a few tense minutes, I couldn't hear them anymore. The creaking of the massive ship filled the silence around us.

"Who was getting tortured?" Zaxis asked.

"One of the pirates. The wendigo arcanist. Apparently he's failed them one too many times."

"Why did you say the name *Kalroux*?"

I shrugged. "The pirate whipping the arcanist said it."

"Kalroux hailed from the north," Luthair said. "He raided ships and burned small towns. He was later taken in by Calisto and made one of his pirate arcanists."

I glanced at the shadows stirring near the barrels. "How do you know of him?"

"Mathis and I were assigned to eliminate him."

"Did you?" Illia asked.

"Indeed."

The wendigo arcanist—Fain—had been the one who attacked us on the Isle of Landin. He had made a show of attacking just Luthair, saying it was for revenge. Fain's brother must have meant a great deal to him, but I didn't have much sympathy for Kalroux, a dastard pirate.

"It sounds like they left," Zaxis said. He rubbed at his eyes. "We should head back. Maybe that's the deck where they keep all their prisoners."

"Be more careful," Traces said with a slight purr.

I stroked her fur. "Of course."

No need for further discussion—we went straight for the stairwell and headed to the next deck and its storage room. The lantern over the door had been snuffed. I reached for the handle and found it locked.

"Luthair," I whispered. "Open this."

He crept under and unlocked it from the other side.

I walked into the storage room, surprised by its size. All the lanterns had been snuffed out inside as well. Dozens of crates filled the corners, and a long table had been nailed to the bulkhead. The rank odor of sweat and blood clung to the air. My hair stood on end as I snuck toward the far door.

The soft sound of sobbing stilled my movement.

Illia stopped behind me, and Zaxis placed a hand on my shoulder, no doubt trying to keep his bearings. We stood frozen in place for a long moment—the sobbing continued.

Then I noticed something opposite the table. Fain, dressed in nothing but a ratty pair of trousers, held his wendigo in his lap. Both he and the mystical creature had lashes across their bodies. The worst of it seemed to belong to his eldrin, though. Wendigo always appeared sickly and thin. This one now had long gashes of flayed skin weeping blood onto the floor. It whined, low and faint.

Fain held his eldrin closer, his frostbitten fingers wrapped up in the fur. Tears ran the length of his face and slipped off his chin.

He hadn't yet detected us. That didn't surprise me. We were shrouded in darkness, and someone as distraught as he was probably wouldn't notice much.

I reached the far door, and Luthair snaked under. I waited while he checked the room. When he returned, he unlocked the door. With slow actions, I turned the handle and crept inside. Illia and Zaxis followed without much trouble.

Again, the room had no light.

When I closed the door, it dulled the sounds of Fain's anguish.

"What was that?" Zaxis whispered. "Someone's crying? Should we help them?"

"It's the wendigo arcanist."

Illia blinked her one eye, but she still couldn't focus on anything. "Why whip him? Can't he heal?"

Traces moved along my shoulders and slid behind my neck, her fur silky and warm. "Calisto uses his manticore's venom to torture arcanists. As long as the venom is in their system, it corrupts magic and prevents an arcanist from healing or performing much sorcery."

Was that how Calisto was killing Zelfree? With his manticore venom?

Curse the abyssal hells. We had to find Zelfree, no matter what.

"So the wendigo arcanist is weak and bleeding out?" Zaxis asked. "We shouldn't just leave him there. We should kill him while we have the chance."

His jump from *should we help whoever is crying* to *let's kill this one* almost gave me mental whiplash. I grabbed him by the collar of his coat, somewhat disgusted by his suggestion.

"He's broken and bleeding. An arcanist shouldn't cut down someone when they're like that."

"Why not? He's a pirate of the *Third Abyss*. You think he would leave us if he found us sobbing? Plus, that's one less arcanist Calisto has at his beck and call. We can easily get away with this. No one else is around!"

"It just... doesn't seem right." I let go of his coat, my words failing me.

"I agree," Illia said. "We should leave this alone."

Zaxis turned his attention to her, an eyebrow raised. "Don't you hate these pirates more than anyone? That's what you told me when we left for Port Crown."

"I do, but we came here for a reason, and that was to get Master Zelfree. We shouldn't risk that just to weaken their ranks. If we could kill Calisto—and bring down their whole operation—it would be a different story. But this is some failed pirate who's helpless in the other room."

Wow. She had articulated most of what I felt about the situation. I still didn't agree with attacking someone as helpless as Fain, though. Despite that, I smiled to myself, thankful Illia had chosen my side over Zaxis's. I knew it was petty, but I still enjoyed it.

To my surprise, Zaxis seemed to mull over the comments. He nodded. "Okay. I get it. Let's go then."

"Zelfree would approve of this," Traces said, a smile in her voice.

I led them through the dark room until we came to another door. To my surprise, it wasn't locked, and when I opened it a crack, a sliver of light pierced the room. I froze, shocked I hadn't seen a glow from under the door beforehand.

Two voices drifted in with the light, their volume an indicator of their close proximity.

"I'm tellin' ya," one man said, his speech slurred. "It's a nice new place. Fancy. Clean women."

A second man huffed. "I'm savin' my leafs."

"Ya don't get it. One lady had jugs the size of melons."

Their bootsteps echoed in the hallway. When they got close to the door, Illia tightened her grip on me, no doubt preparing to teleport. But the men walked by our door. During the half-second they walked by, I noticed they both wore tinted glasses.

Odd.

"I don't care about *jugs*."

"Ah, this's why yur no fun."

"And this is why you itch everywhere below the belt."

We waited until they opened a door and left the corridor. But the light remained, and I didn't like that.

"Luthair, snuff out the lanterns."

Without hesitation, he slithered into the hall and—one by one—killed the lights. I waited a long moment before opening the door, fearing someone would come to investigate, but no one did.

We entered the hallway, and my heart dropped to my gut. There were six doors, *at least*, which meant this deck was larger than I had originally suspected. They had to be storerooms, though. Could Zelfree be in one? Traces could vaguely sense him, but that meant we had to check everywhere. I went to the first and then I turned my attention to Luthair's shadowy form.

"You go ahead of us. Check as many rooms as you can."

"Yes, my arcanist."

Once he left, I slowly opened the first door.

Traces stood stiff, her fur on end and her ears pressed flat against her skull. Her claws dug into my coat, and she clung tight. "I knew it," she growled under her breath. "I didn't want to believe it, but I should've trusted my senses..."

"What's wrong?" I whispered.

"Is that who I think it is?" someone asked from within

the room. Their voice, however... it wasn't quite right. It sent goosebumps across my skin.

The room beyond the door was dark, just like the hall. No light whatsoever.

"Come in," the voice said. "I know you're there."

Illia and Zaxis both snapped their attention to me, the color draining from their faces.

26

BONE CAGE

I didn't recognize the voice, but the tone resurrected terrible memories of the plague-ridden creatures I had fought in the past. They'd all had the same lunacy tainting their words. And their laughter—everything was funny, even the pain and carnage of their own death.

A piece of me wanted to confront the voice. I stepped into the room, even though Illia and Zaxis half-heartedly tugged on my coat.

The new room reminded me of a torture chamber. As the boat rocked, so did the chains hanging from the ceiling. They clacked together, adding to the creaking of the wood and creating a haunting symphony unique to the room. The ceiling had a hatch—one that opened from atop, no doubt to lower larger crates into the hold. But there weren't any supplies in this room, just two massive cages and all the equipment to hold something down.

The first cage, the one nearest the door, sat empty. The iron bars had a sleek polish—a new cage. Unused.

The second cage—I gave it one glance and flinched. A pair of red eyes stared at me from the darkness, their giant orb-like gaze unsettling. It was like... there were no eyelids. Just bulging red eyes, glowing with a sinister hue, an intensity so great I couldn't examine them for longer than a few moments.

The bars of the second cage weren't metal. They were bone.

"What is that?" Illia whispered, pointing to the red eyes.

Traces growled, her fur still on end. "A gargoyle. A tainted gargoyle."

"Not just *any* gargoyle," the disturbing voice said. "A perfect gargoyle. One that needs your help."

Despite the eerie feeling I got when staring at it, I forced myself to glance at the rest of its body. The gargoyle kept itself tightly balled, its leathery wings draped over itself, similar to a fleshy cape. The horns on its head bent forward —so long and sharp I suspected it could skewer a man. Besides the freakish eyes that never closed, its face looked like a skull, its skin stretched tight.

The beast had to be the size of an elephant; I just couldn't get a good look since it kept its wings drawn across its body. A part of me wondered if it was hiding something.

Then the gargoyle reached out a hand. Its fingers had three joints, rather than two, and its thin claws curved— similar to fish hooks—large enough to snare a full grown adult.

"*Volke Savan.*"

I shuddered. The way it said my name—it echoed in my mind. "How do you—"

"Know who you are?" the gargoyle finished. It chuckled, a hint of madness at the edge of its mirth. "The magic that binds all arcanists and eldrin whispers to me. It tells me things. Your name. Your broken sorcery. Your pathetic life. It's all a bit *underwhelming*, to tell you the truth." It continued to chuckle as it dragged its claws along the bars, creating a rhythm of rattles to accompany the clacking chains and creaking hull.

Zaxis placed his hand on my shoulder and squeezed tight. "C'mon. We should go. This thing's crazier than a soup sandwich."

"Ah, *Zaxis Ren*." The gargoyle pulled back its hand. "All the power of a raging inferno and just as subtle."

I nodded and took a step toward the door. "You're right. Let's go."

"Wait. I really do need your help. Isn't that what the Frith Guild's for?"

I hesitated. Why were the pirates keeping this thing in a cage? Was it asking to be set free?

The gargoyle continued staring at me—never blinking, never looking away.

"They locked me in here to drain my blood." It pointed with a claw to the wall.

A handful of glass bottles filled a small crate. Some contained a dark, stagnant liquid, and others were empty. Why would the pirates do this?

Then it occurred to me. All the arcanists on the *Third Abyss* were man-eaters, immune to the arcane plague, so how did they infect Ryllin or anyone else? I knew now. They kept this gargoyle in the hold of their ship so they could use his tainted blood on their weapons. This monster was the source of their corruption.

"It hurts when they come to take my vital fluids," the gargoyle said with a genuine laugh. "Pretty messed up when you think about it. So please. Help me. Let me out of this prison."

Guilt consumed my thoughts. It *was* terrible. No creature—not even this one—should be held in the dark hold of a pirate ship and made to bleed for the benefit of mayhem. I took a step closer, my legs unsteady.

Illia held on to my elbow. "Don't."

"Illia Savan." The gargoyle lowered its voice to a whisper and added, "Or should I call you Illia Delamarre?" It laughed and returned to its normal volume. "Don't fret. I'm not upset with any of you *pitiful* apprentices. Calisto was the one to put me here. It's his head I imagine popping off like a cork—his insides I imagine slurping like a fine wine."

She held her breath and scooted closer to me.

"See? We can help each other. Once I'm free, the pirates won't have access to my blood. Plus, I'll be taking theirs on the way out."

"Can't you free yourself?" I asked as I examined the cage.

The large bones, perhaps eight feet in length, were thicker and straighter than anything I had ever seen. Flat bits of bone made up the floor and ceiling of the cage, like scales or scapulas.

Traces rested back down on my shoulder, a low growl to her voice. "Gargoyles can manipulate stone and metal. These leviathan bones will hold it. They're stronger than normal."

I turned around and stared at the other unused cage. Why have two? Did they have a second creature?

"Oh, don't worry about that," the gargoyle said. "Calisto had the cage made for his *world serpent*. No one else is here but me."

The words sunk into my thoughts. Calisto made a cage for a world serpent? He wouldn't need a prison for a dead body. Did that mean he honestly planned on using the Occult Compass to look for a live world serpent? That was impossible. Maybe he was insane as well.

Zaxis dug his fingers into my shoulder, his grip painful

enough that I grabbed his wrist. He shook his head. "Let's stop talking and go. It's plague-ridden."

The red eyes snapped to Zaxis—jiggling slightly, like they could burst from the gargoyle's head, fly through the bars, and attack someone.

"It's not a *plague*," the gargoyle hissed. "It's a rebirth."

Traces huddled close to my neck. "I don't like the sound of this."

"I used to be a weak, *pathetic* creature. Then... I came upon this boon. The pirates caught me, but they fed me enemy arcanists to keep me alive. That magic added to my own." The beast laughed and shrugged its massive body. "Sure, there was a short period where I was a gibbering mess, but isn't that the same descriptor you could use for a human infant? Now look at me. I've *ascended*. This is my true form."

All the plague creatures I had seen *were* a gibbering mess. Even the white hart I fought in the mire on my home island. They could barely keep it together. But this gargoyle was different. It spoke complete sentences and seemed to have a goal in mind. Was this what would happen if plague creatures consumed enough magic?

Was this a true form creature?

I took another step toward the cage door, my gut screaming at me to leave.

"I can tell you where to find Everett Zelfree," the gargoyle said.

Illia shook her head. "He's lying."

"Why would I lie? I want you to help me, and I want all of Calisto's machinations to fall to ruin. Telling you where to find his new captive incentivizes you to free me *and* harms his plans. Not to flatter myself too much, but I'd say it's a clever strategical move worthy of recognition."

"Where is he?" I asked.

"Release me first."

"No." I inched away. "We'll find him eventually, with or without your help, and—"

"Save your breath, *maggot*," the gargoyle interjected with a laugh. "No one has time for grandstanding. Your broken master is in the captain's cabin, a shadow of his shadow's former self."

I turned to Traces.

She swished her tail. "It does seem... like my arcanist is above us..."

"Now set me free." The gargoyle grazed his massive claws along the length of a bone bar.

I hadn't expected him to actually tell me anything. That changed things. Maybe it *did* just want to get revenge on Calisto—and that was an understandable desire. Perhaps this gargoyle could even act as a distraction while we fled.

I shook free of Illia and Zaxis and walked toward the cage. I didn't really know how I would free it. Was there a lock? A key? Some sort of latch system? I got closer to the bars, wondering if I could somehow break the bone. Would my magic work?

Some of the bars had been gnawed on. The nails in the floorboards around the cage were all missing.

The terrible twisting of my insides never waned. I didn't like this. It reminded me too much of the plague-ridden creatures I had seen in the past. The white hart in the mire had promised me everything I had ever wanted. Power and bonding—the exact things I had desired in the moment. And now this gargoyle promised to kill Calisto and lead me to Zelfree... exactly what I wanted.

The gargoyle's baleful eyes shifted a bit, jiggling as they stared straight into my soul.

"Don't overthink things," he whispered. "I've already given you information. It would be dishonorable to leave me now."

I took a step back. "I never made any agreements."

The beast chuckled, but said nothing.

As I was about to take another step away, the gargoyle lunged out a clawed hand so fast, it skinned its knuckles and forearm on the bone bars. I flinched back, but not quick enough. Its hook-claws caught my coat and easily pierced through the thick fabric. Then it yanked, its strength a shock as I stumbled forward. I grunted as I waved my hand, hoping to manipulate the darkness. Shadow tendrils rose up, but the pain that shot through me unsteadied my feet further.

In the next second—before I fell straight into the bars—flames burst through the room and washed into the bone cage. Then a black sword cut my shirt free, and the shadows dragged me away.

The gargoyle sank back into its prison. The flames did little to its stone-like skin, and the bones remained uncharred.

I took a deep breath, calming my panicked heart.

Traces stood next to me as a knightmare. She sheathed her faux sword. It wasn't difficult to tell her and Luthair apart. Luthair had cracks and scuffs in his armor. Traces didn't, even though she was mimicking him.

Zaxis kept a ball of flame in his palm as he examined the monster behind the bars. The creature kept its wings wrapped tight around its body, hiding whatever lay beneath. "This thing is way bigger than any gargoyle I've ever seen."

"This *thing*," the monster repeated with a snicker. "*This. Thing.* I might have found that insulting if it hadn't come from a cretin."

Zaxis sarcastically held a hand to his ear. "What was that? I couldn't hear you through those bars you'll never escape from."

Illia grabbed me and then Zaxis and headed for the door. We exited the hellhole of a dungeon, but not before the gargoyle called after us.

"Sooner or later, I'll be free. And I'll remember this moment."

With angry movements, Illia dragged us down the hall, Zaxis's flame giving us a small bubble of light. We passed one door, and then another. Traces leapt back to my shoulder as a cat, purring the entire time.

I pulled Illia's arm and stopped her. "Wait. Zaxis, snuff out the light."

He did as I asked.

"Why did you antagonize him?" Illia growled under her breath.

"I wasn't going to let that *thing* insult me." Zaxis adjusted his belt.

"It was trying to upset you. Don't get baited like that. This is exactly what I was talking about back at Port Crown."

He waved away the comment. "Fine. You're right. I shouldn't let it get to me."

His curt tone told me he didn't believe it.

Luthair slinked out of a nearby room and rose from the shadows. "My arcanist. Master Zelfree isn't here."

"We need to get to the captain's cabin," I said. "We have two decks to go before we get outside."

Traces patted my torn coat. "We should find a stairwell. They lead straight to the top deck and then we can get to the captain's cabin."

The main stairwells were found near the bow and stern. I tried to visualize their locations, but it took me a moment to remember where we were. The confrontation with the plague-ridden gargoyle had unsettled me, but at least we knew where Master Zelfree was held.

"This way," I muttered. "Luthair, take point and warn me if anyone is ahead."

He bowed his helmet head and then sank back into the void.

I led Zaxis and Illia down the hall and to the end door. It wasn't locked. With a gentle push, I opened it and continued through the darkness. When I spotted a light from under a door, I went straight for it. Luthair slithered underneath and came back a second later, nothing to report. I opened the door and found the stairwell. The rocking of the ship caused the lanterns to sway, but each was secured by a chain to the bulkhead, preventing them from toppling over.

Luthair snaked up the steps. With light, Illia and Zaxis didn't need me to guide them. We each took the steps two at a time, though I had to slow halfway up to control my breathing. Once we passed the gun deck, I felt myself get tense. The crew quarters were nearby. If someone walked into the stairwell while we were here, I didn't know how we'd explain it.

We'd get into a fight, and while we could kill a mortal pirate, the noise would surely attract more—and eventually Calisto himself.

Zelfree would never forgive me if we were hurt while trying to rescue him. Then again, we'd probably be dead, so it wasn't like I'd have to face him afterward.

Fortunately, we hurried up the steps and made it to the top deck hatch unseen. Water leaked through the cracks, and the wind howled outside with force enough to sound like the world was wailing. I pushed open the hatch just enough for Luthair to shadow-step through. Rain splashed into the stairwell, but I didn't mind. I still felt tense from the gargoyle confrontation, and the cold sprinkling of water brought me back to the here and now.

Traces, on the other hand, hissed. She jumped to my arm and transformed into bangles as she landed, attaching herself to me without any help.

"Come," Luthair said.

I lifted the hatch and cringed. Two men stood by the rigging on the port side, gazing up, a coil of rope in each of their hands. One of the swing guns was near them, partially tied down. It looked like the ropes that held it had broken. The rocking of the boat in this mild storm had no doubt caused them problems.

I ducked back into the stairwell. "Luthair, we can't get caught."

"My arcanist, they won't see the details you see. If you walk with confidence, you can blend in."

The information made me pensive. Hoping no one would notice was a huge risk. What if someone called out to us? What if they wanted us to help? What if we stumbled into another arcanist?

"Get out of the way," Zaxis hissed. "I'll do it."

He moved around me and threw open the hatch. With no hesitation, he stepped onto the deck, tightened his coat around him, and then marched through the light drizzle of rain toward the bow. The two men at the rigging didn't even turn away from their duties. They tugged at the shrouds and threw their rope over the swing gun.

If I had been better with my knightmare magic, I could have just slithered through the shadows like Luthair, but that wasn't a real option since I couldn't control it properly. Cursing myself under my breath, I stepped onto the deck. The cold beating of the rain tamed my hair and plastered it to the side of my face. I stormed off after Zaxis, my hands in my coat pockets.

Illia climbed out of the hold a moment later. With her buccaneer outfit, it was hard to see any of the curves that would identify her as a woman. It wasn't like women didn't become pirates, but it was rare. Spider, the kappa arcanist, was surely aboard—somewhere—but since the number of women would be so much less than men, I was certain we would garner attention if Illia wasn't careful.

The massive quarterdeck had two levels all its own, unlike most of the other ships I has been on. The bottom floor had the officer's quarters and the whipstaff steering room. No one would bat an eye at us entering there.

Zaxis stopped near the quarterdeck door and waited. Illia and I joined him.

"We can go in," I said, the wind taking my voice and scattering it over the open ocean. I had to up my volume. "Then we can find a staircase."

Illia's teeth chattered as she shook her head. "No. Send Luthair. Then I'll teleport us."

Zaxis nodded, and I had to agree.

Without any need for instruction, Luthair slid under the door.

The men at the swing gun secured it in place with tight knots and lots of teamwork. Those cannons often weighed 3,400 pounds. Even with wheels, it took a group of men to move them around.

Luthair returned a minute later. "The captain's cabin is one level above us. Empty. We should hurry."

Illia took Zaxis and me by the arm. Her sorcery transported us to the level above the whipstaff steering room. We hit the floor, but it must have been at the edge of Illia's limits, because I fell forward as we arrived and hit my knees on the hardwood of the floor. Even Illia and Zaxis tumbled, caught off-balance.

Rain battered the glass windows, filling the captain's cabin with anxiety-inducing noise that prevented me from hearing anything outside the room.

"I can't see," Zaxis said.

I stood and glanced at the windows facing the deck. Fortunately, there were heavy curtains. I drew them shut. "You can use your fire now."

Zaxis snapped his fingers and sparked a small flame in his palm. The illumination didn't reach the corners of the impressive room, and I took a moment to glance around. A modest table and a massive desk had been positioned on opposite sides of the room. I suspected the table was for officer meetings, and the desk, along with all the writing instruments, was Calisto's personal property.

A small set of stairs leading downward ended in a door, but there was another door behind the desk, likely connected to the captain's sleeping quarters.

"What is that?" Illia asked as she pointed.

Zaxis and I followed her gesture to the bulkhead by the officer's table. A giant metallic-green object hung on a chain. Flat, diamond shaped, and iridescent, like a soap bubble, it reflected Zaxis's fire in a peculiar way.

Although interesting, I didn't care. I allowed Zaxis and Illia to examine the object while I turned my attention back to the room. The gargoyle said Zelfree was here, but where?

I walked over to the desk. The untidy space reminded me of Gillie's lab, but it was nowhere near as cluttered. As I stared down at the paperwork, however, I caught the edge of a strange scent. It was, unfortunately, quite familiar.

Coppery and stale.

Blood.

WORLD SERPENT SCALE

Tense and unable to relax, I glanced around. Light reflected off bits of metal on the desk. Guild pendants. I pushed some paperwork aside—most of it held down with a paperweight in the shape of a pistol—and I found at least a dozen pendants from various guilds, including Zelfree's silver pendant, his mark as a master arcanist of the Frith Guild.

Were these trophies?

I stepped around the desk, my eyesight thrown off due to Zaxis's flames. If it had been dark, I could've seen fine. If the lanterns had been on, I could've seen fine. But this half-n-half bubble of dim candlelight hindered my ability to make out details.

"Volke," Luthair said from the shadows behind the desk. "Here he is."

I rushed over, confused. Zelfree was here? In the dark? Without anyone around?

My questions answered themselves the moment I laid eyes on him.

Unconscious and lying on his stomach, he didn't move

as I drew near. An ebony piece of metal, like an arrow shaft, stuck out a few inches from his back. The weapon punctured him just below the shoulder blade. His long black hair was matted, and blood stained one side of his face, from the forehead all the way to his chin.

Traces transformed into a cat. She leapt to the ground and went straight for her arcanist.

He wore trousers and nothing else, not even a belt. I didn't want to examine the rest of him, but I knew I had to. The harsh shadows created by Zaxis's flickering flame made everything seem far worse. Bruises, welts, lesions—gouges in his flesh, some so deep I shuddered in empathic pain.

His tattoo—the one of the dragon—had been flayed off his body, leaving a patch of exposed muscle, the skin around it curled and dried.

He was breathing, but shallow and slow.

Damn. It was hard to take in some of the injuries.

Someone had cut the tendons in the back of his heel and the wrists of his hands. A cruel method of immobilizing someone. Slashed like he was, I doubted he could walk or grip anything. Normally an arcanist would recover, healing over time, but his injuries remained, even with Traces right next to him.

I just... couldn't bring myself to stare for long. I looked away, my mind locking up.

Luthair rose from the darkness, forming into his armored self. He said nothing, but offered up his shadowy cape. I shook my head.

"Zaxis," I whispered, my breath gone. I tried again, louder. "*Zaxis.*"

"What is it?"

He hustled over from the other side of the room, his fire

lighting up the cold shadows around Zelfree. I stood and took a step back.

Zaxis slowly knelt and examined Zelfree's body without blinking. "Damn." With an unsteady hand, Zaxis ran his fingers across the shredded skin. The injuries knitted themselves together, but a moment later, the flesh broke open again, like a blooming flower of gore, fresh blood weeping from the wound.

"It's the manticore venom," Traces said. She pointed with the tip of her tail to the black metal shaft sticking out of Zelfree's back. "It prevents magic use. Calisto no doubt laced the weapon."

Zaxis grimaced. "He's a sadist." Then he grabbed the metal device.

"*Stop*," Traces hissed. "It'll be barbed! You need to carefully remove it."

"I can heal him afterward."

"He's so weak." Traces nuzzled Zelfree's blood-matted hair. "Please... Don't hurt him anymore."

Zaxis met my gaze. I shook my head, uncertain of what to do. We had to remove the source of the manticore venom if we were going to heal Zelfree. I motioned Zaxis to take it out, regardless of his eldrin's protests.

He placed his thumb at the base of the weapon and pressed down. The pressure ripped open the puncture wound a bit more, but it allowed for us to see the edge of the barbs. Zaxis pulled on the metal device, taking it out of the flesh at a slow pace.

Traces paced around him, her tail swishing, her ears pressed down on her skull. She made warbling noises, but didn't attempt to physically stop us.

Zelfree flinched as the weapon finally came free from his body.

The thing in his back was an *obsidian thorn*—a torture tool with a hollow interior. People would fill the inside with poison, venom, or other types of liquid meant to slowly drip out into the injury of their victim. I had thought obsidian thorns were found only in legends and exaggerated retellings. I didn't think anyone actually used them.

When Zaxis used his healing again, the injuries knitted themselves together and some remained closed. Others remained visible—like thin lines of white marring Zelfree's body, but they didn't bleed. A handful broke back open.

Manticore venom was still in his system.

Zaxis broke contact and exhaled.

"Keep doing it," I said.

"Can't. That's all I can do."

"Why?"

"I don't know," he growled. "I haven't got this mastered. This is what happened when I tried, all right?"

I gritted my teeth. "Sorry. He still looks..."

"I can see what he looks like." Zaxis glared up at me, his green eyes darker in the flickering light of his fire. "Are we going to move him?"

We didn't have much choice.

As I knelt to lift one side of him, I spotted the red of the phoenix feather around my wrist. Gillie had said it would prevent disease—even magical disease—and while the wendigo could still be a threat, Zelfree needed protection more. I slipped the trinket off my wrist and slid it on to his, hoping that the magic would somehow help him. Would it get rid of existing diseases? I didn't know, but it didn't hurt to try.

Then Luthair offered his cape a second time. I nodded, hoping the silky cloth would be a comfort.

"Volke," Illia said.

I craned my head back and caught sight of her across the captain's cabin. Somehow, she had detached the chain holding the massive metallic-green object that had once been hanging on the bulkhead. She held it close and then motioned me over.

Although I feared for Zelfree, I got up and rushed over to her. "What're you doing? We should go."

"This is the world serpent's scale," she whispered.

I caught my breath, stunned. Then I turned my attention back to the "scale."

It was way bigger than anything I had imagined. Larger than a leviathan scale. About the size of my torso, but flat. Illia held it with no trouble, meaning that while it looked metallic in sheen, it wasn't as heavy.

"How do you know that's the world serpent scale?" I asked.

"Touch it."

Although the scale seemed inviting, I didn't want to delay. I shook my head and declined the offer.

"I believe you." I pointed back at the desk. "But we need to go. We have Zelfree."

"We should take this."

"Why? We don't have time, and if Calisto knows we took it, he'll come after us."

Illia glared. "We're already going to take his compass."

"But he won't know about that until it's too late. If we leave this and the journal, he might think he's won. He'll rush to the wrong spot for the compass and waste time searching."

"Well..." Illia mulled over my words. "I just hate the thought of him having this. I mean, it just feels like... pure magic. It tingles like lightning."

I didn't want him to have it either, but there wasn't

anything we could do about it. If we took the scale right now, he wouldn't bother going in the wrong direction for the compass—he would come straight for us. And with Zelfree in the state he was in, we couldn't afford to have a dread pirate stalking our movements.

Illia turned back to the chain on the bulkhead and fiddled with the attachments. I returned to Zaxis, surprised to see he and Luthair had lifted Zelfree off the floor and supported his weight. Zelfree's head hung forward, and he couldn't seem to stand right. I rushed over and got under Zelfree's arm, hefting half his weight onto my shoulder and relieving Luthair. Zelfree murmured something, but I couldn't tell what.

"He's talking?" I asked.

Zaxis shook his head. "He's delirious. He doesn't even know who I am. Keeps calling me Travin or something."

I didn't like holding Zelfree. He weighed far less than he should have, and it wasn't difficult to feel bone beneath a thin layer of skin, even with the shadowy cape wrapped around most of his body. When I accidently grazed a wound along the ribs that hadn't fully healed, Zelfree grimaced and ground his teeth.

"I'm sorry," I said. "But we're going to get you out of here. I promise."

Traces leapt onto Zaxis's shoulder. "Be gentle."

As Illia finished placing the world serpent scale back on the bulkhead, the door at the bottom of the short stairway opened. Ilia leapt backward and then rushed over to us. It was too late. Spider flew up the stairs, her cutlass drawn and a slight smile on her face.

"Zaxis, extinguish your light," I said. I motioned for Illia to take my place. "I'll handle this."

The fire died, and the room fell into utter darkness. Illia

supported Zelfree. Without a word between us, Luthair slithered over and merged with me, the cool touch of his darkness invigorating.

Spider chuckled ash she sauntered past the officer's table. Her long black hair—damp from the rain outside—hung to her waist and curled at the tips. Although I thought I would have the advantage in the pitch black, her eyes stayed locked on me the entire time.

With a pop and slight flash, Illia, Zaxis, Traces, and Zelfree disappeared.

It was for the best. They could prepare our getaway dinghy, and I could prevent Spider from alerting everyone to our presence.

Don't let your guard down, Luthair said to me, our thoughts now sharing one space.

I held my sword at the ready and tightened my grip on the pommel. Spider narrowed her eyes into a glare.

"Oh, I see," she said, a hint of amusement in her words. "You're the knightmare arcanist that tried to stop us in Port Crown. You must be a friend of Zelfree's."

I didn't want to have a conversation with her. I had been tense since I entered the room—since I found Zelfree—and now I felt the burning need to destroy. Nothing on this ship deserved mercy. Everything here was tainted by a million acts of wanton destruction. They hurt Illia, drove Ryllin to madness, and they tortured Zelfree.

They all had what was coming to them.

Spider tilted her head.

"You smell so... young. Yet your knightmare is full-grown? Interesting."

I lunged forward and swung much harder and faster than I ever had before. Spider sidestepped the attack—barely—proving she could see me. My blade slammed into the wood of the floor, cutting it deep. I ripped the blade free, but I couldn't be so reckless in the future. If Spider hadn't lost her footing, she could've attacked me then, when my defenses were at their lowest.

"Not very skilled, are you?" she asked with a chuckle. "Some amateur thinks he can slay an officer of the *Third Abyss*? You Queen's men never learn."

Spider slashed with her cutlass. I deflected it with my blade, but she reached out her other hand and slashed at my face with her fingers. The shadow armor helmet protected me, but she didn't have fingernails—she had razor claws, like talons. They cut into my defenses, though not through to my skin, burning with the intensity of acid.

The double attack sent me stumbling back. My heart raced.

I didn't know much about the fighting techniques of kappa arcanists.

Spider lunged for me. I channeled my magic, the pain eclipsed by the cold anger running in my veins, and I unleashed my terrors in the room. Spider stumbled to the side and gasped, but unlike many I had fought before, she gritted her teeth and then attacked me regardless.

Her attack had less power, and her legs quaked. I blocked the blow and then stabbed at her weak side. I sliced her shoulder as she slammed into the bulkhead.

As I hefted my sword to attack again, she spat. I saw the attack, but I couldn't react in time. The saliva splashed across my helmet and neck. In an instant, I felt the burn, like the armor itself had a direct line to my nerves, telling me it was dissolving.

Spider spat again. This time I stepped back and avoided it. When she spat a third time, I stepped through the shadows and appeared next to her. She must've expected it, because she whirled around and slashed with her razor claws. I brought my sword up and she cut herself along the blade.

That didn't deter her.

In a quick move that took me by surprise, she thrust with the cutlass and caught me in the upper leg. My armor took most of the blow, but it startled me enough that I tumbled into the officer's table.

Spider spat at the nearby window. It burned through the curtains and then corroded the glass.

I pushed away from the table and readied my weapon again. When Spider stepped close, I swung with an overhand blow, but it was too telegraphed. She sidestepped without a second thought and slashed with her claws.

Then, as I struggled to get proper footing, she bashed into me. With power I didn't think her capable of, she shoved me toward the weakened window. I crashed through the glass and toppled over the sill. The rain battered me as I fell.

THE MANTICORE ARCANIST

W ithin a split second, I was faced with an option. Shadow-step back into the ship through the window, or go straight to the deck. On instinct, I dipped into the darkness and moved as a shadow across the hull of the *Third Abyss*. The magic pulsed through me with a flickering pain, and while I still couldn't "see" where I was going, the deck was a large target to land on.

Sure enough, when I emerged from the darkness, I stood near one of the masts. The rain had become a light drizzle, but the wooden deck remained slick.

I suspected Spider had meant to send me into the ocean. She probably thought I was gone, at least for the time being. I rushed over to the door of the whipstaff steering room and waited, sword in hand, my heart beating fast. She would have to exit here to get to the hold.

A moment later, the door opened, and I thrust forward, anger fueling my power.

I struck Spider in the side of the chest, just as she emerged. Her eyes were wide, her gasp a sweet melody to my ears. She hadn't predicted I'd be here. My blade punctured deep between the ribs, but not all the way through.

In a seeming act of desperation, Spider slashed with her claws and leapt backward toward the stairs, freeing herself from my sword. Blood gushed from the injury, and she doubled over, her long hair tangled with the vital fluid.

I stepped forward, ready to strike again, but I hesitated.

All it took was that moment to catch her breath. Spider glanced up and spat again, this time with much more saliva than a person could normally produce. It came out like vomit and coated my lower legs. The burning happened fast. I stumbled into the rain, hoping the sprinkle of water would wash away the pain.

Spider slinked into the safety of the wheelhouse. I took deep breaths as the soothing chill of the rain eased my agony. The shadow armor I wore shifted and stirred, moving in such a way as to remove the grime. I had never thought of it before, but the armor was alive and capable of dislodging things on its own.

Luthair's irritation soaked into my own mood. *You hesitated. Never second guess your actions when life is on the line.*

I exhaled, and turned my attention to the dinghies. There had been men on deck, the ones tending to the swing gun cannon, but I didn't see them. Illia and Zaxis had one of the dinghies prepped and hanging on the outside of the ship. They lowered it with the cranks, moving with a shaky energy. Zelfree sat on the deck, against the railing, his face tilted up with the rain washing his long hair back.

Despite hating the rain, Traces curled around his shoulders, like she wanted to keep him warm.

I walked over, the clink of my armor hidden under the hum of the weather.

"The two pirates ran to get others," Illia said as I drew near. "We don't have much time."

They couldn't subdue two sailors? Damn. What if—

Out of the corner of my vision, I spotted something rush across the deck. I had just enough time to ready my weapon before it leapt toward me. With a powerful swing, I arched my sword, hoping to slice whatever it was in half.

I hit the creature and splattered green blood across the deck of the ship.

Shaken and a little confused, I took a step backward.

The thing in front of me was a kappa—a humanoid fish-person with dark green scales and gangly limbs. The monster hissed and flashed a row of teeth so thin and pointed they resembled sewing needles.

The kappa moved around on its hands and legs, scuttling across the rain-coated deck with a fearsome speed, in spite of its webbed fingers and toes. Its eyes glowed yellow in the dark, focused on me with a heated intensity.

I readied my stance and weapon, but the kappa scooped up water and flung it. At first I thought it would be like the acid spit, but instead the water hardened and clung to me. There wasn't any chill, yet in a matter of moments, my strength waned.

The kappa lunged, and I slashed again, this time slower.

It brought its needle-teeth down on my gauntlet and chipped away at the shadow. It didn't hurt, though. I kicked the fish-man off and thrust.

A gunshot rang out into the storm. I stumbled and missed with my attack as the bullet grazed over my shadow armor.

Zaxis and Illia stopped what they were doing, their eyes wide.

The kappa laughed as he scuttled away. "Now you'll pay for what you've done to my arcanist."

To my horror, Calisto stood on the opposite side of the deck, his flintlock pistol in hand. His glowing arcanist mark stood out in the gloom and rain. He lowered his weapon, a slight smirk on his face.

"He found us," I heard Illia whisper, her voice strained. She glanced over at Zelfree's limp body, and I knew what she was thinking.

We couldn't teleport away with Zelfree in that condition. We had all swallowed mouthfuls of ocean water getting here, and the three of us had been conscious. Plus, Illia couldn't teleport far enough in one jump to avoid Calisto, not when he had a ship and small boats at his disposal. Perhaps *Illia* could flee if we distracted the pirates, but without a boat of our own, her magic wouldn't save all of us.

Half a dozen men funneled up to the deck from the hold, each with guns and cutlasses. Breen, the snallygaster arcanist, also emerged, his snallygaster shadowing his steps. Breen's peg leg landed on the deck with a hard thud, and he looked us over with a clenched jaw.

My vision tunneled, and it became hard to breathe. Zaxis and Illia didn't have the dinghy in the water yet—and now we had the attention of the entire *Third Abyss* crew. I... couldn't imagine a scenario for escape, and that terrible realization buried itself in my thoughts, chilling my blood.

Calisto slipped his pistol into his holster. Flintlock weapons didn't work well in the wet weather—once water got into the lock, the powder wouldn't fire. Calisto walked across the deck, his irritated gaze shifting from me, to Zaxis, to Zelfree, and then to Illia. His pirates stayed back, including the snallygaster arcanist and the kappa, not wanting to move unless commanded.

Zelfree couldn't fight in his condition, and neither Zaxis nor Illia had their eldrin nearby.

I stepped forward, my sword in hand, my breathing shallow and fast. If anyone was going to fight, it should be me.

"No closer," I said, my haunting double-voice more intimidating than I felt.

Shockingly, Calisto stopped.

"Who are you, exactly?" he asked. "Some corsair-hunting knightmare arcanist with the Steel Thorn Inquisitors?"

I didn't know how to answer that question, and silently tightened the grip on my weapon.

"He hurt my arcanist," the kappa hissed from across the deck. "And he's helping them escape."

Calisto slicked back his rain-soaked hair and lifted an eyebrow. "Oh. I see." He turned his attention to the quarter-deck. "*Hellion*," he shouted. "We have arcanists that need dealing with!"

An answer came in the form of a growl so powerful it rumbled over the ship. The hairs on my spine stood on end, and I knew what he had summoned.

His manticore.

The beast flew off the top of the quarterdeck with black leathery wings. It landed next to Calisto with surprising grace for a creature three times the size of a stallion. Like a lion, it had a mane, but instead of gold or brown, the manticore had a crimson red mane resembling curdled blood. It contrasted harshly with the bone-white fur covering the rest of its body.

When it turned its face to us, I caught my breath.

It... wore a mask. A plain, expressionless mask of the type found in stage plays. The eyes were slits, and so was the straight line representing the mouth.

I had thought the manticore would have the head of a lion, but the mask was designed for a human face—flat and oval-shaped—not elongated like a cat's face. And the mask "grew" out of the manticore, as if it were a body part.

I stared, my mouth open, somewhat disgusted. The manticore had human-like hands, complete with thumbs, but they were fur-covered and tipped with massive claws.

Looking at the beast made me nauseous. It was an amalgamation of freakish parts.

It swished its black scorpion tail back and forth; the limb had to be seven feet long. The stinger at the end was twelve inches all by itself.

Every fiber of my being said I couldn't win against the manticore in a fight. What were we going to do? What could we possibly do?

Calisto lifted his hand and the manticore leaned its mask-face down to touch his palm, nuzzling it.

"I really hate it when arcanists think they can meddle in my business," Calisto said as he stroked his eldrin. "You'd think people would learn from the mistakes of others."

His pirate thugs spread out around the deck, blocking off doors. Trapping us. A few of them wore tinted glasses like the two in the hold, but I didn't have time to dwell on that strange fact. The manticore kept its mask-gaze on me the entire time. I had to tilt my head back just to look at its face. The monster could crush me in its hands if it managed to grab me.

"Hellion loves it when we have uninvited guests. Isn't that right, Hellion?"

The manticore chuckled, its voice emanating from behind the mask. "I do enjoy it when they run."

"I know. Just stay close. If any of them try to escape, you have my permission to do whatever you'd like to them."

Zaxis and Illia shifted closer to me, their movements stiff. Were we going to fight? Was that really our plan?

Luthair, I spoke in my mind. *Please advise me. I have no idea what to do here.*

Stay calm. We know Calisto is arrogant beyond measure. Recall how he allowed Illia to attack him back in Port Crown. Only a man of unchecked confidence would invite an unknown enemy to strike first. Attack when his guard is down.

But what about the manticore? I asked. *What about the—*

Focus, Luthair said, ending my downward spiral. *You won't face those challenges if you don't deal with this one first.*

Calisto smiled and turned to Illia. "I'm surprised you came back. A clever girl would've taken her loss and gone home. Now you'll end up like your pathetic parents—begging for death."

Illia balled her hands into fists. Her whole body shook. She didn't say a word. There wasn't any reason to. This villain just wanted to taunt her.

Zaxis glanced over to me with steeled resolution that told me everything I needed to know. We had to get away.

I lifted my hand and channeled my sorcery without regard to my own safety. I didn't care if it burned—I didn't care if wrecked me—I couldn't hold back.

The terrors I used affected everyone. Calisto, his crew, the snallygaster, and the kappa. Except for the manticore. While everyone else staggered and cried out, the manticore never took its mask-gaze off of me. It didn't even move.

Zaxis, no doubt anticipating my action, recovered quickly. He washed the deck in his flame, but the ocean water and drizzle of rain hampered the effectiveness. It singed the pirates and scared the kappa all the way back to the railing, but otherwise no one seemed harmed.

Illia, recovering just as fast, evoked a white flame far different than fire. It broke apart anything it touched—as if it teleported small chunks away from the whole. Splinters of ghostwood flew away from the deck, and even bits of Calisto's skin, coat, and trousers ripped apart.

"Don't damage my ship, wretch," Calisto shouted, more anger in his voice than I had ever heard. "It's worth more than your life."

He shook off my lingering terror, and his skin knitted itself back together with surprising speed. He had a cold intensity to him.

I lunged forward, used my terror again and slashed with my sword, aiming for the base of his neck. Calisto shivered, but in the split second before I struck him, he reached out and grabbed my wrist.

Too fast—I saw the motion, but I couldn't react.

Then he ripped the weapon from my hand, his strength so vast I had no chance of keeping my grip. I had never been at such a disadvantage when it came to raw muscle—manticore magic gave Calisto the supernatural edge that made the fight feel like a newborn babe versus a gorilla.

Before I could recover, or even change my stance, Calisto stepped forward and grabbed my shoulder. He yanked down as he brought his knee straight up into the center of my chest. Even with armor—even with Luthair's power as part of my own—my vision went white for a half-second from the sheer agony of my ribs breaking.

"*Volke!*"

Calisto planted his boot square in my gut with a powerful kick, sending me out of his grasp. I hit the swing gun cannon and then collapsed to the deck, writhing. I swear he shattered organs. I couldn't breathe. My muscles refused to unclench. I couldn't even open my eyes.

Someone rushed to me, but I was too busy vomiting blood to take note.

When I managed to regain my senses, I realized it was Illia. She had knelt beside me, her hand on my shoulder.

Zaxis got in close to Calisto and unleashed his fire. It blazed hotter than it ever had before, despite the weather. Even in my broken state, the heat registered clearly in my thoughts. Zaxis attacked as though aiming for Calisto's face, getting closer and closer, the temperature increasing with each wild attack.

Calisto stepped back, shielding his eyes with his forearm.

The pirates around the deck cheered for their captain. The kappa laughed, and the snallygaster cried out in animalistic excitement. Breen watched the fight with his arms folded, a smirk on his bearded face.

They had no fear their captain would lose. This was all a show for them—an evening performance. Like schoolyard bullies, they rooted for the strongest to win, delighted with the sheer disadvantage of the other side.

"Kill them!" one of the pirates yelled. "Gut 'em like fish!"

Zaxis threw his arm wide and unleashed a torrent of white-hot fire. He gritted his teeth, and sweat mixed in with the rain on his face. It was apparent from his ragged breaths that such power required a lot from him.

The fire burned portions of the deck and mizzenmast.

"What did I just say?" Calisto growled through gritted teeth. "That's my ship you're wreckin'!"

He shot forward, his enhanced speed far outclassing

everyone here. He grabbed Zaxis by the coat and upper arm and slammed him down on the deck, neck first. I had never seen anyone go ragdoll from a single blow. Zaxis went limp, and his fire died.

Calisto lifted Zaxis's body and squeezed his forearm, crunching bone with his unparalleled strength. Zaxis twitched, despite being unconscious.

The laughter from the crew haunted me more than the images of the fight.

Illia held me close, her muscles stiff as steel. What was I going to do? Luthair had given me advice, but I didn't know what to do with it.

"Hungry, Hellion?" Calisto asked with a chuckle.

A terrifying roar ripped through the night. At first, I thought it was Hellion answering the question, but then I saw the second manticore.

It was Traces. She had transformed into a mimic-manticore.

Unlike Hellion, with his white fur and blood-red mane, she appeared like a normal golden lion in coloration. She didn't have a mask, either—but she had the scorpion tail and leather wings.

Everyone's attention was on the faux manticore, even mine. I didn't notice Zelfree until he was already up close to Calisto. With his mimic magic, he had copied all the powers of a manticore arcanist, including the speed and strength. Although Zelfree hadn't fully recovered, that type of enhanced power was enough to get him back on his feet.

He punched Calisto across the face, the sound of the powerful strike echoing across the deck.

Calisto staggered backward, dropping Zaxis.

Breen rushed forward with his snallygaster, but Calisto recovered in time to hold up a hand. Breen stopped and regarded him with a confused expression. Then he returned to his previous position among the rank and file.

"Oh, Everett," Calisto said, irritation laced in his words. "It seems I can break everything but your spirit." He rubbed his jaw and narrowed his gaze. "Obviously I need to try harder."

Zelfree took a ragged breath and straightened his posture. The rain slicked his long hair down across his face and neck, and the half-healed injuries gave him the appearance of a corpse. His legs trembled, and the old slashes on the back of his legs and wrists began to bleed. Still, he stepped around Zaxis, shielding him from Calisto.

Traces, in her manticore form, rushed forward with her claws extended. She leapt for Calisto, but that's when Hellion stepped into the fight. The real manticore bashed Traces in the chest with the side of its head. Traces screeched, and the manticore slashed with its black claws, cutting into fur and right through flesh.

Blood splattered across the deck, and the sight of the carnage sent excitement through the crew. More of them had come up from the hull. Thirty of them were gathered around the railings, exhilarated by the gore.

Traces whipped her scorpion tail around and tried to strike Hellion.

In one of the creepiest moments of my life, Hellion's mask moved—the mouth upturned into a small smile, and the slit eyes curved to resemble a happy expression.

"Like this," it said.

Hellion's scorpion tail struck from the side, hitting Traces in the neck. In the next instant, Traces untransformed. She reverted back to being a cat-like mimic and fell to the deck with a heavy thud. The manticore venom corrupted magic use—I suspected she wouldn't be able to transform for a short while. She didn't even get back up.

Zelfree collapsed to the deck like a puppet whose strings had been cut. He hit his knees and then slumped over, his breathing heavy. Without the manticore magic to give him added strength and stamina, he struggled to keep his head up. He tried to stand, his whole body trembling with the effort, but he just couldn't.

The triumphant shouts of the crew darkened the situation.

"That's our cap'n," one pirate said. "Not even arcanists of the Frith Guild can stop him!"

Calisto slicked back his copper hair and smiled.

I still couldn't move. My whole body felt bruised and battered. I considered myself lucky whenever I got a sliver of air through my teeth.

Then Illia stood.

I wanted to tell her to run—she could save herself—but words were impossible when my lungs wouldn't cooperate.

Illia squared her shoulders and glowered. "Calisto." She ran a hand over the scars on her face. "This will be settled between you and me. I won't let you hurt them anymore."

The laughter happened instantaneously.

"Is that right, lass?" Calisto asked, his own chuckles mixing with his crew's. "I don't think you understand. The questions isn't, *will you let me?* The question is, *can you stop me?*"

Illia hardened her gaze and placed a hand on the swing gun cannon.

The crew continued their laughter, and Calisto ate it up, even motioning to Zaxis, Zelfree, and Traces sprawled across the deck. No one paid attention as Illia closed her eye and evened her breathing.

The swing gun flickered as sparkles of rizzel magic flitted across it. Illia knitted her eyebrows and gripped the cannon as hard as she could. The next second, the massive weapon disappeared with a *pop*.

I had never seen her teleport something so large—or so far. It appeared thirty feet above a group of pirates, including Breen, near the opposite end of the deck. The cannon fell fast, with almost no warning outside of the second *pop*. All 3,400 pounds came crashing down. It tore through the bodies of the pirates and then continued through multiple decks of the ship, crushing bone and shattering wood.

Splinters flew everywhere. The cracking, ripping, and screams killed all laughter.

The destruction lasted a full thirty seconds as the dust settled over the damp ship. A drizzle of rain fell straight through the new hole in the *Third Abyss*, into the lower decks.

Somehow, the snallygaster had evaded the falling cannon, but Breen, with his peg leg, wasn't so lucky. His eldrin screeched in agony and clawed at the deck, so distraught it slammed its face against the broken planks, its body quaking.

Calisto whipped around and dashed at Illia. He pulled his cutlass with lightning speed, and I thought Illia would be sliced clean in half. She teleported the moment before he struck, and appeared on top of another swing gun cannon farther down the deck. With her palm placed firmly on the cold iron, she glared.

"You've made the last mistake of your life," Calisto drawled, his hatred evident in his slipping composure.

"You took everything from me," Illia said, her fingers

gripping the cannon hard. "Now I'm going to take everything from you, starting with your *precious boat*."

He rushed for her, but it was too late. Illia teleported the
second cannon, this time aiming for Hellion. The massive
manticore managed to flap once and spring out of the way
with great speed. The cannon still plummeted through the
deck—crashing through wood las if it was wet paper. I swear
I heard it break several decks before the debris stopped its
momentum.

Two giant holes riddled the deck of the *Third Abyss*,
causing the whole ship to creak and twist.

Calisto ran a hand through his hair, his fingernails
digging into his scalp. "*Hellion!* Kill this wretch! I want her
insides painted across my flag!"

His manticore eldrin turned his smiling mask on Illia.
When it ran, its impressive weight shook the whole ship,
breaking more of the splintered deck. For a creature so big,
it moved with frightening speed. Illia teleported, but it was
obvious the beast only needed to slash her once for the
whole fight to be over.

I tried to stand, but my body still wouldn't cooperate.

"Should I remove my mask?" Hellion asked.

Calisto clawed at his hair, his hand unsteady. "No. My
crew's around. *Kill her the old fashioned way.*"

To my confusion, haunting laughter emanated from one
of the holes in the deck. The crew backed away, and Hellion
stopped stalking Illia in order to glance behind. The odd
voice, laced with madness, betrayed the identity of the individual in question.

Like it was crawling out of the depths of the abyssal
hells, the captive gargoyle pulled its way out of the hull.
Hellion turned and ran toward it, but the plague-ridden

monster opened its own wings and shot into the air with one powerful flap.

"It's escaped!" one panicked crewmember blurted out. "Run! It'll be comin' for us all!"

The men scattered, all of them rushing toward the hatches that led to the hold. Calisto stood his ground, his hard-set gaze locked on the escapee.

The gargoyle was just as big as the manticore, perhaps larger. Its long tail trailed behind it, and the beast seemed to carry a chain made of nails.

While the pirates and their captain were distracted, Illia teleported next to Zaxis, Zelfree, and Traces. When she touched them, they disappeared in a flash and pop. Then she appeared next to me.

"Volke," she whispered. "Please be okay. We're leaving. Just hang on."

We teleported together, her magic a soothing warmth that helped me catch my breath. We appeared in the dinghy that was still attached to the ship. Zaxis, Zelfree, and Traces were on the bottom of the boat. They looked more like bodies for the charnel house than anything else. And the question still remained—who would lower us?

Illia placed both her hands on the small boat and closed her eye. "You can do this," she murmured to herself. "Focus. *Focus.*"

The dinghy flickered for a second, and I feared we might all be tossed into the ocean. Illia gritted her teeth and dug her fingers into the wood so hard that her nails bled.

"*C'mon,*" she growled to herself. "This one last time..."

Then her magic washed over the dinghy and all of us. Together, as one group, we teleported off the ropes that held us to the *Third Abyss*. In the next moment, we appeared half a foot over the ocean. The dingy crashed into the water, jostling everyone around. Fortunately, we didn't capsize.

The *Third Abyss*, wrapped in fog, continued on, leaving wakes behind it. Our boat rocked and veered away. No one came after us. Screams and shouting were heard on the wind, indicating the crew still had the gargoyle to occupy them.

Illia let out a long exhale and sat on the bottom of the boat.

LOST COMPASS

The dinghy rocked on the soft waves of a calm ocean.

Illia tended to Traces, Zaxis, and Zelfree, making sure they were all still breathing. When Zaxis woke with a grunt, Illia helped him to the back of the boat. He rubbed at the base of his neck and kept his eyes closed, all while Illia whispered soothing words. I couldn't make out what they were, but Zaxis managed a soft chuckle.

I stared up into the mist, my body's pain waning with each passing moment. It took a long while before Luthair had the willpower to detach from me. After I separated from him, everything hurt. I groaned as I leaned against the front of the dinghy, each breath bringing a sharp spike of agony.

Illia moved closer to me. I didn't protest when she unbuttoned my shirt and stared down at my injuries. After a quick glance, I went back to staring at the sky. Purple and yellow bruising stretched from my collarbones to my navel. Looking at it almost made the pain worse.

"I know it hurts right now," Illia said. "But you're going to make it."

I smiled—even that hurt. "Thank you."

She grazed her fingertips across my shoulder. "I thought you were going to die."

"To be honest, I thought we'd never escape. You were amazing, Illia."

"I couldn't let him have you."

I turned my head and stared at her with a furrowed brow. She met my gaze, a weak smile on her face, her chin quivering. Then she hardened her expression, biting back a sharp inhale.

"Calisto already took so much," Illia whispered. "It made me so angry... thinking he would take you as well."

I lifted my hand, and Illia laced her fingers between my own.

"I'm sorry," I said. "For worrying you."

"Don't apologize."

We sat in silence for a long while, listening to the evening ocean singing a melody of distant waves and soothing winds. I enjoyed the splash of water and the slight taste of salt. It reminded me of the Isle of Ruma.

I turned to Illia. "We can't drift around like this forever."

"The fog's thick. I don't know how to find our way."

"Come look at this," Zaxis muttered. Even at a low volume, he was easy to hear. The quiet of our surroundings rivaled a graveyard.

Illia let go of my hand and returned to Zaxis's side. He held up a pair of tinted glasses—ones with perfect-circle lenses and a gold frame. The same glasses most of the pirates wore. Illia took them and placed them on her face. With her single eye, she glanced around.

"What is this?" she asked. "I can see through the fog. And the darkness. It's like daytime."

Zaxis massaged his neck. "It's gotta be kappa magic. I'm

sure that lady officer made these for the crew. That's how they see through the fog."

"She made the crew trinkets?" Illia took the glasses off and placed them back on her face. "I can see the stars with these. Look! Over there. That's west. I can see the guiding constellations."

"We should head south."

"Okay. Hold on."

Illia climbed onto the middle seat and then picked up the two oars. Although rowing a dinghy this size was difficult, Illia didn't ask any of us to help. Gravekeeper William had taught us all about proper boating techniques, and she used them to their fullest to steer the dinghy south. With the glasses still in place, she followed the stars, and Zaxis's instructions, until we were well on our way.

Between Illia's deep breaths and panting, I heard Zelfree stir. He groaned as he shifted positions and sat up, his back against the side of the boat. Traces leapt onto his lap, her purring loud enough to drown out the waves.

Zaxis, already much better than before, got up and sat next to him. His unsteady movements rocked the dinghy, however. He had recovered, but it seemed as though his head spun—he had been hit pretty hard, after all.

"You okay?" Zaxis asked Zelfree as he touched his shoulder.

Zelfree gritted his teeth and jerked away from the touch. "You should've left me." His words came out as a low slur, like it hurt to speak.

"Stop," Traces said. "I don't want to hear it."

Zaxis nodded. "You should sleep."

Although Zelfree didn't answer, I already knew he couldn't sleep. A few times during our trek, it looked as though he had closed his eyes and dozed off. But then he would awake a second later, jolted into consciousness from some terrible nightmare. He couldn't rest. His mind wouldn't let him.

"Worry about yourself," Zelfree murmured.

After a long exhale, Zaxis returned to his seat at the back of the dinghy, his expression one of concern.

Before I could comment, the fog dissipated and we found ourselves gliding through the waters near the rocky skerries. I glanced around, thankful we were close to our desired destination. The cartographer's journal said the ship carrying the Occult Compass crashed on one of these islands and sunk into the depths. Hopefully Adelgis, Hexa, and Atty had found it. Then we could all head back to the guild.

Luthair shifted in the shadows. "My arcanist."

"Yes?"

"How is your health?"

"I'm much better." I opened my shirt and rubbed the fading bruises across my chest. "Won't be long until I can breathe without hurting."

"Once you have your feet under you, we should train some more. As a knightmare arcanist, you have the ability to slip through the enemy's grasp, especially in instances when they attempt to grapple you."

"All right."

"Perhaps I should plan your daily schedule with Master Zelfree to better optimize your time."

I frowned. "Where is this coming from?"

"I feel the same as Illia."

"What do you mean?"

"I've already lost an arcanist to cruel circumstance. I do not wish to lose another."

Their affection weighed heavy on my mind and heart. I hadn't realized they felt that way. I knew neither Illia nor Luthair wanted me dead, but their concern filled me with a deep-seated appreciation. When I had been younger— when my father had been taken, and my mother left me without so much as a goodbye—I thought no one wanted me.

Now I had lots of people in my life.

Gravekeeper William. Illia. Luthair.

I didn't want to lose them either.

Illia huffed as she pulled the oars into the dinghy. "I... need a rest... Then I'll get us to the skerry with the others."

"Let me help," Zaxis said. He sprang to his feet and took a seat next to Illia. "You've been at it for an hour at least."

"I don't need help."

"I never said you needed it. I just want to do it. For you."

She gave him an odd glance, her one eye narrowed, her face pink. She didn't responded. Instead, she moved to another seat and gave him the oars. Zaxis took them up and continued moving us south, weaving through the large rocks that jutted out of the water.

The sun rose over the horizon, lighting up the world with an intensity that lifted my spirits.

Tied to the rocks near a small skerry of red and black rocks, was a mid-sized keelboat. The white sails glowed in the early morning light, and I knew it had to belong to the others. Sure enough, when we got close, I spotted Hexa's distinct shape walking along the stones of the shore. She waved as we drew closer and I spotted the unmistakable blob of white that was Nicholin.

Zaxis rowed us right onto the shore. The dinghy jostled around as it crashed, and I could hear Zelfree suck in air through his teeth.

I walked over to help him. Although he seemed averse to my touch at first, he eventually allowed me to lift most of his weight onto my shoulder. I helped him out of the boat and onto the water-slick rocks. Worried he would fall, I kept him close.

Nicholin popped out of existence and then reappeared on Illia's shoulder.

"You're back!" He wrapped himself all the way around her neck like a fat scarf. "*You have to stop leaving me*! I can't stand not being with you. I don't care if enemies can smell me! I'll wear a coat of bacon if that's what it takes."

Illia chuckled and stroked his soft fur. "I missed you, too."

Nicholin squeaked and swished his tail. "You feel so warm. I'm going to stay here forever."

"I can't believe you did it," Hexa said as she glanced between us. "I... I figured we'd have to go and find you all chained on a pirate boat." Then her gaze settled on Zelfree. "I... hope you're all okay."

Illia shook her head. "We'll be fine. But Volke and Zelfree should get some rest. Have you found the compass?"

"Well..." Hexa turned around and pointed. "You might want to come see this. We have a problem."

"You'll never believe what we found," Nicholin added.

Illia and Zaxis followed Hexa without hesitation.

I turned and headed for the keelboat—a decently-sized vessel for calmer waters that had a flat bottom and a single cabin for the passengers. I was certain there would be a cot or hammock for Zelfree to rest in.

But he had other plans.

"Follow them," he commanded.

Traces leapt to my other shoulder, her claws digging through my shirt and into my skin. "Volke, talk sense into him. He won't listen to me."

"You need to rest," I said. "You've been through a lot."

Zelfree shook his head. "I need to know what's happening."

"Why?"

"Just follow my damn instructions, boy."

The harshness of his words didn't cut as deep as they normally would. He wasn't himself, and that made it easier to shrug off his persistent rage.

Without another word, I helped him across the rocky terrain. Zaxis's healing had helped, and it was good that Traces was nearby, but I doubted Zelfree could walk on his own. He held onto my shoulder with a weak grip, and more than once he urged me to stop so he could rest.

Despite his weakened state, I was impressed with his determination. Back on the *Third Abyss*, I almost couldn't believe that he had managed to stand and confront Calisto, if only for a few moments. Zelfree had been willing to pay the highest price to save us from that lunatic. And now he didn't even want to give himself time to recover.

Thankfully, it didn't take us long to weave between a few boulders and arrive at the opposite shore. Adelgis and Atty were waiting there, both hip-deep in the ocean's waters.

Hexa, Zaxis, and Illia stood next to a knee-high pile of metal objects. The glint of copper, silver, and gold caught my eye, and I helped Zelfree over to examine everything.

I caught my breath.

Compasses.

The pile was nothing but compasses. Some large, some small—some with ornate jewels and others with extravagant artwork—but they were all clearly compasses.

"What's going on?" I asked.

Hexa turned to me and glared. "*As I was just explaining*, we found the shipwreck. That ethereal whelk, Felicity, doesn't need to breathe, apparently, so she floats on down there and finds everything. Raisen can also swim, so he's helpin' out, but it's too deep for anyone else."

"And there was more than one compass?" Zaxis asked. "Are any of them the Occult Compass?"

Hexa shrugged. "I don't know. I'm not sure what it looks like. The eldrin just said there were tons of compasses, so we told them to bring them all up, but Felicity and Raisen are small. They get two or three compasses each trip, and there are still dozens of others."

"I'll do it," Illia said. She turned her attention to the ocean. "I can just... teleport down there and carry all the compasses back."

"Don't," Zelfree growled.

Everyone turned to him. He gripped my shirt tight and shook his head.

Once he caught his breath, he continued, "I swear you're all trying your damnedest to kill yourselves. The water pressure gets intense at great depths. Teleporting straight down, with no way to acclimate, could easily result in you losing consciousness."

Nicholin hugged Illia's neck. "That's what I tried to tell the others when they asked if I could get everything with my magic! Nobody would listen to me, even though I'm clearly the most intelligent one here."

"Just..." Zelfree hesitated a moment, his eyes scrunched

shut. "Get a fishing net. Or the rigging from the keelboat. Have Felicity and Raisen use it to scoop up multiple compasses at once."

While Illia and Hexa jumped to fulfill that demand, Adelgis and Atty walked out of the cold ocean water. They rushed to my side, their attention stuck on Zelfree.

"Will he be okay?" Adelgis asked.

I nodded.

Atty placed a hand on my shoulder. "Will *you* be okay?"

Again, I nodded.

"Please, let me take you to the boat. You can rest there while we gather all the compasses."

BIRTH OF A WORLD SERPENT

The keelboat was smaller inside than it looked from the outside. Fishing gear littered the deck and the sole cabin, giving the boat a claustrophobic feel. I took Zelfree and Traces into the cabin and helped them get settled on the hammock. The ship only had one, but I didn't think I could sleep. Once they were settled, I returned to the deck.

Adelgis and Atty waited for me.

"Where did you get this boat?" I asked.

Adelgis smiled. "We rented it from a fisherman."

"What happened?" Atty asked.

"We were caught while rescuing Zelfree." I rubbed the back of my neck. I didn't feel like explaining every gruesome detail. "We fought our way off, and Illia managed to teleport us away. I don't think the pirates know where we are."

"I'm so glad you all made it back."

I glanced around, the morning sun a welcome sight. "Where are Forsythe and Titania?"

"We sent them to deliver messages." Atty pointed to the south. "We figured we should somehow let the Frith Guild know what's happened. And since the phoenixes couldn't swim..."

"I understand."

I swayed to one side, my exhausted body threatening to quit on me. Atty and Adelgis both jumped to my side, their concern evident in their expressions.

"You should get inside," Adelgis said. "Here. Let us help."

I didn't protest. We went back into the cabin together, and Atty pulled curtains over the three portholes, blocking out the light. Although we didn't have a second hammock, she pulled a cot out from under the captain's desk.

Zelfree had already fallen asleep. Traces rested on his stomach, her long tail wrapped around one of his arms. He twitched a bit, his eyebrows knitted and his body tense. Just like on the boat ride there, the nightmares refused to loosen their hold.

Before Atty and Adelgis left the cabin, I turned and held up a hand. "Wait."

They both stopped.

I motioned Adelgis close. "You... can control dreams, right?"

He walked over and nodded. "Should I help you sleep?"

"No. Help Zelfree."

He glanced over at our master with a slight frown. "You think so? Won't he be upset? I'm just his apprentice, and using magic on him without his—"

"If he gets upset, tell him I forced you to do it," I said. "Zelfree *needs* to get some rest, and he never will if we just leave him be. Please. Just help him."

Adelgis fidgeted with the sleeve of his coat. Then he walked over to Zelfree and placed the tips of his fingers on the man's temple. "What should he dream about?" Adelgis whispered. "Master Zelfree is a bit of an enigma."

"Something happy." Anything to forget his time aboard the *Third Abyss*.

I took off my coat and gently placed it over him. Traces got in the way, but she slipped out from underneath, yawned, and curled up on top. She said nothing as she snuggled into a perfect circle.

"Hmm..." Adelgis waited a long moment, his gaze unfocused.

"Have him dream about talking to Gillie," I said. "They should talk about all the good times in the past. And Gregory Ruma should be there, too."

"Is that a joke?" Adelgis turned to me and shook his head. "He *killed* Ruma."

"Trust me. Just have them all talking about the good 'ol days."

Zelfree had said they were friends. Plus, Gillie made it sound like they had a million adventures together. Perhaps if Zelfree could experience a simpler time, he could unwind and finally get the rest he needed.

Taking a deep breath, Adelgis returned his attention to Zelfree. His use of magic was subtle, and after a few short moments, Zelfree visibly relaxed under his touch.

Adelgis took a step back and exhaled. "There. He should be dreaming about Gillie's lab right now."

With a heavy sigh, I sat down. "Thank you." I leaned back on the narrow cot and stared at the ceiling.

"Do you want me to help you sleep as well?"

"Sure."

I would probably end up with something bizarre, but I didn't care. I didn't want to run the risk of nightmare-infested sleep.

Sure enough, my dreams involved swimming in the ocean with Atty, Zaxis, and Hexa, only I didn't want to get close to them, for fear they would realize how lumpy I was. Illia waited on the beach, smiling as I swam by.

I awoke in a mix of relaxation and confusion. It took me a moment to remember it had all been a magic-induced dream.

My first thought was for Zelfree. He continued sleeping, his eyes firmly shut, his head tilted to one side, a single hand resting on top of Traces's head. She, too, slept soundly. Were their dreams filled with odd occurrences? I supposed that would be better than a nightmare, but still. Perhaps Adelgis just wanted to mess with me.

I turned my head and almost jumped out of the cot. Adelgis sat in the middle of the cabin, his attention on five compasses laid out in front of him. He touched each one, examining it closely before moving on to the next. He didn't seem to notice me as I sat up, but the moment the cot creaked under my shifting weight, he whirled around.

"Volke? You're up faster than I thought you'd be."

I ran a hand down my face. "What time is it?"

"Noon. We still haven't collected all the compasses yet. I apologize."

"It's fine." I eyed the ones in the cabin. "Why do you have those?"

"Well, most of the compasses we found weren't magical —they were just normal tools of navigation. But these ones here are obviously trinkets. We're still not sure which is the Occult Compass, but at least we've narrowed it down."

I kicked my legs off the side of the cot and rested my elbows on my knees. "Why don't you just test it? The Occult

Compass finds mystical creatures, right? Place the compass on one of your eldrin."

"Well," Adelgis looked away and sheepishly laughed. "The compasses all point in a different direction when pressed against a mystical creature. The Occult Compass finds the same creatures, and if both the phoenixes were here, this would be an easy test, but since they aren't, we have no way to confirm which compass is pointing in the right direction. Also, if we still had the cartographer's journal, we could just compare the pictures, since the Occult Compass had a detailed drawing to go along with the directions to the shipwreck."

I leaned forward, unconcerned with the compass situation. We would find the right one eventually—what worried me more was Calisto's ultimate plan.

"Adelgis," I muttered. "We found the scale of a world serpent on the *Third Abyss*."

He perked up and met my gaze. "Really?"

"And we also found a cage. A large one. Someone said it was for the world serpent. Obviously Calisto thinks he'll find a live one with the Occult Compass."

Adelgis mulled over my comment. "Perhaps."

"What?" I balked. "I thought you said he was looking for a corpse? So he could use the pieces for magical items?"

"That's the most likely explanation. But if he has a cage, then I suspect he hopes to find a live one."

"How? They're dead!" I forced a laugh. "I mean, we would've seen one if it had been alive. World serpents are supposedly huge. Bigger than a leviathan. It can't be *hiding* somewhere. Why would it do that?"

"Perhaps it was just born."

His casual suggestion only fueled my outrage. "What?

How? If they're all dead, where did it come from? A random dormant egg? That can't happen."

Adelgis shook his head. He leaned back against the cabin bulkhead. "Um, well, my father classifies mystical creatures by their reproduction method—most researchers do, actually. *Progeny* mystical creatures give birth or lay eggs. They need parents, like we do." He punctuated the sentence with a nervous laugh. "And then there are *fable* mystical creatures. They come into existence after a certain set of criteria are met. Like knightmares, for example."

I had never been taught the breeding requirements of mystical creatures, but it suddenly made sense. Knightmares didn't have *males* and *females* that came together to have children. Knightmares were born when a king was murdered. Well, any sole ruler of a nation—even queens or tyrants. As soon as they were killed, a knightmare would sprout from the shadow.

"So you think this world serpent is a fable creature?" I asked. "As in, some event happened that caused it to spawn into existence?"

Adelgis shrugged. "I'm saying it's a possibility. I don't know anything about world serpents, other than what I read in fairy tales. Maybe Calisto knows. Maybe that's why he's going out of his way to find it before everyone else figures out what's going on."

Damn.

A man like Calisto shouldn't be allowed to find a world serpent. What if he killed it? Or worse—what if he somehow bonded to it? A world serpent arcanist would be... outrageously powerful. Calisto was already so frightening.

"My father knows a lot about mystical creatures," Adelgis muttered, his voice slipping into an absentminded tone. He rubbed at his side, his hand gently touching his

367

ribs. "Maybe he would know what type of creature a world serpent is. He's really knowledgeable."

"Adelgis," I said. "I know this is off topic, but do you mind if I ask you a personal question?"

He looked at me with wide eyes and a slight expression of worry. "Uh, of course not." He took his hand away from his side and placed both of them in his lap.

"When you weave dreams for me, do you have full control of *everything* that I see?"

"In theory. Because I'm so new to this, I sometimes mess up. Like an amateur painter, I don't have solid brush strokes."

"Why do I keep imagining I have lumps under my skin? Every dream it's the same—I'm worried someone might find out. It taints the whole experience with fear. It's hard to describe."

Adelgis's honeyed skin paled. He brushed back his long black hair, his gaze drifting to the floor. "Is that what you see?"

"The last time I walked into your personal room at the guild, I... I saw the thing under your skin. I'm sorry. I should've told you, but I can see in the dark just fine. I could tell you were bruised and there was something in you. Is that what I keep dreaming about?"

Adelgis took in a deep breath and then exhaled. He didn't look at me. "I haven't mastered my sorcery, so I suppose my thoughts are seeping into my dream creations. I'm so sorry."

I shook my head. "I don't care. I'm just worried about you."

He glanced up, one eyebrow raised. "You are? Oh. Well. I appreciate that."

"Of course I'm worried. I've never seen anything like

that." I thought back to the many times that Adelgis insisted on wearing odd clothing—shoulder capes and heavy coats. "Is that lump the reason you didn't want to get into the Sapphire Springs?"

"Y-yes," he muttered. "I, uh, don't want anyone to know. Please keep it a secret between us."

"Keep *what* a secret? Why is it there? What is it?"

Adelgis stood and pulled his coat close, his agitation apparent in the way he nervously paced the tiny cabin. "So... I've told you my father researches mystical creatures. Well, he asked me to help him with some experiments. You see, his ultimate plan is to make everyone an arcanist. A very noble aspiration."

He spoke quickly, his voice distant, like he was talking more to himself than to me.

After a long pause, Adelgis continued, "Obviously, I want to help my father. So, when he asked me to... incubate... a mystical creature for his research, I agreed."

"Incubate?" I asked, both my eyebrows shooting for my hairline.

"There's no other w-word for it." He stopped pacing, gave me a glance, and held up both hands. "Don't worry! The creature has been with me for years now. The worst of it is over."

I wanted to ask a million questions. His father asked him to harbor a creature in his body for research? Why would he do that? And had it somehow harmed Adelgis?

"Like I said," Adelgis muttered. "I'm helping my father. That's all you need to know. I'll try not to infect your dreams with that worry in the future. Everything is fine. Just fine."

The more he said it, the less likely it seemed.

Adelgis stood and turned to the door. "I'm going to check on the compass acquisition. You get more rest." He opened the cabin door and left without so much as a glance over his shoulder. I didn't even get to say anything before he snapped the door shut.

That was... different.

The keelboat creaked with the rocking of the waves.

"You have some bizarre apprentices," Traces said.

Her voice startled me. I snapped my attention to her, my heartrate high. I had forgotten she and Zelfree were sleeping on the hammock. They were both awake now—Zelfree staring at the ceiling, his mimic on his stomach, her tail swishing back and forth.

"What am I going to do with them?" Zelfree asked, his voice rusty. "I swear they're all trying to kill themselves just to spite me." He scratched Traces behind the ear.

She nuzzled into his hand. "It's like trying to save a group of lemmings from going over the cliff."

"I'm sorry if we woke you," I said as I stood from the cot.

I gave him the once-over, surprised by what a couple of hours of good rest could do for a person. Zelfree still looked injured, but he already looked ten times better than he had before.

"How're you feeling?"

Zelfree stared at the ceiling, and with a tone that sounded like he didn't care for my question, said, "I was wondering why Adelgis didn't seem to have the same strength as everyone else. Lo and behold, yet another problem."

"What're you talking about? Adelgis has displayed all kinds of powers. He evokes light and manipulates dreams."

"He's actually older than the rest of you. And while everyone else is improving and developing more advanced skills, he seems to be stuck with the basics. Unlike you—

with the excuse of being second-bonded—he should be excelling."

I crossed my arms, bothered by the information. "Are you saying the thing in his side has something to do with it?"

Zelfree replied with a dry smile. "I know his father. He's a cold-hearted bastard that would throw children to the sharks if he thought it would help him unlock magical secrets. There's no doubt in my mind that *thing* Adelgis is carrying has been the cause of his problems."

Odd. Adelgis always spoke of his father in glowing terms. I had never heard even the whisper of a complaint—just admiration. Was his father really what Zelfree said? I was curious, but now wasn't the time to ask questions.

"I'll speak to him," Zelfree muttered. "Once we're back at the guild." He closed his eyes and groaned as he shifted around the hammock. "Watch everyone while I recover, all right? And... please thank Adelgis for the dreams."

"I will." But I couldn't bring myself to leave his side. The longer I stared, however, the more he regarded me with a cold glower.

"What is it?"

"I... saw how injured you were on the *Third Abyss*. Are you sure everything will be okay?" How long had he endured Calisto's torture?

"I've been through worse," Zelfree said in a melancholy tone. "Don't worry yourself. Just focus on protecting the others."

"If that's what you want."

Concerned about the compasses, I headed for the door. Before I left, Zelfree rolled back over. "Wait."

I stopped and looked over.

"Thank you." He held up his wrist with the phoenix feather trinket. "This helped."

"Of course," I said.

Zelfree returned to his side. No more words were spoken between us.

THE PLAGUE-RIDDEN GARGOYLE

Even with a net, it took Raisen and Felicity several hours to dredge up the valuables from the ocean floor. Apparently, the ship had sunk into a small chasm, making the recovery more difficult than anyone anticipated.

No wonder the cartographer marked the location in his journal and left.

Raisen and Felicity found more than just compasses, however. We had 102 compasses, 13 spyglasses, and 25 bells. Once gathered, we placed them on the deck of our keelboat and separated everything into magical and non-magical piles. Of the magical items, we had 25 compasses, 2 spyglasses, and 10 bells.

While Illia and Atty prepared the boat to set sail, Hexa, Zaxis, and Adelgis regarded the collection with hard stares. Adelgis counted and recounted, muttering to himself the entire time.

"Was that sunken ship some sort of floating museum?" Hexa asked as she eyed all the trinkets.

Adelgis turned to her with a deep frown. "Seriously? A *floating museum*? That was your guess?"

"What? There's a lot of junk here. Reminds me of the museum at the capital."

"Junk? *Junk*? These are magical items!"

"If you're not using them, they're junk."

"This is the prized collection of Sir Henri Fenton! He was having it transported when the ship crashed and sunk into the depths." Adelgis shook his head as though thrown for a preposterous loop. "Sir Fenton had gathered the most beautiful and wondrous nautical trinkets. Not only did he have the Occult Compasses of Master Arcanist Livia Brite, but he also managed to secure a Refraction Spyglass and a Bell of Demise! None of this is junk. They're prized possessions."

"Is this the Refraction Spyglass?" Zaxis asked as he scooped up a bright brass spyglass with writing down the side.

"Most likely," Adelgis said. "But we have no way to test it. The Refraction Spyglass sees through invisibility, and none of us have that kind of magic."

"I'll just assume it's the right spyglass." Zaxis pocketed the item.

"Hey," I said. "Put that back. You heard Adelgis. It belongs to Sir Fenton."

Zaxis sneered. "Don't you know the rule of the seas? Once something's lost to the waves, anyone can claim it."

"We're arcanists of the Frith Guild, not lowborn pirates."

Adelgis offered a nervous laugh. "Well, Sir Fenton hired a ship to transport his collection, but he died shortly afterward. The search for the sunken vessel stopped once Fenton's funding did, which is why Cartographer Martin Mercator was the only one ever looking for it."

"Sir Fenton's collection should go to his family, then," I said.

"I would agree. Except... his family died with him. It was tragic, really."

I shot Adelgis a glare. "Whose side are you on? I'm saying we shouldn't take these things for ourselves."

"Oh, uh, sorry." Adelgis took a step back and pressed his lips together in a tight line, not bothering to weigh in on the actual dilemma at hand.

"Calisto almost broke my neck," Zaxis stated. "I don't think anyone will fuss about a missing spyglass. Especially when all the owners are dead."

Illia gathered a coil of rope and shook her head. "Stop. Just focus on what we need to do to get out of here. Which one is the Occult Compass?"

Everyone turned to the 25 magical compasses. I had seen a drawing of the Occult Compass in the cartographer's journal, but the exact details were difficult to recall. All compasses had the same elements. A needle. The directions. A circular shape.

I knelt close to the trinkets and examined them one by one. Then I came to a compass with an eyeball for the base —the needle stuck in the iris and remained unmoving, no matter which way I turned the thing.

"This is it," I said as I picked it up. "It has to be."

"Why that one?" Atty asked.

"The Occult Compass was made with an eye of an all-seeing sphinx, right? And this looks familiar. It must be the right one."

Hexa balled a fist and smiled. "Then, we got it! Just like that. Long before the pirates."

No one said anything. She glanced around, a clear expression of confusion and disappointment written across her face.

"C'mon," she said. "This is worth celebrating."

Raisen curled around her legs. "You take every moment to bicker, but you won't take the time for victory? Silly islanders."

Although the hydra had a point, I still didn't feel like congratulating ourselves just yet. We hadn't made it back to the Frith Guild, and Zelfree was still bedridden. While we had a few successes, it didn't feel like they outweighed the negatives.

I stared at the Occult Compass for a moment, examining the dead eye. Then I slipped it into my trouser pocket, intent on keeping it safe until we reached the guild.

"Let's get out of here," Illia said. She motioned to the sails and rigging. "We have to prep and head out while the weather is fair."

The keelboat didn't come with a crew, so we had to do everything ourselves to prepare for the journey. It wasn't much, but tending to a ship was more difficult than some people thought. And it was obvious from the way some worked who was familiar with a boat and who wasn't.

Hexa had the enthusiasm, but lacked technical knowledge. She untied everything and got the rope coiled, but she had to wait for Illia to secure the sails. Adelgis was much the same way. They had both been born on the mainland, and neither seemed comfortable with the workings of our vessel. Fortunately, Atty, Illia, Zaxis, and I were practically experts.

Gravekeeper William would've been proud.

Atty stopped unfurling the sails and stared across the ocean with wide eyes. "Wait, do you see that in the distance?"

I whipped my attention to the northern horizon before the words even fully registered in my conscious thought. To my horror, a bank of fog rolled across the waves, heading in our direction at an unnatural pace.

It couldn't be.

"What is this?" Zaxis barked. He walked to the railing and slammed his hands down on the solid wood. "It feels like we've been running from them forever! One encounter after the next—they never relent!" He turned on his heel and glared straight at me. "You said they wouldn't chase us. You said they would take their journal and world serpent scale and search in the wrong spot."

"That was before we wrecked their ship," I muttered. But we hadn't wrecked it enough. The cannons didn't break the hull, so the *Third Abyss* could still sail.

"And you said they wouldn't be able to find us this time!"

"I don't know, okay? I'm not sure what's drawn them here!"

"You destroyed their ship?" Atty asked.

In my original plan, we snuck Zelfree off the ship and then sailed away under the cover of darkness. But Calisto saw us, and we left his prized ship in shambles. Was he coming for revenge? It wouldn't surprise me.

Zaxis shook his head. "We're never going to be rid of these damn pirates! They'll chase us to the end of the world and back, just you watch."

"Luthair," I said. "We almost didn't escape Calisto on the *Third Abyss*, and there's no way a keelboat can outrun a man-o-war. If Calisto corners us on the skerry... Illia might not be able to save us all. What would Mathis do in this situation?"

Luthair's first arcanist fought pirates all the time—maybe he knew of some solution I didn't.

"Mathis never faced a dread pirate as an amateur," Luthair said.

That didn't instill confidence. If anything, the statement

sank into my gut like a rock into water. Luthair had nothing for me? Not even a rare tale of daring escape?

Hexa shook her head. "So, let me get this straight. We left Calisto the journal and the scale, but then you went and wrecked his ship? So now he's coming for us?"

"Our plans haven't worked since we started this journey," Raisen said with a hiss. "It's like this trip is cursed."

Zaxis crossed his arms and then uncrossed them. He glared a hole in the deck of the keelboat, his frustration and fear oozing out of every gesture and movement. Then he pulled out his spyglass—and the dark glasses he got from the dinghy—and pointed them toward the fog.

The dark glasses were made with kappa magic, and were capable of seeing through the barrier of misty obfuscation. The Refraction Spyglass could see through invisibility—could they work in tandem? I didn't see why not.

Adelgis took in several deep breaths. "Volke, what're we going to do? Your thoughts are never this despairing."

"Stop listening," I muttered. It would only get worse from here.

I turned around, and Illia was there, her one-eyed gaze searching mine. She had a stony determination to her expression that I knew well. Did she want to fight Calisto? No. We had lost so thoroughly that we couldn't hope to defeat him in direct confrontation. Did she have a plan? Some tactic like she used on the *Third Abyss*?

"We're going to make it through this," Nicholin said. He perked up his ears. "No way we're gonna let that pirate dastard get the best of us."

Although his bravado didn't come from a place of reality, it did lift my spirits to hear someone say something hopeful.

Zaxis leaned on the railing of the keelboat. "What the?"

Hexa and Atty both gave him questioning glances.

"What is it?" Hexa asked.

"Look."

Zaxis passed around the two trinkets. One by one, the others looked, though their brows furrowed after a few seconds of searching. Then the glasses and spyglass came to me. I used them both to see through the fog. It didn't take me long to spot what bothered Zaxis.

The gargoyle.

It sailed through the sky, exited the fog, and continued at lightning pace toward our island skerry. In its scythe-like claws it held something. For a split second, that something caught the light and shone with an iridescent glitter, betraying the powerful magic held within.

I couldn't believe it. The plague-ridden gargoyle had escaped the pirates and stolen their world serpent scale. Not only that, but I caught sight of the clear glittering power of star shards. A small piece of me wondered if Calisto was chasing that thing rather than us. It was a real possibility.

"The gargoyle," I said as I lowered the spyglass and removed the glasses. "It's heading this way with the scale in hand."

The others exchanged worried glances.

Luthair ascended from the darkness and brushed back his cape. "This explains it. Calisto is chasing the monster."

"I thought the same," I said.

"Then we should leave. Right now."

We had the Occult Compass. Even if Calisto got his scale back, it didn't matter. Running was our best option.

Illia and the others finished the last of the preparation. Zaxis and I helped pushed the keelboat away from the rocky shore, and once we had a clear path, we hopped in and headed for the ocean. We hadn't gone far before the gargoyle flew overhead, its massive elephant-sized body enough to create a dark shadow that swept across the deck.

I held my breath as it glided above on leathery bat wings. I still didn't get a good look at it—not while it was in motion—but the creature flashed its red eyes over the keelboat at the last moment, its gaze chilling.

The monster landed on the skerry and dropped the scale and star shards from its arms. Then it took to the sky again, its long tail lashing about as the beast flew. With each beat of its wings, a strong force of wind disturbed the water and rocks.

It turned toward us.

"It's coming back," Zaxis shouted.

Luthair readied his sword.

In my gut, I had known this would happen. The gargoyle had every right to hate us when we left it to rot in the hold of the pirate ship. Now it would have its revenge.

"It's plague-ridden," I said. "We must be careful!"

But time wasn't on our side. The gargoyle swooped in fast, its granite-colored skin glittering like a geode in the light. When it exhaled, dust came with its breath, as if the insides of its body were lined with crushed rocks.

Both Zaxis and Atty unleashed flames when the gargoyle got close. Both of them failed to create anything hot—no doubt because their phoenixes were so far away.

Illia and Nicholin, however, added their white flames to the mix, blasting the gargoyle for daring to bother us.

The monster didn't care. It allowed pieces of its body to flake away under the flame of teleportation. Then it crashed into the sail of our keelboat, snapped the mast in half, and threw the splintered wreckage into the ocean. Luthair swung at it with his sword, but the gargoyle lashed out with his long tail and punched Luthair back against the cabin of the boat.

Chains made of nails adorned the gargoyle's body, like a disgusting shirt of chainmail armor. Up close, I could see it had a second set of small arms under the ribcage—the fingers were long and adorned with knife-like claws.

And its chest...

It looked like it had taken an axe to the sternum and then healed. A massive wound—a scar?—went from its collarbones to its gut.

"I'm so happy I managed to see you all again," the gargoyle said with a laugh. "Now I can cross off '*watch a grown man cry while I cut up his friends*' from my to-do list."

The monster flapped its wings, knocking everyone off balance, and reached with its clawed feet for Adelgis. Unwilling to let the gargoyle have anyone, I focused my sorcery and evoked terrors.

A scream pierced my ears as the gargoyle collapsed onto the deck of our keelboat, tossing everyone to the deck and rocking the whole ship with its massive weight.

I didn't want the beast to target anyone else—not Zaxis, or Atty, or Hexa—and especially not Illia. She had already done so much for me. It was my turn to repay the favor.

I jumped to my feet and steadied myself with the rocking of the keelboat. "Even out of your cage you're pathetic." I turned to Luthair, and he melted into the shadows. A moment later, he formed up around me, and we were prepared for a fight.

In our new form, I felt what Luthair felt—if we needed to die to protect the others, he thought that acceptable.

The gargoyle thrashed and twisted. It knocked Atty, Raisen, and Illia away with a wild swing of its monstrous tail. Then it stood and flapped its wings once more, glaring at me with sinister red eyes that refused to blink.

"What's wrong?" I taunted, my voice mixed with Luthair's. "Mad?"

A smile crept across the gargoyle's face. "Me? Mad? I'll have you know I'm perfectly sane."

It laughed as it lunged for me, its teeth razor sharp and its claws outstretched.

I wanted to shadow-step away, but I had underestimated the speed and size of my opponent. The gargoyle slammed into me and sent us both overboard. We crashed into the water and sank into the dark depths while its four arms grabbed my shoulders and side, like it wanted to hold me still.

Water didn't frighten me. I had lived on an island my entire life. Even submerged and sinking fast, I kept calm and slashed with my sword, removing one of its smaller arms with a clean slice. A cloud of pink filled the ocean, and I closed my eyes. In the next moment, I slid away into the shadows. Using the water as an aid, I escaped.

When I exited the shadows, I was still underwater. That was when panic set in. I groped at the rocks and dragged myself upward, aware of the water pressure and using it as a guide to the surface.

When I broke through a wave, I gasped, my chest burning with the flames of stale air trapped in my lungs.

The gargoyle burst from the ocean and flew to the skerry. He landed and ran his three hands across the rocks. Before I could get my bearings, the stone all around me shuddered. Magic filled the area, soaking into the crust of the world and shaping it like clay.

Gargoyles had the power to manipulate stone and metal —and I already knew what was happening. I turned my gaze to the distant keelboat. A jagged rock jutted out of the ocean and slammed into the hull. The boat rocked on the waves, on the verge of breaking. The others gathered their things and then leapt overboard before a second attack could sink them. Even Traces and Zelfree managed to escape back to the skerry.

"You're not going anywhere," the gargoyle shouted, his words laced with madness. "You have to pay for what you've done to me. *You all have to pay!*"

Fog rolled over the area, heralding the arrival of our true enemy.

The gargoyle continued shaping the rocks—not just near the shore, but over the entire island—forming a landscape of cracks, twisted mountains, and dangerously sharp edges. His mad laughter echoed off the twisted terrain.

CONFRONTATION IN THE MIST

I still had the Occult Compass. I could feel it underneath my shadow plate armor. For some reason, I feared losing it, though part of me wanted to break it just to prevent Calisto from ever using it.

We could, Luthair spoke to me. *It would defeat his plans.*

I knew that.

But...

What if there really was a world serpent somewhere in the world? Without the compass, I didn't know how we'd ever find it. I didn't want to lose that opportunity, but if Calisto came close to taking it from me, I would smash it against the rocks.

I glanced up, my breathing deep.

Pillars of rock had jutted up all around me, creating a labyrinth of crooked walkways, deep pits, and misshapen steps. With the fog pouring in, the place reminded me of an uneasy dream teetering on the verge of a nightmare. I couldn't see the gargoyle or the others, not through the mire of mist and forest of stone.

It didn't matter. If Calisto really was chasing the

gargoyle, then my goal was to leave this place as fast as possible. The keelboat wasn't completely destroyed in the fight. Even without a sail, we could maneuver it along the shore of the rocky islands until we got close enough to the trading routes. It wouldn't take us long to find someone who would help.

If Calisto *did* know we were here, then we would need to find a way to escape.

In either situation, I couldn't afford to sit around and hope a solution would fall into my lap.

I headed into the fog, intent on sticking close to the shore so I could meet up with the others. The rock formations made everything difficult, however. I slid through the shadows over obstacles, but there were no smooth surfaces, just jagged stones with sharp edges, some hidden under shallow water, almost as if the gargoyle wanted someone to unwittingly step on them.

Fragments of broken mast floated on the waves, crashing into the twisted rocks that protruded from the ocean. In the distance, people shouted. I tried moving faster, but the more I used my magic, the more it harmed me.

Damn my second-bonded magic! This wasn't the time to suffer the ill effects. The others needed me!

Luthair's voice swirled through my mind.

Rest. You can't help them if you push yourself to the breaking point.

Visions of our fight with Calisto filled my thoughts. Illia couldn't trick her way out of this situation. There were no cannons to slam through the deck of a ship.

I breathed deep and was weighing my options when the frigid touch of frost prickled my skin. I stood straight and drew my sword, my heart pounding in my chest. Wendigo magic. I was certain. Did that mean the pirates were already on the skerry? We didn't have much time!

Ice washed over the rocks, coating everything in a second layer of hazardous frost. I tightened my grip on my blade and gritted my teeth.

I had given my disease-preventing trinket to Zelfree.

Careful, Luthair said. *It approaches.*

The click of wolf-claws on stone reached my ears a second later. I turned on my heel, my vision obscured by the fog.

"Wraith," someone shouted. "Calisto said the gargoyle and the scale are our priority."

Everything echoed—even a whisper could be heard far beyond normal range.

"This way, my arcanist," a chilling voice replied. "I can smell the knightmare. It's here."

The wendigo arcanist will come to avenge his brother, Luthair spoke in my mind. *You may need to deal with him.*

Even if I had to fight every single one of the arcanist pirates to get off this wretched island, I would. They weren't going to prevent me from reuniting with the others, nor would they hurt a single other person of our guild.

The wendigo rushed through the fog. It remained invisible, but the mist shifted with its speed, and the click of its claws became louder with each step closer. When the beast got near, I lifted my sword. It dashed to the left and then went in for a bite.

I had seen this tactic before, and acting on instinct, I pivoted and slashed. Blood splattered out of thin air as I struck the invisible wendigo. It yipped and leapt away, but while I was distracted, Fain stabbed at me from behind, his weapon striking my armor with a loud clang of metal. I whirled around. He remained invisible as he slithered away, leaving me with a dent in the shadow armor that quickly coated with debilitating ice.

That was the wendigo strategy—slow and steady. They would chip away at me, infect me with disease, and coat me in hoarfrost. Death by a thousand cuts.

This would have to end soon.

"There's no running this time," Fain said, a chill in his voice worse than the ice. "Your knightmare took my only family. We're going to settle this score once and for all!"

Only family?

For a brief moment, I remembered the moment my parents left. The fear of being abandoned to a world that hated me lingered at the edge of my thoughts. That uncertainty bled into my magic as I lifted my hand and evoked my terrors. Each painful second of burning sorcery added to the power of my magic.

I had lost my family too.

Both Wraith and Fain cried out. Their invisibility flickered and then vanished as they hit the ground. Fain dropped his dagger and grabbed at his head, his eyes scrunched tight. The wendigo shuddered and whined as it backed into the protruding rocks.

With the taste of copper in my mouth, I stabbed at Wraith and plunged my blade into his body. The wendigo didn't move or resist—not while paralyzed with fear—but it tried to leap away afterward. The beast slipped on his own blood and collapsed, his antlers cluttering against the stone. Probably close to death.

"Don't you dare touch him," Fain growled, his voice raw with emotion.

A blast of ice swept over the area, creating icicles and sharp formations of cold crystals. Although ocean water didn't freeze as quickly as fresh water, the puddles on the rocks turned to ice in an instant. My body moved with all the agility of a corpse as I tried to free myself from the rime.

Fain unsheathed his cutlass and slashed at me—his curved sword perfect for fast and long strikes.

I managed to block the attack, but he swung again and again, each hit more powerful and reckless than the last. It took all of my strength to defend against his assault. After the fifth strike, his breathing became heavy. I took the opportunity to strike back hard. He stumbled away, his panting coming out as clouds of mist that mingled with the fog.

I lifted my sword and held it with both hands. "Surrender." My double-voice echoed, creating a haunting command.

Fain forced a laugh. "I'd rather sail through the abyssal hells."

"It doesn't have to be like this."

"I will avenge my brother."

Anger seeped into every ounce of my being. I could see parts of Luthair's past. Fain's brother, Kalroux, had stolen from ship after ship, fighting for Calisto's cause.

"Your brother was a cutthroat not worthy of this revenge," I shouted. "He deserved his fate!"

Fain gripped his cutlass, his jaw clenched. "My brother was a hero."

I was ready to contradict him—to tell him every detail that Luthair could provide—but Fain continued, his own rage evident.

"Kalroux was the only one who provided for us! Our mother, sister, and baby brother... No one cared that our town had frozen over! Not the guilds or the arcanists—*it was my brother who provided for everyone!* And when he was killed... when he stopped sending supplies..."

Fain shook his head as if attempting to dispel the memories, but they clung like poisoned honey. He took a deep breath and stared down at his frostbitten fingers, his gaze unfocused.

I didn't know what to say. His brother had turned to piracy to provide for his town and family, and when he died, I suspected most of them did too. But that didn't justify the actions of the *Third Abyss*. Kalroux wasn't innocent.

Fain snapped out of his spiraling thoughts. He lifted his cutlass and ran for me, uninhibited by the slickness of the ice underfoot. Before he reached me, I manipulated the shadows to grab at his boots. He staggered, as if caught in oil, and slashed at the darkness.

I broke free of the remaining ice and slashed wide with my sword, no hesitation in my strike. My blade cut through his coat, shirt, and flesh, deep enough to gouge bone. For a moment, I was surprised by my own power.

Fain stumbled backward. His injury wept blood onto his belt and trousers. He dropped his cutlass and grabbed at the wound with a shaky hand.

I readied my blade. "I said surrender."

With a ragged breath, Fain planted his back against one of the large rocks and stared at me with a hollow glare. Then he exhaled and slid down the rock into a sitting position.

I waited, my body stiff.

Why do you stay your hand? Luthair asked. *The others could be in trouble.*

I stepped forward, my blade at the ready. "If you report another failure to Calisto, he'll kill you."

Fear flickered through Fain's expression. It disappeared a moment later as he leaned his head back, his frostbitten ears and fingers giving him the appearance of a frozen carcass.

"Do it," Fain muttered. "Get it over with."

I clenched my teeth. "I didn't know about your situation. Let me help you."

He spat on my greaves, his saliva mixed with blood. Then he traced the tattoo on his neck. "This is all I have. You kill me or Calisto does. There is no other option now. I might as well... find my place in the dirt."

With a tattoo that marked him as a pirate of the *Third Abyss*, perhaps he was right. Who would ever trust him? He would be haunted by the evil deeds of the ship for the rest of his life, even if he never participated in the carnage of the crew.

Killing him would be a mercy.

I lifted my blade, ready to finish this feud between Fain and Luthair.

His wendigo limped over and threw himself over Fain's lap like only a dog could. Wraith shielded his arcanist, his skull-like face emotionless.

"Leave me," Fain commanded.

"Never, my arcanist." The wendigo curled onto Fain and pushed his muzzle under Fain's hand. "You may not have your family or brother, but I am with you. And I'll be here at your side, even in the afterlife."

For a prolonged moment, I dwelled on those words, uncertain of my conviction. Although Luthair didn't speak, his emotions bled into mine. He felt no hesitation. Perhaps that was a strength I lacked, because the more I mulled over the situation, the lower I dropped my weapon.

I just couldn't do it.

Mercy. Without it, we cannot help others find redemption.

But I knew I couldn't leave Fain here without a solution. Calisto would finish the deed if I didn't.

What would the heroes of yore do? I had read so many stories and admired their solutions. Gregory Ruma, back when he was a legendary swashbuckler, had made an ally during one of his pirate raids. But the specifics of that tale didn't apply here.

Then it struck me.

I sheathed my blade, Luthair's disapproval at the corner of my thoughts. I shook my head and willed him to separate from me. His black armor melted away and formed as a separate being.

"You can do whatever you want," I said. "But know that you don't have to die. There's a woman in Fortuna—the grand apothecary—who needs to do more research with wendigo magic. If you go to her and tell her I sent you, I know she'll take you in."

She had helped so many people in the past, why wouldn't she help Fain? I was certain this was the solution. If Fain wanted to live, this was the way.

`I walked away without giving him a second glance. The situation was out of my control now. I needed to find the others.

Luthair slithered into the shadows and followed me as a phantom, almost a breath away, as if ready to lunge at a second's notice.

We made our way through the fog and the twisted terrain. Gunshots in the distance cracked like thunder, and I turned toward the sounds of fighting. Whenever I lost my footing or stumbled into a crag, I shadow-shifted to solid ground. Although using magic stung, I was slowly becoming accustomed to it. Maybe one day—once it didn't hurt any more—I would come to miss the stinging sensation, but for now, it clawed at my focus.

I dashed around a pillar of rock and caught sight of two

terrible situations: Hexa fighting the snallygaster, and Atty fighting a pair of pirates.

In the half-second I had to contemplate the situation, I decided the snallygaster was a bigger threat. I ran to help Hexa, but stopped when she evoked a cloud of noxious poison. The snallygaster flapped its wings, stirring the fog and vile purple fumes into a deadly mix.

Then Raisen leapt through the poison gas—unaffected —and crunched his fangs on the snallygaster's leg. The monster retaliated and bit Raisen's neck, digging in deep. It didn't matter, though. I already knew the fight was over.

Hydra venom wasn't as lethal as king basilisk venom, but it incapacitated its victims quickly. Sure enough, the snallygaster wobbled on its feet. In a last-ditch effort to harm its opponent, the snallygaster thrashed its head, ripping apart Raisen's flesh and damaging his neck.

Hexa lunged for her eldrin and freed it from the snallygaster.

"Luthair, finish this," I commanded.

In one swift motion, Luthair emerged from the shadows and plunged his sword into the snallygaster's chest. The creature writhed and twisted as it fell to the ground.

Hexa held her hydra close. Raisen went limp in her arms, yet his gold eyes remained alight with amusement.

"I did good?" Raisen asked.

Hexa smiled. "Course."

Luthair pulled his sword from the snallygaster and threw his weapon into the shadows. When he withdrew it, the blade showed no blood. He sheathed the weapon and then turned his empty helmet to "look" at Raisen's bleeding body.

Raisen continued to breathe. "Don't worry," I said. "I'm sure Zaxis can heal this."

Then I glanced over my shoulder. Atty stood over the smoldering lumps of dead pirates. She took in ragged breaths and rubbed her upper arms. I was tempted to approach her, but I returned my attention to the injured hydra.

"A scratch like this... can't stop me," Raisen said between bloody coughs. He growled and hissed at the same time, aiming his glower in my direction. "I'm a *hydra*. I don't need healing."

"You have gotten older," Hexa muttered. She placed Raisen on the rocky ground. "Volke, would you mind if I borrowed that blade of yours?"

With a lifted eyebrow, I turned to Luthair. "Well, uh, it's not technically mine."

Luthair handed the sword over. "This was once Mathis's. I consider it yours now that you're my arcanist. I simply hold it for you until you master it yourself."

I gave the blade to Hexa, still uncomfortable calling it *my own*. I hadn't made the blade, like Mathis had, and I preferred to think Luthair had ownership of it as well.

With no uncertainty in her actions, Hexa brought the point of the shadow sword down on Raisen's injured neck. She sliced clean into the bone and muscle and then twisted to make a perfect cut, decapitating her eldrin.

I knew the stories of hydras. *I knew.* But it didn't dull the shock of seeing one bleed out a puddle of crimson after losing a head. I held my breath, unable to look away. A second passed, and that was all it took for panic to grip my thoughts.

What if he *wasn't* okay?

But then the red puddle of vital fluid slithered back to Raisen's body. His dead head rotted away in a matter of moments as his eyes sunk into the skull and then disintegrated into a mass of lumpy flesh. The carnage clung and jiggled back to Raisen's body as two heads slowly emerged from the injury of the old one—first bone, then muscles, then scales, and finally, two faces and tongues.

It happened so fast—but it still felt like an eternity.

Raisen rocked onto his side and then looked at himself, both heads examining the new limbs.

Hexa patted both at the same time. "Told you that you were old enough."

"Old enough for what?" I asked.

"Multiple heads." Hexa stood and offered me a half-smile. "A hydra's body will always form an extra head for each one cut off, but if the hydra isn't old enough, it'll get a withered head and possibly die."

Raisen gave Hexa a four-eyed golden glare. One head spoke and said, "We'd appreciate it if you didn't talk about killing hydras in front of us."

"Sorry."

Hexa's arcanist mark had changed. The star on her forehead always had a hydra intertwined with it, but now the hydra had two heads.

The second head spoke with a hiss and added, "We should regroup with the others."

The distant sounds of fighting had not ceased, but they hadn't registered in my thoughts until Raisen mentioned the others. The gunshots and shouts played tricks with my imagination. Steeled for combat, I ran over to Atty and touched her shoulder.

She glanced up from the charred corpses and nodded. "Yes. We should go."

Together—Atty, Hexa carrying Raisen, and I—maneuvered through the fog and rocky environment. Hexa slowed us, but I didn't mind. It gave me a chance to shake a lingering feeling of dread.

Both Calisto and the gargoyle were nearby.

Atty kept close. When we stopped to allow Hexa to catch up, she turned to me, taking in deep breaths.

"My fire has gotten so hot," she whispered. "Even without Titania nearby..."

I nodded.

"I was... a little surprised." She placed a hand on her chest. "My heart is pounding. Will it be like this every time?"

Two thugs with pistols and daggers came around a large rock. The fog and echoing noises prevented me from noticing them until they were mere feet away. Luthair sprang up to merge, but Atty acted before I did. She unleashed her flame.

The pirates stumbled over themselves. One fired, but the bullet ricocheted off the rocks and sailed off harmlessly.

Hexa reached us and tossed Raisen to the ground. Her hydra lunged for a pirate and bit him with both heads, the venom reacting so quickly that the man collapsed in mere moments, his legs too weak to support him.

During their panic, Atty used her fire again, crippling the non-poisoned pirate.

"*Calisto!*"

The shout stopped everyone in their tracks.

The gargoyle.

"I'm killing your men one by one, but I've grown tired of effortless victory. Face me! I can't enjoy consuming your scale unless I garnish it with your insides."

A SHIELD OF DARKNESS

They weren't far off—if I closed my eyes, I swear I could've smelled the gargoyle's breath.

Atty and Hexa both regarded me with intense looks. What would we do? Run to see the confrontation between pirate and monster, or head in the opposite direction? If it were just me, I would leave these two villains to kill each other, but Illia was here somewhere. Given her passion to see Calisto dead, I imagined she would be attracted to the promise of this fight.

"We should head in their direction," I said.

Although I hadn't articulated my reasoning, Atty and Hexa nodded. In Atty's case, I think she understood my goals, but Hexa had a slight smile on her face, like she just wanted a front row seat to the battle of the century.

We took off through the fog. The ice from the wendigo fight clung to me long after the confrontation. I shivered as I ran, the beating of my heart not enough to warm me.

It didn't take us long to reach the battlefield. Rocks jutted from the ground around a wide area, creating an arena of sorts. Hellion, the giant white manticore, flapped his black leather wings, stirring the fog and clearing the area.

Calisto, Spider, the manticore, and three pirates stood close together. The gargoyle flew around overhead, his tail trailing behind him, dripping blood. The corpses of ten pirates littered the ground like mounds of fresh dirt before a newly-dug grave, but they were already cold and forgotten.

The gargoyle, still missing the arm I had cut off, flew to the ground and touched the rocks with one of his clawed feet. The stone in the area began to shift and move. It took me considerable effort to stay upright, but I managed.

"So, you thought you could cage me?" the gargoyle said, smiling. "Let me return the favor."

Calisto leapt back, easily clearing a distance of five feet with little effort. Spider also kept on her toes as she moved away, her attention on the ground.

I didn't know why until one of the pirates didn't move fast enough. The stone grabbed him by the ankle and then pulled him down into the rocky island, swallowing his leg up to the knee. The man screamed and clawed at the stone in a poor attempt to escape. When that didn't work, he held out his hand.

"Help! Someone!"

Spider leapt to his aid, but no matter how hard she pulled, she couldn't get him out.

Then the stone holding his leg crushed inward, smashing the man's limb in one sick twisting movement that sounded similar to the squishing of an overripe fruit. When Spider pulled again, she managed to free him, but he was missing the leg and on the verge of passing out from shock.

A chain made of nails adorned the gargoyle's body, and the monster slung it off to use as a cruel whip. It lashed out at one of the other pirates, and the snap of the chain took a chunk of flesh from the man's arm.

"Come now," the gargoyle drawled. "Don't you remember doing this to me? Maybe it wasn't memorable enough. *We'll fix that.*"

I hid behind a tower of rock, certain that no one had yet noticed me, or Atty, or Hexa.

"He'll kill us if he catches us," Atty whispered. Then she turned to me. "What should we do?"

Hexa shook her head and held Raisen close. "We should let these blackhearts fight. As long as we aren't caught by the gargoyle's stone-manipulating magic, we'll be fine."

"Spider," Calisto said. "Find my scale. I'll deal with this."

That one command halted all other thoughts. I couldn't allow Spider to find the world serpent scale. Instead of sitting idle, *I* would find it first. I had seen the gargoyle with it, after all, but where had it gone?

"You two stay safe," I said. "I'm going to search around."

Before Atty or Hexa could respond, I took off around the outside of the stone arena. I shadow-stepped when I could, taking small leaps so I didn't get lost. I'd master this magic one tiny step at a time. I had to practice, after all. I had to conquer my fear and hesitation. I had to.

The fight between Calisto and the gargoyle continued. The scraping of rock and the cry of pirates covered the island like a dark cloud. A piece of me hoped they would all kill each other by the time I returned.

Then I came to an odd structure—a crude dome made of giant stone slabs—obviously set up to protect something within. I had found what I was looking for. I peered through the cracks between the rocks. With my ability to see through even the darkest of shadows, I spotted the glint of the scale inside.

I also spotted something else.

Star shards. The same ones the gargoyle had been carrying while fleeing the *Third Abyss*.

Although not strong enough to move the stone slabs—they must've weighed over a ton—I again used my ability to shift through the shadows and slipped between the cracks. I emerged inside the cramped space a second later. I couldn't stand fully, not without hitting my head, and no light managed to seep into the stone dome.

I chuckled, amused with my ability to bypass obstacles that I never could have when I was younger. The crack between the rocks was no more than an inch, perhaps less. A thumb couldn't even fit between the slabs.

Thankful I had found the scale so quickly, I knelt and scooped it up without a second thought. A surge of power—like a flash of lightning—shot through my fingers and up to my elbows. I dropped the scale with a gasp and backed into the rocks. Illia was right. It definitely was a scale of a world serpent. No other mystical creature had so much latent power brimming in every piece of its being.

After a deep breath, I picked up the scale again. The power coursed through me, but I was prepared. I held on tight, determined to keep this out of Calisto's hands.

Then another thought struck me. I fumbled through my trouser pocket and withdrew the Occult Compass. Would it work? Could I use these two items to find a mystical creature? My pulse raced as I held up the compass. The needle was completely still.

"Luthair," I said. "Touch the compass."

He entered the stone structure and stood next to me, hunched over. This small space didn't suit either of us, but I didn't care. All I needed was his cooperation.

Sure enough, when Luthair touched the compass, it

reacted. I gritted my teeth as the eyeball at the base of the compass glowed gold, and the needle spun. A moment later, it pointed south-west. Was that the direction of the nearest knightmare to us?

Luthair removed his shadowy gauntlet and the compass spun once again. This time, the needle went dead and the eye stopped glowing.

Satisfied that it worked, I touched the compass to the top of the scale. With bated breath, Luthair and I watched the needle spin again. Then it stopped—pointing south.

"Curse the abyssal hells," I muttered.

Luthair shook his helmet. "Calisto somehow knew of this world serpent, but I suspect not many other people do. I think it would be best if we at least informed the Frith Guild."

I nodded.

He continued, "Under no circumstance should Calisto ever get his hands on a creature that powerful."

"I agree."

"Good. Mathis would have said the same."

Intent on taking it out of the stone dome, I slipped into the shadows and slithered through the crack. When I emerged, however, I didn't have the scale. With adrenaline icing my veins, I glanced around. Nothing. I looked back into the rocks and found the scale had fallen out of my grasp. I slipped back inside and retrieved the scale, my eyebrows knitted in confusion.

"What's wrong?" I asked.

Luthair motioned to the scale. "It's too large for you to take into the shadows."

The scale was three feet in length and at least two and a half feet wide.

I grazed my fingers over the powerful object. "I've gone

into the shadows with other things before. My clothes and—"

"They're smaller and part of you. This scale is far too massive."

"Your sword is long, maybe even longer than the scale, and I can take that."

"The sword has been imbued with knightmare magic. Anything crafted from our sorcery can freely enter and exit the shadows."

We weren't strong enough to move the gigantic stone slabs, which meant there was no way to free the world serpent scale. At least, not physically.

"You said the sword moved through the shadows because it was imbued with knightmare magic?" I asked.

Luthair replied with a nod.

I glanced over to the star shards. Could I imbue the scale with my knightmare magic? I had never done anything like create a magical item. What if I messed it up? What if I somehow damaged the scale? What if we couldn't use it to find the world serpent if I imbued it with my sorcery?

Wait—Luthair had said Mathis crafted his sword from a behemoth fang. I motioned for him to hand it over. Once I had the blade in my hand, I placed the Occult Compass on the hilt. Would this work? The needle spun and then ticked to a stop—pointing east. Not in the direction of the knightmare or world serpent.

Which meant it was pointing to a behemoth.

"Luthair, do you know how to create magical items? Can we... turn this scale into one and then hide it in the shadows so Calisto could never track it?"

For a long moment, Luthair said nothing. When I was about to ask again, he said, "What would you turn it into?"

"I, uh, don't know. I just thought of the idea."

Someone had told me knightmares made unparalleled weapons and armor, but could the scale be turned into a weapon? Unlikely, though I supposed it was possible. Not a weapon I would know how to wield, however. It couldn't be a rifle or another sword. But I didn't dwell on the problem long before the solution came to me.

"A shield," I said. "It could be a shield."

Luthair placed his gauntlet on the scale. "Hm. That suits you."

"What do you mean?"

"I mean, a knightmare and his arcanist typically make their first magical item together—a weapon. Mathis and I made a sword, and that suited him as a person. He lived his life to fell the wicked. But you... I say you're similar to Mathis, yet you have always been reluctant to shed blood in the name of justice."

"Well, I—"

"A shield protects the innocent."

I caught my breath.

"A shield defends against injustice," he continued. "Which is why it suits you better than any weapon."

"I never thought of it that way... Maybe you're right."

"I should warn you, though. Once you use this scale to create your shield, you'll never be able to make it into anything else. Your amateur hands and sorcery will likely create an inferior magical item. If you wait until you're a master—or if you give it to a powerful arcanist—it could be a magical item beyond compare."

Anything was better than Calisto having it. Or the gargoyle, for that matter.

I gripped the scale tight. "I want to do this."

"Let me guide you."

Luthair melted into the darkness and formed around

me, his cold metal a comfort I was learning to anticipate. When acting as one, I had control, but Luthair had attempted to lead in the past. His physical actions hurt me—much like the second-bonded magic that coursed through my being. It reminded me of being a child, as though my limbs were being yanked and pulled by an adult.

This time, however, when he took control, it was simply to guide our gauntleted hand to the scale. His thoughts bled into mine, and the scene glowed with a nostalgic warmth. He and Mathis had been so much younger when they first attempted their imbuing powers. They had... messed up a couple of times before it worked. Luthair remembered the event with such clarity, like it was an event he recalled often.

We placed the scale on the ground and gathered the ten star shards. Then I channeled his thoughts in order to understand the imbuing. The jumbled mess of Luthair's past experiences helped a little, but I suspected whatever I crafted now would be far below even an amateur attempt. It would be like handing a perfect piece of marble to a child and telling them to craft a statue.

But I had made my decision—I would do this.

I touched each of the star shards, and darkness seeped from my finger and flowed over the glittering crystals, the inky magic coating the gems completely. Then I placed my palm on the scale and took in a deep breath. Allowing my magic to pour into the scale required a great deal of concentration. I closed my eyes and tried to imagine something calming.

I pictured the ocean on a peaceful day. The way the waves lapped against the white sand beaches always soothed me. With that picture in mind, I gritted back the pain of the imbuing. The scale was taking some of my sorcery—Luthair's memories told me this wasn't permanent, but it would weaken me for a time.

That was fine. Our goal was too important to abandon over trivial matters like that.

While the magic drained from my core, I imagined the types of shields I was familiar with. Heater shields and kite shields were both the kind carried on an arm, while tower shields and double-arc shields were typically set down, since they were so large.

The scale wasn't big enough for the largest ones, but a heater shield seemed appropriate. I imagined the design with as much clarity as I could muster.

The scale... it kept taking magic, like a large sponge in a small puddle. After a few moments, I ripped my hand away, unable to handle the pain and loss anymore. It wanted more —and if I had given it, maybe I could've created something grand—but I just couldn't. Even now, my arm felt charred and blistered, worse than if I had plunged it into an open fire.

I opened my eyes. The scale and the star shards were no more. Instead, a shield made of darkness sat in its place— pure black and smooth. Like the sword, the outside of the shield resembled the void of a dark night without stars.

I touched the object, unable to stop smiling.

"We did it," I said, my voice both my own and Luthair's. "We crafted a magical item."

Luthair split from me, but that only hurt my arm even more. I gasped and flinched backward into the stone.

After picking up the shield and attaching it to his left gauntlet, Luthair turned to me. "I'm impressed."

I chuckled. "Thank you. It was... because of your memories. I knew how to do it because of you."

"Regardless. Some arcanists pull their hand away too

quickly, or fail to stitch their magic into the object. Although this is a crude object at best, I still feel it deserves commendation."

After a long moment of regaining my strength, I gave Luthair a nod. He stepped up close, put a gauntlet on my shoulder, and returned to the darkness in order to merge with me once again.

At first I didn't understand why he had left me in the first place. Then I sensed that he wanted to congratulate me personally—*me*, and not *us*. I appreciated the sentiment.

We shifted through the shadows and exited the stone dome. The fog surrounding the skerry remained thick, but when we emerged, it didn't prevent me from catching sight of Spider.

She stumbled back, but not far. She carried a pistol and cutlass, and there was acid corroding the stone of the dome. I smiled, grateful I had made the decision to get the scale myself. If I hadn't, Spider would no doubt have found it first and taken it back to Calisto.

I unsheathed my blade and held the shield with my weak arm. The scale-shield didn't weigh much—it almost seemed weightless—but it was still a struggle to hold my elbow at a 90-degree angle.

Without warning, her fish-man kappa leapt off the rocks above me and landed hard on my shoulder. It dug its needle-teeth into my armor. It failed to piece to my skin, but acid leaked from its mouth at a steady rate, burning the shadows.

I grabbed at the beast and threw him off. While I did that, Spider took that moment to attack. She was only a foot from me when she fired her pistol, her aim dead for my forehead. The bang and metal clank shot through my ears, making them ring far longer than they ever had.

I staggered away, disoriented.

She swooped in with her cutlass and stabbed at the joints where my shadow armor connected. Her blade went into my underarm, and I grunted from the burning sting.

Familiar with her basic tricks, I lifted my new shield just as she spat acid.

The resulting magic—I'm not even sure what happened —felt as though the shield absorbed the destructiveness of the acid sorcery and unleashed a backlash of magical energy. Spider was knocked away and even fell to the ground.

Her kappa leapt to her side and then offered me a hiss as it flashed its disturbingly thin, sharp, teeth. Its fish-scale body glistened in the fog, but its yellow eyes offered nothing more than a malevolent glare.

"You found it," Spider said, breathless. "And you ruined it."

The ringing in my ears almost prevented me from hearing, but her words were clear enough. Spider and her kappa stood—and to my surprise—took off in the opposite direction. The vertigo from my damaged ears prevented me from giving chase.

Where was she going? To inform Calisto?

The laughter of the gargoyle drowned out all my other thoughts.

"Now is the final curtain call for your pirating career," the monster said with a giggle.

Desperate to stop Spider and make sure Calisto fell to the plague-ridden beast, I attempted to run back to the others.

34

FREEDOM

The rocky island skerry had changed during the few minutes I had spent dealing with the scale. The rock formations had been twisted around the arena where the gargoyle had lured Calisto. It made finding my way back more difficult, but I arrived in time to see the crescendo of their confrontation.

Calisto, Hellion, and the gargoyle had torn the place asunder with their magic. The stone of the island was warped, like magma, and Hellion's mask, once pristine and white, had been cracked open to reveal his mouth underneath. It was a human mouth, but unnaturally large, with three rows of teeth—all sharp, as if stolen from a shark.

At some point during the fight, Calisto's coat and shirt had been torn, exposing a good portion of his back and chest, including his unicorn horn necklace. It looked like the work of claws. I didn't concern myself with his wardrobe, but I did take note of the tattoo on his shoulder blade.

A dragon design similar to Zelfree's.

No.

Identical.

I shook the thought from my head and took note of one last disturbing detail. Although his clothes had been shredded, his body remained uninjured. Had he healed? Or was he just that impervious to damage?

The gargoyle wasn't.

It bled from a hundred cuts across its rocky skin. And its chest—I had thought it damaged down the sternum—was now opened wide. The sharp points of the ribs acted as fangs to a vertical mouth that opened and closed. The gargoyle swooped close to Calisto and bit his arm with the ribcage maw, holding him close.

That was when the gargoyle attacked with it claws. Every attack, however, tore through Calisto's clothes but left him unharmed. Instead, Calisto raised his cutlass and sliced off another of the gargoyle's arms. He did so with such ease. He almost looked annoyed.

The gargoyle screamed and backed away with a few quick flaps of its wings.

"I'm perfect," the monster growled. "Made strong by this plague magic. I should be tearing you apart while in my true form."

Calisto, covered with the gargoyle's diseased blood, brushed off his arms and slicked back his copper hair. "You're nothing. Hellion, finish this piece of trash. I need to know if Spider found our scale yet."

"As you wish, my arcanist," the manticore growled.

The gargoyle exhaled a breath of rocky dust. Then it set a clawed foot back on the ground and twisted the terrain again. Calisto leapt out of the way, not caught by the crushing stone underneath.

"Once I eat you and your manticore... I can only get stronger," the gargoyle rasped. "I'll just... grind you up and drink your flesh and bones."

Hellion flapped his wings and lunged for the gargoyle. Perhaps the gargoyle had been faster at the start of the fight —nimbler than the bulky manticore—but exhaustion had taken its toll. The gargoyle tried to fly off, but couldn't. Hellion pounced on the creature and slammed it into the stone island. Although they were roughly the same size, Hellion had bulk to back him up. The skeletal and misshapen body of the gargoyle didn't offer much in terms of total weight.

With monstrous cries, the gargoyle thrashed and clawed. Its wings had hooks at the tips and it used them to slash at the manticore's side.

Hellion didn't seem to care. Unflinching, it grabbed both sides of the gargoyle's ribcage mouth and then pulled them apart in one brutal motion. It broke the ribs and removed half of the maw, rending the gargoyle practically in two.

The manticore hadn't struggled—or even broken a sweat. It was just that strong.

The plague-ridden beast still moved, though, but with less energy and more laughter.

"You're fools," the gargoyle said, giggling. "Misguided maggots. All of you should embrace this plague. You'll have to, eventually! There's no stopping it. None of you will be able to—"

Hellion bit down on the head, silencing the gargoyle once and for all. Then Hellion stepped off the corpse and licked his human lips, his tongue long and spindly.

"*Spider*," Calisto shouted. The thick fog lingered. His ship had to be nearby. "Spider, I need you to find that scale, dammit!" He rubbed at the scruff on his chin and his eyes narrowed as he glared at the mutilated gargoyle. "Why don't scum ever learn their lesson? No one messes with my operation. *No one.*"

Illia leapt out of the fog and climbed to the top of a rock overlooking the area. She stood confident, her shoulders squared, Nicholin wrapped around her neck. That was when she held up a compass—one that sparkled, even in the dim light of the ominous fog.

"Calisto," she said. "Looking for something?"

He slowly turned around and glanced up at her, his usual bravado replaced with a cold look of malice. "Hellion. Kill her."

"Your crew isn't here," the manticore said. "Can I remove my mask now?"

"Do it."

His manticore eldrin stepped away from the gargoyle corpse and reached for his half-destroyed mask. The human-like hands of the creature gripped the cracked operatic accessory and peeled it away from his skin, revealing the face of an old man. The skin tone matched the unnatural white of his fur, and the wrinkles ran deep from the corners of his eyes. His mouth, large enough to fit three rows of teeth, literally reached the bottoms of his ears.

The manticore glanced in my direction for a split second, but that was all it took to meet its eyes. That's when I felt it—my heart clenched, and my whole body seized.

Forgive me, Luthair said. *This paralysis—I had no idea manticores had such power.*

Some mystical creatures had those abilities, like basilisks and cockatrices, but manticores? It made sense, in a twisted way. Manticores were the hunters of mankind, and their magic suited that role. The more I thought about Hellion, the more I realized he wasn't just a normal manticore—he was a true form manticore. That had to explain Calisto's glowing arcanist mark that matched our guildmaster's, and why his magic was so powerful.

And it also explained why Zelfree's mimic-manticore didn't look the same. Zelfree didn't copy the effects of the true form, or the plague-ridden monsters. Even back when Zelfree fought Ruma and had Traces transform into a leviathan—Ruma's leviathan had been sickly and covered in eyes, but not Zelfree's.

I wanted to yell at Illia, and warn her of the danger, but I couldn't move. The manticore's gaze kept me frozen in place, a slight tingle running from my spine to the tips of my toes and fingers.

Illia closed her eye. Nicholin covered his face with his paws. Did they already know of the danger?

With powerful movements, Hellion ran across the cracked rocks of the island. As he neared Illia, she lifted the compass over her head, and threw it as hard as she could to the ground. It shattered—magic burst out between the cracks of glass, creating a tiny pop of fire and sparks.

Although I couldn't move, the weight of the Occult Compass in my pocket told me she was bluffing.

But Calisto didn't know that.

He balled his hands into fists so tight his palms bled. His expression never changed, however. His seething rage only manifested in the form of crimson droplets, dripping from his knuckles to the skerry.

Hellion flapped his leathery wings and lunged. Illia teleported a second before the beast reached her. Then she reappeared between Calisto and his manticore, much to my surprise. Such brazen arrogance would only serve to agitate him further.

Calisto walked forward, his whole body visibly tense. "Do you know what I've done to get that compass? All the obstacles I overcame?"

"I told you," Illia said, playfulness in her voice. "I'm

going to take everything you care about, one piece at a time."

Nicholin arched his back, his fur on end, his ears laid flat against his skull. "We'll make you regret every decision that led to you becoming a pirate. No one hurts my arcanist and gets away with it!"

The tingling in my body waned and I knew the paralysis wouldn't last forever.

When Calisto leaned forward to attack, I wanted to stop him, and the most frustrating—nightmarish—part of the scene was my inability to do a single thing.

Calisto jerked to a halt, his shock apparent as he glanced around. His boot had sunk into the rock, and he continued to be pulled deeper and deeper. He glanced over his shoulder at the dead gargoyle, his confusion mounting.

Even I didn't understand—who was controlling the stone?

Illia and Nicholin smiled.

Hellion whipped around to attack Illia, but he also got trapped, his four limbs sinking as though caught in quicksand. He roared in defiance and attempted to lift his legs free. The stone twisted in on his ankles, crushing them.

Someone stepped out from behind a small mountain of rocks. If I could've moved, I would've laughed aloud.

Zelfree.

Although he walked with a weak step, he, too, smiled wide. His arcanist mark had the form of a gargoyle twisted around the star points. Judging by his confidence and Illia's actions, the two of them had planned this all along. Illia distracted Calisto and Hellion so that Zelfree could trap them with the gargoyle magic.

Hellion glared in Zelfree's direction, but Zelfree shielded his eyes with his forearm.

THE DREAD PIRATE ARCANIST

"Everett," Calisto said through clenched teeth. "What do I need to do to rid myself of you?"

Zelfree shook his head. "I can't let you hurt my apprentices, but I'll let them hurt you."

With her back to the manticore, Illia opened her eye and picked up a flintlock pistol from the corpse of a nearby pirate, the heavy type of dragoon pistol meant to kill large men or horses. She fumbled for a moment as she checked to see if the powder and ball were loaded. Once certain, she aimed the weapon and pulled the trigger.

Dragoon pistols could pierce wood and bone, but the ball of iron hit Calisto and did nothing more than tear his already shredded coat. Illia threw down the weapon with a frown.

In another attempt to end Calisto's life, she lifted her other hand and unleashed her white flames of disintegration. They washed over the rocks, breaking them apart by teleporting small bits around, and tore a bit through Calisto's impervious flesh. But even after a full five seconds of her evocation, it didn't do much harm. She was just too weak an arcanist—a mere amateur—and she would accidently free Calisto from his stone prison before she killed him.

"When I get my hands on you," he growled. He thrashed and half dragged himself out of the rocky island, his strength so great the stone cracked. "*Hellion*."

Calisto was strong, but his manticore was in a league of his own. Hellion roared as he struggled against his restraints. He even managed to rip a front paw from the rocks, though his human hand came up mangled.

Zelfree used his sorcery to sink the pirate further, trapping Calisto up to his waist. Then the manticore sunk to his stomach.

"We should go," Zelfree shouted to Illia, his voice almost lost to Hellion's screams.

Illia turned away, and Nicholin shook his head.

"You made your point, but we're not going to kill him like this."

The way Zelfree said it made me think he didn't have the strength to keep Calisto and his manticore trapped for long. And if Calisto broke free, he would never relent.

Illia hesitated, as if leaving had never been an option for her.

"The others are weak and injured," Zelfree continued. "If we're all going to make it out of this, we have to go now."

How did Illia think she would kill Calisto? Even though he was trapped, she just didn't have the magic or weapons. She had wounded his pride, not once, but twice, and I suspected she would take delight in doing it a hundred times over, but we didn't have that option either. If she insisted on staying, we would have to contend with the rest of his crew, including Spider.

"Fine," Illia said. "You're right. We should go."

Calisto clawed at the ground, his fingertips leaving bloody trails as he shredded his own skin against the rock. "I'll kill you both. *Mark my words.*"

I hadn't realized it until then, but the paralysis had drained from my body. I shadow-stepped away, protecting my eyes as I fled.

Illia, Nicholin, and Zelfree left as well, but not before sinking Calisto and his eldrin another few inches into the cold skerry terrain.

I found Zaxis and Adelgis at the edge of the deformed

skerry. They had our damaged keelboat tied to a rock. It still floated, which was the most important element of a boat, but without the sail or long oars, there was no way to direct the vessel through the waters.

Luthair melted away and back into the shadows at my feet, taking the sword and shield with him. No one would be able to get the scale while it remained in the depths of darkness.

"There you are," Zaxis said to me as he hopped over a few slick boulders. "Are you okay?" He examined me the moment he got close. Satisfied I wasn't hurt *that much*, he smacked my upper arm and smiled. "You had us worried."

I shrugged. "Somehow I managed."

"Zelfree told us to get the keelboat ready, but I haven't seen him since."

I glanced around, certain Illia and Zelfree had come this way. To my relief, they both emerged from the fog, followed closely by Atty and Hexa. The small group hustled to the keelboat and greeted each other with quick nods.

Zelfree no longer wore the arcanist mark of a gargoyle. Instead, there was a kappa wrapped around his star, and I almost laughed aloud. Kappas could control waterways, and that was how he intended to use our little keelboat, despite its damage.

I even spotted Traces gliding through the water in her new kappa form.

"Everyone get aboard," Zelfree commanded. "We're returning to the guild, and this time I mean it."

During all three days it took us to reach Fortuna, I worried we would see a bank of fog heading our direction. It never came, so I suspected that Calisto either didn't know where we were going or didn't manage to escape the island in time to catch up with us. Even if Calisto was powerful, he wasn't capable of attacking the Frith Guild directly.

Both phoenixes reached us when we neared the Fortuna. Apparently they had managed to inform the guild of our activities and master arcanists had been dispatched to help us, but that was all moot now. Still, Titania and Forsythe seemed happy to be reunited with their arcanists.

Zelfree had slept most of the voyage. Adelgis's ability to manipulate dreams helped him rest, and when we reached the capital, he looked much better than I had ever seen him. The bags under his eyes weren't as pronounced, and he smiled more often.

The moment we reached the docks, Hexa leapt off our rickety keelboat and hugged the land. Raisen waddled his way over to the dirt and planted himself in the sun like a sleepy cat.

"I think I hate islands," she muttered with a contented sigh. "Too many crazy things happen out here."

Adelgis smoothed his clothing, but nothing he did corrected the wrinkles, stains, or smudges of food. "I need a month-long bath."

I went to get off the keelboat the same time as Atty. She stuck close and reached out her hand as she stepped over the threshold to the docks. I offered her my shoulder, and she used it to steady herself to get off the boat.

"It's a shame we didn't get the world serpent scale," she said. "I would've liked to see it."

I held my breath, half-tempted to tell her the story, but I decided against it. It would be better for everyone involved if people didn't know about the scale in my shadow.

Spider knew, which meant Calisto knew, but I doubted

they would spread that information around. It was bad enough having one set of pirates out to get me; I didn't need any more.

Illia and Zaxis disembarked together, engaged in a quiet conversation I wasn't privy to. I offered Illia my hand, but Zaxis took it instead as he hopped over the railing.

"Thanks." He tapped my chest with the back of his hand. "You're pretty dependable, you know that?"

"You're not too bad yourself," I muttered.

Forsythe flew over, his soot raining down as he landed on the deck. "I'm so glad you made it back. I feared you would all meet gruesome deaths."

"Thankfully that didn't happen."

"Yes. The arcanists of the guild filled my head with stories of Calisto's conquests. He mutilates his victims, or so I was told."

"E-enough," I said. "Let's just focus on celebrating our return."

Calisto hadn't been defeated, after all. I didn't want to fuel my nightmares with thoughts of him exacting revenge.

Nicholin climbed to the top of Illia's head and popped his head out of her wavy brown hair. "Ha! Just let that stupid pirate come. He's never met an eldrin like me."

"We'll be better prepared next time," Illia said. She patted Nicholin and smoothed her hair, but when the ocean winds whipped by and exposed the scars on her face, she didn't move to hide them. Instead, she offered me a smile. "Isn't that right, Volke?"

I nodded.

Nicholin perked his ears up and snuggled close to Illia's neck. "You know what we should do? Spread our story all around the port towns. *Dread Pirate Calisto beaten by a little girl, his precious artifacts destroyed right in front of him.* I bet he'd be so angry. Can you imagine his face?" Nicholin squeaked out a laugh, and Illia joined him.

"*No,*" Zelfree drawled as he got off the keelboat. "Under no circumstance should you goad that lunatic into hunting you down. As a matter of fact, I forbid you to talk about this event to anyone outside of the guild. Do I make myself clear?"

Nicholin deflated on Illia's shoulder. "Hmpf."

To my surprise, Illia didn't argue. Instead, she smiled. "I won't speak of it."

"Good," Zelfree said as he ambled past us. He stopped at the end of the dock and then glanced over his shoulder. "Well? Are you two coming or not?"

Illia hesitated for a moment, and it was only then that I remembered she was no longer part of the Frith Guild. Would she be welcomed into the guild manor house?

Zelfree exhaled and turned his attention back to the road leading into town. "As my apprentices, you two shouldn't take too long before reporting in. It'll reflect poorly on me."

He said each word with a slow precision and exactness. I knew what he meant, and so did Illia.

She took my elbow and motioned to the road with a nod of her head.

Together, we headed back to the atlas turtle. I couldn't wait to relax and get my life back to normal.

35

CELEBRATION ON THE ISLE
OF RUMA

I loved riding the atlas turtle across the ocean. It was far safer—and more reliable—than any ship, no matter how impressive the craft. Gentel, our guildmaster's eldrin, kept her head high as we glided through the waves, never slowed by wind or rain.

We were almost to the Isle of Ruma, the place of my birth. Giddiness flowed through me like blood, and I stood out on the fields of the atlas turtle shell, admiring the azure waters and sapphire skies. It looked as though one bled into the other—two parts of a single whole. Our guildmaster, Liet Eventide, stood next to me, her long braided hair flowing in the breeze.

She wore a coat with scales and phoenix feathers patched over every inch. It only occurred to me then that they were magical items. Trinkets and artifacts. Powerful objects that no doubt protected her, much like Calisto's necklace. I had thought her eccentric, but now I realized I just didn't understand everything there was in the world.

Guildmaster Eventide had spoken with all of us at one point or another. She wanted everyone to recount their experiences with the pirates and on the skerry. I told her everything, including the fact that there was a world serpent somewhere south of us. She seemed to find that information amusing, but never asked to see the Occult Compass or my scale shield.

"—and in the end," I said, finishing up my story, "Hellion removed his mask and attempted to paralyze everyone with his gaze."

"Frightening," Guildmaster Eventide said.

I shrugged. "I don't know. That's a powerful ability, but why didn't he use it on the deck of the ship when we were fighting him? We never would've gotten away then."

She crossed her arms and mulled over my comment. Then she turned to me. "There was no reason for Calisto to think he needed it."

"But if he *has* the ability, why would he refuse to use it?"

"Calisto didn't become a dread pirate by giving away all his tricks. Never play an ace when you can win with a two and your enemies will never know what they're really up against."

I opened my mouth to retort, but I stopped myself cold. I hadn't thought of that. And he did surprise me on the island with it later. He just wanted to save his tricks.

"Guildmaster," I said as the Isle of Ruma appeared on the horizon. "I have a question for you."

She offered a half-smile. "Of course."

"Your arcanist mark glows."

"It does."

Her mark had the giant turtle with a tree wrapped around the star. The glowing lines went up into her hairline and down around to her neck. She seemed to be both arcane and mystical—it was hard to describe it any other way.

"And Gillie told me your eldrin has reached its true form," I said.

"That's right."

She answered without any hesitation or mystery. I liked that about her.

I tucked my hands in my pockets. "Calisto has an arcanist mark that glows. His manticore is in its true form, isn't it?"

"That's right."

"Why? I thought that only happened if you were a good arcanist."

She laughed, but it wasn't patronizing—it almost seemed sad. "It has nothing to do with how good you are, contrary to what some may believe. You just have to embody the magics of your eldrin. When you realize you've become one, then it just happens."

"What does an atlas turtle embody?"

"Protection and growth," Guildmaster Eventide said. "And guess what? Gentel and I discovered her true form when I became the leader of the Frith Guild. I'm always looking to grow and protect new arcanists. It's my calling in life—the same as hers."

"So... what about Calisto? What does a manticore embody?"

She looked away, her gaze distant. "Manticores consume and take. They embody a tyrant's mentality—someone who answers to no one. When Calisto took up the black flag of a pirate and embraced the thrill of greed and consumption, he discovered the true form of a manticore."

Hm.

A comfortable silence settled between us and I wondered what it meant to embody the magics of a knightmare.

"There's just one more thing," I muttered. "The plague-ridden gargoyle claimed he was also in his true form. Was he correct? He didn't even have an arcanist."

Guildmaster Eventide had this way about her expression —she always looked deep in thought—but my question obviously disturbed her. She pushed back her silver hair and stared out to the horizon.

"Gillie warned me about this. She said those plague creatures got stronger when they consumed magic. They think they're becoming perfect, but nothing could be further from the truth. For the time being, Gillie says these are their *dread forms*. The exact opposite of a true form, really. Monsters."

"Where does this arcane plague come from?"

"If I knew, I'd stop it." She smiled. "For now, it's best to worry about your own health and training. Your life is a little too chaotic at the moment."

"But what about the world serpent?"

"All in due time, Volke. I need to discuss that with the rest of the master arcanists in the guild. Please, just enjoy your time at home."

We arrived at the Isle of Ruma a little after the sun had set. The evening blanket of stars covered the sky as we took a dinghy from Gentel's docks over to the island. Only Illia, Zaxis, and Zelfree accompanied me. Adelgis and Hexa didn't know my island, and Atty said she didn't want to see her mother so soon after leaving.

Zaxis stared at Zelfree for most of the short trip across the water.

"You look a lot different," Zaxis said.

I agreed.

Zelfree had cut his long hair. The sides were shaved down and the top cut short. It gave him a more striking appearance—someone with a hard-edge. His eyes seemed more focused as well. He hadn't been drinking, and his clothes fit properly. When he walked, he moved like someone who knew his way around a fight. And he wore gloves, which he hadn't before, as though covering as much skin as possible.

Traces sat on his shoulder, her long cat tail swishing from side to side. "He's fancy now." She purred and offered Zaxis a smile. "You could get your hair cut too, ya know."

"It's already short." Zaxis touched his red hair. It hadn't been properly cut in over eight months, and it did have a disheveled look about it. "Well, maybe..."

Once we got the dinghy secured to Ruma's tiny dock, we disembarked. A few dozen people came to meet us, including the city guards. It didn't hit me until then, but my home island was tiny compared to the rest of the world. Port Crown had been ten times the size and lively, like the whole island had a pulse of excitement.

The Isle of Ruma seemed so... quaint.

"I'm back," Zaxis announced to the crowd.

Sure enough, they answered with cheers and clapping. Forsythe swooped around the citizens, adding to their delight. I had forgotten how much they adored Zaxis.

Technically, Illia and I had been banished from the island by the schoolmaster, but since I didn't see him, I decided to head straight to the graveyard. I was certain I'd find Gravekeeper William in his cottage. He kept an exact schedule, thanks to his time in the navy, and after the sun set, he made himself a snack and went to bed.

The small crowd didn't bother with anyone other than

Zaxis. They led him through the streets, taking him straight to the Ren Family home. To my surprise, Zaxis did offer us a wave and a nod, as though acknowledging that we would meet up later.

"I'll go watch him," Zelfree said with a sigh. "You two stay out of trouble in the meantime."

He followed after the crowd without another word to anyone.

Illia walked next to me, and Nicholin hummed a little song as we traveled. The familiar roads, the pleasant company—it felt like traversing one of Adelgis's dreams. If someone offered to dance with me or I found lumps formed under my skin, I would know this wasn't real, but for the time being, I enjoyed it.

We reached William's cottage sooner than I expected.

The Isle of Ruma really was tiny.

I knocked on the door, but by the time I reached the third bang, it swung open.

William stood on the other side, his massive frame unmistakable. Before I could get a word in, he reached out and embraced me with his tree-trunk arms. Although I considered myself tall—at least six feet—he had a good six inches on me. I always felt like a child when next to Grave-keeper William.

"My boy," he said, his voice thick with emotion. Then he noticed Illia, and he pulled her into the embrace as well. "And there's my girl."

His gut protruded more than I remembered, but his muscle remained the same. I returned the embrace, happy to hear his voice again. It had been so long...

"Happy birthday," he said as he released me.

I stared up at him, a tightness forming in my chest. "That's right... You remembered?"

"Of course. I wouldn't forget." He turned to Illia and pointed. "And yours was last month." He stepped aside and motioned us into the kitchen. "Come in, come in. I've got presents for the both of ya."

The smells, the visuals—I knew the cottage well. The rush of nostalgia hit hard. I even gave thought to asking to stay, but I knew that was foolish sentimentality. I just... didn't want to leave.

Illia and I took seats at the table, right in our old spots.

While Illia and I soaked up our childhood home, William rushed around the kitchen with a grace unbefitting someone his size. He kept everything organized—a habit from his time as a naval officer—which made cooking a bit easier. He pan-fried some bacon and then toasted some bread in the oil. In a matter of minutes, we had hot food and some beverages.

William lit a couple of lamps, giving the cottage a warm glow of hospitality.

"And here ya go," he said as he placed a small wooden box in front of me. Then he turned to Illia and gave her a pouch. "And this one is for you."

I chuckled to myself as I turned the box over. "You had presents waiting for us?"

"Ya keep talkin' like I wouldn't do this, but I never missed a birthday." He took a seat at the table and waggled a fork in my direction. "Never."

"That's true," I muttered. "I'm just surprised. We don't live with you anymore."

"I'm a sentimental man." William tapped at his heart. "Ya live with me in here."

I didn't know what to say, and by the looks of it, neither did Illia. Nicholin, however, leaped over Illia's shoulders and made grabby-hands for the pouch. "*Open it, open it.*"

She untied the strings and opened the pouch with shaky hands. Then she withdrew a piece of elaborate cloth. While she held it, I didn't know what it was, but then she laid it out across the table.

It was an eyepatch, but not just any simple patch. It was triangular and large enough to be considered half a mask. A rizzel had been stitched into the side using white and silver threads. The craftsmanship impressed me—the details of the ferret-like rizzel were unmistakable.

"I know you don't like folks seein' your scars," William said. "And maybe you've gotten over that now, but I think it'd be best if ya didn't have to worry about it. Plenty of sailors wear eyepatches. Nothin' to be ashamed of."

"I love it," Illia whispered. She grazed her fingers over the fine stitching.

Nicholin nodded, a smile on his weasel-face. "Yes. I concur. A beautiful accessory adorned with a handsome likeness of yours truly."

"It took me a few weeks to get it right," William said. "But I'm pretty sure it'll fit snug as a bug."

Then everyone turned to me. I picked up the box and undid the latch. What would he give me? I had no idea—no expectations or real desires. I just enjoyed the moment as I opened the lid.

Inside sat a folding razor blade. A stamp of the Queen's Navy had been embedded in the steel, and the handle was made of auburn wood.

"It's an officer's gift," William said, a nervousness to his voice. "They give it to young men who pass the academy. For shaving your face, obviously."

I rubbed at my chin, amused I already had stubble. I had shaved yesterday, after all.

"This is yours, isn't it?" I asked.

"Well, it *was* mine, but I figured I have to pass it down the family line."

His initials had been engraved in the wood—WJS.

I didn't know what to say. William had given me so much, even though he never had to. No one would've faulted him for refusing me as an apprentice. No one would've cared if he had just treated me as a worker, rather than a son. No one had expected him to give me his last name. Yet here he was, a better father to me than my real father had ever been.

My throat tightened, and I wanted to apologize for not getting him a gift. His birthday had been three months back.

He placed a large hand on my shoulder. "Don't get that look. This is a happy time."

I forced a nod. "Sorry. I just... really appreciate this."

William leaned back in his wooden chair. The sturdy little thing had held his weight for decades, and I suspected it wouldn't give out anytime soon.

"So," he said. "What brings you two here? Surely it wasn't for the birthday gifts."

"Zaxis wanted to see his father," Illia said. "And since the Frith Guild was moving through the area, we figured we'd come to see you."

"Is that right? Tell me all about your time in the Frith Guild. I can't wait to hear what ya'll have been up to."

I sat at the edge of the island, staring out over the ocean as though I were at the end of the world. The crescent moon hung high in the sky, reflecting off the waves that splashed across the shore. My legs dangled off the edge. If I scooted further out, I could see the rocks at the bottom of a forty-foot drop.

Illia sat next me. After a long while of staring at the stars, she rested on her back, the grass poking up through her sprawling hair. Nicholin scurried around to her legs and jumped between them.

I rested on my back as well, just to be near her.

This would be our only night on the Isle of Ruma. Tomorrow we would go back to the guild and continue our training as arcanists.

Nicholin glanced between us. Then he hopped onto Illia's stomach and rubbed her shirt. She stared down at him with a quizzical expression.

"What're you doing, Nicholin?" Illia jerked to the side. "That tickles!"

He stopped and tilted his head to the side. "Belly rubs always make me feel better. I thought it would make you feel better too."

"I'm fine."

"No you're not. You've been like this all night! You said you were going to talk to Volke, but you haven't said a word."

"Shh," Illia hissed. "I was getting to it."

Nicholin scurried off her and then curled up in the grass. "Hm-kay. If you say so."

We returned to stargazing, no one saying a word. And while I admired the beauty of nature all around us, I couldn't help but wonder what Illia wanted to talk about. Time passed, but she made no effort. Soon I would find myself too tired to hold a conversation.

Illia tucked her hands behind her head and laced her fingers together. "I admire you, Volke. You've always known what you wanted, and you worked to get it. Even when people told you it was a fantasy or a farce. You just kept working toward your goals anyway."

"You work hard as well."

She shook her head. "That's not what I meant. I just..."

I remained quiet while she gathered her thoughts. Then Illia exhaled.

"I hate myself for everything I want," she whispered, the ocean breeze threatening to steal her voice before I could hear it. "For years, I just wanted revenge, but when Zelfree yelled at me about what it meant to be an arcanist with the Frith Guild... I felt foolish." She turned to me, her eyepatch covering the scars, but her one eye searching mine. "And I've always wanted love, but even then... I'm not sure I can have the person I want."

"Illia..."

I sat up, flustered. No position seemed comfortable anymore, so I leaned forward and took a breath.

Illia sat up as well.

Nicholin glanced between us, but he refrained from speaking.

"Where is this coming from?" I asked. "You've never spoken to me like this before."

"I don't know." She petted Nicholin, her gaze set on the waves. "I wanted to tell you everything I felt. I didn't want any anger or problems to come between us because I hid all my thoughts. Does that make any sense?"

I nodded, but I still didn't know what to say.

"We're arcanists now," she continued. "Life is different than when we were gravediggers, but sometimes I wish we could just go back."

I turned to her and lifted an eyebrow.

She smiled. "I think I was more afraid of change than I realized."

"Nothing has to change between us."

"Maybe."

"What does that mean?"

"It means you don't get the birthday gift I got you," she said, waggling her finger. "I don't know what I want to do yet, and this conversation has told me you don't know what you want either, so it'll just have to wait."

"Wait? For what? What is it?"

"I'm not going to tell you."

Her childish tone—and the way she looked away from me—reminded me so much of our time as kids. She *always* did that after I had done something to annoy her.

Illia shook her head. "I want a goal that I pursue relentlessly, like you. Something I refuse to give up. It could be anything, but I want to make sure it's something I really want first."

"Are you going to leave the Frith Guild?" I asked.

"What?" She glared. "No. I really like training with Master Zelfree. I think... he and I... we might have a lot more in common than I thought. But I am talking about my personal goals. I need more time."

"That's fine." I reached into my trouser pocket, a little confused about how I should handle our future. After a moment of contemplation, I decided I would ignore this. She didn't know what she wanted, and I didn't want to risk anything coming between us. "I have a birthday gift for you."

"You already gave me one," she said. "Back on my actual birthday."

"Well, this is special." I handed over the Occult Compass. "I know you smashed the other compass to trick Calisto, but I think you should have this one now."

Illia held the trinket in her hands, her eye wide.

I shrugged. "Calisto wanted it, so I think you should decide its fate. I have the world serpent scale, and if you have the compass, maybe we could find the world serpent. Together. But if you think it'd be better to destroy the compass..."

"I'm keeping it," she said. "But I do think we should tell Master Zelfree."

"Well, yeah, that's what I meant. Not just *us*. Everyone."

"Oh." Illia twirled the compass in her palm. "I'm still going to keep it. There are no other compasses like it in the world, right? I'm not going to break something this rare and unique."

The thought of adventuring across the world in search of mythical creatures of old had a certain amount of excitement that couldn't be adequately described. It was like living through a fairy tale.

I leaned closer to Illia, glad she would experience the adventure with me.

THANK YOU SO MUCH FOR READING!

Please consider leaving a review—any and all feedback is much appreciated!

Adventure. Competition. A duel to the death.

While on a journey to the famous city of Thronehold, Volke Savan learns of the Sovereign Dragon Tournament. The massive celebration involves hundreds of arcanists competing for fame and glory, and Volke is determined to win.

Dark forces dwell in the city, however, and rumors of the legendary world serpent spread amongst the shadows. Whoever bonds with a god-like mystical creature will gain magic beyond compare, and the queen's guards suspect cutthroats will use the chaos of the tournament to hide their plotting.

Unsure of who to trust, Volke investigates the terrible rumors while advancing in the ranks of the tournament. Unfortunately, the true villain may be closer than he realizes...

Continue the Frith Chronicles with the third book, Coliseum Arcanist!

ABOUT THE AUTHOR

Shami Stovall grew up in California's central valley with a single mother and little brother. Despite no one in her family having a degree higher than a GED, she put herself through college (earning a BA in History), and then continued on to law school where she obtained her Juris Doctorate.

As a child, Stovall enjoyed every portal fantasy, space opera, and magic series she could get her hands on, but the first novel to spark her imagination was Island of the Blue Dolphins by Scott O'Dell. The adventure on a deserted island opened her mind to ideas and realities she had never given thought before—and it was the moment Stovall realized that story telling (specifically fiction) became her passion. Anything that told a story, especially fantasy series and military science fiction, be it a movie, book, video game or comic, she had to experience.

Now, as a professor and author, Stovall wants to add her voice to the myriad of stories in the world. Everything from sorcerers, to robots, to fantasy wars--she just hopes you enjoy.

To find out more about Shami Stovall and the Frith Chronicles, take a look at her website:
https://sastovallauthor.com/newsletter/

Or contact her directly at:

s.adelle.s@gmail.com

OTHER TITLES BY SHAMI STOVALL: